Here's what *Romantic Times* had to say about

ELIZABETH BEVARLY

"Ms. Bevarly does an excellent job
of combining wit and humor
with an underlying sense of poignancy...."

"Ms. Bevarly creates vivid characterizations and
a touching emotional ambiance...."

"Elizabeth Bevarly's irrepressible pen dishes up
equal servings of love and laughter...."

and

KATHLEEN CREIGHTON

"...Kathleen Creighton shines!"

"...Kathleen Creighton...
will touch your heart...."

"Ms. Creighton knows just how to
set our pulses pounding in delight."

ELIZABETH BEVARLY

was born and raised in Louisville, Kentucky, and earned her B.A. with honors in English from the University of Louisville in 1983. Although she never wanted to be anything but a novelist, her career side trips before making the leap to writing included stints working in movie theaters, restaurants, boutiques and a major department store. She also spent time as an editorial assistant for a medical journal, where she learned the correct spelling and meanings of a variety of words (like *microscopy* and *histological*) that she will never, ever use again. When she's not writing, Elizabeth enjoys old movies, old houses, good books, whimsical antiques, hot jazz and even hotter salsa (the music, not the sauce). She has claimed as residences Washington, D.C., northern Virginia, southern New Jersey and Puerto Rico, but she now resides with her husband and son back in Kentucky, where she fully intends to remain.

KATHLEEN CREIGHTON

has roots deep in the California soil, but she now resides in South Carolina. As a child, she enjoyed listening to old-timers' tales, and her fascination with the past only deepened as she grew older. Today, she says she is interested in everything— art, music, gardening, zoology, anthropology and history, but people are at the top of her list. She also has a lifelong passion for writing, and now combines her two loves in romance novels.

ALL I WANT FOR CHRISTMAS

ELIZABETH BEVARLY

KATHLEEN CREIGHTON

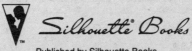
Silhouette Books

Published by Silhouette Books
America's Publisher of Contemporary Romance

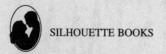 SILHOUETTE BOOKS

ISBN 0-373-23016-8

ALL I WANT FOR CHRISTMAS

Copyright © 2003 by Harlequin Books S.A.

The publisher acknowledges the copyright holders of the individual works as follows:

JAKE'S CHRISTMAS
Copyright © 1992 by Elizabeth Bevarly

ONE CHRISTMAS KNIGHT
Copyright © 1997 by Kathleen Modrovich

Visit Silhouette at www.eHarlequin.com

Printed in U.S.A.

CONTENTS

Dear Reader,

I'm so happy to see *Jake's Christmas* in print again, since it's always been one of my favorite books that I've written for Silhouette. Of course, a lot of that could be because Christmas is my very favorite holiday. So much so that we celebrate it for more than a month at my house. The tree goes up the first weekend in December (sometimes as early as the weekend after Thanksgiving), and stays up until the week after New Year's Day. We have hundreds of ornaments spanning decades that we've collected in our travels, and they all find their way onto that tree. Somehow. Then we thoroughly study all of our holiday recipe books for the most luscious cookies and the most savory wassail. Everything just feels so warm and cozy this time of year, because I think Christmas brings out the best in all of us.

It's a lesson Jake Raglan hasn't quite learned yet, but Rebecca Bellamy is about to teach it to him. In spades. She'll teach him the true meaning of Christmas if it's the last thing she does. I had a lot of fun writing *Jake's Christmas*. I hope you have as much fun reading it.

Happy holidays!

Elizabeth Bevarly

JAKE'S CHRISTMAS
Elizabeth Bevarly

For my two sisters-in-law, Maritza and Laura,
who took on the toughest jobs of all.
Much love, and good luck.

One

"The wedding was wonderful, Rebecca, even lovelier than your last one."

"Yes, dear, they just keep getting better and better. How many have there been now?"

Rebecca Bellamy listened to the praise of the two elderly women seated at her table and smiled modestly. She gazed out at the collection of people dancing and laughing in the cavernous white greatroom of the Peterson-Dumesnil House—her favorite place to hold her receptions—and sighed contentedly. Fluffing her long, dark curls discreetly and smoothing a hand over the lapel of her shell pink suit jacket, she replied proudly, "Twenty-two. And would you believe I'm already in the planning stages for number twenty-three?"

The other women exchanged meaningful looks and nodded their approval.

"Keep up the good work, dear," one of them said as she patted Rebecca's hand.

Murmuring her thanks, Rebecca excused herself from the table with the explanation that she needed to check on how the food was holding out at the buffet. Her weddings were indeed some of the most talked-about events in virtually every Louisville social circle, and she couldn't help but feel a tremendous sense of pride and accomplishment. She had come a long way in five years.

Planning weddings for other people almost made up for never having been able to plan one of her own. Still, Rebecca knew deep down that she was saving all of her best ideas for the nuptial celebration she hoped to enjoy herself someday. Just because her first hastily executed marriage had ended up in a shambles didn't mean she had to remain alone for the rest of her life. All she had to do now was find the perfect mate. Unfortunately, she was beginning to wonder if that particular aspect of her wedding plans might take some time.

The new Mrs. Daphne Duryea-Prescott, Rebecca's most recent employer, swooped in on her then, looking like a white, poofy cloud with her platinum blond hair and elaborately decorated wedding gown topped by an eight-foot-long veil. It was an ensemble that probably cost more than a number of Rebecca's clients spent on their entire wedding budget. At twenty-three, Daphne was only seven years Rebecca's junior, but the look of complete innocence and excitement that lit her eyes indicated a youthfulness that Rebecca could scarcely recall experiencing herself.

"Rebecca, come quick," Daphne said anxiously.

Rebecca snapped to attention. "What is it? What's wrong?" She knew things seldom ran entirely smoothly at weddings, and Daphne's should certainly be no different. But whatever was amiss could surely be corrected. She hoped.

Daphne clutched a fold in her white lace gown in one hand and lifted a battered bunch of flowers with the other. "I'm getting ready to throw the bouquet."

Rebecca smiled indulgently. "That's more a matter for the photographer, Daphne. I'm sure you'll do fine without me."

"But you're a single woman," Daphne protested. "You have to be there. I kind of wanted you to be the one to catch it."

Rebecca's heart kicked up a funny rhythm at hearing Daphne's declaration. The last time she'd caught a bridal bouquet, she'd wound up with a husband before the year was through. Five years after that, she'd found herself divorced. Another five years had passed since then, and Rebecca was just starting to reap the benefits of all the hard work she'd put into building her business. Despite the fact that she certainly had no aversion to marriage, she still wasn't sure she was ready to risk an investment like that again just yet.

"Oh, I don't think so, Daphne," she hedged, "but thanks, anyway. Grappling with bridesmaids for the bouquet isn't exactly in my job description."

"Oh, come on," Daphne pleaded. "You said you'd

do anything for me where my wedding was concerned.''

''And your parents are paying dearly for it,'' Rebecca pointed out. ''I'm here as your wedding planner. And as much as I've enjoyed doing it, it is, after all, my job.'' Her expression softened as she smiled and took Daphne's hand in hers. ''Throw your bouquet to someone who will cherish it. Now, I really must go and check on the buffet.''

''Rebecca…''

''It is what you hired me for, Daphne.''

''I know, but I want to do something nice for you, because you've made my wedding day so memorable.''

Rebecca, ever the astute businesswoman, replied with a wide grin, ''Then recommend me to your friends.''

Daphne's shoulders drooped in defeat. ''I already have,'' she told Rebecca petulantly. ''You know, for someone who plans weddings for a living, you sure aren't every romantic.''

Rebecca's grin grew broader. ''On the contrary, I'm all for romance. It keeps me working.''

''You know, you're as bad as my Uncle Jake,'' Daphne muttered. ''You guys would get along just swell.'' Her eyes widened then, full of speculation, as she added, ''Hey, by the way, have you met my Uncle Jake yet?''

It was perhaps one of the most dreaded questions a single or divorced woman in her thirties wanted to hear, rivaled only by the one about someone's nephew. Or cousin. Or brother. Or barber. ''Oh, gee, Daphne,

I really do have to check on the buffet,'' Rebecca assured the other woman as she began to back away in fear for her personal safety. ''Maybe some other time, okay?''

''But—''

''I'm sure we're starting to run low on crab puffs and stuffed mushrooms. Gotta go.''

As she threaded her way through the crowd of well-wishers attending the Duryea-Prescott affair, Rebecca's panic at being cornered by a paunchy, balding uncle who probably worked as an undertaker or door-to-door salesman began to ebb, and she began to feel festive once again.

There was simply something magical about weddings, Rebecca thought. Her own had been prepared on the spur of the moment and had claimed none of the flourish for which she had become famous in Louisville. As college students, she and her ex-husband had found themselves spending spring break in Bermuda during her junior year. One night, in a fit of romantic nonsense resulting from too many piña coladas, they had rounded up the first clergyman they could find, and had gotten married on the beach at sunrise.

Her parents had been extremely upset by the revelation when Rebecca had announced the deed, a reaction for which she had been fully prepared. Ruth and Dan Bellamy had never approved of Eliot, had worried from the start that he was only interested in Rebecca because of the Bellamy wealth. Upon learning of the marriage, they had offered an equally upsetting revelation of their own—their daughter and her new husband would be completely cut off from them financially.

Thinking back now, Rebecca supposed the action had been her parents' way of making sure Eliot's affections were genuine. Had the two of them remained married and been able to prove to the world that love was indeed what had kept them together, her parents would have no doubt reinstated Rebecca's ample allowance. But Eliot had proved instead that his affections were anything but genuine. And thankfully, when the marriage did fall apart, her parents had lovingly welcomed her back into the family circle, and to their credit had never issued a single word of reproach.

But that was in the past now, she reminded herself. Eliot was living with his wife in California, where he had set up a law practice, and was about as far removed from Rebecca's life as he could possibly be. Why, she scarcely even thought about him anymore. Except occasionally, late at night sometimes, when she was watching TV and saw all those commercials for sleazy, unethical, ambulance-chasing attorneys. Only then did Eliot's impression brave even the tiniest entry into her brain.

Rebecca was so preoccupied by thoughts of the past that several moments went by before she realized she had been halted on her journey to the buffet by a group of women who were casually chatting in the middle of the greatroom. At first, she didn't understand exactly what they were all doing there, just standing around. Then, when she heard someone cry out her name, she glanced up quickly, startled to find a large collection of gardenias, white roses, calla lilies and

ELIZABETH BEVARLY   15

sweetheart ivy descending rapidly in her direction. Instinctively, she threw up her hands to ward off the
projectile…and discovered much to her dismay that
she had just caught the bridal bouquet.

"Gotcha!" Daphne called out with a chuckle.

Rebecca had the decency to look caught, then gra-
ciously lifted the flowers to her nose. They smelled
sweet and fresh and alive, exactly how a marriage between two people should be. For just a moment, Rebecca allowed herself to believe such a state of wed-
ded bliss was in store for her someday.

"I'll get you for this, Daphne, if it's the last thing
I do," she assured the blushing bride quietly, only half
joking.

"Invite me to your wedding," Daphne replied, clap-
ping her hands in delight.

Rebecca shook her head hopelessly, lifted the bouquet to inhale its sweet aroma one final time, then
settled it against her shoulder as if it was a burden to
be borne. She promised herself she would put the
flowers in water as soon as she got home. But in the
back of Rebecca's mind, all she could think was that
before the week was through, the tender, fragile blos-
soms would surely all wither and die.

On the other side of the room, Jake Raglan sat at
the bar savoring his Scotch and water and watching
the byplay on the greatroom floor with much disgust.
God, now there was another one out there—another
woman looking to land a husband she could drain dry
and suck the life out of. He should probably finish his
drink and get the hell out of there before she set her

sights on him. There was no way he was going to get caught in another mantrap like the one his ex-wife had set for him. He'd chew his own foot off first if he had to.

"Would you care for another drink, sir?"

Jake looked up at the bartender's question and told himself he should say no, that he had to get going before something terrible happened. Instead, he nodded, reasoning that since he was Daphne's favorite uncle, his niece would certainly notice his early departure, and then he'd never hear the end of it from the mouthy kid.

Involuntarily, his gaze traveled back to settle on the woman who had just caught Daphne's bouquet, lingering as he took in the tantalizing curves her suit did little to conceal. She was some piece of work, he'd grant that. He watched as she silently saluted the bride and spun on her heel, carrying the fragile white flowers as if they would dissolve before she took two steps.

He wondered how she knew Daphne. The woman looked to be several years older than his niece, so therefore probably hadn't been a classmate or sorority sister. And because Daphne had majored in landing a husband in college rather than focusing on career training, the recipient of the bouquet couldn't be a co-worker. Daphne didn't have a job. The two of them probably enjoyed some social tie, Jake decided, showed up at all the same parties or did the same charity work. The other woman looked like she came from a moneyed background.

When he realized the object of his appraisal was approaching the bar, Jake's earlier apprehension returned, and he suddenly felt like a deer on the highway, caught in the headlights of an oncoming semi. He chuckled quietly at his analogy. No, he would be a *stag* on the highway of life, he corrected himself with masculine pride, and from the slight build of the woman coming his way, he would be caught in the headlights of a sputtering moped. He'd probably do considerably more damage to her than she could ever do to him.

Frowning, he wondered where in the hell that idea had come from and took another swallow of his drink. Still, he continued to study the woman as she neared, because she was without question someone worth studying. Small but slender, she gave the impression of height, regardless of the fact that she was probably no more than five-three in her stocking feet. Her hair was a tousled mane of near-black curls that spilled down her back in a tangle. As she came nearer—and was that incredible smile meant for him?—he realized that her eyes were a magnificent color he'd never seen on another human being, a dark olive green that hinted at a deep-seated passion.

He watched while she exchanged pleasantries with the bartender, then turned on his stool to face her fully. As soon as she had been close enough to do so, she had set the bouquet of flowers on the bar and now avoided looking at them. Jake thought such a response intriguing. Wasn't catching the bouquet supposed to be the ultimate feminine achievement? Wasn't that matrimonial trophy what every single woman strove to win at wedding receptions?

As the bartender placed a glass of club soda before

the woman, Jake couldn't help the devilishly playful thoughts that bounced around in his head. Before he realized what he was doing, he had risen from his place at the bar to move closer to the woman.

"Run while there's still time," he said quietly as he took his seat on the bar stool beside her.

She glanced over with an expression of genuine surprise and stammered, "I...I beg your pardon?"

Jake noted then that her eyes weren't completely green. The part of the iris around each pupil was stained with brown, looking like a scattering of winter leaves. The color made her seem more...unattainable, somehow. He suddenly wanted nothing more than to pull her as close as he possibly could without getting himself arrested.

Pointing to the neglected bouquet, he grinned as he repeated, "Run. While there's still time." Only at this point, Jake wasn't sure if he was talking to her or to himself.

The woman smiled back at him, a little uncertainly at first, then with what Jake for some reason suspected was a rarely displayed shyness. He was ridiculously pleased that he seemed to have scored a point with her.

"Is it that obvious?" she asked.

The smile that punctuated her question threw him off guard for a moment. It was a disconcerting realization. No woman had caught Jake Raglan off guard since his ex-wife. And look how that had turned out.

"Is what that obvious?" he finally asked, still reeling from the odd sensations burning up the air between them.

Rebecca considered the man who had made himself at home beside her, trying to conjure a polite reason to excuse herself from this conversation before it could get started. Not because she didn't want to talk to the man—he was, after all, rather breathtakingly handsome—but because she had only come over to the bar to check the wine situation on her way to the buffet and didn't have time to dawdle.

"Never mind," she replied absently to the question she couldn't remember now.

She had seen him earlier, of course, at Daphne's wedding ceremony, the moment he'd entered the cathedral. He was the kind of man a woman couldn't help but notice. At roughly six feet in height, he would tower over her, she knew, if he were standing beside her instead of sitting. As it was now, she stood eye to eye with him, even in heels. And what eyes they were—as dark blue as an early nightfall, and full of any number of suggestive ideas. His hair was dark, too, claiming more hints of nighttime color—black threaded with bits of silver. Even his suit was dark, complemented by a discreet dove gray necktie. He looked to be in his late thirties, and was, to put it mildly, a very attractive man.

"I'm sorry, Mr...."

"Raglan. Jake Raglan."

He *would* have a name like that, Rebecca thought absently. "Mr. Raglan," she repeated a little breathlessly. Then his first name registered, too, and her eyes widened in surprise. "You can't be Daphne's Uncle Jake?"

Jake, too, was surprised by the question, but smiled indulgently as he rejoined, "Why can't I be?"

"Well, because you're supposed to be paunchy and balding," she blurted out before she realized what she was saying. "You're not supposed to be so..."

Now Jake's smile became dangerous. "Not so what?"

Rebecca felt herself blushing, and bit her lip to prevent any more blathering that would cause her to further embarrass herself. Feeling more and more flustered with each passing second, she said hastily, "I really do have to run, Mr. Raglan. I'm on my way to the buffet."

"You're that hungry?"

Why, all of a sudden, did everything he said sound like a sexually charged come-on? Rebecca wondered wildly. "No, I..." What was it she had to do, again? "I have to check on the, uh, crab puffs and...and the stuffed mushrooms."

"Delicious," Jake told her in a very smooth, very seductive voice.

Rebecca didn't pause to ponder what exactly Jake Raglan might be thinking was delicious. She only knew she had to be going, and the sooner the better. "I, ah... Excuse me, will you?"

Without waiting for a reply, Rebecca spun around and headed for the buffet, completely forgetting that she had left her club soda and the bridal bouquet on the bar.

Jake chuckled to himself as he watched her leave, enjoying the fact that he could still fluster a beautiful woman, in spite of his much despised and all-too-quickly-approaching fortieth birthday. As he turned to pick up his drink once again, Jake saw his niece's bouquet lying on the bar and realized the woman had forgotten to take it with her. It was a good sign. It meant the ultimate symbol of impending matrimony meant very little, if anything at all, to her. She might be just the kind of woman he was looking for. And he didn't even know her name.

Jake was about to get up and make a little trip to the buffet himself when he saw the woman in question penetrate the crowd on the dance floor to begin an unsteady journey toward the bar once more. He told himself he had *not* breathed a sigh of relief at her reappearance, but merely wanted to clear his lungs in preparation for that tantalizing scent that had clung to her when she'd stood so close to him before.

She approached him slowly, uncertainly, casting her gaze everywhere except on him, as if she was trying to sneak past without alerting his attention. Fat chance, Jake thought. Gingerly, she extended her left hand toward the white flowers that lay in a heap on the bar. The moment she touched the delicate leaves, Jake gently circled her wrist with long fingers and lifted her hand for his inspection. Only then did she meet his gaze, and only then did he realize the mistake he'd made in touching her.

She was soft. Her skin was warm and smooth, and the bones in her wrist and hand felt as small and fragile as a child's. Below his thumb, he could feel her pulse quicken and dance at his touch. But her eyes were what held his interest most of all. They were dark and full of longing, and as panic nearly overcame him,

Jake realized the desire he saw flickering to life in her eyes must only reflect his own. Oh, boy, was he in trouble.

"No ring," he said softly, trying to quell his own pulse rate as it threatened to run wild at the realization that she responded to him so quickly, so completely.

Rebecca's heart felt as if it were about to burst behind her rib cage. Somewhere deep within her soul, a flame that had smoldered to life when she first beheld Jake Raglan exploded into a raging wildfire. She took a deep, unsteady breath, but told herself she wouldn't succumb to him so easily this time.

"No, no ring," she replied levelly.

"So that means you're single?" Jake assured himself he had no further interest in her answer beyond casual curiosity, but for some reason, the thought that this woman might be joined to another man made his heart do funny things.

"Divorced, actually," Rebecca confided reluctantly.

He nodded in silent understanding, then laced her fingers through his. "You don't have a ring, but you must have a name."

"Yes..."

The silent pause between them seemed to grow until it was a dangerous, limitless chasm. Jake didn't quite seem certain he wanted to know her name, and Rebecca wasn't quite certain she wanted to offer it.

Finally, he put an end to their silent queries by commanding simply, "Tell me."

"Rebecca," she replied without hesitation. "Rebecca Bellamy."

For one long moment, they looked at each other as

if neither could understand what was happening between them. Rebecca felt herself falling into the dark blue depths of his eyes and spinning out of control as if caught in a hot, raging whirlpool. The fingers wrapped around her wrist were warm and rough in texture, but gentle in their embrace.

"So, Mr. Raglan—"

"Jake."

Her heartbeat quickened again at the thought of being more familiar with this man than she already felt she was. "Jake," she repeated quietly in an effort to break the spell that seemed to have settled over them. "What…what kind of man are you that you can make people reveal things about themselves they weren't necessarily willing to surrender?"

His lips curled into a smile at her surprisingly accurate observation. "I'm an attorney."

Jake felt Rebecca's skin temperature drop about twenty degrees at his statement, watched as her entire posture changed. Her eyes darkened dangerously, and her body became rigid. Slowly, effortlessly, she withdrew her hand from his loose grasp to grip the bar tightly, and for some bizarre reason, Jake got the impression that she clung to the bar because to let go would cause her to wrap her fingers firmly around his throat. Suddenly his tie felt extremely constrictive, and almost as an involuntary reaction, he fumbled to loosen it.

"An attorney. How nice," Rebecca said blandly. "Well, it was very nice meeting you, Mr. Raglan. Now, if you'll excuse me, I really must be going."

"Hey, wait a minute," Jake protested, taking her

wrist in his hand once more. This time he was less willing to release it when she made the move to do so. He studied her intently, but she refused to meet his gaze. "Rebecca, what's wrong?"

Rebecca's shoulders slumped in surrender. It had happened again. Every time she met a man who identified himself as a lawyer, she set her interior temperature to frostbite and walked away. As much as she might try to deny it, Eliot Madison still influenced her life, even after being absent from it for five years.

"I'm sorry, Mr. Raglan," Rebecca apologized. "I didn't mean to be rude. I'm…" She waved her hand at nothing. "You just took me by surprise, that's all."

"Yeah, well, I'm not the only one who came as a surprise here. You don't exactly seem like the type of woman who would scorn weddings. Of course, now that I realize you're divorced—"

"Who says I scorn weddings?" Rebecca asked, drawing her eyebrows down in confusion. "I don't understand."

Jake was also puzzled. "I… No one. No one *said* you did. I just meant… Well, you walked off and left Daphne's bouquet sitting here after going to all the trouble to catch it. I just figured that meant you weren't real keen on the topic of matrimony."

Rebecca stared at him thoughtfully for a moment before replying. "In the first place, I didn't go to all the trouble to catch it. Daphne threw it at me. In the second place, I didn't leave it here because I don't want it, I left it here because I forgot to take it with me." She neglected to add that the reason she forgot was because she had been so addled by Jake's imposing presence. "And as for the topic of matrimony, Mr. Raglan, no one could be more supportive than I am of the institution of marriage. I plan weddings for a living. I planned this one. Someday, I even hope to plan one for myself."

Jake tamped down the desire to make a cross out of his two index fingers and back away from Rebecca, but instead wondered at the vehemence with which she delivered her words. "But you said you were divorced," he mumbled lamely, not knowing what else to say.

"Yes, I am that," Rebecca agreed. "I worked three jobs for five years to put my husband through school, only to have him dump me the day after he earned his degree. Despite that, I still believe it's worth celebrating when two people find each other and want to spend the rest of their lives together."

Jake had stepped on more than a few toes in his time. In his profession, it was impossible not to. But he had never once felt guilt or remorse for hurting someone else's feelings or for putting them on the defensive. Yet as he looked at Rebecca Bellamy, saw her attempt an aggressive stance despite the pain in her eyes she couldn't hide, Jake suddenly felt like the worst kind of creep. And then he got angry, too. Because he didn't like it when someone else had control over his emotions.

"Yeah, well, I'm beginning to understand why hubby took a powder," he shot at Rebecca in retaliation, damning himself for feeling even worse when the pain in her eyes made them appear even larger.

"If the poor sap had to listen to tirades like that one all the time, I can sympathize with the guy."

Rebecca chuckled humorlessly before snatching the bridal bouquet viciously from the bar. "That doesn't surprise me for a moment, Mr. Raglan. Because the school I put my husband through was *law* school, and his degree was a *law* degree. *He* was trained to be a coldhearted bastard, too."

Before Jake could say another word, Rebecca turned her back on him and disappeared into the gradually thinning crowd. What had begun as a day meant to celebrate the lifelong union of his niece and her new husband had ended up bringing Jake together with someone only long enough to thoroughly drive them apart. He told himself he was better off, that women like Rebecca Bellamy were nothing but trouble. Unfortunately, all he could think about instead was the way she'd looked at him when he'd told her he sympathized with her husband.

It had been a lie, of course. Jake couldn't begin to imagine any man having Rebecca Bellamy and then letting her go. Only an idiot would do something like that. An idiot or a bastard whose heart was indeed cold. As he drained the last of his drink from the glass, Jake had to admit grimly that maybe Rebecca Bellamy's assessment of him hadn't been so far off the mark, after all.

And that, more than anything else she had said to him, made Jake Raglan feel like a fool.

Two

"**Y**ou're going to do *what?*"

"Alison and I are getting married. And keep your voice down, will you, Jake? She's over in my office right now."

Jake glared at his partner, Stephen Flannery, then down at the array of paperwork scattered across his desk. He'd been working all morning on the Sinclair divorce case—one that was making headlines throughout Louisville thanks to the local businessman's wealth and prominence—and he had come to the conclusion that any man with even half a brain would never, ever, allow himself to get roped into marriage unless he was the worst kind of masochist. Now his partner and best friend was admitting that he was in fact just such a madman.

"How could you possibly let that woman talk you

into something like this?'' he demanded caustically. ''You, above all people, should know better.''

''Jake…'' Stephen began, his voice edged with warning.

''Just think of Gordon Sinclair,'' Jake continued, jabbing a finger pointedly at the clutter on his desk as he rose to move in front of it. ''The poor sap gets tangled up with some bimbo half his age, and the next thing you know, she's got him down on his knees proposing to her. Less than two years after that, his lovely wife is leaving him, tearing every strip of flesh from his bones as she goes.''

''Knock it off, Jake,'' Stephen cautioned. ''For one thing, Alison is nothing like Elaine Sinclair. If you'd ever taken the time to meet her, you would have realized that by now. And as for Gordon Sinclair, the guy robbed a cradle, begged the kid to be his wife, then spent the next two years sleeping around on her. If I were Elaine, I'd want a piece of his hide, too.''

''You're missing the point,'' Jake objected.

''No, *you're* the one missing the point. Just because you suffered a messy divorce at the hands of your ex-wife—whose brother, incidentally, happened to be as brilliant a divorce attorney as you are and went for the jugular on an already-wounded man—it doesn't mean every woman in America is suspect.''

''I never said every woman in America is suspect,'' Jake corrected him. ''I said every woman in the *world* is.''

Stephen shook his head hopelessly. ''Look, will you just come out and meet Alison? She's really nervous about making a good impression.''

"Yeah, I'll bet she is," Jake muttered. To himself, he added, She's probably afraid I'll be able to see her for what she really is, and not with the muddled, foggy outlook of a man besotted by what he thinks is true love.

"I'm busy right now," Jake hedged. "I promised Gordon I'd have this financial statement prepared by this afternoon."

"You're going to have to have to meet her eventually," Stephen said wearily. "And it would be especially convenient if the introductions took place before the nineteenth."

"Why then?"

"Because that's the date of the wedding—"

"*In three weeks?*"

"—and I want you to be my best man."

Any other objection Jake might have voiced was cut off by his partner's request. Best man? In a ceremony he could never condone? Uh-uh. No way.

"Forget it, Stephen," he said simply. "You want to wreck your life, that's up to you. But don't expect me to be there facilitating it."

"I'm not wrecking my life."

"Yes, you are," Jake told him. "You're not even thinking this through. Three weeks isn't long enough to consider all the implications that come with marriage."

"Alison and I have been talking about getting married for over two months," Stephen informed him. "Last week, we finally set the date."

Jake could tell by the expression on his partner's face that there was no way he would be able to talk him out of the horrible mistake he was about to make. In a last-ditch effort, however, he stressed, "Three weeks isn't long enough to plan a wedding. You need more time."

Sensing his friend was weakening, Stephen braved a smile as he replied, "The wedding planner Alison hired said she could organize a very nice celebration in only three weeks."

The words "wedding planner" caught and held Jake's attention more than any others his partner had uttered. Immediately, his brain filled with images of a dark-haired, green-eyed beauty in a soft pink suit, a woman who had possessed his dreams for more than three months now, ever since Daphne's wedding in June.

Jake had never been plagued by such an experience before—meeting a woman once, and very briefly at that, only to have her totally bewitch him until he could scarcely think of anything else. Even after three months, he could picture Rebecca Bellamy very well, only instead of seeing her in the simple pink suit she'd worn that day, Jake usually conjured her up in something dark and lacy and thoroughly arousing. It had caused him to suffer more than one sleepless night.

"Wedding planner?" he heard himself repeating out loud, his voice sounding tinny and hollow, as if it were coming from someplace far away.

Stephen nodded, his smile broadening suggestively. "A real knockout, too. Now *she* might be able to change your mind about being in the wedding. Come on out and meet her. She's with Alison in my office."

"Is she…?" Jake caught himself before he said

anything further. No, it couldn't be. A city this size must have a number of women who did what Rebecca Bellamy did for a living. Just because Stephen had said she was a knockout... "Oh, all right," he finally relented, hating himself when he realized he was unconsciously straightening his tie and fingering his hair back into place.

"I knew it," Stephen said with a triumphant chuckle. "All it takes is the mention of a beautiful woman, and you're hooked."

Jake grumbled something unintelligible under his breath, but followed his partner out of his own office and across the reception area to Stephen's. Their secretary had left to run an errand, and an eerie silence hung over the room, foreshadowing, Jake was sure somehow, what would be an equally eerie situation.

"It's okay, Alison," Stephen said as he opened the door. "Jake promised to be on his best behavior."

Jake was about to state emphatically that he had made no such vow, but was silenced when he saw the two women who stood to greet him. His eyes skimmed briefly over the one he knew must be Alison, taking in her short blond hair and tailored dark suit. She was...cute, he mused. Really...very cute. Somehow, he had expected a loud, overbearing, fire-breathing vixen with long red fingernails perfectly honed into hooks that could seize a man by the loins and never let go. Instead, Stephen's fiancée looked like a well-educated, even-tempered, normal, everyday kind of woman.

On the other hand, her companion did indeed turn on the heat, no less intense now than it had been three months ago. Rebecca Bellamy was still an exceptionally beautiful woman, Jake reflected, and she still touched a part of him deep down inside that he hadn't known existed—a raw nerve that shuddered and burned simply because she was present in the same room.

Today she wore loose-fitting brown wool trousers and a man's-style tweed jacket over an ivory blouse. Her hair was bound loosely at her nape with a gold clip, cascading over one shoulder like a wild, night-drenched river. But her eyes were what held Jake's attention most, fascinating him with the play of emotion that she was clearly unable to hide. He couldn't mistake the fact that she was surprised by his appearance, nor could he deny that she was obviously none too pleased as a result of it. Before he could comment on what either of them might be thinking or feeling, however, Stephen launched quickly into introductions.

"Alison, this is Jake Raglan. See? I told you he wasn't a monster. Not around women, anyway." Hastily, he qualified, "Except, of course, for those women who are married to his clients. And Jake, this is my fiancée, Alison Mitchell. Just for the record, she's not a monster, either. Except around the month of April. CPAs are like that sometimes. Taxes…you know what I mean."

"Alison," Jake managed impatiently by way of a greeting. Somewhat reluctantly, he extended his hand, prepared to leap on whatever faults he could find in Stephen's fiancée. He was surprised to discover that Alison had a very firm, self-assured grip, one that mirrored his own.

"Jake," she replied in a tone of voice similar to the one he'd used with her. That surprised him, too.

"And this," Stephen continued, indicating his fiancée's companion, "is—"

"Rebecca," Jake interrupted, his voice softening involuntarily when he turned his attention to her. He extended his hand to Rebecca as well, and couldn't help but smile when she unconsciously swiped her palm across the leg of her trousers before settling her hand in his. Her skin was every bit as soft as he remembered it being, but her grasp on his hand wasn't nearly as confident as the attitude she tried to project. Again, Jake was delighted that he was able to set her off kilter.

"Mr. Raglan," she replied coolly.

"Jake," he corrected her.

"You've met," Stephen said quietly, clearly aware that he was intruding on something.

"Mr. Raglan," Rebecca repeated meaningfully, avoiding the use of Jake's first name.

Stephen raised his eyebrows in speculation. "She knows you well, then," he mumbled to his friend.

"Not as well as she's going to," Jake responded just loudly enough for everyone in the room to hear. After a pregnant pause during which no one said a word, he added, "Since I'm going to be in the wedding, I mean."

The others nodded quickly, mumbling agreement.

"Of course," Rebecca repeated after swallowing with some difficulty. She hurriedly explained for the others' benefit, "I planned Mr. Raglan's niece's wedding some months ago. That's where he and I met."

"It was a terrific bash," Jake said enthusiastically. "Especially the, uh, little set-to that ensued after the bride threw her bouquet."

"How is Daphne?" Rebecca asked before Jake could say any more.

"She and Robby are doing fine. She's putting on weight, though." He grinned wickedly as he added, "My sister is terrified that her daughter might be in a family way. At forty-five, Ellen is less than willing to become a grandmother."

"And that would make you a great-uncle, wouldn't it?" Rebecca asked conversationally.

Jake wasn't sure, but he could almost swear her eyes sparkled when she posed her question. He hadn't thought about that when he'd made the teasing remark about his sister. However, the suggestion—and realization—that he himself was old enough to be of the "great" generation was less than grand.

"Yeah, I guess it would," he replied thoughtfully.

"Hey, Alison, do you feel like we've intruded into a conversation that started a long time ago?" Stephen asked suddenly.

Both Jake and Rebecca started visibly, as if each had forgotten that the other two people were in the room.

"Kind of," Alison agreed with a grin. "Look, since Jake and Rebecca know each other, why don't you guys join us for lunch? We were just going to walk down the street to Charley's."

Jake noted that Rebecca was shaking her head as vigorously as he was when he said, "No, I don't think so."

"Oh, come on," Alison cajoled. "We'll be talking about plans for the wedding, and you'll both need to be briefed on them, anyway. We'll be killing two birds."

Somehow Alison's choice of cliché seemed very appropriate to Jake. Whenever he was around Rebecca Bellamy, he did indeed feel as if someone had dashed a stone against his head. He only hoped the dizziness and nausea he was experiencing now wouldn't wind up being a permanent condition. He knew he should decline the offer, knew it was foolish to spend any more time with Rebecca than he absolutely had to. Then he imagined what she might be wearing under her man's-style clothes and smiled dangerously.

"Lunch sounds good," he finally said quietly, throwing Rebecca the hungriest look he could manage. He only wished it would be Rebecca Bellamy, and not something as bland as a club sandwich, that he would be sinking his teeth into.

For Rebecca, lunch was only the prelude to what she was fast becoming to think of as the wedding from hell. She had thought it would be a wonderful challenge, planning an elaborate celebration for fifty people in less than four weeks. She had thought it would be fun. Alison Mitchell and Stephen Flannery had seemed like such nice people, she thought, as she gazed over her spinach salad at the two of them seated on the other side of the booth. How could they be doing this to her now?

"What do you mean, you want to have the ceremony at Jake's house?" she heard herself asking in disbelief, shocked by her own rudeness, but helpless to disguise her distress.

Ever since she had stood up in Stephen Flannery's office to find Jake Raglan entering her life again, Rebecca had been unsteady on her feet and ready to bolt at any moment. Wasn't it bad enough that she had remembered him looking so incredibly handsome in a dark suit? Now she had to see how gorgeous and sexy he was in a light-colored one, as well? For three months the man had haunted her thoughts and dreams, and for three months, Rebecca had been telling herself it was only a matter of time until she would weed him out of her system.

But her preoccupation with him hadn't ebbed at all. In fact, the more she had tried to deny how attractive she'd found him, the deeper her thoughts of him seemed to take root in her mind. She had told herself she was blowing his physical attributes out of proportion, that no man could possibly be as handsome as she was remembering him. And now she had to admit uncomfortably that her recollections of Jake Raglan didn't even begin to do the man justice.

The blue eyes she had found so compelling then were now lit with easy humor and fun as he witnessed her obvious anxiety, and the dark hair sprinkled with bits of silver called to her traitorous hands like a siren's song, urging her to bury her fingers there and pull him close until they could lose themselves in each other.

Almost as if he sensed the avenue her thoughts had taken, Jake shifted his position on the seat beside her in the booth, and his thigh brushed briefly against hers.

Immediately, Rebecca wondered what the same action would feel like if they were both undressed, then felt her cheeks flame in horror that she was entertaining such uncharacteristic thoughts. Oh, no, Rebecca hadn't forgotten Jake Raglan at all. And now she would have to start trying all over again.

She wasn't sure if he was doing it on purpose when he changed positions again and this time let his leg linger against hers, but his smile was suspicious when she glanced over at him. For some reason, though, she did nothing to put a little distance between them.

"I think it's a great idea," Jake said in reference to his earlier offer. He still wasn't sure why he'd made it, but now that it was done, it seemed appropriate. "I've been living in that house for six months now, and I have yet to entertain anyone. There will be plenty of room, and weather-wise, late October is generally a beautiful time of year around here. There will still be flowers in the backyard." And that, he told himself, was the only reason he was doing this. It had nothing to do with the fact that now Rebecca would be forced to spend a good deal of time at his house and, consequently, with him. Nothing whatsoever.

"But…" she began to object.

"Rebecca, you have to see this guy's house to appreciate it," Stephen told her. "It really is a showplace since he had the decorators in. You'll love it."

Rebecca's smile was hollow as she tried to calm her frantic thoughts. This was not going at all as planned. When she and Alison had spoken on the phone last week, the bride-to-be had described a dream she had embraced since childhood, to have her wedding occur outdoors, against a well-manicured, parklike backdrop.

Immediately, Rebecca had thought of Gardencourt at the Presbyterian Seminary, a beautifully landscaped and recently renovated location. It would have been magnificent. Mid-autumn weather, chrysanthemums of yellow, gold and amber springing up amid leaves of red, ocher, copper and plum, a color scheme for the wedding of scarlet and ivory and black.... She sighed inaudibly at the memory. It would have been so lovely.

But now... *Now* Stephen was suggesting mutiny, and Alison was going along with him. Had the words "Jake Raglan's house" come up during their conversation last week, Rebecca would have slammed the telephone receiver down into its cradle and bolted every door and window in her office, then would have placed the Out to Lunch sign in the window indefinitely and caught the next flight to Tierra del Fuego.

"Of course, Alison will want to have a look at the house before deciding," Stephen was saying when Rebecca finally pulled herself back into the conversation. "But it was awfully generous of you to offer, Jake. I must say, you're taking a more active role in this wedding than I thought you would."

Jake waved a hand negligently and replied magnanimously, "Well, that was before I realized what a wonderful woman you were marrying."

However, it wasn't Alison who claimed his attention as he spoke, Rebecca noted uncomfortably. It was she herself. "I'll need to approve the house, as well," she spoke up softly, turning away from his lingering

gaze to address her clients. "It may not be appropriate
for fifty people. The size of the yard—"

"Over an acre," Jake told her. "No problem."

"We'll also need to consider the size of the
kitchen—"

"It's big enough."

"Whether there's one room large enough to seat all
the guests, just in case it rains—"

"I have a huge dining room. We can just move the
furniture out."

"If Mr. Raglan has pets, there are guests who might
be allergic—"

"No pets. Don't worry."

"And, of course, we must make sure no one will
be…ah…inconvenienced," Rebecca concluded a little
awkwardly.

Unwillingly, she turned to face Jake once again, and
found him staring back at her with obvious confusion.
She cleared her throat delicately before explaining.
"I…I know you aren't married," she stammered,
"but there may be someone who is a…a frequent,
um…*visitor* to your home and who may be, as I said,
inconvenienced by fifty people invading the premises."

Jake laughed outright. "Are you trying to find out
whether I have a girlfriend, Rebecca?"

She could feel heat seep up from her breasts to her
cheeks, and cursed herself for being so easily embarrassed. "Why, no, I, uh…I just want to make sure all
the bases are covered, that's all."

His smile turned smug as he replied, "There's no
one in particular who spends weekends with me, and

I don't have a girlfriend, if that's what you want to know.'' He leaned toward Rebecca until their shoulders touched and whispered further, ''But you never know who might turn up.''

Then with a wicked grin, he straightened in his seat again, and Rebecca had to stifle a strangled groan when she felt his thigh rubbing slowly and deliberately against hers once more. Now she knew he was doing it on purpose. But strangely, she kind of liked it.

''When would you like to see the house?'' he asked the other couple, still smiling cryptically.

''As soon as possible,'' Alison said, her words laced with excitement. ''Tonight?''

''That's fine with me,'' Stephen agreed.

''I can't,'' Rebecca told them. ''I'm sorry, I have another engagement. It's business…another wedding.''

She told herself she added the explanation for the benefit of her clients—who were entitled to know why she was unable to be present—and not because Jake threw her a look that was rife with suspicion. Damn him, it's none of his business, she told herself. So why did she feel as if she owed him an explanation, more than she did the others?

''Stephen, you and Alison can come over this evening, and Rebecca can come when her schedule permits,'' Jake suggested. ''Tomorrow night?'' he asked her casually.

Rebecca wanted more than anything to be able to tell him no, but that was impossible. She would definitely need to see Jake's house if that was where Alison decided she wanted to have her wedding. In a fit of futile optimism, Rebecca told herself, Maybe Alison wouldn't like Jake's house. Maybe the bride-to-be would decide to go with Gardencourt, after all. Maybe she herself was worrying in vain. Tomorrow morning, her clients could very well call to say that they had decided not to have the wedding at the best man's home. Maybe this time, Rebecca concluded her pep talk hopefully, the gods would smile on her instead of laughing at her, and pull her out of harm's way. Harm in this case, of course, being Jake Raglan.

"I think tomorrow evening will be fine," Rebecca finally replied, telling herself in the meantime that their rendezvous might never take place. "Say, six-thirty?"

"Better make it seven o'clock," Jake said. "I seldom leave the office before six-thirty."

He gave her directions to his house, and Rebecca was surprised to discover it wasn't far from her own. But Jake's address in Bonnycastle, near Cherokee Park, indicated his home was probably worth five times what her modest Crescent Hill tollhouse had cost her. Still, his was a beautiful neighborhood full of old houses, huge trees and lush yards boasting colorful gardens. A wedding at Jake's house might indeed be a splendid celebration. So why didn't Rebecca feel more festive?

Jake's *was* a beautiful house, Rebecca decided immediately upon pulling up in front of it the following evening. A sprawling structure of yellow creek stone with a pale gray tiled roof, Jake's house looked warm and inviting in the dying rays of the setting sun. She was surprised to see a yard full of flowers and a porch populated by pots of flowering plants, normally an indication of feminine influence, then decided quickly that she shouldn't be. Naturally a man like Jake Raglan was going to know lots of women, and she suspected one of them probably claimed a hand in teaching him to care for the place.

Rebecca felt depression settle over her as she realized that Jake must share an intimate tie with at least one other woman. Then she chastised herself for considering herself in the running to begin with. There was absolutely no reason that would warrant getting involved with the man whose home she would be invading for the next three weeks. Jake had made it more than clear how he felt about the topic of matrimony, and it was completely at odds with the intentions Rebecca herself embraced.

Now all she had to do was keep repeating that over and over in her head so that no other thought of Jake Raglan would dare brave entry. Unfortunately, at that moment, the front door to the big house before her opened, and the man she swore she would be able to ignore stood framed in the arched doorway that offered entry into his home. For a single, crazy moment, Rebecca was overcome by the feeling that she belonged exactly where she was, that this scenario was one that should be played out every day. Coming home to a man like Jake, to a house like this, just seemed right somehow. Taking a deep breath, Rebecca closed her eyes and, with no small amount of effort, willed the feeling to go away.

How had she allowed herself to get roped into this?

Rebecca asked herself as she began what felt like an endless journey up the walkway toward the front door. A few days ago, she had been looking forward to a couple of weeks off. Her most recent clients had canceled at the last minute the wedding ceremony she was planning for them, opting instead to elope in an effort to escape the parental meddling that was threatening their relationship. As a result, Rebecca had planned to use her sudden break from work and the couple's non-refundable deposit to do a little skiing and unwind.

Then Alison Mitchell had called, hoping against hope that Rebecca Bellamy was free to plan a wedding in three weeks, because she wanted more than anything in the world to be married in October, outdoors, before the chilly weather set in. Rebecca had thought, Why not? Skiing would be around all season, and she really did love doing autumn weddings—the colors, the sounds, the smells, the onset of the holiday season. It would be fun, she had thought then. It would be a good time for a celebration.

Now, as she approached an awaiting Jake Raglan, she felt strangely detached from the real world, as if she was no longer in control of anything that was happening to her. When he pushed the storm door outward, she saw that he was wearing clothes like none she had ever seen him wear—faded, form-hugging jeans and a slouchy navy blue sweatshirt. The fingers of one hand were curled around the stem of a glass half-full of ruby-colored wine, and as she drew nearer, Rebecca could smell the bouquet of the burgundy mingled with something rawly masculine and potently intoxicating.

Crazily, the only thought that went through her head was that she was overdressed in her forest green suit. But instead of wanting to be dressed as casually as he, Rebecca had the wild, uncontrollable desire to simply step out of her clothes and into his arms.

"I halfway thought you wouldn't show," he murmured when she was close enough to hear him.

His voice was low, deep, smoothly intimate, as if he knew exactly what she was thinking and couldn't wait to help her carry out her intentions.

"That wouldn't be very fair to my clients, now, would it?" she countered a little breathlessly, trying to still the ragged thumping of her pulse.

"Ah, yes. You're only here because of business, right? No pleasure allowed."

Normally, Rebecca would have denied that such was the case at all, because she took great pleasure in her work. If she was honest with herself, she would even admit to a few thrills of excitement and anticipation in planning *this* wedding. But she knew Jake would choose to misinterpret any enthusiasm she might show for this project—after all, there was pleasure, and then there was *pleasure*—so she only smiled at him and said, "No, no pleasure allowed. Not tonight."

"Then I guess there's no point in asking you if you'd like to take your coat off and stay awhile, maybe have a glass of wine?"

Again, Rebecca found herself wanting to answer differently than she actually did. "No, I guess there wouldn't be."

He sighed in resignation and invited her to come in,

closing the door behind them when she was safely inside. Rebecca stared in amazement at the room in which she found herself, trying to align the inside of Jake's house with the outside. The living room was large and spacious, and the furnishings were dark, expensive and beautiful, but something was missing, something very important—warmth.

Where the flowers outside attested to loving care and domestic tranquillity, the arrangement of Jake's things inside were in no way evocative of such tenderness and affection for one's surroundings. Although the room looked like something from the pages of a glossy magazine, it wasn't…real. There was no soul here, no feeling. It didn't appear as if any living went on in the living room, and Rebecca wondered if maybe it was because he just never used it.

"The dining room is this way," Jake said, jumping right to the point of her visit. "And then I'll take you out back."

Through each room they passed, Rebecca noted curiously that Jake's house simply did not exhibit any kind of personal touches. There were no photographs, no mementos, no souvenirs, no awards. Her own house was very small, but was crowded with the tokens she had earned to commemorate her rites of passage through life—from the Raggedy Ann doll and homecoming mum in her bedroom, to her Best of Louisville award in her living room. And on her hallway walls were photographs of just about every relative she had, right down to her four-week-old niece.

Rebecca's house reflected everything in Rebecca's character, everything in her very soul. Jake's house was like the backdrop for a stage play—paint and fabric and wood, and not much else.

Upon entering the dining room, Rebecca saw that it would indeed be commodious enough for fifty people with the removal of the table, chairs and china cabinet. With further exploration, she also decided that the kitchen—a sprawling white room full of high-tech appliances—would be ample enough for the caterer. And when they stepped through the back door and wandered out into the yard, Rebecca confirmed that it, too, would be large enough to hold both the ceremony and reception outside if the weather was agreeable. She also couldn't help but note that it was as lovingly planted and painfully tended as the front, as lush and full of warmth as the house was lacking in it. Jake's home was, to say the least, an enigma.

"It's beautiful out here," she said softly, genuinely. The sun had nearly dropped completely from the sky, and in the pink-and-amber twilight of another gorgeous Kentucky sunset, Jake's backyard was awash with red and gold. "You must have some green thumb to keep everything in such good shape. Me, I've never had much luck with anything except house plants."

"Oh, I don't take care of the yard," Jake told her. "I have someone come in to do that. I bought the house from an elderly couple who were moving to Georgia to be closer to their kids. Mrs. Eddleston was the real gardener. She's the one who put all the flowers out and everything. It all looked so nice, I hated it that everything would choke and die at my hands. So I have a gardener come in once a week to take care of everything. As you can see, he works wonders around here.''

That explains a lot, Rebecca thought with a silent nod. Obviously, Jake was a very busy man, and it would be crazy to think of him out tending to his roses in the manner of a gentleman-gardener on a warm Sunday afternoon. Still, despite his assurances to the contrary—which he offered frequently—Rebecca sensed something about Jake Raglan that was indeed nurturing and domestic. She wasn't sure why she should think such a thing—certainly he had never shown any indication of hearth-and-home tendencies—but Rebecca couldn't shake the feeling that there was some secret place in his soul that wanted very badly to be part of a family. Before she could ponder the suspicion further, though, his voice distracted her, posing a question she didn't quite hear.

"Hmm? What?" she replied absently, still gazing with unseeing eyes out at the yard.

"I...I asked if you wanted to go back inside."

Jake was watching Rebecca closely, wondering what it was that kept her thoughts so faraway. There was a dreamy, thoughtful expression on her face, and for the first time, he knew he was seeing her without her guard up. In the quickly fading light, her skin was almost translucent, rosy with warmth and as fragile-looking as porcelain. The breeze kicked up then, nudging a stray lock of hair across her face, and before he realized what he was doing, Jake lifted his hand to push it back over her shoulder. When he did, she turned to look at him, her expression still hazy and distant, her defenses still dropped.

Cupping her cheek gently in his palm, Jake thumbed another curl back from her face, unconsciously parting his lips as if to speak...or to kiss her, which was what he really wanted to do. Before he could commit to either, however, Rebecca's eyes focused on his again, and he was surprised when she didn't push him away. Instead, she placed her own hand softly over his, smiling sadly, sympathetically, as if she felt exactly what it was that tore him up inside. Then she slowly moved his hand away, and turned to go back into the house.

"I think Alison and Stephen will have a lovely wedding here," she told him without looking back. "I'll get together with the florist and the caterers this week, and I'll arrange for the photographer. They may or may not want to see the premises before the wedding day, so I'll be in touch to let you know. If it will be inconvenient for you—"

"Why don't I just give you a key to the house?"

His question stopped Rebecca in her tracks, and she pivoted to face him with an expression that indicated his offer couldn't have shocked her more.

"That isn't really customary—" she began.

"That's okay," he stammered with a shrug. "I trust you. And I know you're probably going to need access to the house on a number of occasions over the next three weeks. I'm in and out of my office all the time, and I usually work well past normal business hours, so you might not be able to reach me, and I might not be available every time you need to get in."

"Jake, I don't think it's a good idea."

It was the first time she had called him by his first name since Daphne's wedding, and Jake decided he had missed hearing it from her lips. Just why had he suggested that she take a key to his house? *No one* had ever been offered a key to Jake's house, not even members of his family. But then, he had never been particularly trusting of anyone in his family, and no one in his family except Daphne had ever really expressed an interest in seeing his home to begin with. Yet here was a woman he'd met on only three occasions, and he was ready to allow her access to everything he owned. For some reason, it seemed perfectly acceptable for Rebecca to have a key. More than that, it just seemed…right.

"I don't know," she hedged. "I'm not sure I'm comfortable with an arrangement like that."

Fearing that Rebecca would make an excellent argument, Jake quickly approached her, placed his hand gently in the small of her back and propelled her back into his house. Setting his wine on the kitchen table, he strode purposefully toward a corner hutch and lifted the lid on a canister marked Tea.

"I never drink the stuff," he explained as he withdrew the one spare key he possessed. Until now, he had always assumed that if he ever needed to give the key to anyone, the recipient would be Stephen, on some occasion when Jake had to be out of town for a protracted length of time. Never in his wildest dreams had he thought he would be surrendering his spare key to a woman.

"Really, Jake, I—"

Taking her hand in his, Jake turned it up to drop the key into her palm, closing her fingers gently over it after he did so. "Don't worry about it," he told her. "I'm not going to."

And surprisingly, he wasn't, Jake realized as a strange kind of serenity settled over him.

"Call first, if you can," he concluded. "But even if I'm not home, you're welcome in my house anytime, Rebecca."

With a slight lifting her shoulders, Rebecca smiled shyly and said, "Thanks, Jake. That's nice of you. I promise not to take advantage of the situation."

Which, of course, was more than he was willing to do. In the back of his brain, Jake wondered if maybe he hadn't simply orchestrated this entire escapade so that he could take advantage of Rebecca Bellamy. All he knew was that he looked forward to finding her in his house. The sooner the better.

Three

_____

It wound up being sooner than Jake thought. Three evenings after telling Rebecca Bellamy goodbye at his front door without so much as a handshake, Jake came home to find her in his dining room, crouched on the floor with tape measure in hand, scribbling in a notebook. Apparently she hadn't heard him come in, so he took advantage of the opportunity to study her unobserved.

Instead of her usual working uniform of tailored suit, tonight Rebecca was dressed casually in a deep scarlet sweater and faded blue jeans, and her dark hair was woven into a thick braid that swung over her shoulder like a length of rope. As Jake leaned silently in the doorway, she turned on her knees away from him, placed one end of the tape measure against the wall opposite his position, and began to crawl backward, unwinding the measure as she did so. Her movements provided him with an intriguing picture, to say the least. Jake bit his lip to keep from speaking out loud the suggestive comment he wanted to utter as he beheld the exquisite curves and motions of Rebecca's backside coming toward him. Instead, he focused on trying to stem the rush of heat that invaded and overtook some very dangerous parts of his body.

Only when Rebecca backed into his shin did she finally realize she wasn't alone. As if jabbed by a cattle prod, she leapt forward awkwardly, trying to turn around and identify what had obstructed her progress as she did so. The result of her action was to send her sprawling onto her bottom, hands outstretched behind her to break her fall, legs spread wide. When she looked up to find Jake Raglan laughing at her, Rebecca's relief that he wasn't a burglar quickly turned to annoyance that he found so much humor in something that had scared the living daylights out of her.

"What are you doing here?" she demanded, still shaken by his appearance and sounding, she realized belatedly, very proprietary.

Jake smiled down at her as he continued to lean lazily in the doorway. "Gee, how quickly they take possession," he said mildly. "In case you've forgotten, Rebecca, I live here."

"Sorry," she apologized sheepishly. "I didn't mean to snap. I just wasn't expecting to see anyone. I called your office before I came over, but Stephen said you were having dinner with a client and couldn't be reached, and that you'd probably be tied up for most of the evening. If I'd known you'd be home, I would have waited until you were here."

It had felt very strange to come over to Jake's house and use his key to gain entry. An unsettling, lonely silence had greeted her when she'd opened the door, and Rebecca had been uneasy the moment she set foot inside. When she came home from work to her own house, her two cats, Bogart and Bacall, immediately raced to the front door and loudly demanded her attention, each rolling around on the rug and vying to see whose tummy would get rubbed first. There was always some interesting dialogue or commentary sounding from the radio, because Rebecca left it tuned to National Public Radio during the day so that the cats would have human voices to listen to. Between that and the wind chimes on her front porch, and the Benny Carter tapes she listened to when she was home at night, Rebecca's house was never, ever, quiet.

But Jake's was. Even now that he was home, except for the sounds of their voices, a silence still hung over the house that was anything but comforting.

"My client was called away between cocktails and ordering so I came on home to eat," Jake told her. He didn't bother to add how much he detested eating in restaurants alone.

Although he rather liked the position into which Rebecca had fallen, he reluctantly extended his hand to offer her assistance in getting up. "Imagine my surprise to find a vintage roadster parked in my driveway," he added as he pulled her toward him. "That's some car you've got there, Rebecca."

The pressure Jake exerted in helping her up was a little more than was actually necessary to successfully complete the task. As a result, Rebecca found herself nestled quite perfectly against his chest, her hand still captured by his, his palm settled intimately against her hip in an effort to steady her. She had sought balance by splaying her hand over the front of his shirt, and she marveled at the hardness and warmth of the flesh she felt beneath her fingertips. Suddenly, the air around her, which she'd considered so empty before, was filled with a tension and electricity like nothing she'd ever experienced. Suddenly, Jake's house was warm indeed.

For a moment, neither of them moved or spoke, but their gazes met and held as if magnetically drawn. Then gradually, hesitantly, Jake pressed his fingers more firmly into Rebecca's jeans-clad flesh, and raked them down her thigh with maddening slowness. Rebecca gasped softly, her eyes widening in surprise, but she did nothing to stop his motions. Without thinking, she bunched a fistful of his shirt and tie in her hand, as if willing him closer. Jake responded with a quiet groan, dragging his fingers up the back of her thigh until his hand cupped over her derriere. With gentle pressure, he urged her hips forward until they were settled against his own, then he bent his head down toward hers.

Instinctively, Rebecca lifted her face to receive Jake's kiss, senseless to everything around her except him. At first, he only brushed his lips softly against hers, nipping, teasing, leisurely tasting, as if asking her permission to go further. Rebecca's eyelids fluttered downward at the tantalizing sensations that went zinging through her body with every brief, feathery caress. And when she felt the tip of his tongue tracing a slow circle around her mouth, Rebecca nearly collapsed in his arms, issuing a single, soft sigh of surrender.

That quietly uttered sound was Jake's undoing. It was as if a dam of emotion split open inside him then, and all the pent-up frustration of wanting Rebecca for three months without having her finally gushed forth without control. His kiss deepened perilously, became a sensual foray that challenged Rebecca, dared her to go as far as her desires would carry her. In the back of her mind, she knew that things were going way too fast, that nothing could have prepared her for the position she was in now, and that nothing good would come of it. Still, she was as active a participant as Jake was, and his passion only mirrored her own.

Then, without warning, the kiss ended. And Rebecca was chagrined to realize she hadn't been the one to end it. Jake seemed to tower over her when she looked up to meet his gaze, his chest rising and falling raggedly and rapidly. For just an instant, Rebecca was shocked to see fear—real fear—glinting in the depths of his blue eyes, but as quickly as she had detected it, the frightened expression was gone, replaced by the easy humor that seemed to be such an integral part of his character.

"Hi, honey, I'm home," he mumbled softly, his words punctuated by quiet, unsteady laughter.

Rebecca didn't know what to say. Her heart was pounding like a jackhammer, her blood racing like a roller coaster, her nerves as jagged and jumpy as a chain saw. "I...that..." She took a deep breath and tried again. "That shouldn't have happened," she finally stated shakily. Then to her horror, she realized she was still grasping the front of Jake's shirt as if he were her most prized possession, and she released him as if he were something poisonous. "I'm...I'm sorry," she whispered quickly, nervously smoothing her fingers over the soft fabric. "I have to get home."

She jerked away from him then, scrambling to pick up her coat and portfolio from the dining room table, stuffing her notepad and tape measure unceremoniously into her purse. As she tried to push past Jake, he reached out calmly and wrapped his fingers gently around her wrist, halting her attempt to flee.

"Don't go."

Those two little words stuck in Rebecca's heart like nothing she'd ever experienced before. So much pleading, so much sorrow, so much...loneliness... permeated them, that she couldn't help but look up into his face.

He wasn't gazing down at her, but instead focused his attention on the empty wall opposite them. His jaw was rigidly set, and he swallowed with some difficulty. All the while, his thumb stroked over the rapid pulse in Rebecca's wrist, his loose grip telling her she was more than free to go if she insisted.

"I'm sorry, too," Jake said, still not looking at her. "You're right. It shouldn't have happened." Then he did turn to observe her with quiet scrutiny. "Not yet, anyway. But I'm not going to promise that it won't happen again."

She really should go, Rebecca thought. She'd only come because she wanted to get the dimensions of the dining room and kitchen for the florist and the caterer, who would need to know how much space they had to work with, should the ceremony and reception wind up being held inside. Now that she had the information, there was no reason to stay. None except for the fact that she simply didn't want to leave. None except for the fact that she honestly wanted to spend more time with Jake Raglan.

"That's okay," she finally told him. In an effort to dispel the uncomfortable tension that still stained the air so heavily, she added playfully, "Who says you're going to get another opportunity, anyway?"

Jake smiled, but he was feeling anything but happy. Just what the hell had come over him, anyway? Good God, he hadn't come on to a woman as quickly and uncontrollably as he had with Rebecca in his entire life. What was it about her that tied his libido in knots? Why couldn't he keep his hands to himself where she was concerned? And why, dammit, did it feel so good to come home from work and find her here?

"I bet I do," he rejoined, as relieved as she that the uneasy moment had passed.

Rebecca shook her head slowly, but knew deep down that hers was an empty promise. She was going to be spending the next three weeks planning a wedding that was to take place in his home, and for which he was to be best man. Certainly a number of opportunities would arise between now and the nineteenth. She just had to decide once and for all what she was going to make of them.

"Have you eaten dinner?" Jake asked her.

He still hadn't released her wrist, so Rebecca glanced down at it meaningfully. Reluctantly, Jake let go and lifted his hands in surrender, then crossed his arms over his chest to await her reply.

Rebecca adjusted the strap of her purse on her shoulder, as if such an act would help her insist that she had to leave. "No, I ate a late lunch today, then spent the rest of the afternoon sampling wedding cakes and treats at a new bakery that opened in the Highlands, so I haven't been hungry for a while.''

That's funny, Jake wanted to reply. I've been starving for something ever since I met you. He wondered idly how she managed to stay so slim when she must attend dozens of functions where rich, high-calorie foods were served. Oh, how he'd love to help her burn a few of those calories off now and then.

"So, are you hungry now? We could go out for something," he suggested. "Or order in."

Rebecca hesitated before responding, telling herself she was making a big mistake as she asked, "What would you have done if I hadn't been here when you came home?"

Besides be utterly disappointed and thoroughly lonely? he wondered. Pushing the thought away, he replied, "I'd have called China Joe's for Hunan shrimp and a couple of egg rolls."

Rebecca grinned. "That's closer to my house in Crescent Hill. I didn't think they delivered out this far."

"I'm one of their best customers."

She nodded as her smile grew wider. "Make it three egg rolls, and throw in an order of cashew chicken, and I'll stay."

Jake grinned back. "Evidently I have competition in the 'best customer' category."

"I work a lot of evenings," Rebecca explained. "It's easier than cooking."

Actually, she just hated cooking when it was only for herself. Invariably, whatever she whipped up in the kitchen went bad before she had a chance to enjoy the leftovers, and grocery shopping for one was often a futile expedition. Everything seemed to be family-size these days—side dishes, main dishes…even canned soup provided two servings. She couldn't get fresh produce in quantities suitable for one, unless she waited until the store clerks turned their backs and provided her with an opportunity to break up bunches of bananas or divide the rubber-banded stalks of asparagus. She had come to feel like a criminal whenever she went to the grocery store, so she had simply opted to eat out or order in most of the time.

While they awaited the arrival of their dinner, Jake and Rebecca retired to the living room. Jake had changed clothes after making the call, and now crouched in front of the fireplace in jeans and a Berea College sweatshirt. Rebecca observed him intently as he tended to the tiny flames flickering to life amid the kindling, pondering what few things she knew about him, curious to discover more. He had opened a bottle of chardonnay to enjoy with their simple carry-out dinner, and now as he sat back against the hearth, he twirled his glass thoughtfully at the base, gazing unseeingly into its transparent depths.

"You went to Berea?" Rebecca asked conversationally, indicating the word stretched across his chest.

"For my undergraduate degree, yes," he told her. "My law degree is from Vanderbilt."

"But you wear your Berea sweatshirt," she pointed out. It was a remarkably good school, but one that was little known outside collegiate circles. Berea was noted not only for its academic excellence, but because it provided an opportunity to underprivileged students who wouldn't otherwise be able to pay for college. Virtually everyone enrolled at Berea was required to work in some capacity to oversee the cost of tuition, most opting for the arts and crafts that generated a good portion of the university's income. Others worked in Boone Tavern, a hotel and restaurant well-known for its local fare. She was surprised that Jake Raglan had attended such a university. The vast majority of the students at Berea were from rural, economically depressed areas, particularly Appalachia.

"I liked Berea a lot," Jake said as he sipped his wine. "It's a wonderful school. Ellen and I both went there."

"Are you from Louisville originally?" she asked curiously.

Jake shook his head. "Nope. Hazard County. A little smudge on the map called Acorn Ridge."

"No kidding?"

"No kidding." His voice was flat as he spoke, indicating quite clearly that Jake harbored absolutely no affection for his hometown. When he'd voiced the name of the community, he had almost spat it out.

"You, uh, you don't have a rural accent at all," she said softly.

"No, I followed Ellen's example and worked hard all through college to get rid of it."

Rebecca was puzzled. "But why? Some of those accents are lovely."

Jake shifted uncomfortably in his position on the floor, threading the fingers of one hand restlessly through his hair. He didn't look at her when he spoke, and his thoughts seemed to be far, far away. "Because, Rebecca, nobody takes you seriously when you talk like a hick. And for a lawyer who wants to make it big outside his hometown, a Southern accent is nothing but a hindrance.''

"Do you go home very often?"

"Home is here now."

"But what about your parents?"

"Dead."

His voice was low, and Rebecca had to strain to hear it. She wasn't sure exactly when it had happened, but Jake had almost completely withdrawn from her. Not that he had been especially generous with himself before, but this side of Jake Raglan was one even she wouldn't have anticipated. It was as if he had placed himself on automatic pilot and was replying to her questions without considering the import of his answers. He displayed no emotion whatever in relation to the images of his past that must be vivid in his memory.

"I'm sorry," she said quietly.

Jake waved a hand airily in her direction, but still didn't look at her. "It was a long time ago. Life in the mountains wasn't the easiest in the world. My old man contracted black lung long before he was my age and died about fifteen years ago. My mother held on for a couple more years, but she finally gave up, too.''

Rebecca was at a loss. She'd never met anyone who had seen the passing of both parents at such a young age. Except for the death of her grandmother when she was seventeen, she'd never experienced the loss of a family member herself. She couldn't imagine how she would react to such a tragedy. It would be devastating. Yet here was Jake Raglan talking about the deaths of the two people who had given him life as if he hadn't even known them.

"Well, at least you still have your sister, Ellen, and her family."

Jake drained the ample amount of wine left in his glass before responding. "Yeah, thank God for Ellen," he ground out bitterly. "At least she did one thing right when she decided to keep Daphne."

"Jake, what are you talking about?"

"Look," he muttered impatiently, "would it be too much to ask that we change the subject?"

"No, of course not." Rebecca remained silent for some moments, confused about everything Jake had just revealed, and intrigued by all the things he hadn't. She posed the first question that came to mind, one that seemed perfectly harmless and conducive to less volatile discussion. "So, what's your undergraduate degree in?" She still wanted to discover as much about this man as she possibly could, despite the fact that he didn't seem overly inclined to conversation.

"English."

"Really?" She couldn't hide her astonishment. She might have expected anything else, but this came as a surprise.

"I know you like to think that all lawyers are an insensitive bunch, Rebecca," he said bitingly, "but one or two of us actually do have an appreciation for the finer things in life."

Her back went up automatically, defensively. He could see immediately that he had hit a nerve. "Oh, you'll get no argument from me there. The finer the better, I'd say. Louisville wasn't good enough for Eliot's practice, so he took off for San Francisco. I wasn't good enough to be Eliot's wife—ironically enough, because I wasn't a college graduate—so he became involved with a graduate student in sociology who was more intellectually stimulating.''

"Rebecca…''

"And coincidentally, she was from a wealthy family, too,'' Rebecca went on relentlessly, nearly choking on her words. "I'm sure that was a big bonus as far as Eliot was concerned. Her folks probably didn't pull the plug on her finances, either, the way mine did.''

"Rebecca…''

He rose from his position on the floor as if he intended to approach her, but the doorbell rang then and startled them both back to reality. When Jake had paid the deliveryman and closed the door behind him, he stared at Rebecca for a moment in the soft amber glow of the fire.

"I'm sorry I overreacted,'' he finally said quietly. "You just touched on a sensitive issue.''

Rebecca lifted her chin defensively. "So did you.''

"Truce?''

She nodded, braving a small smile. "Truce.''

"Then let's eat.''

They passed the remainder of the evening in companionable conversation, skirting questions and topics that might lead to unwelcome probing, sticking to the small talk that people pursue when they don't know each other very well. It was awkward, Rebecca thought, because she at least didn't feel as if Jake was a stranger to her. The kiss they had shared only a short time ago still lingered on her lips like a warm, familiar caress, and she continued to marvel that she could have reacted so quickly, so heatedly, to a man she barely knew. What she experienced with Jake Raglan was truly puzzling.

The awkwardness became an almost-palpable discomfort when it came time for Rebecca to leave. Having already kissed once, it seemed perfectly realistic to expect the evening to end with another one. Yet at the same time, both had agreed that their earlier embrace shouldn't have happened. Because she wasn't sure how she should act, Rebecca wound up staying later at Jake's house than she would normally have done, simply because she was uncertain, and not a little fearful, about what would occur. When the grandfather clock in Jake's hall tolled eleven times, however, she knew she couldn't put it off any longer.

"It's late," she said softly after the last chime had faded away. "And we both have to work tomorrow."

Jake nodded, but remained silent, rising from his position on the floor. It wasn't that he had nothing to say to Rebecca—just the opposite, in fact. He wanted to tell her how wonderful it had been to come home from work and have someone to talk to for a change. He wanted to plead with her not to leave just yet, that there was so much they had left to discuss. He wanted to describe the strange stirring of desire her presence in his home aroused in him. He wanted to laugh with her some more, to be with her a little longer. He wanted… He wanted so much. Perhaps too much.

So Jake said nothing. He was afraid that if he opened his mouth, one thing would lead to another, and he would wind up telling Rebecca things he wasn't sure he was ready to acknowledge to himself. Instead, he moved silently to the front door, opened it while Rebecca gathered her things together, then waited restlessly for her to say goodbye.

But Rebecca didn't say goodbye. She paused before stepping outside, turned to Jake and asked uncertainly, "How about dinner at my house Friday night?"

It probably wasn't a good idea, Jake thought. His odd thoughts and feelings tonight aside, there were other things to consider. Rebecca Bellamy simply wasn't the kind of woman to have a brief affair with a man. She had made it quite clear on their initial meeting that she was indeed the marrying kind—more specifically the kind who was looking forward to it ASAP. If she was inviting him over to her house for dinner, it was no doubt because she wanted to get to know him better—better in the sense that she wanted to discover his husband potential. He owed it to both of them to stress that he had absolutely no potential in that department at all.

"Friday," he repeated, trying to come up with a good excuse why he was unavailable. "Friday, let's see…"

Rebecca felt her heart drop. She'd been single long enough to know when a man was stalling. Come to think of it, she'd been married long enough to know when a man was stalling, too.

"That's okay, never mind," she said quickly, throwing up a hand to affect an indifferent goodbye. "It was a bad idea. I know you must be very busy." In an awkward rush, she started to push past him, adding hastily, "I probably won't have to bother you again for a couple of weeks, so you won't have to worry about me invading your house again. I'll be in touch, Jake. Goodbye."

Jake blocked her retreat by stretching a muscular arm across the doorframe, at a height that coincidentally fell right below Rebecca's breasts. She was able to stop herself just before she would have barreled right into him. When she looked up at him, his expression was bland, offering her no insight into what he might be thinking or feeling. His eyes were dark and assessing, however, and Rebecca began to feel like an insect trapped beneath a microscope.

"Friday sounds great," he said finally. "But there's something you have to remember about me, Rebecca, something I have to make perfectly clear. I enjoy spending time with you. You're attractive, intelligent and fun to be with. But I'm not looking for anything long-term. I'm not looking for a relationship. I can't stress it enough—I'm not going to marry anyone, ever again."

Rebecca studied his features long and hard. Hadn't he already told her that once? Hadn't he reemphasized by his words and actions on numerous occasions since then that those were his precise feelings? It should matter to her, she told herself. She wanted to find a man with whom she could settle down for the rest of her life. But suddenly she didn't want any man but Jake Raglan.

"I didn't ask you to marry me, Jake," she heard herself say playfully, scarcely recognizing the flirtatious fluffiness her voice carried with the statement. Even Jake seemed surprised by her lighthearted response. "I just asked you if you wanted to have dinner with me."

"What time?"

Rebecca shrugged. "Seven?"

"Seven it is, then."

Before he dropped his arm so that she could pass, Jake leaned toward Rebecca with a predatory smile. All he could think about was how much fun it would be to unwind her braid and bury his hands in her hair, then wondered if the opportunity to do so would arise again on Friday. And because he was so overcome by the anticipation of making advances toward Rebecca, instead of taking her mouth hungrily with his, as his desire demanded he do, he only pressed his warm lips against her cheek and murmured his good-night.

Maybe he'd been wrong about Rebecca, he thought, watching the easy sway of her hips as she strode down the walkway toward her car. Maybe she was no more ready to settle down just yet than he was. So she wanted to get married. So what? She hadn't put a time frame on her intentions, had she? She hadn't said she insisted on being married by a specific month of a specific year. Maybe she just wanted to have a good time until the right guy came along. And maybe, Jake concluded as warmth filtered to every part of his body, he was just the guy to help her.

Four

Rebecca couldn't remember the last time she had cooked a meal for a man. Even when she and Eliot had been married, they'd usually cooked together. It was the one memory of her marriage that she carried fondly. She scarcely knew how to go about performing the task now. Briefly, she had entertained the thought of calling China Joe's for delivery, but had quickly dismissed the idea. No, she was determined to do this right. Jake Raglan was an interesting man, one she definitely wanted to get to know better. It had been too long since she'd met someone she even wanted to go out with, let alone see more than once. Jake just might turn out to be a man she could see a lot of. He might even turn out to be a man that she could love.

Don't do it, Rebecca ordered herself, as she sliced the ends from asparagus stalks. Don't even allow yourself to hope that something substantial might result from your time with Jake. He's already told you he has no intention of ever marrying again. Don't expect much from him in the way of reciprocity.

Although Rebecca's head assured her such was the case—Jake had, after all, spelled it out for her in no uncertain terms at his house earlier this week—in her heart she sensed that there was another part of him, a deeper, stronger part, that would assert just the contrary.

As if conjured up by her musings, a series of rapid knocks at the front door announced his arrival. Rebecca shouted out that she was coming, finished the last of her preparations, tossed aside her chef's apron and smoothed a hand over her hair to tuck a few errant strands back into her braid. After a quick glance in the mirror, she opened her front door to find Jake Raglan looking polished and handsome in dark corduroy trousers and a creamy fisherman-knit sweater, a bottle of wine in one hand, and a huge bunch of amber spider mums in the other.

"The last ones in the garden," he told her.

Rebecca's pulse rate skittered erratically at the sight of him. *Might* turn out to be a man that she could love? she asked herself again. That was a laugh. She was already three-fourths of the way there.

"Thank you," she murmured a little nervously as she took the bouquet from him. She tried not to think about the other bunch of flowers that had come between them three months ago—Daphne's bridal bouquet. Instead, she invited Jake inside, belatedly remarking, "I hope you don't mind cats."

Jake gazed mildly down at the two felines—one black and one white—twisting and curling between his legs, moaning and purring for attention. "What if I do?" he asked mischievously.

Rebecca grinned. "Then I'll have to ask you to leave."

He lifted his eyebrows in surprise. "One of those, are you?"

Rebecca shrugged. "Hey, love me, love my cats."

"You'd choose your cats over the city's most eligible bachelor?"

She feigned surprise. "Oh, so *you're* Louisville's most eligible bachelor. I've been wondering who was."

"Planning on making a play for me?"

"Why? You planning on resisting?"

"Not a chance."

Laughing, she replied, "Well, let's just put it this way—my cats have seen me in the morning before I have my coffee and they're still around. I can't say that about many men."

Jake pushed the door closed behind him, disengaged himself from her cats, and strode into Rebecca's house with a proprietary air. "Just how many men *have* seen you in the morning, Ms. Bellamy?" he asked with a playful wiggle of his eyebrows.

Rebecca felt herself color. "No, I meant… I mean, I *didn't* mean…" She sighed in exasperation, surrendering to her inability to be eloquent when someone's presence was making her extremely nervous. "Eliot, okay? Eliot's the only one besides Bogart. Bacall is a female cat."

Jake thought about that, wondering if it was true. Was her husband the only man Rebecca Bellamy had slept with? If so, then coming here tonight had been a big mistake, and it could make things between them complicated. He himself had been anything but discriminating in girlfriends before he was married. And although he had enjoyed a number of relationships with women since his divorce, none had been anywhere near serious enough to call exclusive, nor had they been particularly fulfilling.

As a result, Jake had adopted an attitude that simply prohibited him from attaching too much significance to any romantic dealings he might have with women. Sex was nice. Sex with someone he liked was even better. But even to suggest that something permanent might result from such a liaison was ridiculous. If Rebecca had been with only one other man in her life, she was liable to place far too much emphasis on emotional entanglements, and far too little on physical satisfaction.

However, that wasn't something he really needed to be thinking about right now, he told himself. Instead, he should be focusing on how delectable she looked in her full, shin-skimming skirt of sage green beneath a loose, belted shirt of pale yellow. Her hair was plaited again, hanging between her shoulder blades to the center of her back, and all Jake could do was rejoice in the fact that he would indeed have another chance to tug it free and untangle the mass of curls over Rebecca's ivory, naked skin. He took a step toward her, uncertain of his intentions, but was held up by the fat, furry presence of two cats rolling around on the floor in front of him.

Rebecca chuckled when she noted his dilemma. "Sorry, but no one gets past that front door until the cats have been amply satisfied."

Jake bent to give each a perfunctory rub on the stomach, then stepped over them until he was face-to-face with Rebecca. "And what about their mistress?" he asked in a dangerously soft voice. "When do I get to satisfy her?"

His eyes were so blue, Rebecca thought absently, suddenly feeling as if she were dangling precariously in the most fragile of webs. A dark, midnight blue like none she'd ever seen before. But instead of being cool and detached, the way they had been the first time she'd seen him, now his eyes were filled with a heat and intensity that seemed to underscore his desire for the most intimate kind of bonding. Before she could stop herself, Rebecca lifted a hand to trace the lines that fanned out from his eyes, letting her fingertips glide into the silver-touched hair above his ear. All she could think about was how much she wanted Jake to kiss her, and instinctively, she turned her face up toward his.

Jake set the bottle of wine down onto an end table by the couch, then he, too, raised his hand to cup Rebecca's cheek gently in his palm. Slowly, he skimmed his fingers down her jaw to the back of her neck, and pulled her braid forward over one shoulder. Rebecca trembled at the caress of his fingertips on her heated, sensitive flesh, but told herself it was only because his skin was cool from the temperature outside.

As Jake ran his thumb down the length of her braid, his knuckles casually brushed the fabric of her shirt and paused at the scrap of yellow satin that bound her hair. He lifted the braid slightly away from her body, his hand hovering just above her breast, and although it seemed a harmless-enough gesture, Rebecca felt a shiver rush from her scalp to the tips of her toes. It was as if his touch sent a part of his spirit spiraling through her body, stealing a little bit of her soul for himself in the process.

For long moments, Jake gently fingered her dark hair, his eyes never leaving hers as he studied the face that had haunted him all week. If she were any other woman, he could free her hair as he had in his fantasies and they could both be writhing naked on the couch in no time. But Rebecca Bellamy wasn't any other woman. And Jake was more than a little astounded to discover that, deep down inside, he didn't want to treat her like one.

Rebecca never replied to the question he posed, so Jake didn't press his luck. Instead, he jumped track and took off in an entirely new direction when he asked, "What's for dinner?"

Rebecca blinked in confusion several times, as if he had just spoken to her in a foreign language. "What? Oh. Oh, yes. Dinner." She stepped away from him resolutely, tossing her braid back over her shoulder when it fell from his fingers. She took a very deep breath and expelled it before she continued. "Lamb chops, new potatoes, asparagus, baby carrots and corn bread. If you'd like to open the wine, I'll just get everything going. Shouldn't take long."

As Rebecca arranged the flowers in a vase and placed them in the center of the table, Jake hastened to do as she instructed. When he had poured glasses of merlot for them both, he added, "What else can I do?"

Rebecca shook her head. "Nothing. You're my guest, so relax. Have a seat and talk to me."

Jake did talk to her, but instead of sitting down, began to prowl around Rebecca's living room. Her Crescent Hill neighborhood was one of the many in Louisville in which the very wealthy mingled with the not-so-very-wealthy, in which the socially and artistically advantaged took up residence right alongside those whose day-to-day existence consisted of simply earning enough to stay alive. When Rebecca had first told Jake where she lived, he had assumed she must be of the former group. But when he had pulled up in her driveway, it had struck him that perhaps she wasn't very successful in her business, after all. Otherwise, why would she be living in such a tiny, tiny house, something that was little more than a cottage, complete with gingerbread trim and a wraparound porch?

However, now he was beginning to change his mind again. Although it was true Rebecca's house was considerably smaller than his own, comprised perhaps of a third of the rooms he himself could claim to wander around in, it was by no means indicative that she was unsuccessful. The interior—like the exterior—was immaculate, her furnishings immediately identifiable as genuine, quality antiques, even to an unpracticed eye like Jake's. The living room dimensions couldn't possibly have exceeded ten feet by twelve feet, but she had made use of every bit of space available. The walls were covered with paintings and awards—another indication that she was indeed successful—and the bookshelves and end tables were stacked with every variety of reading material. There were knick-knacks and mementos everywhere Jake looked, and he realized that simply by standing in her living room, he was learning more about Rebecca Bellamy than she had ever told him.

The living room abutted the kitchen, the two rooms separated simply by a counter. The kitchen itself was a mere corridor with cabinets and appliances on one side. Beyond it was a door opening onto a small hallway that must lead to a bedroom and a bathroom, but from the size of the exterior building, Jake speculated that there could be space for little else inside. Despite the close quarters, though, he was surprisingly comfortable in Rebecca's house.

Jake had always sworn that once he was out of school, he would never be satisfied until he bought a house that was huge. Growing up in Acorn Ridge, he and Ellen had actually been forced to share a bedroom, because his parents' house hadn't been much larger than Rebecca's. It was probably one of the reasons he and Ellen hardly spoke to each other, even today. As teenagers, they had come to resent each other because neither had ever enjoyed any privacy. Ellen had grown up with the same intentions Jake claimed. When she had married Leonard Duryea twenty-four years ago, it was only because the guy had money, and more important, could provide her with a big house.

Ellen hadn't even wanted to share it with children. The first Christmas she and Leo had spent as husband and wife, she had invited Jake up from Acorn Ridge to show off her big new house to him. Over the holidays, she had discovered she was pregnant with Daphne, and one night, because she was feeling frightened and insecure, she had desperately confided her condition to her brother, voicing her reluctance at the prospect of becoming a mother. Jake had experienced a number of mixed emotions. He could sympathize with Ellen, because he didn't want to have children, either. But the thought that his sister might provide him with a niece or nephew had done funny things to his insides, even as a teenager. He'd told Ellen the decision was hers to make. Then he'd been very relieved when she'd informed Leo and the two of them had worked through it together.

And when Daphne was born, Jake had made himself available whenever necessary to baby-sit, telling himself it was because his sister needed a break now and then, and not because he simply enjoyed doing it. Once a month, he would drive to Louisville from Berea for the weekend to visit his niece. Babies, he quickly discovered as a college student, defied any preparation university studies or life experience could offer. His niece's antics had made him view the universe from an entirely new perspective, and offered him a much-needed diversion from his studies. He'd loved baby-sitting for Daphne.

But he'd hated doing it in Ellen's house. He wasn't sure why. Maybe because he and Ellen never got along as kids, or maybe because she, like he, was very ter-

ritorial in relation to her home. Perhaps it was a combination of the two. But for some reason, Jake had
simply never felt welcome in his sister's home.

And it was a feeling he continued to experience to
this day. He could count on one hand the number of
times he'd entered Ellen's house in the past ten years.
Despite the fact that she issued an invitation to Jake
to spend his holidays there every year, he knew it was
only because she felt it was her obligation to do so,
as Daphne doted on him. But Jake had always avoided
the tension that inevitably ensued when he visited his
sister and her husband by beginning a tradition of taking Daphne out to dinner every Christmas Eve—even
during the years that he was married.

Now that *she* was married, would she continue their
tradition? he wondered. Probably not, because Daphne
was married to someone who cared as much for her
as she cared for him. Unlike Jake, who had married
someone more concerned about her own entertainment
than about the comings and goings of her spouse.
Daphne would doubtless spend the holidays with
Robby. So where did that leave Jake for Christmas?

The thought hadn't even occurred to him until this
moment. Now that his niece was married and had begun her own family, Jake's ties to his sister were effectively cut. Ellen probably wouldn't even issue him
an invitation this year. Not that he would accept it,
anyway, but still… It was odd to think about being
alone over the holidays and beyond. Of course, Jake
had in effect been alone since his divorce, but in the
back of his mind, he had still claimed a family tie to

Daphne. Now she claimed a tie to someone else's family. Which left Jake well-and-truly alone.

When his brain formed the startling realization, for some reason, Jake instinctively glanced up at Rebecca. She had her back to him as she stirred something on the stove, and didn't seem to realize she was singing along to a jazzy instrumental rendition of "Sweet Georgia Brown." As the music grew more lively, she began a little dance of her own creation, and Jake felt himself drawn to her as if she were winding an invisible thread attached to his heart. Before he knew what was happening, he was standing beside her at the stove, and she looked up quickly, seeming as surprised as he was by his appearance.

"I want to help," he said simply.

To Rebecca, Jake seemed to stumble over his words, until it almost sounded as if he'd said, "I want help."

"It…it's done," she replied, speaking as hesitantly as he. "I'm just getting ready to bring it in. You can help me carry these things to the table."

He nodded and extended his hands to take whatever Rebecca might offer him. Her cheeks were flushed from the heat of the stove, the hair around her face curling from the humidity. The kitchen was filled with the most delectable aromas that could only result from food that wasn't prepackaged, and the jazzy, danceable music had faded into a slow, bluesy number that spoke to some dark part of Jake's soul. Outside, the wind whipped against the house suddenly, savagely, and all he could think was that he was so damned grateful to be exactly where he was.

Home.

For some reason that word jumped instantly into his head. Despite the fact that this house was even smaller than the one he'd so detested growing up in, despite the fact that nothing, absolutely nothing he owned could be found under this roof, in this tiny room with Rebecca, Jake felt more at home than he'd ever felt in his life.

The realization frightened him. And then, he acknowledged reluctantly, it comforted him. After admitting that, Jake refused to speculate further. He carried the plates full of food to the table, lit the candles, topped off their wine, and sat in the chair opposite Rebecca.

Rebecca wasn't sure what was going on, but she could swear that things had suddenly, drastically changed between her and Jake. Gone was the casual banter and sly innuendo in which he loved to indulge, and gone was the easygoing humor in his blue eyes. Jake suddenly seemed so serious, so anxious, and she wasn't sure what she had done to make him change.

They ate in rather stilted silence, but all through dinner, neither could stop looking at the other. When they did chat, it was amiable, though a little stiff, covering a variety of topics before finally lighting on Rebecca's job.

"How did you get started doing this?" Jake asked. "It's kind of an unusual occupation. And, no offense, but you seem to harbor a few negative feelings about your divorce. The fact that you take so much pleasure in planning weddings seems a little contradictory."

"No offense taken, and incidentally, I do plan other

things besides weddings—I can organize *anything,* any kind of celebration you might conjure up." Rebecca thought for a moment before continuing. "As far as my divorce is concerned, I simply married the wrong person. It wasn't so much that my marriage was bad, as it was that my *husband* was bad."

Jake began to object, as she'd known he would, so she put up a hand to stop the flow of words. "No, wait, let me finish. Eliot was a jerk—that's all there is to it—and I was too young, too naive, and too ignorant to notice or accept it."

"Why do they always blame the men?" Jake posed the question in exasperation to no one in particular.

"I'm not blaming men," Rebecca stated adamantly. "If I'm blaming anyone, it's myself for putting up with Eliot for as long as I did." She'd never told anyone else about everything that had gone on between her and Eliot, only that her husband had married her for her money, and when it had run out, he'd left her. She wondered if maybe that's all she should tell Jake. Then she decided, hey, he was a big boy. He took pride in taking off the gloves, so why couldn't she?

"Eliot married me because I came from a wealthy family," she began. "And he stayed with me when my parents cut us off only because I offered to quit school and find a job that could support us both while he went to school full-time. I wound up taking three jobs to do that, Jake. I worked more than eighty hours a week most weeks for the entire time I was married. I hardly ever saw Eliot. But a lot of my friends did see him. Mostly at parties and bars, and nearly always with other women.

"But when my friends told me that, did I listen?" Rebecca shook her head. "No way. I was so sure there was some reason for it. I even made up excuses for it. Oh, Eliot has a tough time of it in law school. Those tests are so hard, he has to study all the time. He deserves a little R & R, he deserves to go out and party sometimes. I never once thought that maybe I deserved a little of that, too."

Jake said nothing, only looked at her from across the table. Rebecca reached for the nearly empty bottle of wine and divided the rest between their two glasses.

"You know, I think back on it now, and I'm amazed at how surprised I was when Eliot said he was leaving me. I can't believe how stupidly I behaved for five years. Five years," she repeated for emphasis. After a moment, she added, "And now you think I'm going to try to rope you into marriage, don't you?"

Jake decided that honesty was the best way to go here. "The thought had crossed my mind, yes."

Rebecca smiled sadly, then lifted her wine to inspect it in the candlelight. "I've learned the hard way that it's better to be alone than to be with someone who's wrong for you." She paused for a moment, then seemed to recall that she had set out to tell him something completely different. "But then, you were asking how I got involved in my job, weren't you? Not whether you'd be getting out of my house alive and unattached, right?"

That *was* what he had been asking her about, wasn't it? Jake tried to remember. He couldn't recall further than thinking about how much he'd wanted to pull Rebecca into his arms to console her as she'd described what had gone on in her marriage. He didn't dwell on how many things Eliot seemed to have in common with his own ex-wife, nor did Jake think about how much he'd like to deck the son of a bitch if he ever met up with the man.

"I only brought up my marriage because my job is a direct result of it," Rebecca went on after a thoughtful sip of her wine. "Because I hadn't graduated from college, I wasn't really skilled in anything. I wound up working in a local department store, in the china department of the bridal registry. I also got on part-time with a bakery and a florist. As a result, I was surrounded by all things matrimonial whenever I went to work. I learned a lot about the different businesses and gained a lot of insight into what people were doing for their weddings these days. Suddenly I realized I had some pretty good ideas of my own, too.

"My parents were more than willing to lend me enough money to get my business off the ground. I think maybe they still felt guilty for cutting me off while I was married to Eliot. Since then, I've repaid that loan with interest, and the business has really taken off."

"And I bet your folks are extremely proud of you," Jake guessed.

Rebecca smiled a little sadly, as if she was remembering something long past. "Yes, they are. They're wonderful people. We had some tough times while I was married, but it was only because they saw Eliot for what he was when I couldn't. When he took off, they never uttered an 'I told you so' or 'It's about time.' They only told me I was welcome if I wanted to come home.''

"Do you have brothers and sisters?" Jake asked, telling himself he was only making idle conversation, that Rebecca's family couldn't have mattered less to him.

"An older sister and brother."

"Do you get along with them?"

What a question! Rebecca wanted to shout. Then she remembered how he had described his own up-bringing and the tension he and his sister shared, and instead she only smiled. "Yes, we get along very well. We've always been very close in my family. My sister and brother are both married with children, and I baby-sit frequently for them. They have great kids," she added parenthetically, forcing herself to refrain from stating that they were just like the children she hoped to have for herself someday.

But Jake seemed to know what she was thinking, anyway. "I don't want kids myself," he stated in a matter-of-fact tone.

It didn't surprise Rebecca at all, but still she asked, "Why not? I think you'd make a terrific father."

He couldn't hide his astonishment at her assessment of his character. "You have got to be kidding."

"No, I'm not."

"What could you possibly find paternal about me?"

She shrugged, as if she was about to voice the obvious. "You're strong in your convictions. You seem to have a solid grasp on what's right and what's wrong. You're intelligent and relatively open-minded—"

"What do you mean 'relatively?'"

"—And, well, look at you—you obviously come from a terrific gene pool," she finished with a laugh.

That got Jake's attention. "Oh? And just what makes you say that?"

Rebecca realized suddenly that she had somehow managed to sink herself in far too deeply this time. Jake was gazing at her across the candlelight as if she was to be his dessert, his expression suggesting any number of intimate prospects. She tried to squash down the part of her that wanted to explore more fully whatever he might have in mind, but try as she might, the fires stirring inside her grew incandescent. "You...you have nice eyes," she finally whispered in response to his question.

Jake rose from his chair and slowly circled the table until he stood behind her. Rebecca's stomach exploded into a swirling fireball at having him so close, and her heart began a ferocious tattoo behind her rib cage.

It was going to happen, she thought feverishly. And nothing she might say or do could stop it, even if she'd wanted to. Which, of course, she did not. Making love with Jake simply seemed like the most obvious course of nature, like the first law of the jungle. Deep down inside, part of her knew they were meant to be together. And deep down inside, part of her knew it wouldn't be for long.

"I want to make love to you, Rebecca," Jake rasped out above her. He cupped her shoulders with his hands and gave them a gentle squeeze. "I haven't been able to stop thinking about you since the moment I first saw you."

Rebecca closed her eyes against the fiery sensations his words and his touch sent blazing through her body. "It's nice to know I'm not the only one who's been afflicted with that particular obsession," she whispered roughly.

The hands on her shoulders raked slowly down Rebecca's arms, the subtle friction starting little fires all along the way. At the juncture of her elbows, which she had rested on the arms of her chair, Jake pushed back her sleeves and formed soft circles on the tender flesh with his thumbs. Then, flattening his palms over her forearms, he continued his intimate journey farther, until his hands were covering the ones she had settled limply in her lap. As Rebecca marveled at how warm his skin was, Jake curled his fingers around hers and lifted her hands, crossing her arms over her chest and urging her to stand, kicking away her chair as she did so.

For long moments, he only held her against him in a warm embrace, luxuriating in the feel of having her so close, rejoicing that they would finally be together. Then, with a final squeeze and the gentlest of tugs, Jake lifted her arms above her head, and spun her slowly around like a ballerina until they were face-to-face.

Rebecca almost felt as if they were moving in slow motion, as if what they were doing was indeed a dance of sorts. Without releasing her wrists, Jake lowered her arms again, behind her back, until she was willingly held prisoner in his embrace. Tangling his fingers with hers at the small of her back, Jake urged Rebecca forward until nothing separated them but the thin barrier of their clothing. He dipped his head and brushed his lips softly, ever so softly against hers, then pulled back to gaze at her expression before he continued.

When he saw that she was every bit as lost as he was, Jake smiled and leaned forward again. At first, he barely touched Rebecca's lips with his, rubbing gently, tugging softly, only tasting her until their breaths mingled as one. When he could stand it no longer, he pressed his mouth to hers more insistently, urging her lips to open with his, exploring her deeply, kissing her to the depth of her soul.

Rebecca reacted with equal fire and passion, feeling more alive, more enraptured, than she had ever felt in her life. It was as if this embrace with Jake was her initiation into the realm of the senses, as if she'd never truly *felt* anything before now. His lips pulled persistently at hers, demanding a response, and Rebecca gave him whatever he wanted, taking for herself what she desired in return.

For long moments, they remained entwined, releasing all the pent-up passion, desire and emotion they had been forced to hold in check since meeting three months before. But instead of satisfying their needs, their actions only intensified them. As their quiet kisses turned to heated demands, as their tender explorations became insistent needs, each began to forget anything that had come before. All that mattered now was quenching their thirst for each other, extinguishing the flames that had turned so quickly into raging wildfire.

Before Rebecca realized what was happening, Jake had lifted her into his arms and was carrying her through her house. Vaguely she wondered if he knew where he was going, but she couldn't make herself stop kissing him long enough to offer him directions. However, it didn't seem to matter, because all too quickly he was releasing her, laying her on her back in the center of her bed. It was only when he stood towering over her, gasping for breath and gazing at her hungrily, that Rebecca finally began to regain some semblance of coherent thought.

"What's happening?" she asked herself more than Jake. "Where did all that come from?" More important, she wondered, where was it going to lead them?

Jake took a moment to steady his breathing before he replied. "I think we both know the answer to that. What's happening is that we're about to make love. And where all this came from is one of those mysteries of life I don't think anyone will ever be able to solve."

Rebecca didn't know what to say. Rationally, she realized what they were about to do was probably a big mistake. She hadn't been with anyone since her divorce, was almost uncertain how to go about all this man-woman business now. What was it about Jake that made her throw caution so utterly to the wind? Why did he shake her so profoundly where other men had left her completely cold? There had been others who had expressed an interest in Rebecca beyond the sexual, a number of men who had made it clear to her that they were available for a lifetime commitment. But none of them had seemed exactly appropriate for one reason or another. None had seemed quite…right.

But Jake Raglan did. God knows why, because he had done absolutely nothing but discourage her, but after only a few meetings, Rebecca felt better with Jake than she had with any man, even with Eliot. Especially with Eliot. When she was with Jake, bits of the puzzle of her life just seemed to slip right into place. Things fit with him. Things felt good. So why did he have to be so completely wrong for her?

"What do you want, Rebecca?" he asked her suddenly. "You call the shots here. What do you want?"

I want a life with you, she thought immediately. I want a house full of children and warm feelings and holidays, I want the white picket fence and flowers, I want cats and dogs and canaries. I want everything, Jake, I want it all.

"You," she replied simply. "Oh, Jake, I just want you."

It was all he needed to hear. With one savage tug, Jake yanked his sweater over his head, then pulled Rebecca up off the bed and into his arms once again. As she tangled her fingers in his hair, he unfastened her belt and tossed it to the floor, then undid all the buttons on her shirt. Beneath it she wore a breezy confection of champagne-colored lace, something that clung lovingly to her body and only hinted at what was to come. Jake groaned in delight that she had turned his fantasies about her into reality, then pushed the soft fabric of her shirt over her shoulders until it, too, was pooled on the floor.

Rebecca gasped when he slid his hand down her warm back and spanned her derriere, then her eyes grew wide as he stroked his hand over her skirt and the back of her thigh, cupping his hand behind her knee to lift her leg. Pulling her toward him, Jake raked his fingers down her calf and around her ankle, then pushed her shoe from her foot. Grinning the predatory smile that sent Rebecca's temperature skyrocketing, Jake let her foot go, then performed the exact same service for her other leg.

This time, however, when her shoe hit the floor with a delicate thump, Jake continued to hold Rebecca's foot for a moment. Ever so slowly, his hand skimmed up to circle her ankle, then his fingers raked back up over her calf, under her skirt, to curve at the bend in her knee once again. Rebecca's eyes widened in shock when Jake tugged on her leg to jerk her body forward against his, moaning out loud as her torso came into contact with his.

He was already ready for her, she realized, as heat coursed through every part of her body. All ready. But apparently he still wasn't willing, because instead of hurrying them into bed, Jake only rubbed his open palm up the length of Rebecca's thigh and over her hip, curving and pressing his fingers into the soft flesh above.

"Oh, Jake" was all Rebecca could manage in response, but her fingers flexed in his hair, then dropped to squeeze his shoulders. When Jake wrapped her leg around his waist, Rebecca instinctively tightened her hold on him, until she wasn't sure where her body ended and his began. However, as his fingers crept back up her thigh to explore her further, initiating a gentle, insistent, intimate caress, she realized all too well, and she could only gasp for breath as she shuddered with exquisite delight.

Jake continued with his ministrations as he unfastened Rebecca's skirt, pausing just long enough to push it and her thigh-high stockings down her legs until she stood before him in only her brief, ivory teddy, shaken and delirious at what had just happened and what was to come.

"You are so beautiful," he whispered when he could trust his voice not to quiver.

Rebecca smiled a little shakily. "You're not so bad yourself."

That was an understatement, she thought feverishly. Jake Raglan was, in a word, glorious. His broad chest was a collection of the most wonderfully placed muscles she had ever seen, corded and hard and covered with a dusting of black curls that spiraled across his abdomen and down to his trousers. Almost involuntarily, Rebecca reached out and unfastened the button resting below his navel, noting triumphantly that he sucked in an unsteady breath as she did so. Ever so slowly, she tugged on his zipper until it would open no farther, and feeling more reckless than she ever had in her life, tucked her hands deep inside his waistband.

Jake didn't resist when Rebecca curled her hands around his waist to cover his hips and pull him close. Instead, he leaned forward until they both lost their footing and fell onto the bed. He propped himself up on his elbows to gaze down at her, stunned to see fear lurking in her green eyes.

"What is it?" he asked her softly, laying his palm flat against her cheek and stroking her hair back from her face. "Why do you look so frightened?"

Rebecca swallowed hard before answering him. "Because I *am* frightened. Jake, I..."

He kissed her temple gently, then brushed his hand down to cup her jaw. "You what?" he asked her softly.

"I haven't been with a man since my divorce," she confessed quickly. "It's been five years…"

He stopped the flow of nervous words by placing a finger over her lips. "Shh. I know that."

"You do?"

He nodded. "I suspected, anyway. A woman like you…"

When he said no more, Rebecca prodded, "A woman like me…?"

Jake just shook his head, looking a little melancholy as he clarified, "A woman like you wouldn't sleep around. You need something more than a physical attraction."

"Yes."

"You need a little emotion."

"Yes."

"You need a lot of emotion."

"Yes."

Hearing her confirm his suspicions so honestly, Jake knew he should stop what he was doing and be honest with her, too. But the fact of the matter was, he wasn't sure what the truth was anymore. Before Rebecca, he would have sworn he couldn't offer a woman anything more than sex, that emotion would never play into the game. But now… Ever since meeting her, he had reacted to things in ways he never would have thought possible. He had experienced *emotions* unlike anything otherwise within his grasp. Why shouldn't he make love with Rebecca? he thought selfishly. Why shouldn't he explore this further?

He didn't say anything in response to her admission, but gazed down at the pearl buttons that kept her teddy together. He lingered for a long time over the first one, as if making the most important decision of his life, then he slowly slipped it through its hole. One by one, he undid each of the tiny buttons until the lacy fabric gaped open between her breasts. When he leaned down to place a warm kiss over her heart, Rebecca sighed in contentment and buried her fingers in his hair once again.

"Don't stop," she pleaded softly. "Please, Jake. Don't ever stop."

Ignoring the little voice at the back of his brain demanding that he consider the repercussions of what they were about to do, Jake pushed aside the fabric covering her breast and kissed Rebecca's ribs one by one. Gradually he moved upward until he found her breast, then, cupping her warm flesh in his hand, he circled the dusky peak with his tongue before drawing her more fully into his mouth.

Rebecca's breathing grew rapid and uneven as he tasted her, and she cried out loud when he cupped her other breast and gave it a gentle squeeze. Instinctively, deliriously, she scored her fingernails down his back until she found the waistband of his trousers, and she pushed insistently until he finally understood her demand.

Lifting himself away from her long enough to shed the rest of his clothing and help her out of her teddy, Jake took a moment to gaze at her once more. The only illumination in the room came from the yellow rectangle of light spilling through the bedroom door, and in it, Jake could see how rosy Rebecca's skin had become, how fragile she seemed to be. Vaguely, he realized he had never even thought to free her hair from her braid, but her dark tresses had somehow come loose anyway and lay spread across the pillow like dark fire. He knew he shouldn't do this, knew he was going to wind up hurting Rebecca. Then she lifted her arms to him, inviting him in, and he knew he would only hurt himself more if he didn't have her.

Jake was as helpless to stop himself as the doomed sailors of lore had been upon hearing the sirens' song. It was no longer a matter of wanting Rebecca. Now it was a matter of needing her.

Like a man possessed, he came to her then, taking Rebecca with all the passion, all the fire, all the intensity his body commanded. Deeper and deeper he drove himself, until every fiber of his body melted with hers, until each was consumed in a burst of white-hot combustion.

And as incoherence turned to rational thought once again, Jake knew he had done the wrong thing. It wasn't just that he had heard Rebecca cry out that she loved him. It was that he had heard himself cry out that he loved her, too.

Five

It was dark when Rebecca awoke, feeling fuzzy and unsure of her surroundings. She was in her own bed, she realized vaguely, in her own house with all of her own things surrounding her. But somehow they didn't seem like her home and her possessions any longer. Everything felt…different than it had before. And the silence surrounding her—that was new, too. Too many nights during her marriage, she had lain awake in tension-filled silence waiting for Eliot to come home. After her divorce, the silence every night had become intolerable, and Rebecca had taken to sleeping with the radio on, tuned to a nerve-soothing classical-music station. So why was her house so quiet and lonely now?

All at once, Rebecca recalled what had happened. She had made love with Jake Raglan, had experienced the heights and depths of a passion she had never known she was capable of enjoying. As memory after memory washed over her, she smiled at the heated sensations seeping into every cell in her body. Instinctively, she reached across the bed to touch him, finding the space empty, yet still warm from his presence. Pulling his pillow sleepily into her arms, Rebecca squeezed it to her breast and inhaled deeply the aroma of Jake Raglan that still clung to it. He had been so loving, so tender, so sweet. And she had fallen madly, desperately, hopelessly in love with him.

Surprisingly, Rebecca wasn't alarmed by the recognition of her feelings. It was as if a part of her had known from the moment they'd met that things would develop between them as they had. Somehow, making love with Jake just seemed like the natural conclusion to an association that had begun a long time ago, and now had come full circle. To her, such a realization brought with it comfort, and an almost serene outlook. She was sure, however, that Jake would react a bit differently. How was she going to make him understand that they were meant to be together? And what was she going to do if she couldn't?

Rebecca rolled onto her back, still clutching Jake's pillow to her heart, and stared unseeingly at the ceiling. Where was he now? she wondered. Was he out in her kitchen, carelessly opening another bottle of wine for them to enjoy, to share in their newfound romantic intimacy? Or was he out in her living room, pacing nervously, pondering all that had passed between them and puzzling over his feelings as she was? Her heart sank as the next thought entered her brain.

Or was he perhaps already on his way home, driving along with the stereo turned up, dismissing what they'd just shared together as another night's adventure, worrying over what awaited him at work Monday morning?

Only one way to find out, Rebecca told herself reluctantly.

She rose from bed and went to her closet to wrap herself in a blue chenille bathrobe. Not the most revealing piece of clothing in her wardrobe, she reflected, but the room had grown cold without Jake's presence there to warm her, and at the moment, for some reason, she wasn't feeling particularly sexy, anyway.

Padding from the bedroom in bare feet, Rebecca made her way silently down the short, narrow hallway and peeked through the door leading to her kitchen. The light above the stove was on, as it usually was at night, but the radio was off. That accounted for why the house was so eerily quiet. The reason it felt so coldly empty was even more obvious.

Rebecca's gaze wandered around her living room, slowly, deliberately, so that she wouldn't miss a thing. She took in the remnants of her meal with Jake that lay cold and unappealing on the table, the odd shadows cast by the tree-obscured light from a streetlamp outside, and the silent forms of Bogart and Bacall sleeping serenely on the back of the sofa, oblivious to her turmoil. Pulling the collar of her robe more snugly around her throat, Rebecca lowered her eyes to her bare feet rooted nervously against the chilly wood floor, willing the tears she felt welling to subside. No,

there was no question why her house was so cold tonight.

Jake Raglan was gone.

How could I have been so stupid? she berated herself viciously. How could I have thought he would be
different? How could I have told him that I loved him?
And as she shuffled slowly into her kitchen, Rebecca
asked herself the final, most persistent question. How
could I have *felt* that I loved him? The evening that
had caused her to feel hopeful for the first time in five
years had left her with nothing more than a table full
of dirty dishes and an arctic cold that surrounded her
heart. Rebecca shivered involuntarily and swiped at a
trickle of water that tumbled down over her cheek.

"Damn lawyers."

Moving automatically, she turned her radio on to
drown out the silence that had begun to deafen her,
then went to run water in the sink. There was nothing
worse than waking up to dirty dishes that should have
been done the night before, she thought.

Nothing except waking up cold and alone.

It was only because she'd been sleeping so soundly
and he hadn't wanted to wake her, Jake thought rationally, emphatically, and not because he'd scared the
hell out of himself. As he lay awake in his own bed,
scarcely aware of the approaching sunrise, he repeated
to himself yet again the reason he had left Rebecca
without saying goodbye some hours ago. So he had
cried something out in a moment of passion that he
shouldn't have, he told himself. So what? Every day
people said things they didn't mean. Every day men

told women they loved them when they really didn't. Lots of men did that.

But Jake didn't.

At least, he hadn't before. Maybe he was just imagining things, he tried to reassure himself. Maybe he only thought he'd told Rebecca that he loved her. They'd both been so consumed by feverish ecstasy, neither one of them could have been too coherent about the things they were saying. Hell, she probably hadn't even meant it when she'd said it to him. She'd told him over dinner that she knew better than to get involved with a man who was wrong for her, hadn't she? And who could possibly be more wrong for a marrying kind like Rebecca Bellamy than a forever-unattached bachelor like himself?

Because forever unattached was precisely how Jake intended to remain. Attachments led to entanglements, then entanglements led to involvements, then involvements…well, involvements invariably led to relationships. And everyone knew where relationships led—straight into marriages. Jake had already been down that crooked path once. There was no way he would ever be stupid enough to follow it again.

Jake tossed restlessly onto his side and stared blindly out at the gray light of dawn creeping into his bedroom. He recalled another morning similar to this one, the morning after a night when he had lain awake alone in bed thinking, worrying, wondering. Only it hadn't been Rebecca Bellamy who had inspired his troubled thoughts. It had been his wife, Marie. They had argued when he'd arrived home from work late and had missed a dinner party Marie had thrown for her mother's birthday. Jake had truly forgotten all about it, had been so caught up in a case, that he had worked until nearly nine o'clock before realizing what time it was.

He'd come home to find Marie seated alone in her cocktail dress, elbows on the dining room table still heaped with the remains of dinner. Everyone else had gone home. Marie only stared at him for a moment, then blew out the candles and rose from her seat in silence. She went to the hall closet and collected her coat and purse, then turned to speak to Jake one final time.

"This was your last chance, Jake," she'd said in a quiet, even tone of voice he'd never heard her use before. He recalled thinking that she'd sounded almost…defeated in some way. "I'm going to spend the night at David's. I'll collect the rest of my things later."

Jake had suspected that Marie had been having an affair, but he hadn't known with whom. To hear her state it unequivocally, to hear her offer the man's name with such casual familiarity, tore like a dull knife at something inside him. David. David what? Jake had never bothered to find out. To this day he had no idea who the man was or where Marie might have met him. And a part of him still couldn't believe that his wife had betrayed him so thoroughly. It had hurt him, hurt him badly. And Jake had sworn to God that it would never, ever, happen to him again. He would go to great pains to see to it that no woman ever touched him that deeply again, that no woman ever reached the secret part of him that Marie had once warmed and then so brutally chilled. No woman. Not even Rebecca Bellamy. Especially not her.

She'd have to be crazy to get involved with a guy like him, thinking it would lead to something substantial, Jake reminded himself viciously. Hey, he'd made it clear where he stood with her, hadn't he? He hadn't led her on, encouraged her to believe he was anything other than what he said he was. Jake Raglan was *not* going to marry, ever again. And Rebecca knew that unequivocally. If she had consented to carry their little attraction to each other further, then she had no one but herself to blame.

So why did Jake feel so damned guilty? Why did he feel like he should crawl over to her house and promise on bended knee to make an honest woman of her? Why, dammit, did he want nothing more than to call her on the phone this instant and apologize for running out on her the way he had? To call her and murmur silly, romantic bits of nonsense to make up for hurting her?

Because Jake was absolutely certain that he had hurt Rebecca. And that knowledge only made him feel even worse about what they had done. He tried to convince himself that he wasn't behaving like a coward when he decided it would be best not to see her again. Then he remembered that his closest friend was to be married in his house two weeks from today, and that the woman he sought to avoid would be orchestrating the entire event. There was no way Jake could refrain from running into Rebecca. He had no choice but to see her again. However, that didn't mean he couldn't put it off as long as possible.

And put it off he did. Jake didn't see Rebecca for nearly two weeks. Once, only once, did she leave a message on his answering machine. It was three days after they had made love, a Monday when Jake came home from work feeling detached, defeated and depressed. The red light on the machine in his kitchen flickered at him once, twice, three times, before he looked away from it. Cautiously, he pushed the replay button as he shed his coat and loosened his tie. After a moment, Rebecca's quiet, steady voice filled the room, and suddenly the day didn't seem quite as gloomy as it had before. Her tone was light, breezy, just the way he remembered it, as if nothing in the world had changed between them. She simply told Jake that she was thinking about him, and would he please give her a call when he got the chance.

He didn't return her call. But he did come home from work one evening and knew immediately that Rebecca had been in his house while he was at work. The moment he opened his front door, he picked up the scent of her perfume, something sweet and delicate and reminiscent of a Victorian garden. Foolishly, he hurried through the house looking for her, certain she was still there measuring a room or laying out decorations for the wedding. But she was gone. Without a note, without a trace. And Jake couldn't get over how cheated he felt at the realization. He assured himself his own reaction couldn't have been anything like what Rebecca must have felt at finding him gone that Saturday morning.

Even when Jake settled into bed that evening, it somehow seemed as if her fragrance was there, too.

He knew he must be imagining things, but his dreams that night had been filled with images of Rebecca and those exquisite moments when they had hit the heights of passion together. And he hadn't been able to stop thinking about her since.

It wasn't until the evening before the wedding, when Stephen and Alison hosted their rehearsal dinner at a local restaurant known for its good food and avant-garde ambience, that Jake saw Rebecca again. The first thing he noticed when he saw her enter the restaurant was that she looked more beautiful than he had ever seen her, and the second thing he noticed was that she wasn't alone. She had come with a date. A man. A man who was young, good-looking and exceptionally well dressed. A man Jake was sure he knew from somewhere.

"Oh, there's Rebecca," Alison said, rising slightly from her seat between Jake and Stephen to beckon to the other woman. "Over here, Rebecca! You and Marcus can sit across from me and Stephen."

Marcus, Jake muttered to himself. What kind of man allowed himself to be called by a name like that? And then it hit him. Marcus Tate, a divorce attorney who worked in town and was well known for two reasons: he was utterly amoral, and he went through women faster than most men went through underwear. Why he was with Rebecca—a woman who professed to despise lawyers—was anyone's guess.

Rebecca had promised herself not to lose her composure at seeing Jake again. She tried to remain calm and unruffled, tried to forget about the fact that this was a man who had made love to her and left under cover of darkness, and who hadn't even bothered to call since doing so. But it was very difficult to remain cool in the face of someone so handsome and intimidating. Someone to whom she had bared a part of her soul no one else had ever seen. Someone she loved who didn't love her back.

The past two weeks had been perhaps the dreariest and the loneliest Rebecca had ever experienced. Even the days following Eliot's rejection hadn't left her feeling as empty and achy inside as Jake's abandonment had. How could she have been so wrong about him? she asked herself for perhaps the hundredth time. Why were her feelings for him clearly so much stronger than his were for her?

Rebecca thought back to the afternoon when she had left a message for him on his answering machine. She had felt like an adolescent with her first crush, her stomach balled up into a painful knot as she listened to his phone ring at home. She had chosen a time when she'd known he would be at work, because she simply hadn't been sure she could react rationally if he had actually answered the phone. So, like a frightened, insecure teenager, she had pretended his night flight meant no more to her than a stubbed toe, had airily, coyly mentioned that she was thinking about him, and had left the simple request, "Call me when you get a chance."

And thus she had thrust the responsibility for their relationship onto Jake's shoulders. And he, evidently, had simply let it drop into the dust. So much for being so certain he was the right man for her. So much for hoping what he'd told her at the peak of their love-making was true.

Apparently Jake was one of those men who could tell a woman anything without regretting it later. He probably wasn't even aware that he'd said it, probably told all of his partners that he loved them. The word ''partner'' bothered Rebecca terribly. To think that she was Jake's partner only in sex and nothing else made her feel sullied and cheap, just one more in a string of affairs.

And now to take her seat across from him, at a table full of people who had met to celebrate the union of a couple so much in love they had decided to marry... Well, it was something of a blow to Rebecca's al-ready-battered ego. It helped little to realize that Jake had come alone. It helped even less to realize he had yet to look at her. It only served to reinforce the mis-givings she still harbored about having invited Marcus to come with her this evening.

Normally, Rebecca wasn't the kind of woman to orchestrate elaborate setups as she had done tonight. And really, it hadn't been her idea. Not entirely, any-way. Although she had asked Marcus to come with her strictly because she knew what kind of man he was and hoped it might rattle Jake, this wasn't the first time he had been her escort to some function. He and Eliot had been good friends in college, so Rebecca had known him for years. She was well aware of the fact that Marcus was considered a womanizer in social cir-cles, and a coldhearted snake in legal circles.

But he was also a damned effective attorney who succeeded in doing exactly what he'd been hired to do. And, although most people would shake their heads in disbelief, Marcus was Rebecca's friend. He was the only one of her acquaintances in college who hadn't treated her like a pariah after her divorce. Instead, he had turned his back on Eliot, deeming the man a fool.

Rebecca was perhaps the only person in the world Marcus felt tenderly toward. And she was probably the only person in the world who felt tenderly toward Marcus. It was why she had been able to confide in him about Jake. And why Marcus had been able to hatch a plan to make the other man feel jealous.

Now she felt as if her behavior tonight was as childish and ridiculous as it had been when she'd left the message on Jake's machine. No good would come of trying to manipulate a situation, Rebecca thought. She probably should have simply declined Alison's invitation to attend the rehearsal dinner and stayed at home with a good book. But Alison Mitchell was a very persuasive woman, and when she'd told Rebecca she was welcome to bring a date, Rebecca had thought, Why not? Obviously Jake Raglan had no intention of seeing her again. And although she knew it would be a very long time before she had worked through her feelings and was over him, Rebecca thought perhaps she could take some consolation in knowing she had left him with the impression that he meant as little to her as she evidently did to him.

And the evidence was in. He hadn't even noticed that she had taken her seat directly opposite him. Beside her, Marcus smiled encouragingly and pushed back a pale blond lock of hair, his gray eyes twinkling merrily.

"You look beautiful tonight, Rebecca," he murmured just loudly enough for Jake to hear.

His comment provoked the desired response from the man across the table. Out of the corner of her eye, Rebecca saw Jake's attention wander from Alison to Marcus, then to herself. His gaze was indifferent, however, his expression revealing nothing about what he might be feeling.

"Hello, Rebecca," he finally greeted her amiably, as if they were the most casual of acquaintances. "Marcus. Long time no see."

At first, Rebecca thought Jake had offered his offhand greeting to her, and she wanted to slap him unconscious for being so cavalier and uncaring. But when Marcus responded with a less-than-enthusiastic chuckle, she realized the two men must be sharing some private joke.

"Not long ago, I beat the pants off Jake in court," Marcus told Rebecca, leaning toward her much closer than was necessary.

Jake's hand clenched involuntarily around the old-fashioned glass in his hand when he observed the other man's proprietary gesture, nearly shattering the delicate crystal. So that was what Marcus and Rebecca had in common, he thought idly. They'd both had him out of his pants lately, one figuratively, the other literally.

"My client," Marcus continued, adopting a pathetic tone of voice, "was a poor, downtrodden, helpless woman whose husband was a total sleazoid. I won a settlement that proved to the world women wouldn't tolerate being victimized by such scum any longer.''

Jake rolled his eyes toward the ceiling. ''Oh, please. Your client was a scheming, conniving ex-*hooker,* for God's sake, who panicked when her husband found out about her past. You won that case by the skin of your teeth and you know it, Marcus,'' he concluded evenly, successfully disguising the effect the other man had on him.

Marcus grinned, shook his head knowingly and pointed a finger at Jake. ''You know, if you wouldn't focus so heavily on clients who are tired, bitter old men who feel like they've been shafted by the very women they drove away to begin with, you might enjoy your work a little more. But then, I guess, birds of a feather... Right, Jake?''

Rebecca saw Jake flinch as if he had indeed been slapped, saw a nerve in his jaw twitch once, then go rigid. He downed his drink, mumbled, ''Excuse me,'' and pushed himself away from the table without offering any indication that he would return. All eyes followed as he threaded his way through the maze of tables and up the steps toward the bar, but no one uttered a word. The members of the wedding party simply looked at one another, then went back to the various conversations they'd been enjoying when the interruption occurred. Only Rebecca turned to Marcus and silently demanded an explanation.

''Trust me,'' Marcus said softly. ''Guys like Jake Raglan don't take kindly to hearing the truth. Give him a few minutes. He'll be back.''

But when ten minutes passed without bringing

Jake's return, Rebecca began to worry. "Just what were you trying to imply by your comments to Jake?" she asked Marcus insistently.

Her companion swirled his drink casually in the glass and replied, "There's something you should know about your friend, Mr. Raglan."

"Oh?" Rebecca asked mildly. "And what might that be?"

"He went through a *very* nasty divorce about three years ago."

"That's not exactly a secret, Marcus."

Marcus eyed her skeptically. "Are you telling me Jake told you about his divorce?"

"Well, no. But it doesn't take a genius to figure out it must not have been pleasant. He's more soured on the institution of marriage than anyone I've ever met."

Marcus said nothing for a moment, then posed a question to which he already knew the answer. "Your own divorce was pretty awful, wasn't it, Rebecca?"

She sighed. "You know how awful it was, Marcus. You represented me, remember?"

"Yeah, I remember," he muttered distastefully. "And I could have won you a bundle, too, if you hadn't been so damned softhearted where that bastard, Eliot, was concerned. I still can't believe you declined alimony and any kind of settlement after the way he treated you. It's incredible how you—"

"Marcus, it doesn't matter," Rebecca interrupted, her voice edged with the finality she felt toward her own disastrous marriage. "It's over now. There's no need to rehash it. We were talking about Jake's divorce, not mine."

ELIZABETH BEVARLY 109

"My point is that you both suffered at the hands of your spouses, yet you've gone on to bear no grudge, to harbor no ill feelings at all."

"Oh, I have ill feelings toward Eliot," she began to confirm.

"But they don't cloud your perception of life," Marcus pointed out. "You don't live every day colored by your experiences with your ex-husband."

"I thought we decided not to talk about my marriage, Marcus."

Reluctantly, Marcus let the subject drop and explained, "But Jake Raglan's everyday life *is* colored by his feelings toward his ex-wife, and what he sees as his mistreatment at her hands."

"What do you mean, 'what he *sees* as his mistreatment?'"

Marcus thought for a moment before he began to describe the gossip that had burned up the legal grapevine a few years back. "Jake's wife left him for another man three years ago," he told Rebecca. "But not because she was the screeching siren he tries to make her out to be. Marie Raglan was just a lonely woman. Jake worked constantly, put his job before everything else, including his wife, and Marie went to bed alone too many nights, waiting for her husband to come home from work. Then one day, she met a nice man who put her first in his life, and she began to see what a farce her marriage was. So she left.

"Her older brother represented her, and, as big brothers are wont to do, he set out to protect his sister in any way he could. That meant airing the whole dirty business for the entire legal community, painting Jake as a complete ogre, and exploiting his pain and guilt to win a very hefty settlement.''

Marcus paused for a moment before continuing. ''It was a lousy experience for everyone involved. No one's fault, really, just one of those things. Happens every day. But Jake Raglan took it to heart. Marie hurt him, and he's been a bitter, vengeful man ever since.'' After a moment, Marcus concluded, ''But I'll tell you something else—the episode turned him into one hell of a divorce lawyer. Obviously, he prefers clients who have been through what he sees as experiences similar to his own.''

Rebecca shook her head in disbelief. ''And true to form, you went for the throat, too, just to make him squirm.''

''Rebecca, I was only trying to make him see how unfair he's been to you and to himself.''

''Oh, Marcus, how could you? I'm going to look for him,'' she said suddenly, rising from her chair before Marcus had a chance to stop her.

Rebecca followed the route she had seen Jake take, stopping at the entrance to the bar. It was dark and hazy with blue smoke, filled to capacity on a Friday night. Despite that, she had little trouble making him out, seated at the bar with one hand wrapped around a drink, the other bunching a fistful of hair over his forehead. Silently, she made her way through the crowd until she stood behind him, then she placed her hand gently on his shoulder.

The moment she touched him, Rebecca felt Jake relax. Muscles that had been bunched beneath her fingers eased and rolled, as if bands of steel melted into fluid mercury. For a long moment, he didn't turn around, but the fingers in his hair smoothed the dark locks back and settled calmly on the bar. Only then did Jake turn in his seat, and for the first time in two weeks, he looked Rebecca squarely in the eye.

"Trying to make me jealous?" he asked softly, almost wearily, the ghost of a smile playing around his lips.

Rebecca smiled back, feeling the ice that had encircled her heart for two weeks begin to trickle away like a warm stream. "Why? *Are* you feeling jealous?"

Instead of answering her truthfully, Jake glanced down at the floor, and evaded her question by replying, "I never made any promises to you, Rebecca."

She shook her head almost imperceptibly and lifted her shoulders in a slight shrug. "I don't recall ever saying that you did."

"You knew where you stood with me."

Rebecca said nothing for a moment, then told him, "You made it clear as crystal."

"What's that supposed to mean?"

"Nothing, Jake. It's not supposed to mean anything." She sighed impatiently, wishing they could go back to the first moment they'd seen each other at Daphne's wedding. "I...I don't guess there's any chance we could start all over again, is there?"

Jake had found himself wishing the exact same thing a number of times over the past two weeks. "No, I don't guess there is."

Rebecca nodded in resignation. "So I guess we just chalk it up to one of those things?"

Jake studied her face for a long time before responding. "I guess we do."

The minutes dragged into an awkward silence, and Rebecca knew there was nothing she could say that would change the way things were between them. "I'm sorry about Marcus," she finally said quietly.

Jake didn't know if she was sorry she had brought the other man, or if she was apologizing for what Marcus had said. Either way, it didn't really matter. Ultimately, it all boiled down to one thing: he and Rebecca wouldn't be seeing each other socially any more. The realization brought him none of the relief or serenity he had thought it would. Instead of feeling as if he could close a chapter of his life and move on, he somehow felt as if there were loose threads dangling everywhere.

It didn't feel good to Jake. It didn't feel right.

Six

The Mitchell-Flannery wedding went off without a hitch the next day. Rebecca had never felt more drained or more relieved to be through with an affair than she did by Saturday night. Long after Alison and Stephen had left Jake's house to pursue their marital bliss, Rebecca was still working, corralling the most festive guests who were unwilling to end their revels, thanking and paying the musicians and the clergyman, and double-checking to be sure that the cleanup crew she had scheduled would arrive early Sunday to work on the house. As per her own suggestion and with Alison's blessing, Rebecca made sure that what was left of the catered food went to a downtown shelter that night, and the flowers were delivered to a local hospital.

By 1:00 a.m., everything was again peaceful and

quiet in Jake's house. Rebecca stretched like a cat and sank down onto the overstuffed burgundy-and-hunter-green striped couch in his living room, kicked off her shoes, and rubbed her eyes. She had removed her cinnamon-colored suit jacket earlier, and at some point in the evening had untied the lace collar and unfastened the top two buttons of her ivory silk blouse. Now she sat with her elbows on her knees, her face in her hands, hovering at the edge of consciousness because she was so exhausted.

It wasn't that this wedding had been a particularly difficult one to arrange, she reflected wearily. On the contrary, Alison had been a remarkably easygoing bride, and Rebecca had planned a number of other weddings infinitely more difficult. Nor was it that the day had been an especially long one. Alison and Stephen's ceremony and reception had been no more time-consuming than those for any other couple of Rebecca's acquaintance.

No, the reason Rebecca felt so beaten and weary was that she had been forced to spend the day in continuous contact with Jake Raglan. At every turn she had found herself confronting him for one reason or another, and there were times when she almost felt he had even orchestrated situations, simply because he wanted to talk to her. Of course, she told herself that such suspicions were ridiculous—after all, *he* had been the one to run out on her—but she still couldn't shake the uneasy feeling that, despite their conversation of the evening before, there were too many important things that had remained unsaid between them.

All in all, Rebecca had been left feeling as if every

cell in her body had been drawn out, trampled over and replaced in the most painful manner possible. She hurt everywhere, in every possible way—physically, emotionally, psychologically and spiritually. And deep down inside, she wasn't certain she would ever feel good—honestly *good*—again.

Because her hands were doubled into loose fists over her eyes, Rebecca heard more than saw Jake come into the room. She remained motionless and silent, however, willing him to go away and leave her alone. But when she heard the sound of something being set on the coffee table before her, she reluctantly removed her hands and opened her eyes. Before her, a long-stemmed crystal flute sparkled with pale gold champagne, looking at once harmless and inviting, and very, very dangerous. It was champagne meant to celebrate a new beginning, a new life for two people very much in love. Rebecca was torn between wanting to drain the glass dry with thirsty sips and wanting to dash it violently against the wall.

"Last of the champagne," Jake said softly as he took a seat much too close beside her on the sofa. "Cheers."

Rebecca stopped herself from laughing derisively out loud. Cheerful was perhaps the last word she would use to describe the way she felt. Nonetheless, she curled her fingers around the stem of the glass and lifted it to her lips.

"Cheers," she rejoined in a hollow voice when she had swallowed.

"You look beat," Jake told her. He slid one hand across her back, wrapping his fingers over her upper arm, turned her to face slightly away from him, and began massaging her shoulders lightly in a gesture that was at once strange and familiar.

"That's because I feel beat," Rebecca murmured on a tired sigh, loving the feel of Jake's hands so gentle and warm on her aching body.

She should tell him to stop, she thought, as his fingers kneaded the taut flesh stretched over her shoulder blades. But what he was doing felt so good. Rebecca sighed again as he circled his thumb at the base of her nape, closing her eyes to enjoy his touch more fully. Little by little, she felt herself growing sleepier, until she wasn't quite sure if she was conscious or dreaming. When her head rolled forward, Jake skimmed his fingers up her neck and into her hair, and before Rebecca realized what was happening, he was loosening the pins that held her chignon in place, tangling his fingers playfully in her dark curls.

"Jake, don't," she protested halfheartedly as her scalp began to tingle everywhere his fingers touched.

"Shh" was all he offered in reply.

When her hair cascaded to the center of her back in an unruly mass, Jake bunched a fistful in his hand and swept it aside, pushing it over her shoulder. Rebecca groaned softly when he began to rub his hands over her neck and back once again, moaning quietly in contentment at the vibrations tingling throughout her body as a result.

This is nice, she thought, as a warm, fuzzy fog surrounded her brain. She'd never had someone to come home to after work, someone who would pamper her and speak softly to her and put her needs before his own. Eliot had usually been in bed by the time Rebecca got home from work, or else he'd been at the library studying until well past her own bedtime. At least, back then she'd thought he was at the library. Now, of course, she realized he had probably been out trying to impress some sweet young coed with his extensive legal knowledge.

But Jake was nice to come home to....

For long moments Rebecca only allowed herself to feel, to become caught up in the sweet sensations wrought by Jake's soft caress. And when his lips joined his fingers in wreaking tender havoc on her senses, she could only smile in dazed satisfaction. Still caught up in the hazy sensation that she was lost in the most exquisite kind of dream, she unwittingly murmured Jake's name in an intimate whisper, uncertain whether she had asked him to please cease his assault or to never, ever, end it.

"Rebecca," Jake ground out on a ragged breath.

He wasn't sure what had possessed him to touch her in the familiar way he had been for the last several moments, but suddenly all he wanted to do was become lost in her warmth and softness as he had two weeks ago. With quiet, deft maneuvering, he tugged gently on Rebecca's shoulders, dragging her across his lap until he could gaze down at the face that had haunted him for months, dreamy looking and glowing in the pale amber light from the fireplace. Her hair fell back over his arm like a black waterfall, and her eyes glistened like expertly cut gems. She was so beautiful, so desirable. And with no small amount of panic, Jake realized he wanted her more than he'd ever wanted a woman, any woman.

Cupping her jaw with his hand, he smoothed her hair back from her face and leaned down to kiss her. He expected her to push him away, expected her to bolt, but Rebecca did neither. She reached up and threaded her fingers insistently in his own hair, and pulled him down to receive her kiss instead. Jake complied willingly, eagerly, rejoicing in the knowledge that they would make love once more, completely forgetting that he had sworn it wouldn't happen again.

As their kiss deepened, Jake leaned forward until Rebecca lay beneath him on the sofa. His hands began a subtle exploration of curves and valleys he remembered well, starting at her hip, then fingering each rib as if counting them, only to curve below the swell of her breast. Rebecca arched upward then, positioning herself until Jake was cupping his fingers snugly over her breast, then flexed them open and closed them again. When he thumbed the rigid peak to even riper fullness, Rebecca moaned, placing her hand over his and urging him to venture downward.

Jake's smile was full of promise when he gazed down at Rebecca again. There would be time enough for that later. They had the rest of the night together, and he wanted to go slow. He wanted to make sure nothing was overlooked, wanted to be sure that ultimately they were both completely satisfied.

As Rebecca stared back at him silently, heatedly, her chest rising and falling in ragged gasps for breath, Jake rose enough to pull her blouse from her skirt and began to unbutton it. One by one he slipped the fabric-

covered buttons through their holes, then he pulled
Rebecca's blouse open and discovered to his joy the
front closure clasp of her lacy brassiere. Immediately
he hooked his finger beneath it and unfastened it, then
flattened his palms against her warm skin and pushed
his hands up over her breasts, shucking the linen and
lace as he did so.

Rebecca's fingers were still tangled in his hair, and
when Jake lowered his head to leave a chaste kiss over
her heart, her hands fell down to his neck and rubbed
uneven circles across his back. Gradually, Rebecca let
her fingers dip lower, and the more intimate her ca-
resses became, the more insistently Jake tasted her.
When she curved her palms over his taut hips, he
opened his mouth wide and drew as much of her breast
inside as he could, flattening his tongue against her.
Rebecca cried out softly and squeezed her hands into
fists, pulling his hips against the cradle of her thighs
with anxious insistence, entwining her legs with his.

The feel of her softness so close, yet so unattainable,
nearly drove Jake into an uncontrollable frenzy. Instinctively, he pushed himself more intimately against
her, and instinctively Rebecca arched her body upward, crying out his name as she did so. It was only
then that Jake realized how close they were to making
love again, and it was only then that he began to think
coherently about what they were about to do.

"Rebecca," he gasped out, his breath hot and damp
against her skin. "I'll make love to you again, but you
have to know that I don't—I can't love you."

His words were like a bucket of icy water on Rebecca's inflamed emotions. She looked dazedly down

at their partially undressed and intimately entwined bodies, observed in shock the carnally possessive manner in which she cradled him against her, and nearly choked on her horror. Oh, no, how had she let this happen to her again? How could she have allowed things to progress this rapidly, to this extreme, between them? Her brain was inundated with questions to which she could provide no answers. But louder and more insistent than any of the others was the one that had bothered her subconscious for weeks. Why couldn't Jake love her?

For a moment Rebecca remained helplessly silent. Then, without thinking, she uttered the first thing that launched itself into her brain. "But…but you told me you loved me," she said in a very small voice.

It was the last thing Jake wanted to hear, the last thing he wanted to be reminded of. Slowly releasing a breath he had scarcely been aware of holding, Jake dropped his head forward in defeat. The action simply served to offer him a view of Rebecca's delectable, pink flesh, reddened now by his relentless mauling. Reluctantly, he disengaged himself from her long enough to push her clothing back into place, and then he sat up straight on the couch. Dangling his hands between his knees and dropping his gaze to the floor, he looked every bit as weary and defeated as Rebecca had only a short time ago.

"Rebecca," he began quietly, uncertain exactly what he had planned to say. He felt the sofa shift beside him and knew that she, too, had risen to remove herself from the dangerous position into which they had put themselves.

"Don't, Jake," he heard her say softly. "Don't say anything. I understand. Just let it go."

God, what had she been thinking? Rebecca asked herself caustically as she buttoned up her blouse too quickly, noting when she reached the neck that she had skipped a buttonhole somewhere along the line. Dropping her arms to her sides in frustration, she doubled her hands into fists and quickly released them, then began to stuff her shirttail furiously back into her skirt.

Jake was nice to come home to. That was what she'd been thinking about when she'd allowed things to go too far.

But this wasn't her home, she reminded herself viciously. And Jake wasn't hers to come home to. She would have been smart to remember that, would have been smart to remind herself what had happened the last time she'd felt so comfortable, so cozy with Jake Raglan. She'd gotten hurt. Badly hurt. And it wasn't going to happen again.

"Rebecca, don't... Don't do that," Jake said when she circled the coffee table until it lay as a barrier between them. "We need to talk."

She chuckled without humor, trying to fight back the tears she felt threatening. No, she would not cry. Not now. Not yet. "Talk," she repeated coolly, her voice edged with something akin to cynicism. "No way, Jake. You've said more than enough."

"Rebecca..."

"It's late," she stated brusquely, yanking her jacket from a chair near the fireplace and thrusting her arms into its sleeves. "I think I'm pretty well finished here.

If there's anything I've forgotten, let me know and I'll take care of it in the morning.''

"Rebecca—''

''It was nice of you to let Alison and Stephen use your house for the wedding,'' she added in an effort to keep him from saying anything further about their situation. ''It's a beautiful house, Jake. I know you'll be very happy here.'' She wished she had the nerve to add the word *alone* in a meaningful way, but at the moment all Rebecca wanted was to be gone.

Reaching into her coat pocket, she closed her fingers over the key he had given her two weeks ago. Without a word, she placed it on the coffee table, picked up her purse from the chair where her coat had been, then turned and headed for the front door.

Jake made a halfhearted effort to go after her, wondering why he was even bothering. ''But—''

'''Night.''

And with that, Rebecca hurried out the front door, jarring the entire house as she slammed it behind her, and leaving Jake silent and dumbfounded in the middle of his living room. After a moment he heard the sound of her sports car roar to life in his driveway, and the squeal of tires as she rushed away from his house. And then, Rebecca was well-and-truly gone, effectively removed from Jake's life forever. All that remained was the scent of her perfume, a scattering of hairpins lying on his coffee table, and a head full of memories that wouldn't even begin to keep him warm at night.

"Dammit,'' he bit out angrily.

Everything had been moving along nicely between

him and Rebecca all day, and Jake had begun to think that maybe, just maybe, they would be able to salvage something—God knows what—from their time together. So what the hell had he done wrong?

Everything, he answered himself immediately. He'd done everything wrong. Slumping back onto the couch in the spot Rebecca had just vacated, Jake sighed wearily, just as she had. He felt as if he'd lived a lifetime in the past three weeks. Rebecca Bellamy had careered into his life from out of nowhere four months ago, had invaded his thoughts and his libido until he could think of little else, then had exploded onto the scene again in all her glory. Then as quickly and thoroughly as she had gotten under his skin, she had retreated, and this time he was sure she wouldn't be coming back.

But that was good, wasn't it? Jake asked himself. That meant he didn't have to worry about being roped into a wedding by a woman who was determined to get married, right? No more having to defend himself and his position on the topic of matrimony. No more feeling guilty about wanting to stay single every time she looked at him with those huge green eyes of hers. No more catching himself wondering what it would be like to wake up next to Rebecca every morning and see her looking soft and vulnerable as she had that night two weeks ago. As she had again tonight. He could continue to wake up every morning completely, blissfully alone. Wasn't that exactly what he wanted?

Jake wove his fingers viciously through his hair, then slammed his fist down hard onto the coffee table. Yeah, that was what he wanted, all right. To be alone.

Leaning forward from his position on the sofa, he

lifted the glass that was still filled with softly bubbling champagne. There was a pale scarlet, crescent-shaped stain on one side, and Jake turned the glass until that side faced him. Placing his lips exactly over the spot where Rebecca's had tasted the wine, he drank deeply and scowled. It tasted a little flat to him. Slowly, he walked to his kitchen and approached the sink, then tipped the glass and watched with much disinterest as the champagne cascaded downward into the drain.

It had been a nice wedding, Jake reflected morosely, as he turned out the kitchen light and headed off to bed. Too bad such celebrations always had to end in marriage.

Rebecca was having trouble concentrating. In fact, she'd been having trouble concentrating for nearly a month now, ever since severing any ties that might remain to Jake Raglan. As she sat at her desk in her Frankfort Avenue office, chin in hand, staring out the window, she realized absently that she was daydreaming again. Normally Rebecca didn't have time for daydreams. Usually November was a very hectic month for her because of the upcoming holiday season. But more and more often this month, she had found herself turning down clients who requested her services to plan both weddings and holiday gatherings, citing a busy agenda and full schedule instead of the physical fatigue and spiritual weariness that actually caused her to decline.

What was it with her lately? she wondered. Gone was the enthusiasm she had once felt for her profession, and gone was the happy zeal with which she had undertaken every project. Ever since the Mitchell-Flannery affair, Rebecca had taken little interest in any prospective nuptial celebration she might be asked to plan, thinking instead that she had grown tired of organizing weddings. What was so great about two people declaring their lifelong devotion, anyway? Statistically speaking, half of them were going to wind up alone again in the long run, so really, what was the point?

Rebecca sighed and toyed with a pencil on her desk blotter, noting vaguely as she continued to stare out the window that it had started to rain. Might as well call it a day, she thought. She couldn't focus on anything, anyway.

As she rose to collect her black greatcoat from the hook behind her door, she heard someone enter the outer office, heard her assistant, Claire, say that, yes, Ms. Bellamy was in her office and able to accept a client. Rebecca sighed again and went back to her desk, smoothing the wrinkles out of her plum-colored wool suit and assuming a posture she hoped made her look terribly busy. But when her office door opened and she glanced up to find Jake Raglan entering, Rebecca knew any facade she tried to erect around herself would fail miserably. So she only stared at him silently, and wished he were nothing more than a hallucination.

"Hello, Rebecca," he said quietly, as he closed the door behind him. Instead of walking toward her desk, he leaned back against the door, clinging to the knob as if to prevent her escape.

"Hello, Jake," she replied cautiously, amazed that she was able to keep her voice level and indifferent.

"Aren't you going to ask me what I'm doing here?"

Rebecca shook her head. "I figure you'll get around to telling me eventually. You've never been one to beat around the bush. You'll make your intentions clear right off."

Jake wasn't sure how he had expected Rebecca to react upon seeing him again, but "cool, calm and collected" hadn't been in his top five choices. He had hoped she would react differently. Evidently, however, his hopes had been in vain. Apparently, Rebecca Bellamy had already put him behind her, and now what he'd come to do wouldn't be as easy as he'd thought. But he was here and it was too late to turn back, so he might as well get to the point.

"I want to hire you."

Rebecca's heart nearly stopped beating at the announcement. "You're getting married?" she asked in a shallow voice, her breath having left her lungs in a steady rush.

"Married?" Jake asked incredulously. "God, no, I'm not getting married."

Inhaling deeply, Rebecca discovered she could only nod silently in response.

"No, I want you to plan a Christmas party for me," Jake clarified. "In fact, I want you to plan my entire Christmas. That is, if you're not already booked up for the season."

Rebecca gazed at him thoughtfully for a long time before replying. Just what was he up to? she wondered. Why would he hire her to perform such a service when a number of other people in town could do it for him? He had made it clear that there was no reason to pursue their relationship any further, had been more than open in his assertion that they wouldn't be seeing each other anymore after Stephen and Alison's wedding. Why her? Why now? Why ever?

"I've got a pretty full calendar, Jake," she lied reluctantly. "Corporate parties, social soirees, even a couple of weddings."

Jake tried not to let her see how deeply her rebuff unsettled him. Although he told himself he should simply accept things for what they were between them—over—and go along on his merry way, instead he heard himself asking, "You couldn't grant me a few weekends? An extra weekday here and there?"

"I won't be *granting* you anything, Jake," Rebecca reminded him. "You'll have to pay me for my time."

"So you'll do it?"

It was only then that Rebecca realized her words had indicated she was willing to accept him as a client. She tried to tell herself her acquiescence had resulted from nothing more than a slip of the tongue. But if she was brutally honest with herself, she knew that deep down inside, nothing would have pleased her more than seeing Jake Raglan again.

She drummed her fingers restlessly against the surface of her desk before voicing her assent. "What exactly did you have in mind?"

Jake had given much thought to his wishes, surprising himself immensely when he first came up with the idea to have a big Christmas celebration at his house. The night following Stephen's wedding had been full of introspection for Jake. He had lain awake in bed for hours, marveling at what a good time he'd had during the wedding and reception, and at how much it had pleased him to see his house full of people having a wonderful time. And at how good it had felt to know Rebecca was responsible for it.

When he'd first bought his house seven months ago, Jake had never once entertained the thought of ever having anyone over. He had simply liked the size of the massive creek-stone structure—especially the fact that it was even larger than the house Ellen shared with her family—and he had liked knowing he would be living in one of Louisville's most prestigious neighborhoods. It would impress his clients, he'd thought then. And it would get under Ellen's skin. That was all. Those were the only reasons for buying that particular house. Not because of any entertainment potential, and certainly not because it would provide enough room for a big family.

But oddly enough, both of those ideas had careered into his mind the night after Stephen's wedding. For the first time since Jake had moved in, his house had been full of people. And even though those people were friends and relatives of someone else, Jake had realized another first—his house felt like a home. The place had simply felt warm, comfortable and full, reinforcing how thoroughly empty it was when he was home by himself. And somehow it had also occurred to Jake then that only Rebecca Bellamy would be able to make it feel that way again. It had taken him almost a month to actually admit it.

"I want you to do everything," he told her.

Rebecca raised her eyebrows in speculation. "Come again?"

Jake finally released the doorknob and moved across the room to take a seat in the chair opposite hers. "You once told me that the 'Plus' in 'Weddings Plus, Inc.' could be anything. You told me that you had even organized a Christmas once, everything from the shopping to the decorating to the wrapping to the cooking. I want to hire you to do that for me."

"Why?" Rebecca thought it was a fair-enough question. Jake was a grown man who had come far in life. Surely this wasn't the first Christmas he had celebrated. Surely he knew how to go about performing the usual tasks. But his answer proved she was mistaken.

"Because I've never really celebrated Christmas before, that's why."

Rebecca eyed him doubtfully, but said nothing.

"It's true. When Ellen and I were growing up in Acorn Ridge, my family couldn't afford to have Christmas. Oh, we went to church, and chopped down some sorry excuse for a tree, but there were no gifts, no parties, no eggnog or Santa Claus. Then when we got older, Ellen...well, Ellen wanted to spend Christmas with her new family, not with me. I carried too many reminders of what she'd left behind. When Daphne was old enough, she and I would go to dinner every Christmas Eve, but that was the extent of my holiday revels." He paused for a moment, fixing Rebecca with an almost desperate expression. "I've never had a Christmas before, Rebecca. Not the way most people do."

He looked so forlorn seated across from her that Rebecca wanted to reach over and take his hand in hers. Here was a man, one of the most successful attorneys in town, wealthy beyond his dreams and completely unable to enjoy a holiday. How could she turn him down? she asked herself. She, who knew better than anyone in the world how to celebrate, she who found celebration in *everything* life had to offer…how could she say no to such a simple request as his?

"Okay, I'll do it," she said with a smile.

Jake hadn't been aware he was holding his breath until he let it out on a long sigh. He smiled back at Rebecca with genuine relief. "When do we start?"

"Right now," she told him as she went to a file cabinet and pulled open the top drawer. "Let's see now," she said to herself as she began to thumb through manila folders. "Anniversaries, babies, birthdays, bridal…ah, here it is. Christmas."

She held the folder aloft as if it were a trophy, returned to her desk and spread it open before her, then glanced up at Jake again. "You sure you want me to do it all?"

"Absolutely positive," he assured her with a firm nod.

"Then I'll need you to supply a few things for me."

"Such as?"

"A list of people for whom you'd like to buy gifts and how much you'd like to spend on each. If you can supply me with a few ideas, it would be an enor-

mous help. If you want to entertain, I'll also need a
guest list, and I'll have to go over menus with you.
You'll need to tell me about any food allergies or dislikes you or your guests might have, any specific di-
etary needs that might have to be met—vegetarian,
low-salt, diabetic, that sort of thing....'' Her words
trailed off as she sifted through more papers. ''I'll
need price ceilings, dates of availability—''

''Rebecca?''

It was the voice Jake had used when he'd made love
to her, and it almost made Rebecca want to cry at
hearing it once again. Slowly, she lifted her gaze from
the papers on her desk to the man who sat before her,
and slowly, her senses began to go berserk. He was
looking at her as if he cared for her, gazing at her as
if all he wanted to do was hold her close and never
let her go. Oh, how she wished he would. Oh, how
she wished Jake Raglan was a man who could love
her until her dying day. But that was a futile wish, an
empty dream. Jake would devote himself to no
woman. Jake Raglan would never marry again.

''Yes?'' Rebecca asked faintly.

For long moments he said nothing, only continued
to stare at her with that maddeningly tender expression. ''Thanks,'' he finally uttered quietly.

Rebecca's heart hammered hard in her chest. ''For
what?''

Jake's smile became softer then, and his voice was
so low when he answered her that she almost didn't
hear. ''For everything.''

For a moment, Rebecca didn't—couldn't—respond.
Her mind was too muddled, her thoughts too confused.

Gradually she calmed herself down, took a deep breath, and spoke in a voice that surprised her with its evenness and composure. "There's something we need to get straight, though, Jake."

His expression indicated nothing as to what he might be feeling or thinking. "What's that?"

"What happened between us before…it won't happen again."

She waited for him to respond, but his posture remained unchanged, and he only gazed at her, unfazed, as if demanding that she clarify her intentions.

"I'm serious, Jake. If I take you on as a client, there's to be no flirting, no innuendo, no longing looks…in short, no hanky-panky."

She could tell he was biting his lip in an effort to prevent his laughter from erupting. "Hanky-panky? Now there's a phrase I haven't heard in a couple of decades. Hanky-panky… Golly gee whillikers, is that still around after all this time?"

Rebecca ignored his sarcasm and explained, "I'm going to be spending a lot of time at your house, Jake, and I want you to promise me that you won't try anything funny."

Jake rose from his chair and leaned over her desk, so close that she could smell familiar scents that evoked dangerous memories. His eyes were dark, stormy and very, very serious when he told her, "Rebecca, I can safely say that you won't find anything I try funny. Erotic, maybe, arousing, certainly, but… funny? No way."

"Jake…"

"Okay," he finally conceded. "No funny stuff. No

hanky-panky, whatever the hell that is. I'll be your client, and you'll be my holiday organizer. Nothing more. Is that what you want?''

''Yes.'' She tried to sound assertive and strong, but Rebecca's voice was breathless and ragged when she replied.

''Are you sure?''

Not trusting her voice to comply with her demands, Rebecca simply nodded silently.

''Okay, then. We've got the record straight.'' Jake returned to his seat, and assumed once again the pose of a successful man who wanted to employ her expertise for his holiday entertaining. Gone was the heated gaze, the promise of pursuit. In its place, Jake had inserted a bland expression of neutrality.

Rebecca thought back to how he had looked and sounded when he'd told her thanks only moments ago, then cautioned herself not to overreact. He had simply been thanking her for taking him on as a client, nothing more. Still, deep down inside, she couldn't prevent the little flame of hope that flickered to life in her heart. No matter how often she tried to squelch it with the waters of reason, the spark sputtered back to life again. Rebecca called herself foolish and naive. She called herself a dupe. But she couldn't help feeling excited that she'd be there to plan Jake's Christmas.

And, despite the warning she had given him only moments earlier, in the most secret chamber of her heart, Rebecca couldn't help but hope that she might be there to enjoy it with him, too.

Seven

─────

By the middle of the third week of December, Rebecca had completely transformed Jake's house. He had told her he wanted to have a cocktail party and open house for his neighbors and a number of his associates that evening, and she was well ahead of schedule in her planning of the night's festivities.

The color scheme in Jake's living and dining rooms was perfect for the season—deep crimson and forest green—so Rebecca had simply added accessories to enhance the rooms. Over the fireplace she had hung an enormous wreath made of grapevines interwoven and sprayed with holly and greenery and a huge golden bow. A garland of twisted pine and spruce boughs touched with the same golden ribbon adorned the mantel and bannister leading to the upstairs. Opposite the fireplace and tucked into a corner created by the stairway and wall, she had placed an eight-foot-high Scotch pine decorated completely in gold—glittery gold trim, twinkling gold lights, shiny gold balls and glistening gold tinsel. Beneath it lay the gifts Rebecca had purchased as Jake had indicated—every one of them for clients, save the one he'd ordered for Daphne, Rebecca recalled dryly—all wrapped in foil paper of green, red and gold. Rebecca had always loved shiny things. She supposed that in her next life she would probably come back as a magpie.

Now as she stood in the center of Jake's living room studying her handiwork, she smiled to herself in satisfaction at what she had accomplished in such a short time. Jake had been more than generous in his price ceiling. For the most part, he had told Rebecca that money wasn't a concern, that he simply wanted to make up for all the Christmases he had ever missed, and that she should do whatever necessary to make such a celebration memorable.

She had taken him at his word and organized a holiday celebration that would surpass even her own family's revels. Christmas for the Bellamys had always been, to put it mildly, a very big deal. And the only celebrations Rebecca threw herself into with the zeal she embraced for weddings were her Christmas festivities. She found great joy in bringing to other people's homes many of the traditions and holiday treats she had enjoyed herself as a child. And for some reason, sharing these things with Jake, in his house, caused Rebecca to feel even more joyful than usual.

Lifting her nose to inhale the spicy aromas coming from the kitchen, she remembered that she needed to

see how her holiday libations were coming along and
went to check on them. Simmering on the stove were
two large stockpots—one filled with dark beer, cloves,
orange peel and cinnamon for wassail, and another
with apple juice and similar spices for a non-alcoholic
hot cider. In the refrigerator were three one-gallon jugs
filled with Rebecca's own recipe for eggnog that she
had perfected over the years—two of them containing
enough liquor to qualify as "Rebecca's Killer Eggnog," as her father liked to call it. She had also made
arrangements for a caterer to provide the requisite holiday foods and preparations—ham, turkey, mincemeat,
pumpkin pie, fruitcake, jellies, candies and the like—
and she had personally undertaken and nearly exhausted herself with the annual baking of a dozen va-
rieties of Christmas cookies from recipes handed down
by her great-grandmother.

As she stood at the stove, tasting the wassail one
last time before straining it off into the huge crystal
punch bowl that had been in her family for years, Rebecca felt oddly at home. Because she had found
Jake's kitchen and china cabinet to be sadly lacking
in many of the pieces necessary for large-scale entertaining, and since she was reluctant to spend what
would amount to a small fortune to buy him things he
might never use again, Rebecca had opted to bring
many of her own special belongings to Jake's house
for use at his party. Rented china was always so boring
looking. Hence her great-grandmother's crystal punch
bowl and cups. Hence her grandmother's fine china
and crystal stemware. Hence her own silver flatware.

Rebecca told herself that her actions were not unusual in any way. She had often used her own things when she herself catered small parties, because people almost never had enough of their own to entertain in numbers larger than those in their family, or else they were often unwilling to risk the breakage and loss of their fine china, crystal and silver to casual acquaintances. However, Rebecca had never, ever, used her older and more-valuable pieces—the heirlooms that had belonged to generations before her. Only with Jake had she felt it acceptable, indeed even desirable, to use her most beautiful crystal, china and silver. And now, seeing her things mingled so comfortably with his own, a feeling of strange serenity settled over her like a soothing hand.

You're doing it again, a little voice in the back of her head piped up unbidden. You're beginning to feel at home in Jake's house.

Rebecca couldn't honestly deny it. Because Jake was the only client she had agreed to take on this holiday season, and because Jake's Christmas was the only project she had to organize until almost February, she had thrown herself into the planning of this celebration with all the fervor she normally saved for her own holiday. With no small amount of chagrin, Rebecca had to admit that she had probably spent more time in Jake's house this week than she had her own. In fact, she realized uncomfortably, here it was only one week before Christmas, and she hadn't even put up a tree at her home.

But of course, that was because she had been so busy lately, getting things organized at Jake's house, trying to make sure everything ran smoothly here. Her lapses in getting her own home decorated went no further than that, Rebecca assured herself. And if it felt different now going home at night alone, if her house had suddenly begun to feel like a strange place to her, well, that was simply because she'd been under a lot of stress lately. It was perfectly understandable. Any woman would react the same way under the circumstances—planning a holiday celebration for a man who had made love to her only to turn his back on her romantically. Thinking about it now, Rebecca realized she must have been mad ever to accept Jake as a client to begin with.

It wasn't the first time the thought had occurred to her. But Rebecca was beginning to understand exactly why she had agreed to take on Jake's Christmas. There was still a part of her deep down inside that thought—hoped—that Jake might change his mind about marriage. And although she had lain awake at night wondering if she would ever have a second chance with him, wishing that he would take her in his arms just one more time, she knew it was ridiculous to dream. She should be delighted that Jake had stuck to their agreement and hadn't so much as touched her since she'd entered his house again, Rebecca reflected morosely. It had kept her from making a complete fool of herself.

Glancing up at the clock on the wall, Rebecca realized she had been lost in thought longer than she could afford to be, and would be cutting her time too close if she went home to change her clothes. Fortunately, she had brought her entertaining outfit with her in anticipation of just such an emergency. The party didn't start until eight, and it wasn't yet five, and Rebecca had discovered that Jake made it a habit never to leave his Main Street office before six-thirty. Therefore, if she started now, she knew she could be more than ready by the time he got home. Dusting her hands off absently on her pants, Rebecca grabbed her garment bag from its hook on the inside of the kitchen door and headed upstairs.

To say it was unusual for Jake to leave the office early in order to go home would be a gross understatement. Although it wasn't customary for him to leave the office at all before the end of the workday, if he did, it was to perform some function that directly pertained to business—dinners with clients, depositions, case-related appointments, that sort of thing. But today for some reason, Jake had been feeling restless and edgy, had been nearly overcome by the desire— almost a *need*—to get home as soon as possible.

It had begun around midmorning, when Jake discovered that he was scarcely listening to the verbal meanderings of a newly acquired client. Mr. Landrow was an older gentleman who suspected that his wife— a woman from one of the city's most prominent families, a woman who was noted throughout the community for her selfless charity work—had been cheating on him for some time with the strapping young teenager who delivered the groceries, despite her assurances that such allegations were ridiculous. Normally Jake would pounce on the potential a case like Landrow's seemed to have, but today, he simply wasn't interested.

Instead of paying attention to the less-than-convincing reasons the other man had for his feelings, Jake found himself lost in thoughts of his own, all of them centering around Rebecca Bellamy and what she was doing in his house at that very moment. Every night this week he had come home to find her there, either on her way out or putting the finishing touches on her day's work and preparing to leave. Every night he had asked her to stay for a little while, maybe have some dinner with him. And every night she had said no.

What had he expected? Jake asked himself. She had made it clear from the beginning that she wouldn't tolerate any *hanky-panky,* as she'd so archaically put it. And she had made it clear that what had happened between them before would *not* happen again. In other words, Jake thought, angry with himself, Rebecca wouldn't allow herself to be hurt again. Not by Jake Raglan, anyway.

When he came home at night to find her there, his house seemed fuller and more inviting than he ever would have imagined it could feel. And as soon as she left, the warmth and welcome vanished with her. Then Jake's house became lonelier and more silent than he'd ever noticed it being before. Then Jake's house became empty.

What was she up to right now? he wondered, still sitting idle at his desk hours after Landrow had left him. For the life of him, Jake couldn't even remember what the other man's beef about his marriage had been. Poor old guy simply couldn't believe that his wife still loved him, even after forty-two years of marriage.

The thought caught Jake off guard for a moment, then he pushed it away, suddenly remembering quite clearly what the other man's problem had been. An unfaithful wife. Yet another woman who couldn't be true to the man who loved her. Why shouldn't Mrs. Landrow dump her husband for some young stud? Jake asked himself with all-too-characteristic suspicion. Women did that every day. She had money and connections and was reasonably attractive. And face it, he himself knew Landrow left a lot to be desired in the conversation department. There was every reason in the world to believe that Mrs. Landrow was a wandering wife. And if Mr. Landrow wanted to divorce her because of it, that was his business. All Jake had to do was provide the best legal counsel he could for his client.

But he would have to do it tomorrow.

Because today, Jake wanted to leave the office early and go home. Home to his house, home to the holidays, home to Rebecca. He refused to contemplate how much his feelings had changed over the past two months, refused to consider how important she had become to him, refused to accept that he might honestly be falling hard for this particular woman. He only knew he wanted to go home. And in his mind, that meant being wherever Rebecca was.

Rebecca paused in her preparations when she heard the front door open and close downstairs, followed by the sound of heavy footsteps crossing the living room floor. It couldn't possibly be Jake, she thought. It was barely past five o'clock. She'd scarcely had enough time to step out of her cooking-and-baking clothes and stuff them into a duffel bag heaped in the corner of the bathroom, and now stood barefoot, dressed in only a lacy slip. Her cosmetics lay scattered about on the pedestal sink, her dress hung on the shower-curtain rod still enclosed in its garment bag, and some intruder was downstairs.

With a sudden sense of relief, she realized it must be Donnie, who drove the truck for his father's catering company, and who was supposed to be stopping by with some canapés he'd forgotten to bring with the other food earlier that day. Rebecca had told him she'd leave the front door open in case she was out of hearing range. Opting to simply call downstairs to the teenager that he should put the items into the fridge and tell his father she'd telephone him later to settle up, Rebecca looked around for something to throw quickly over her slip and saw Jake's bathrobe hanging on the back of the door. Oh, what the heck, she thought. It would only be for a minute.

Thrusting her arms into dark blue velour sleeves that hung down well past her fingertips, Rebecca threw the bathroom door open and rushed toward the stairs, all set to bellow out her instructions to the caterer. But the moment she came around the corner and saw Jake topping the highest step, she skidded to a halt and stood rooted to the spot, feeling like a naughty child with her hand in the cookie jar.

At a quiet, oddly strangled sound, Jake glanced up from scanning over the day's mail in his hand and saw what he told himself must surely be a figment of his extremely overactive imagination. There in his upstairs hallway, bundled up in and swallowed by his bathrobe, her toes digging nervously into the lush, dark gold pile carpet, stood Rebecca Bellamy. She looked vulnerable, panicked, uncertain and adorable. And, Jake thought, taking a few reluctant steps toward her, she also looked very desirable.

"Jake," she said, drawing his name out on a long, breathless sigh. "What are you doing home so early?"

"Hi," he said quietly, willing his feet to stop before he got close enough to take her in his arms and scare the hell out of both of them. "I'm sorry. I didn't mean to surprise you like this. I just... I had a light load today, and since the party was tonight, I thought I'd leave early and see if there was anything I could do to help you."

Rebecca seemed to realize then that she was wearing his bathrobe, and fumbled with the sleeves until her hands appeared, so that she could tug the collar up more snugly around her neck. After clearing her throat delicately, she said softly, "I...uh...I was expecting the caterer."

Jake knew full well that her announcement didn't imply what it in fact suggested, but he couldn't help but smile when he replied, "So this is how you greet the caterer. I was wondering how these professional deals worked. I hope he gives you some substantial discounts for this."

Rebecca's eyes widened when she realized how her statement must have sounded, and she fumbled over her words as she tried to explain. "No, wait....

That…that came out wrong. What I meant to say was that I was expecting the caterer's son—''

Jake's eyebrows rose in speculation.

"No, I didn't mean that, either.'' Rebecca sighed in exasperation, tangling a hand in her hair to push it back off her forehead. "I wasn't expecting to run into anyone. I was planning on just calling out to him down the stairs to leave the stuff in the fridge.''

"I see.'' He gazed at her for a long time in silence, until he finally seemed to remember where they were and what they were doing. "The house smells wonderful,'' he told her softly.

"Thanks,'' she responded a little breathlessly.

"And you look wonderful.''

Rebecca laced her fingers together nervously, then unlaced them, then began to twist them up restlessly in the sash of the robe. Her heart beat in irregular rhythms beneath her breastbone, and her stomach knotted into an anxious fist. "I'm…I'm sorry I have on your bathrobe. I…it was handy.''

Jake's grin broadened. "You wear it well. I don't think I'll ever be able to look at it in quite the same way again.''

Rebecca felt heat seep into every fiber of her being, and little sparks of fire flashed like tiny explosions throughout her body. Jake was gazing at her the way a starving man studies a sumptuous banquet, the way a parched wolf eyes a sparkling mountain stream. More alarming than that, though, Rebecca thought, was her realization that her own feelings of hunger and thirst at the moment were even more demanding.

"I'll…I'll just go change,'' she said quietly.

Jake followed her as far as the bathroom and let his gaze rove past the door to where she had scattered her feminine weapons all over his sink. Marking her territory? he wondered. For some reason, the thought that she might be doing just that did little to raise his hackles. In fact, he reflected, as she closed the door and he headed farther down the hall to his bedroom, it occurred to him that Rebecca Bellamy had probably marked his house the moment she had entered it, and he honestly didn't mind at all.

He should, Jake tried to remind himself viciously. He should mind a lot. Before he'd bought his house, when he'd been renting apartments, he had hated it when he'd discovered a stray lipstick or hair clip or earring tucked discreetly into his medicine cabinet, or between his couch cushions, or under the pillow opposite his in bed. It had meant the owners of the items were leaving a message for any other woman who might happen along, stating that the premises were already covered. It was why he had never invited a woman into his house for a romantic evening and had instead insisted on either going out or going to her place. Jake hadn't wanted his house to be marked the way his apartments had been.

But now it was. Rebecca Bellamy was there in every nook and cranny, and had been for months. Ever since that first night that she had come to inspect the suitability of Jake's house for the Mitchell-Flannery wedding. Ever since she had told him his house was beautiful. Because when Rebecca was there, it was indeed a beautiful house. When Rebecca was there, it was a home.

Just as it was now. For Jake, it had been wonderful to come home every night this week and find Rebecca performing her job downstairs in the most public rooms of his house. But coming home tonight to find her upstairs, in the more private domain of his home, enveloped in a garment as personal and intimate as his bathrobe…it stirred flames so deeply buried inside him that he had nearly forgotten a fire could still burn there. Oddly enough, he realized, as he closed his bedroom door to change clothes, at the moment, there was one burning brighter than it ever had before.

Eight

"Uncle Jake! Uncle Jake! I have the most wonderful news!"

Jake had been speaking at length with one of his neighbors when he heard Daphne's voice coming breathlessly from behind him, and he turned to find her approaching him with eyes as shiny as the Christmas tree behind her and cheeks as red as the velvet cocktail dress she had on. He recalled the first Christmas Eve that he had taken her out to dinner. She had worn a red velvet dress then, too, but as a five-year-old had opted for a much more modest style than the off-the-shoulder number she had on now.

Five years old, Jake thought, with an almost indiscernible shake of his head. That had been nineteen years ago. In an effort to impress his only niece, he had taken her to one of the most expensive restaurants in town. Daphne had deemed the Caesar salad and coq au vin yucky, but had found the raspberry torte to be very much to her liking. Last year when he'd taken her out, she had behaved like nearly every other date Jake had ever escorted to dinner—she'd chosen the garden salad and poached salmon, cooing enthusiastically over both, then had skipped dessert because they were all so fattening. If he hadn't been feeling so strange at the moment, Jake might have laughed at the changes. But all he could do was wonder when Daphne had grown up to become such a beautiful woman.

"Hi, Daphne." He greeted her with a smile, noting that the warm feelings he felt whenever his niece was around were still as strong as ever. "How's married life treating you?"

Daphne's grin couldn't have been broader if she'd put her fingers in her mouth and stretched it. "It's fantastic," she told him. "I never thought I could have this much fun with another person."

"How's Robby?"

Daphne's smile became almost coquettish, and she blushed a little more deeply. "He's fine. He just got a promotion at work. He's regional sales manager now. Takes care of the entire southeast."

"Where is he?" Jake asked, glancing around to inspect the guests. "I'll congratulate him."

"No, wait!" Daphne objected, tugging on Jake's sleeve as he caught sight of his nephew-in-law and began to head in that direction.

Her insistence surprised Jake, and his voice reflected his feelings when he turned back to face her. "Why? What's wrong?"

For a moment, Daphne only stared at her uncle, biting her lip nervously. Finally she blurted out, "You'll have two reasons to congratulate him, Uncle Jake. I'm...I'm going to have a baby."

His expression probably would have been the same if she had just told him she was migrating to Antarctica. "You're *what?*"

Daphne was suddenly overcome by a wave of shyness, and she shrugged a little nervously as she clarified, "I'm going to be a mother, Uncle Jake. And you're going to be a great-uncle."

Whoa, whoa, whoa, Jake wanted to say. He was only...he was only...oh, dammit, go ahead and say it, he told himself. He was only forty years old. That was way too young to be a great-anything. Unless, of course, it was a great lover.

"A baby?" he asked softly. "You and Robby are going to have a baby?"

Daphne nodded vigorously. "If it's a girl, we're naming her Carmen, after Robby's mother. But if it's a boy...if it's a boy, we'd like to name him Jacob. That is, if that's all right with you."

Jake didn't know what to say. A baby boy named after him running around in the world? It was something to which he'd never given thought. After his debacle with Marie, he had simply assumed he would never have children of his own, obviously because he would never marry again. Certainly he would have liked to have children of his own. In fact, if he had ever allowed himself to think about it, Jake would probably have felt great remorse that he would never hear the word "Daddy" used for him. But he had consciously forced himself *not* to think about it. At least, he had until now.

"I'm flattered, Daphne. Of course I don't mind if you name your son after me. How could you think that I would?"

"I just figured that when you have a son of your own, you might want to name him Jake, Jr. or something. I didn't want there to be any confusion when my little Jake and your little Jake play together."

His little Jake? he thought wildly. *His* little Jake? "I don't think you have to worry about that ever happening, Daphne."

"You're not one of those guys who insists his name be carried on, is that it?"

Jake shook his head. "I'm not one of those guys who will ever have children."

Daphne smiled at him knowingly. "Don't count on it, Uncle Jake. It might take you longer than most, but you'll be up to your elbows in diapers and strained carrots. Just you wait."

Before he could contradict her again, Daphne spun on her heel and went to find others of her acquaintance to whom she could deliver the good news. Jake watched her leave, feeling oddly happy, though for the life of him he couldn't put his finger on exactly why. Telling himself it was simply because Daphne always brought out a gentler side of him, he sipped his drink and tried not to smile like an idiot.

When Daphne's husband, Robby, strode past, Jake

caught his eye and congratulated him on both his promotion and his impending state of fatherhood.

"Thanks," the other man said with a huge smile. Like Daphne, he was blond and blue eyed, and Jake couldn't help but think that their child was probably going to look like an angel from a Renaissance painting. "We haven't told my parents yet," he continued. "We're going to spring it on them on Christmas Eve."

The announcement took Jake by surprise. "Christmas Eve?" he asked, puzzled. His reaction must have been obvious, because suddenly Robby seemed to become very nervous.

"Uh, yeah, Christmas Eve. Oops. Didn't Daphne mention it? She wanted to be the one to tell you, Jake, because I know the two of you always spent Christmas Eve together. But my folks want us to celebrate with my family at their house. Dinner, drinks, holiday reveling, the usual. Boy, Daphne's going to kill me when she finds out you heard about this from me." Robby paused for a moment, clearly reluctant to dig himself in any deeper than he already had. In what Jake supposed was an effort to change the subject, he added, "My mother's going to go bananas when she hears the news."

"Christmas Eve," Jake repeated absently.

Robby nodded, prepared to apologize further, when someone called his name. "Oh, excuse me, Jake. There's someone here I really have to talk to."

And with that, Daphne's husband vanished, along with Jake's plans for the holidays. Certainly he shouldn't be surprised that his niece would want to spend Christmas Eve with her new husband and his family, and certainly he didn't condemn her for wanting to. It was just that now he was going to be alone during the entirety of the holidays. And the idea simply didn't sit well with him.

Lifting his drink for an idle sip, Jake glanced over the edge of his glass and saw Rebecca on the other side of the room, speaking to one of the guests, and paused. Her dark green, long-sleeved dress was cut low in the back, and when he'd first seen her wearing it, he'd realized the color made her eyes seem even deeper than usual. Her hair was bunched atop her head in a careless sweep, a few short ringlets tumbling down her neck and over her forehead. She was indeed a perfect hostess, Jake thought. She had mingled quite successfully and seemed to have a warm smile and a nice word for everyone who had come. Everyone, that was, except for him.

Each time he had tried to draw Rebecca away from the crowd to attempt a moment of privacy, she had suddenly remembered something that needed attending to. First it had been the dip, then the cheese ball, then the wassail, then the eggnog. When she'd run out of edible items, she'd begun to get more creative, first citing the capacity of the hall closet for the guests' coats, then the size of the centerpiece, then a lost earring. Before long she would be losing the guests themselves, Jake thought dryly. Anything to keep her from having to talk to him.

Well, Rebecca Bellamy was about to learn that there were some things in life she simply couldn't avoid. And while she was in his house, at his party, she was going to have to realize that he himself was one of those things. Setting his glass down on a cocktail table near the fireplace, Jake began to take deliberate strides in her direction.

"You know, I've been wondering all this time about the people who moved into the Eddlestons' house." Jake's across-the-street neighbor, Mrs. Dorset, eagerly popped a stuffed mushroom into her mouth and took her time to suck the remainder from her fingers before she continued. "It was so nice of you and your husband to have a holiday open house for the neighborhood, Mrs. Raglan. Although it would have been nice to meet you both sooner."

"Mrs. Dorset, as I told you twice earlier, I'm not Mrs.—"

"Do the two of you have any children, dear? My two grandchildren, Eddie and Sophia—my son's little boy and girl—are ages seven and five, respectively, and they always seem to be lacking in playmates whenever they come to visit."

Rebecca finally surrendered to the other woman's insistence, and simply sighed. "No, Mrs. Dorset, we don't have any children."

Mrs. Dorset reached for one of the nut nibbles heaped on her plate, put it to her mouth, then withdrew it again as another thought struck her. "Well, you don't want to wait too long, you know. No offense, dear, but you realize of course that the two of you are no spring chickens anymore. You don't want to wind up at the last minute with a full heart and an empty bassinet, do you?"

Rebecca closed her eyes and rubbed her forehead in

an effort to dispel the migraine she felt threatening. "No…"

"My Alicia did just that thing. Wanted to get settled in her career first, then have a family. Well, of course you know what happened."

Rebecca was about to say that no, of course she did not, having never met Mrs. Dorset's Alicia, but Mrs. Dorset saved her the trouble.

"My Alicia discovered too late that she was…well, that she had put all her eggs in one basket, so to speak—no pun intended—and then had dropped the basket on her way to market."

Rebecca gazed at Mrs. Dorset through eyes narrowed in confusion, wondering if she had just spent the last fifteen minutes conversing with a recently released mental patient. The other woman seemed like a sane-enough person. Still, one could never tell these days.…

"Ah, there you are."

It was the first time this evening Rebecca had been relieved to hear Jake's voice. As she had watched him weave in and out of his guests, looking so incredible in an exquisitely cut dark suit, her heart had hammered like rain on an empty drum, bouncing around behind her rib cage as if it were about to shatter. She simply didn't trust herself around him. Ever since running into him while wearing his bathrobe, she had felt as if she'd become oddly intimate with him all over again. Now she feared that if he said just the right thing, or looked at her in just the right way, she would damn the consequences and follow him straight to bed.

It was just that he was so handsome, Rebecca

thought, feeling her mouth grow dry as she looked at him. When she had ordered the table arrangements from the florist, she had been struck by a fit of whimsy and had ordered a boutonniere for him to wear, a trio of red berries nestled in a sprig of holly. Now he looked festive and happy and at home, more satisfied than Rebecca could ever recall seeing him. It was all she could do not to sigh dramatically, throw an arm to her forehead and swoon into his arms.

"Excuse me, won't you, Mrs. Dorset?" Rebecca asked her companion, trying to make a quick break before the other woman said something bizarre.

"Mr. Raglan!" Mrs. Dorset exclaimed, when she realized the identity of the man who had joined them. "I was just telling your wife how nice it is to finally meet the two of you and be able to welcome you to the neighborhood. You could have done something like this earlier, you know."

Jake looked first at Mrs. Dorset, then at Rebecca, then back at Mrs. Dorset again. "I'm sorry?" he said softly, clearly in the dark about what the other woman was talking about.

Rebecca closed her eyes and drew in a deep breath, then linked her arm fondly with Jake's. "Excuse us, Mrs. Dorset," she repeated patiently. "Jake? May I have a word with you?"

Before he could decline, she gently eased him away, glancing over her shoulder only once to see if Mrs. Dorset was following them. Jake's neighbor had already latched on to someone else, and Rebecca couldn't help but smile when she realized it was

Daphne. The two of them should have plenty to talk about, Daphne's condition being what it was.

"Congratulations on becoming a great-uncle," she told Jake as they ventured out of the living room and into the hall. She wasn't sure where they were going, but only knew it was well away from Mrs. Dorset.

"You heard," Jake said, his voice flat and emotionless.

"Are you kidding? Daphne corralled everyone she could with the news. I don't think she even had her coat off before she blurted it out to me."

Jake nodded but said nothing.

"Jake? Is something wrong?"

They were at the end of the hall now, in a part of Jake's house into which Rebecca had never before journeyed. The sounds of voices and Christmas music and clinking glasses raised in holiday cheer were muted and distant behind them; here the lighting was somewhat dark and recessed. Rebecca halted in her steps when she realized how alone she was with Jake, and involuntarily began to take a few steps backward. Before she was able to complete even two, Jake tugged gently on her arm and pulled her into a room that appeared to be a library, closed the door behind them, and then settled Rebecca against the door and himself against Rebecca.

"Jake, what are you—?"

He kissed her then, long and hard and deep, and the last thing Rebecca remembered thinking was that it felt so good to be this close to him again. Instinctively, she circled her arms around his waist and pulled him toward her, spreading her hands open against his back, skimming her flattened palms upward until she could cup one at his neck.

At her encouragement, Jake crowded his big body even closer to hers, arching one arm above her head, as if daring anyone to try to open the door, cupping his other hand possessively over her hip. Rebecca moaned softly from deep inside her soul, bunching a fistful of his jacket in her hand.

"Mrs. Dorset thought we were married," he murmured raggedly when he finally tore his lips away from hers.

Rebecca didn't trust her voice, so she only gazed at the floor and nodded mutely.

"Where would she get an idea like that?" Jake wondered aloud further.

He didn't sound angry the way she would have thought he would, so Rebecca braved a glance up at his expression and discovered much to her surprise that he didn't look angry, either. "Jake, I swear I never told her we were. In fact, I denied it three times. She's just one of those people who has her own view of the world and refuses to see it otherwise."

"You don't have to get defensive, Rebecca. I know you wouldn't do something like that. I thought maybe Daphne had put some weird notion into her head, that's all."

Now Rebecca was confused, too. "Why would Daphne do something like that?"

Because she's just dying to see me married with children, Jake wanted to say. And dammit, ever since she'd brought it up, he hadn't been able to completely push the thought away. Now, as he looked down at

Rebecca leaning against the doorway, her fingers still playing with the hair at his nape, her breathing still as ragged and edgy as his own, some window opened up in the back of his mind, filling it with sunlight and fresh air. Immediately, Jake slammed it shut again, and in the darkness that ensued, told himself his next question was only idle curiosity.

"Are you doing anything Christmas Eve?" he asked suddenly.

Rebecca couldn't prevent the rapid-fire beating of her heart, couldn't prevent the flicker of hope that sprang to life inside her. She wasn't sure what Jake was doing or why, but she couldn't help thinking he might be presenting her with precisely the chance she'd been wishing for.

"I'm spending it with my family," she told him. "I always do."

His hand on her hip slipped lower then, down to her thigh, then back up to her waist. Leaning forward again, he gently, lightly kissed her lips, then her jaw, then her forehead. Rebecca's eyes fluttered closed as she tipped her head back against the door. Jake took advantage by rubbing his lips softly against her neck, tasting her collarbone where it peeked out from the neckline of her dress.

"Oh...oh, Jake."

"Could I maybe make you change your mind about that?" he asked in a rough whisper.

Heat seeped into Rebecca's body everywhere he touched her, and she brought her hand around from his back to splay across his chest and toy with his necktie. "No can do," she told him regretfully. "I'm catering it."

He pulled away from her then, studying her intently to see if she was serious. "You're making that up," he finally said with a doubtful smile.

Rebecca shook her head. "Nope. Sorry. It's where I try out new stuff. New recipes, new activities, new music, new floral arrangements, new color schemes, you name it. I use my family for guinea pigs, and what they like I incorporate into my work."

Jake sighed in resignation. Oh, well. He was going to have to get used to spending his holidays alone sooner or later. Why not sooner? There must be something good on TV that night. Didn't they usually save up the Grinch or Charlie Brown or something for Christmas Eve?

"You could come over, if you want," Rebecca offered experimentally, uncertain how he would react to her invitation. "My parents' house will be loaded down with relatives. There will probably be more than thirty people there. No one's going to notice one more." Except me, she added to herself. You'll probably drive me to distraction.

Jake told himself he should turn her down, that he had been crazy to even ask her what she was doing Christmas Eve in the first place. Instead, he thought once again how quiet the house would be without her. There would be no luscious smells coming from the kitchen, no platters piled high with festive food, no punch bowls full of wine and garnishes of oranges studded with cloves, no Rebecca wandering around his upstairs in his bathrobe. It would be a lousy holiday.

"You sure no one would mind?" he asked hesitantly, still feeling for some reason that he was doing the wrong thing in accepting her invitation.

Rebecca tugged on his necktie until his face was near hers again. Feeling inordinately playful, she smiled and kissed him quickly, then cupped his jaw in her hand. "My family will love you," she told him honestly. Probably almost as much as I do. Then, as an afterthought, she added to herself, I only hope they don't pull a Mrs. Dorset on you.

Nine

Jake wasn't sure what he was expecting where meeting Rebecca's family was concerned. Hell, he still wasn't altogether sure what had made him agree to meet Rebecca's family in the first place. Yet he had come willingly, had taken pains to make himself look presentable in dark trousers and a forest green sweater over an ivory shirt and discreet necktie, and had even dug into his limited wine cache to find a bottle that might impress Mr. Bellamy, who, Rebecca had told him, had rather a fondness for expensive Pinot noirs. Now, as Jake stood beside Rebecca at the front door of a house in Shelby County that was more than twice the size of his own, he was finally beginning to wonder what he had gotten himself into.

He couldn't remember the last time he had been taken to a woman's home to meet her family. Oh, wait.

Yes, he could. It had been Marie's family on their sprawling Thoroughbred farm outside Lexington nearly ten years ago. Jake had been forced to spend the evening dodging blunt questions about his financial status and plans for his newly formed partnership with Stephen, and for two hours had been trapped by Marie's father in his study, trying not to gag as he sampled some of the old man's expensive cigars. To top the evening off, Marie's parents had gotten into one of their usual arguments about God-knows-what and had called each other names Jake never would have uttered to his worst enemy.

Ah, yes, he remembered it all now. All too well. Just when he was wondering if he had enough time to cut and make a run for his car, the front door before him opened to reveal a woman in her early sixties, with silver hair, laughing green eyes exactly like Rebecca's, and a huge smile on her face.

"Sweetie!" the woman cried as she pulled Rebecca into her arms for a ferocious hug. "Welcome home!"

Rebecca's smile was contented, unresisting and full of love as she hugged her mother back and replied, "Oh, come on, Mom. I was here just yesterday. You're going to make Jake think I'm a horrible daughter, never coming to see you and Dad."

Mrs. Bellamy circled her arm around Rebecca's waist as she turned to Jake and extended her hand. "And of course, you must be Rebecca's friend, Jake. Welcome to our home."

Hearing himself referred to as Rebecca's friend came as a surprise to Jake. He'd been prepared for interested looks as he was less-than-jokingly referred

to as her "boyfriend," or her "young man," or some
other parental term to indicate that Mrs. Bellamy
wanted to know his intentions toward her daughter.
But to be labeled something as innocuous and vague
as "friend" simply threw Jake for a loop. He was
going to have to readjust his perspective on things a
little now. He'd been ready to feel defensive while he
was visiting Rebecca's family, fielding questions about
any future they might have together. Instead, Rebecca's mother made him feel like nothing more than
a guest who was welcome in her home.

"Mrs. Bellamy," Jake said, nodding in greeting as
he shook her hand.

"Oh, please, call me Ruth."

"Ruth," he repeated obediently as her smile grew
broader.

"Come in, come in," Ruth instructed them further,
stepping back into the house to allow them entry. "It's
so cold outside today. Your father thinks we'll get
snow tonight. Wouldn't that be wonderful? I can't remember the last time we had a white Christmas around
here."

"Dad and his snow," Rebecca said as if it was an
old joke, chuckling with her mother. "He's probably
already got the sled out and waxed and sitting at the
top of Edgar Hill, ready for the kids."

"Well, of course he does," Ruth replied in a tone
of voice that suggested Rebecca's was a silly speculation to begin with. "Everyone is back in the solar-
ium sampling Rebecca's new treats," she continued.
"Give me your coats and go on back and say hello.
I'll be right there."

Jake and Rebecca shrugged out of their coats and handed them to Ruth as she requested, then wandered into the living room off the foyer. Jake tried to be discreet as he gazed at everything, still unable to get over the size of the Bellamy homestead. He had received the impression from Rebecca some time ago that she came from a moneyed background, but he'd had no idea it was something like this. For a man who judged a person's success by the size of the house he lived in, Jake assumed the Bellamys were indeed more successful than most.

Yet there was something else about this house that struck him as he followed Rebecca through it. For a building so large and roomy, there didn't seem to be any empty spaces. Jake's house was only half this size, yet felt almost vacant, even when he was there. But the Bellamy home was a huge house that felt utterly full, despite the fact that he and Rebecca still hadn't stumbled upon any other people who might be visiting. There were photographs on every wall and every table, plants that had obviously been growing for years tumbling from every nook and cranny, books on every subject crammed in bookcases in every position imaginable, knickknacks, magazines, games, toys....

The house looked like someone was not only in residence there, but actually *lived* there—enjoyed life, celebrated life, squeezed every ounce of pleasure possible out of life. And that, Jake realized with no small amount of panic, was precisely why his own house felt so empty all the time. No one who resided there really lived life to the utmost. No one had ever brought

that to his house except Rebecca. Only under her influence had his house come alive.

"When you said you were catering this thing, I was
afraid I might only see you in passing today," he told
her as they strode down a hallway toward the back of
the house.

"No way," Rebecca assured him, turning back to
face him fully. She looked festive and beautiful in a
red sweatshirt that was painted and bejeweled with a
Christmas-tree design, her hair caught up in a tousled
ponytail, shiny red and green bells dangling from her
ears. "I never, ever, miss out on a Christmas celebration. I prepare everything in advance and put it in
Mom's fridge. Then she gets it all out in the morning,
and for the rest of the day we all take turns refilling
the bowls and platters. So far, it's a tradition that's
worked out well."

"Your family seems to have a lot of those," Jake
said thoughtfully.

"A lot of what?"

"Traditions."

Rebecca smiled at him, a smile that was warm and
affectionate and full of fond remembering. "Yeah, we
do. And it's never too late to start new ones."

Before he had a chance to ask what she meant by
that, Jake and Rebecca entered a room full of laughing,
chattering people. Everything that could be decorated
was, from the enormous fireplace behind them to the
floor-to-ceiling windows boasting fragrant evergreen
wreaths that must have been three feet in diameter.
Even the people were decorated, all dressed in red and
green, some sporting Santa hats, some wearing bells,

others with sprays of holly tucked in headbands and lapels and behind their ears. The Bellamy clan, it appeared, consisted of more than a few party animals.

Jake and Rebecca were met by cries of ''Merry Christmas'' and ''Welcome'' and ''It's about time you arrived,'' then were plied with punch, eggnog and wassail. Jake found himself being introduced to people whose names he would never be able to remember, shaking hands, receiving brief kisses, being slapped on the back. Never did any of Rebecca's numerous relatives refer to him as anything other than Rebecca's friend, and never did he feel uncomfortable.

''Uh-oh, here comes my father,'' he heard Rebecca say beside him as the last of her relations wandered away, leaving Jake feeling dizzy and maladjusted, having had all of his expectations of feeling matrimonial pressure thoroughly shot to hell.

''What?'' he mumbled. Then her words registered, and he thought, Ah-ha, here it comes. The official meeting of the father. Now he would begin to feel the pressure, Jake thought. Now he would be getting the treatment. He was really going to get worked over... but good.

''Dad, over here!'' Rebecca called out to a distinguished but festive-looking man in his late sixties.

Mr. Bellamy was tall and slim, and carried himself like one who was supremely at home in his surroundings. In a single glance, Jake could tell everything about Rebecca's father that he needed to know. He was a powerful, successful man who in no way lacked confidence, a man who would speak his own mind and be able to read those belonging to other people. He was the kind of man who would insist that his daughter be treated right. And he would stop a suitor dead in his tracks if he came up lacking in any way.

"Rebecca, dear." Rebecca's father swept her into a hug and kissed her warmly on the cheek. "So you've finally arrived. This must be Jake."

For the first time since arriving, Jake wondered what Rebecca had told her parents about him. Had she intimated that they were romantically involved? Had she led them to believe their relationship might turn into something substantial? Had she gone so far as to tell them there might be wedding bells in the future? Nothing in anyone's behavior so far had indicated she might have said anything other than that he was her friend, but Jake couldn't help wondering if there was something everyone else knew that he himself did not.

Trying not to gulp audibly, Jake extended his hand to Rebecca's father and shook it firmly. He felt an inexplicable need to let the man know he would not be overrun, wanted to be sure Mr. Bellamy knew Jake Raglan wasn't a man to be taken lightly. He wanted him to know that although he had feelings for the youngest Bellamy daughter, they were feelings of Jake's own, feelings over which *he* had control, and they concerned no one else but Rebecca. Then he proceeded to offer the other man a bribe.

"Mr. Bellamy," Jake greeted Rebecca's father staunchly, pressing the bottle of wine into his hand after shaking it. "This is for you and your wife to enjoy later. Rebecca told me you favor Pinot noirs."

Mr. Bellamy studied the label closely, arching his eyebrows in obvious admiration for Jake's choice.

"Yes, I do. This is a wonderful vintage. Thank you very much. And please, it's Dan. All that 'Mr. Bellamy' business is completely out of place in this house."

"Dan," Jake replied, thinking the other man's observation about formality a very astute one. This house did indeed inspire one to relax and take it easy.

"Rebecca tells me you're a lawyer," Dan continued.

What else had she told him? Jake wondered. "Yes, I am. A partner in Raglan-Flannery Associates."

"Do you specialize?"

"Divorce," Jake replied simply.

Dan Bellamy seemed to be honestly surprised by his vocation, and Jake was puzzled. Perhaps, like Rebecca, they didn't much cotton to the profession because of her experiences with her ex-husband, he mused. Or perhaps Rebecca truly hadn't told her family much about him, after all. Maybe she hadn't thought him important enough to go on about at length. Hadn't considered him a part of her life worth mentioning. Jake couldn't understand why the realization bothered him so much.

"Well, we certainly could have used your services around here about five years ago, let me tell you," Dan said frankly.

"Daddy, don't you dare bring up Eliot...." Rebecca began.

"I was talking more about Marcus and the crummy way he represented you, Rebecca."

"Marcus represented me exactly the way I wanted to be represented. Now let's—"

"Becca, he didn't even win a financial settlement for you. The least that jerk you married could have done was—"

"Daddy, I didn't *want* a financial settlement from Eliot. I didn't want anything from Eliot. At that point, I just wanted to be rid of him. Now let's drop it."

Dan Bellamy treated his daughter to a stern look, then his face softened and he smiled. Draping an arm over Rebecca's shoulders, he pulled her close and turned to Jake. "She's an independent cuss. Simply drives her mother and me into a frenzy sometimes. But she's such a wonderful cook, we can't possibly turn our backs on her."

Rebecca smiled, too, rolling her eyes heavenward. "Gosh, thanks, Daddy. It's so nice to be wanted."

Jake watched the byplay between Rebecca and her family with much interest. This was a side of her he'd never witnessed before, a side that was fully contented to the point of playful. He couldn't imagine what it must be like to be this close to one's family. But, Jake admitted reluctantly, it looked like it might be kind of nice.

Then his thoughts rewound, and he was struck by what Rebecca's father had just revealed. She had turned down the opportunity to receive a financial settlement from her ex-husband. And with what was probably a good deal of evidence that Eliot had indeed been unfaithful to her, and considering the amount of financial support Rebecca had offered him during their marriage—not to mention having a shark like Marcus Tate as her attorney—her settlement could have been a hefty sum indeed.

But Rebecca had instead chosen to return to her family for help and support, and had simply put aside any feelings of vengefulness or vindictiveness she might have entertained about her lousy marriage. It was a realization that told Jake he should think hard about a lot of things.

What's he thinking about? Rebecca wondered. Jake had been thoughtful and not a little distant ever since entering her parents' house, and for the life of her, she couldn't even begin to guess what might be causing his preoccupation. She hoped he wasn't as attuned as she was to her family's intense curiosity about him. She had told her mother yesterday that she would be bringing a friend with her today, that her friend just so happened to be male, and, too, just so happened to be single.

But she had cautioned both of her parents sternly about snooping. Jake Raglan was a man who had hired her to plan his holiday, Rebecca told them, and when she had discovered that he would be spending Christmas Eve alone, she had invited him to share it with the Bellamys instead. That was the extent of their tie to each other, she had stated emphatically. There was absolutely no need for her parents to think there might be anything more to it.

However, she'd seen the expression on her mother's face when she'd opened the door, Rebecca recalled now. The moment Ruth Bellamy had seen what Jake Raglan looked like, it was as if a little light had switched on in each eye. Her father also appeared to be more than a little speculative right now, and was obviously impressed by Jake's gesture with the wine.

Oh, great, Rebecca thought miserably. Now she would never hear the end of it from either of her parents.

"Jake, will you give me a hand in the kitchen for a minute?" Rebecca asked suddenly, feeling for some reason that she had to get Jake out of there right away before her father asked some probing question like, "So, when will the two of you be tying the ol' knot?"

Jake glanced over at her, a curious expression on his face, but didn't immediately respond, as if he was still lost in thought somewhere.

Rebecca looped her arm through his and urged further, "I want to check to be sure that I didn't put too much dark rum in the eggnog."

Jake, like every other guest at his party, had fallen madly in love with Rebecca's eggnog. She hoped by mentioning it now, it would serve to bribe him into accompanying her as she requested. As further incentive, she added, "I also want to make sure the alterations I made to the recipe haven't ruined it."

That got his attention. Jake turned to her with an expression that was almost crushed. "You changed the recipe?"

Rebecca smiled at him. "Only a little. Come on."

The remainder of the day passed just as every other Christmas Eve at the Bellamy homestead had. The Bellamys made much merriment, opening gifts and playing games, passing the wassail and joining in song.

And just before dinner it started to snow. And snow. And snow. And snow...

The children in particular seemed to enjoy themselves most, running in and out of the house, indecisive about whether they wanted to play with their new toys or out in the snow. Some carried their new toys out into the snow, but most remained inside, content to drink hot chocolate and enjoy the warmth of family ties.

Rebecca found herself continuously trapped by one toddler or another on her lap. Her big brother, Michael, and his wife had three children, and her older sister, Catherine, and her husband had two. Also present were the children of a number of Rebecca's cousins. None was older than eleven, but all were equally demanding of her attention.

"Aunt Becca, Aunt Becca, will you come and play dolls with us?" was the constant cry of her nieces, while her nephews and second cousins of the masculine persuasion insisted more on video games. But Rebecca secretly favored the company of her newest niece, three-month-old Grace, who was, as far as the Bellamy clan was concerned, the most beautiful baby on earth. Every chance she had, Rebecca cuddled the baby on her lap, cooing and gurgling and making silly noises in an effort to arouse the contented little smile that Grace offered so frequently for her Auntie Becca.

It was in such a position that Jake found Rebecca some hours after a dinner of enough food to feed a small sovereign nation, and enough wine to make Bacchus sleepy. He had looked out the window and discovered to his surprise a countryside covered in sparkling white, and snow still plummeting to earth in fat, festive flakes. A white Christmas, he had thought whimsically. Who would have thought? Somehow it topped the day off perfectly. However, he had realized reluctantly, if he and Rebecca wanted to make it back to the city in one piece, they probably should be leaving right away.

Jake was feeling mellow and contented and very much at ease among Rebecca's family when he stumbled upon her in her parents' library, sitting by the fireplace and humming quietly to her infant niece. She hadn't seen him arrive, so he took a moment to observe the scene, wondering why it tugged so insistently at some dark, unnamed part of him.

He should turn right around and pretend he hadn't found her, Jake told himself. Should run screaming in fear for his life and much-cherished bachelorhood. Instead, he found himself taking slow, careful, silent strides forward, though he wasn't sure if it was a sign of his unwillingness to disturb the baby or Rebecca or himself. Only when he stood beside the big, overstuffed club chair did Rebecca look up to meet his gaze, and only then did Jake realize what a mistake he'd made in approaching her.

Her eyes were full of a shining emotion that was without question love at its purest and most powerful. Baby Grace lay motionless and slumbering in the cradle of Rebecca's arms, blissfully oblivious to everything that made the world so unbearably confusing. Before he realized what he was doing, Jake dropped a finger to stroke softly over the baby's cheek, smiling when she turned her face in the direction of his hand and pursed her lips with a sigh. He was suddenly reminded of all those weekends baby-sitting Daphne when she was just a baby, and he was suddenly reminded of something else he hadn't allowed himself to recall for years.

Suddenly Jake remembered how desperately he had once wanted to have children of his own. And now, because of his determination to stay single, it would never happen.

"She's beautiful," he murmured. "How old is she?"

"Three months," Rebecca told him.

"She's Michael's daughter?"

Rebecca nodded.

"He must be very proud of her."

Rebecca chuckled softly. "You can't imagine. After two boys who scuffle all the time, he nearly busted his buttons when Diana told him amniocentesis revealed they were expecting a girl the third time around." She snuggled the baby on her lap a little closer and added, "You're going to be such a daddy's girl, aren't you?"

The words tore at Jake's heart more than anything else Rebecca could have uttered. It occurred to him then that perhaps his devotion to Daphne was as much from his realization that he would remain childless as from his love for his niece.

"Can I hold her?" he heard himself asking, as surprised by the question as Rebecca seemed to be.

Without replying, she rose from her chair and silently bid Jake to take it instead. When he had situated himself comfortably, Rebecca placed the baby gently in his arms, showing him how to support Grace's head and balance her miniature body. Immediately after Rebecca let go, Jake wished he had never given voice to his desire to hold the baby. Grace was tiny and fragile and soft, and having her enfolded in his arms took him back more than twenty years, to all those evenings marveling at Daphne as she slept.

"God, she doesn't weigh anything," he said quietly, still amazed by the size of the infant in his embrace.

In response to his voice, Grace opened her eyes and gazed up at him, and Jake wondered what she was thinking about, waking up in the arms of a total stranger. He was prepared for a bout of very loud crying, but instead, Grace smiled softly and closed her eyes again, perfectly at ease in the big man's keeping. The understanding of her complete trust touched Jake in a part of his soul he'd never known existed.

"She likes you," Rebecca stated unnecessarily, easing down onto the arm of the chair beside him, settling her hand casually along the back of the chair. "But then, that's not surprising, is it? Every woman here today has fallen for you, Jake. Even my mother has a crush on you."

Jake didn't know what kind of madness was coming over him to make him pose his next question, but he was as helpless to prevent it from coming as he was to keep his heart from beating. "And what about you, Rebecca? Does 'every woman here today' include you, too?"

Why couldn't she simply ask him? Rebecca wondered. Why couldn't she just look him straight in the eye and demand to know what his feelings toward her were? *Jake, I love you, and I need to know if you love me, too.* Why couldn't she just say that? Why was a short string of monosyllabic words so difficult to utter?

Immediately, Rebecca answered her own question. Because she was afraid to hear his answer. She was afraid of what he would tell her. *No, Rebecca, I don't love you. I'll never love you. I can't love you.*

"Have you looked outside lately?" she asked instead, her words sounding rushed and overanxious. "Dad said snow, and he got snow, didn't he? I heard Michael say something about pouring the rest of the hot wassail and cider into a couple of thermoses and heading for an all-night sledding session at Edgar Hill. What do you say?"

When she finally turned to look at Jake, he had dropped his head back down to study the baby, so she was unable to gauge his reaction to her evasive maneuvering. However, when he replied, his voice was quiet and even, touched with just a trace of disappointment.

"I can't. I have to work tomorrow."

"On Christmas Day?"

He nodded, his attention still focused on the baby.

"But no one works on Christmas Day," Rebecca objected. "Everyone sits around feeling fat and reading the paper and eating more food than they normally would in a week."

"The movie theater and restaurant workers of the world, not to mention a host of others, would loudly disagree with your statement, I'm afraid."

"But you're not a movie theater or restaurant worker. You're an attorney who owns his own partnership and who can easily give himself a day like Christmas off. Have you ever gone sledding in the middle of the night?"

Finally Jake looked up at Rebecca, just the trace of a smile playing about his lips. "No, Rebecca, I've never gone sledding in the middle of the night."

"Not even on Acorn Ridge?"

He shook his head. "My parents kept a pretty tight rein on Ellen and me when we were kids. Nine o'clock curfew, even in high school."

Rebecca grinned at Jake, helpless to stop herself when she pushed back a lock of dark hair that had fallen over his forehead when he'd had his head bent. "Well, then, Mr. Raglan, you're in for a treat."

Ten

"**W**hy is this called 'Edgar Hill'?" Jake asked as he stood at the top of a snow-blanketed bump on the earth, staring down into what would have been a black abyss if not for the bright full moon overhead. "Does this have anything to do with your Uncle Edgar? More specifically with the fact that your Uncle Edgar's arm is in a cast?"

Rebecca laughed at Jake's reference to her mother's brother, who had come to the Bellamy Christmas celebration straight from having his arm encased in plaster from shoulder to fingertip. "Yes, this hill is named after my Uncle Edgar, and, yes, he has wiped out here on a number of occasions over the past sixty years. However, today's incident stemmed from his waking up thinking it was Christmas morning and moving a tad too quickly to get downstairs to see what Santa

Claus had left him. He slipped, and…well, let's just say that everyone at Mercer General Hospital is on a first-name basis with Uncle Edgar.''

Jake shook his head doubtfully. ''I don't know about this midnight-sledding thing, Rebecca. It's awfully dark to be racing at breakneck speed over an icy surface and into the black beyond, isn't it?''

Rebecca sighed in mock disgust. ''Oh, come on, Jake, don't be such a coward. My mother and her brothers and sisters grew up in that house and have sledded this hill for decades. Michael, Catherine and I have carried on the tradition for the past three ourselves. Only minor injuries, I swear. No lives lost at all.'' After a moment's thought, she added, ''None that have been recorded, anyway.''

''Terrific.''

Rebecca gazed around at the group of people who had gathered at the top of the hill and then slowly began to smile devilishly. ''Come on,'' she instructed Jake in a soft whisper. ''Grab your snow saucer and follow me. It's going to be too crowded to really get good speed up here. I know a better spot.''

''Good speed?'' Jake repeated skeptically, reluctantly allowing himself to be led as Rebecca tugged insistently at the sleeve of the down-filled jacket he had removed from the trunk of his car before they'd departed on their hike. ''Frankly, a crowd sounds like an excellent idea to me. I'm not so sure I want 'good speed' to begin with.'' Lifting the fluorescent orange plastic disk he held in his gloved hand, he further demanded, ''And what's this 'snow saucer' you shoved into my hands out in your parents' garage? Is this thing actually supposed to transport a human body? I mean, am I expected to believe that this flimsy little piece of plastic is actually supposed to be considered *safe?*"

"Oh, Jake, will you quit complaining?" Rebecca said, halting in her tracks and spinning around to face him fully. "You're the one who wanted to experience Christmas to its fullest, remember? And in the Bellamy tradition, to top off the holiday right, you have to do something really fun. In my opinion, sledding at Edgar Hill is about as fun as it gets."

"But we're not at Edgar Hill anymore," Jake pointed out unnecessarily. "We're out in the middle of nowhere."

True enough, they had managed to thoroughly distance themselves from the other late-night revelers and now stood at the top of what seemed to Jake an even bigger hill than the first. All around him, the earth was at peace, no movement, no sound, nothing stirring at all. Even the silence seemed more quiet than usual, muffled, he supposed, because of the way the ground was blanketed by several inches of snow. The night was surprisingly bright with the moonlight reflecting off the white hills, and hundreds of stars winked at him from billions of miles away. If he had been a whimsical man, Jake would have bent an ear and listened for the sound of sleigh bells and eight tiny reindeer. But, of course, he wasn't a whimsical man, he reminded himself. Besides, those reindeer had flown at midnight, and by now it was well past one.

"It's beautiful, isn't it?" he heard Rebecca say

softly, almost reverently, her voice easing through the still night like a warm wind.

Jake nodded. "It reminds me of…" He cut himself off when he realized he had almost said the word "home." "Of Acorn Ridge," he finished softly. "We didn't get a lot of snow there, but when we did, it looked like this. Clean, untouched, almost mystical in its beauty…and full of possibilities." Still staring out at the countryside, he added so quietly he wasn't sure Rebecca would even hear him, "Too bad life isn't like that."

"Oh, life is very much like that, Jake," she replied immediately, confidently, and he knew he must have spoken more loudly than he had thought. "You just have to know how to approach it."

He turned to her then, loving the way her dark curls framed her face beneath the red knit cap she wore. Her cheeks and nose were pink from the brisk air, and her eyes shone with a light to rival that reflecting off the hillsides. Bundled up in a navy blue ski parka with a thick red scarf wound around her neck what appeared to be a half-dozen times, her hands swallowed by two monstrous red mittens, Jake thought she looked more wonderful than he'd ever seen her before. And he'd seen Rebecca looking pretty wonderful in the past few months.

"And just how should I approach it?" he asked finally.

Instead of replying, Rebecca grinned broadly and lifted the fluorescent yellow snow saucer she had been carting for the entire half-mile trek from the house. Tossing it casually onto the snow just where the hill they stood upon began to curve downward, she plopped herself unceremoniously onto the disk, fanny first. The action was orchestrated in just such a way that the force of the movement propelled the saucer forward, and before Jake realized what was happening, Rebecca was skimming quickly and easily along the top of the snow, maneuvering her mount with expert dexterity, whooping loudly with delight.

"Hey!" he shouted after her. "Hey, wait for me!"

Jake tried to mimic precisely the same execution of movement Rebecca had so elegantly performed, but wound up somehow with one leg tucked beneath the other, one arm flailing wildly in the air while the other gripped the suddenly very tiny disk for dear life, rushing backward down the hill at a speed much greater than any he would have thought a snow saucer could achieve. As a result he landed some distance away from Rebecca, in a position that reaffirmed all too well the fact that he had never been snow saucering in his life: facedown in the snow, beneath a brambly thicket, behind a huge hickory tree that he was certain had almost ended his life.

"I call it the Rebecca Bellamy approach to life," Jake heard a familiar, feminine voice say from behind him as he licked at the dusting of snow on his upper lip. "Just throw yourself into it with all the force you can muster and hope for a safe landing."

Turning awkwardly onto his back, Jake stared up at Rebecca for a long time without speaking, wondering how she could be so damnably annoying and adorable at the same time. Then he lifted his hand toward her as if soliciting help, and when she took it to pull him forward, yanked her down on top of him instead.

"You know, I think it's about time somebody put snow down your pants," he told her meaningfully.

Rebecca's eyes widened in surprise, and he suspected it wasn't so much because of what he was suggesting as it was that he was so blatantly teasing her.

"Now, Jake…" she began to protest.

"No, really, Rebecca," he continued, unobtrusively digging his fingers into the snowdrift pushed up around them by the weight of their bodies. "I'm of the opinion that there's simply no better way to humble someone who's behaving smugly than to put a big handful of cold…"

"Jake…"

"Wet…"

"Jake…"

"Icy…"

"Jake…"

Without further ado, and with as much dexterity as he had lacked controlling the snow saucer, Jake grabbed a fistful of snow, pushed aside Rebecca's open parka, and carried out his threat quite capably. Rebecca shrieked with laughter and surprise, then grabbed a mittenful of snow and plunged it down the front of Jake's shirt, thankful that he had removed his necktie some time ago. For a moment, he lay stock-still, as if he couldn't believe what she had just done. Then, with a burst of energy and laughter, he shoveled more snow into one hand, tore off Rebecca's ski cap with the other, and unloaded a pile of snow onto her head.

"Okay, that does it, buster," Rebecca warned him playfully. "No more Ms. Nice Gal. Now it's time to take off the gloves and get rough."

As if to illustrate, Rebecca pushed herself awkwardly up on her elbows—settling them on Jake's chest because there was nowhere else to settle them—and put forth a great deal of effort to remove her mittens. Jake watched in amusement, thinking he was having more fun with Rebecca now than he'd ever had in his life. But when one of her elbows slipped off his chest and brought her upper body down hard on top of his, Jake's amusement quickly fled, to be replaced by a very demanding need. Without thinking, without planning, he wrapped both arms around her, rolling their bodies in the snow until they had reversed positions.

Rebecca wasn't sure exactly when things had taken a turn from playful to sexual. She only knew that one minute she and Jake had been participating in the harmless, silly kind of teasing couples sometimes enjoy, and the next minute they were gazing into each other's eyes with the most desperate kind of longing. Where once there had been nothing but cold night air, now there was heat, and Rebecca thought vaguely that the snow around them would surely be turning straight into steam at any moment. Before she had a chance to utter a protest she didn't want to voice, Jake lowered his lips to hers for a kiss that left no part of her chilled.

After that, everything ceased to exist for Rebecca except for the night, the snow, the thicket behind the hickory tree, and Jake. Together, they combined to form a kind of haven for her, a sanctuary to which she could escape from everything that had ever caused her harm. With Jake she felt truly alive and happy and safe for the first time. She had always considered herself a woman who enjoyed life to its fullest, yet with Jake Raglan she had found something else to celebrate, the most important thing of all—love, true love in its purest, most perfect form.

Circling her arms around his neck, she pulled him closer, then was disappointed when she realized they were still separated by the barrier of their clothing. Mindless of the cold and snow, Rebecca pushed at Jake's sweater until her hands were beneath it, unbuttoning his shirt enough to feel the warm skin stretched across his taut muscles beneath.

At the feel of her cool fingers on his hot skin, Jake groaned aloud, intensifying his kiss until neither of them was sure where one body began and the other ended. Then, mimicking Rebecca's actions, Jake, too, began to let his hands go wandering, first up under Rebecca's sweater, until he could cup his palm over the lacy brassiere beneath. She, too, sighed with pleasure at the contact, arching her body upward as she pulled him even closer.

When he first touched her skin, Jake's fingers were cold, but Rebecca soon realized he was a man who warmed up quickly. Flexing his fingers over her softness, he kneaded her tender flesh with the persistence of a man who has gone a lifetime without any human closeness. Spanning his hand over her breasts, he captured one peak with his thumb, the other with his ring finger, and with maddening circles drove Rebecca into a near frenzy. Then, wedging his thigh between hers, he urged her legs apart and settled himself intimately against her.

This time it was Rebecca who groaned aloud, loving the feel of having Jake so close and full, so heavy against her. Pushing her hands around over his back to cup his buttocks, she pulled him toward her, pressing herself against him as she did so. She remembered how exquisite it had felt to make love with Jake Raglan, and all she wanted now was to feel that way again, damning the consequences, whatever they might be.

Jake let his body drop fully onto Rebecca, rubbing himself sinuously against her over and over again, until they were both crying out in frustration at being unable to consummate their passion. Knowing only that she wanted to be joined with Jake in the most intimate union two souls can share, Rebecca tugged at his belt and unbuttoned his trousers, exploring him with gentle fingers as she freed him, marveling at his strength and softness, remembering his tenderness the first time he had made love to her. She touched him gently at first, then with more insistence, until he pulled away from her with a ragged gasp.

''Not yet,'' he muttered with something akin to exhaustion. ''Not just yet.''

Jake took Rebecca's wrists in one hand, and held them over her head, cradling them in his palm so that it was his skin buried in snow instead of hers. Then, his eyes never leaving hers, he unfastened and unzipped her blue jeans, and flattened his palm against her belly. Slowly, he moved his hand downward to the waistband of her panties, dipping his fingers quickly inside to the depth of his knuckles.

"No snow this time," he promised softly. "Only heat."

And with that vow, he plunged farther, stroking over Rebecca's hot skin like a penetrating balm. With long fingers he explored her, touching her more deeply, more intimately than any man had ever done. Rebecca could only feel, could only luxuriate in what he was doing to her. Gone was the winter night, gone was the snow and cool breeze. Instead, she was plunged into an incinerator, consumed by a fire that burned white hot.

"Oh, Jake," she whispered when she felt herself close to the edge, turning her face to the snow in an effort to cool herself off, slow herself down.

Suddenly she felt herself being lifted, and somehow realized that it wasn't into a heated swirling vortex of sensual desire, but into Jake's arms. Unaware of how it had happened, Rebecca realized that Jake had removed his jacket and spread it open on the snow, and was now bending to place her back on it. As he did so, he tugged her jeans down from her hips until they tangled above her boots around her ankles. When Rebecca understood that they were about to make love still fully clothed, out in the middle of a snow-drenched landscape, she nearly cried out in celebration at the wild recklessness of it. It was the act of two people thoroughly consumed with passion, she thought dizzily. Two people who embraced a lust for life and each other.

Jake bent one more time to place what he intended

to be a chaste kiss over Rebecca's heart before plunging into her warm, welcoming depths, but when he realized once again how soft her skin was, he had to linger for a taste. Closing his mouth over her breast, he circled the dusky peak with his tongue slowly, leisurely, thoroughly, then drew it more deeply into his mouth. Rebecca sighed in contentment, cradling his head in her palm as if willing him never to stop. Reaching lower to touch her in intimate promise one last time, he positioned himself atop her and plunged himself deep inside.

Rebecca gasped at being so filled by him again, but before she could wrap her arms around him and pull him closer, he withdrew, then plummeted deep inside her again. She curled her arms up over his back to keep him from going too far away, but again Jake withdrew completely before hammering into her again. Finally he seemed to have propelled himself deeply enough, and he initiated a slow, methodical rhythm that began to drive Rebecca slowly, deliciously mad.

"I love you, Jake," she heard herself whisper amid gasps for breath. "I love you."

Jake said nothing in reply, but continued his assault on Rebecca's senses until they were both delirious and dazed. Higher and higher they climbed, until there was nowhere else to go but down. Their culmination came amid an explosion more incandescent than any the heavens had ever seen, and like fireworks that dissolved against a night sky, so, too, did Jake and Rebecca slowly descend to earth, feeling as if they were part of a fiery cascade.

When they lay entwined on Jake's coat, panting for

breath and groping for thought, Rebecca found to her surprise that she wasn't disappointed Jake hadn't cried out that he returned her feelings when she had voiced her love for him. She realized then that she didn't need to hear him say the words, because she had felt his love in the way he had kissed her and held her, in the way he had shown such gentleness and care in making her his. Jake Raglan loved her. Rebecca knew it as well as she knew her own name.

She recalled the time when he had indeed cried out in a moment of passion that he loved her, then had stolen away without so much as a simple goodbye. This time, he had kept his words in check. But somehow Rebecca knew that his emotions had been as wildly uncontrolled as her own, knew that the feelings of love and passion coursing through her were rampaging through Jake's system, as well. He loved her. The knowledge filled her with contentment, and for the first time in years, Rebecca felt honestly good about the course her life had taken.

"Are you all right?"

She heard Jake's voice coming to her from a very great distance away, sounding warm and soft and filled with a quiet tenderness. It made Rebecca smile. Gazing up at his handsome face, angular and strong against the star-spattered sky, she lifted a hand to push back a lock of dark, damp hair that had fallen over his forehead.

"I'm fine," she whispered with a soft chuckle, unable to quell the happy feelings bubbling up inside her. "I'd be hard-pressed to think of a moment when I've felt better than I do right now."

Jake smiled, too, cupping his hand along Rebecca's cheek, pushing her hair back from her face. "It won't last if we don't get up and get ourselves dressed. The heat of the moment wears off fast when you're lying in snow."

"What snow?" Rebecca asked languidly, letting her eyelids droop and her body relax. "We just survived a forest fire. There couldn't possibly be any snow around here."

"Tell that to the others when they happen across our cold, frozen bodies, fused together in a very unlikely survival pose."

That brought Rebecca's attention around. She had completely forgotten that they had left her parents' house with a dozen of her relatives who were still wandering around the countryside. Immediately, she disengaged herself from Jake and rearranged her clothing, trying not to blush when she remembered how incredibly erotic it had been to make love in the great outdoors, the way it was meant to be. The cold winter wind danced across parts of her body never exposed to the elements, and Rebecca shivered with chilly delight.

Jake saw the action and dropped his arm over her shoulders, pulling her close to wrap his coat around both of them. He couldn't believe what they had just done. He had never, ever, submitted to such a spontaneous desire in his life. Making love in the great outdoors was unlikely enough for him, but in the snow? It was completely unlike him. However, Jake had to admit that what he and Rebecca had just shared together also surpassed any other life experience he had ever enjoyed.

What could possibly exalt the act of living and enjoying life more than succumbing to one's most primitive instincts in the most primeval of surroundings? As he stood with his arms wound around Rebecca's shoulders, drawing from her heat and offering his in return, it occurred to Jake that he had just completely veered from the path he'd chosen for his life.

It also occurred to him that he'd never enjoyed another Christmas more than this one. And it wasn't simply because of Rebecca's presence, although obviously it all led back to that. It was a combination of everything—the holiday itself, the festive atmosphere at the Bellamy home, the decorations, the food, the children, and the close, loving kinship of her family.

But mostly, it *was* Rebecca who was responsible for the warm feelings wandering through Jake's body at such a leisurely, comfortable pace. It was Rebecca who had made him fall in love when he had sworn for years that it would never happen again. However, there was still one tiny problem. Jake had absolutely no idea what he was going to do about those feelings.

"Warming up any?" he asked her, his quiet voice seeming to boom like thunder across the silent hills.

When Rebecca met his gaze, Jake saw that her expression was one full of love and contentment. To see her looking at him that way—with such unadulterated emotion, such complete and uncompromising trust— twisted a dull knife deep into his gut. He wanted to order her to stop looking at him that way, wanted to command that she stop loving him, because he wouldn't love her back. The trouble was, Jake knew he would be lying if he said that. The trouble was, he wasn't honestly sure he wanted her to stop.

"They've built a fire at Edgar Hill," Rebecca said quietly, her words muffled against Jake's thick cotton sweater. "I can smell it. Hickory branches."

Looking over her head, Jake discerned a faint, distant amber glow warming a section of the night sky and nodded. "There seem to be a lot of fires burning tonight," he murmured against her hair, kissing the crown of her head soundly. "Bonfires, fires of passion…"

"Home fires," Rebecca finished for him. "Those tend to burn brightest and hottest, you know."

Jake wanted to reply that, no, he didn't know, couldn't possibly know, because he'd never felt their warmth. But tonight he had. Tonight, Jake realized, he had experienced everything he'd been missing out on in life, everything he had hoped to achieve with his marriage to Marie and hadn't come close to winning. A month ago, he had told Rebecca to make his Christmas one that would include everything he had never enjoyed with Christmases in the past. And like a Dickensian ghost, she had complied with more than ample provisions.

But could it last? he asked himself. Was it enough? December was a month full of holidays notorious for making people do things and act in ways they wouldn't even consider during the other eleven months out of the year. Christmas was a magical time, a special time. What he was feeling now was also magical and special. But could it last? Jake asked himself again. Or, like Christmas, would it be temporary and finite, ending with the melancholy that always follows a holiday?

"Come on, we'd better go rejoin the others," Rebecca said with obvious reluctance, interrupting his troubled thoughts. "They're probably wondering if we're lying sprawled at the bottom of a hill with every bone in our bodies broken."

However, when they had wandered back to the group of nighttime revelers, Jake and Rebecca discovered that they had scarcely been missed. Between the continuous up- and downhill movement of sledders and the freely flowing wassail, no one seemed to have noticed that two of their number had snuck off to enjoy a more intimate diversion. Instead, Jake and Rebecca were welcomed back as if they had just returned from a trip to the foot of Edgar Hill, with cries of congratulations that they had survived their ordeal.

It was nearly daybreak by the time the Bellamy clan returned to the house. Ruth and Dan had long since gone to bed along with the younger members of the family, but a pot of coffee was still hot and fragrant on the back of the stove. Most of the group ignored it, and with wide yawns and extravagant stretching made their way toward the stairs. Only Jake and Rebecca remained in the kitchen to sip their coffee and exchange longing glances, both fully comfortable with the silence that enveloped the house, both thoroughly uneasy about the way things were between them.

"I hate to leave when everyone else is sleeping," Jake finally said after draining the last of his coffee from its mug. "But we really should get back to the city this morning."

Rebecca set her own mug on the table, feeling an inexplicable sense of dread slinking over her. "You weren't kidding when you said you had to work, were you?"

Jake shook his head but said nothing.

"You're entirely too dedicated," Rebecca told him as she stood up. "Anybody ever tell you that you work too much, Mr. Raglan? It'll ruin your life someday."

Rebecca hadn't meant anything by her carelessly offered comment, had intended it to be nothing more than a simple, nonjudgmental observation that anyone else would have taken with a grain of salt. Instead, she recalled too late what Marcus had told her about Jake's ex-wife, about how Marie had left her husband for another man because she felt neglected when Jake spent more time at the office than at home. More than anything, Rebecca wished she could take her words back, mentally kicking herself because she hadn't thought before she'd spoken.

But when she looked up to gauge Jake's reaction, she could tell by his expression that nothing she might say would make amends for those words. Nor was there any way she could apologize without revealing that she knew more about Jake's past than he had told her himself. Caught in a dilemma she had no idea how to escape, Rebecca simply remained silent, hoping in vain that he would just ignore her comment and say something to alleviate the tension straining the air between them.

Jake stood, too, but instead of treating Rebecca to

some sharp retort, he pulled her into his arms and pressed her against the doorjamb of the entryway leading from the kitchen to the dining room. Before she could voice her puzzlement, he leaned down and kissed her, a kiss that was bone-crunching, soul-searching, and seemingly without end.

With one hand on each wall behind her, Jake's arms formed an effective trap, one Rebecca was unwilling to escape. She wrapped her arms tightly around his waist to bring him closer, helpless to stop the little cry of surrender she uttered when he rubbed himself insistently against her. Instinctively, she thrust her hips forward in response to his gesture, and when she did so, Jake deepened his kiss, mimicking the act of lovemaking with his tongue because he was unable to fulfill their desire any other way without rousing the entire household.

It was as if he was trying to brand her in some way, Rebecca thought dazedly. As if he was trying to leave his mark on her so blatantly that she would never be able to think about another man for the rest of her life. No problem, she wanted to assure him. As if there could possibly be another man for her besides Jake Raglan.

When she gradually began to remember that they were standing in her parents' kitchen and could be interrupted at any moment, Rebecca pulled her lips away from Jake's and dipped her head into the hollow created beneath his chin. Trying to still the rapid beating of her pulse and steady her ragged breathing, she spread her palm open over his heart, smiling when she realized it was racing as unevenly as her own.

Hugging herself to him, she closed her eyes and murmured softly, "What was that all about?"

"Mistletoe," Jake whispered in reply.

He felt her place a warm, chaste kiss on his neck, and knew that she was smiling. "What?" she asked in a voice that was almost a purr.

Curling his index finger below her chin, he tipped her head back and pointed up at the bunch of greenery dangling from a hook on the doorjamb above them.

"Mistletoe," he repeated.

"Mmm. Potent stuff."

"I'll say."

Jake had no idea what had come over him to kiss Rebecca so insistently, so demandingly. But when he'd heard her accuse him of working too much, it had brought back all the painful memories of losing his wife that he thought he'd buried forever. Only this time there was a slight difference in his reaction. This time the pain wasn't caused by his loss of Marie. This time Jake realized it was Rebecca he'd be losing, and that had made the pain all the more unbearable. He'd realized then that he and Rebecca had no future together, because he realized what Rebecca had said was true. He did work too much, and it had ruined his life once. He simply couldn't risk it happening again.

He had never noticed until that moment how much Rebecca and Marie had in common. Like Marie, Rebecca liked to socialize. Hell, that's how she made her living. She was a woman who celebrated everything life had to offer, and Jake was a man who had never had the chance to learn how to do the same, a man whose entire identity was wrapped up in his job. Like

Marie, Rebecca would surely tire of his long hours and all the time he spent away from home. Eventually she would probably wind up in the arms of another man, one who could treat her the way she deserved to be treated.

That's when Jake realized he was going to lose Rebecca someday. And he decided it would be better if it happened now instead of later. That way it wouldn't be quite so painful, he told himself. Although what could be more painful than the gut-wrenching sensations tearing up his insides right now, he didn't know. He had promised himself he would never allow himself to be hurt by another woman again. But he should have known he couldn't trust his own promises. That one about never falling in love again had been nothing but a lie, too.

Eleven

"**O**h, ho, look who's been caught under the mistletoe."

Rebecca and Jake both started at the sound of another voice in the long-silent kitchen. Tearing their gazes away from each other to look in the direction from which the noise had come, they found Ruth and Dan Bellamy standing in the opposite doorway, wearing matching robes and pajamas of burgundy silk, grinning slyly and suggestively from ear to ear.

"I knew that 'friend' business was just a red herring you threw us so that we wouldn't put Jake on the spot," Dan said, shaking his finger playfully at his daughter. "Now, how long has this been going on, and when can we expect the nuptials to take place?"

Rebecca cringed inwardly, trying to stifle the groan she wanted to utter. Don't overreact, she told herself firmly. She knew her parents had good intentions, knew they wanted nothing more than for their little girl to be happy. They had assumed—and correctly at that, she reminded herself—that things between her and Jake must have progressed well beyond the casual acquaintance stage. As the heat of embarrassment crept up from her breasts to her neck, it also occurred to Rebecca that, depending on how long her parents had been standing in the doorway, they probably had very good reason to suspect that she and Jake were even intimately involved.

"Dad, don't—"

"Now, Dan," Rebecca's mother intercepted for her.

Good ol' Mom, Rebecca thought. Ruth Bellamy was the most tactful, soothing person she knew. If anyone could smooth ruffled feathers and ease a tense situation, it was Rebecca's mother. With a few simple words, Ruth would be able to call off Dan and reassure Jake that the elder Bellamys were in no way suggesting that he marry their daughter.

"You know better than to put the kids on the spot that way," she said softly. As her smile broadened, she added, "When they set a date, they'll let us know."

Rebecca rolled her eyes heavenward. Thanks a lot, Mom, she said to herself. Nothing like putting the poor guy completely on the spot. This was just great. Now Jake would really feel uncomfortable around her family.

"Who's getting married? Rebecca and Jake?"

Now it was Rebecca's brother Michael and his wife,

Stephanie, who entered the room with baby Grace in tow.

"Jake and Rebecca are getting married?" Stephanie asked, delight obvious in her tone. "How wonderful! Congratulations!" Holding up the baby in her arms, she continued, "I could tell by the way you are around Grace that it wouldn't be long before you'd be scouting out a man who was good father material. I must say, though, Rebecca," she went on with a sly wink at Jake, "that you certainly outdid yourself with this one."

"No, you guys, wait—" Rebecca tried to interject.

"Welcome to the family," Michael said, extending his hand to Jake with a brotherly smile.

Rebecca closed her eyes and willed the scene to go away, wishing this were nothing more than a bad dream, and wondering when such a magical evening had gone so utterly, completely awry. She waited for Jake's reaction with her breath held, half of her wondering if maybe, just maybe, he would laugh and take her brother's hand, then thank her parents for inviting him into the family so readily. But the other half of her knew better, and she tried to tell herself that's why she didn't fall apart when she heard Jake's reply.

"Uh, listen," he began, his words drawn out as if he was trying to be very careful in choosing them. "I'm not sure what Rebecca has told you about us, but…we haven't even talked about getting married, let alone starting a family."

"Well, then maybe it's about time you did," Dan Bellamy told him with characteristic frankness.

"Dan…" Jake took a step away from Rebecca as

if putting physical distance between them might make what he had to say easier. "You have a wonderful daughter.... She's terrific.... But...but we're *not* getting married."

"Why not?" the elderly Bellamy asked pointedly.

"Daddy, please," Rebecca whispered with some difficulty, having grown more and more miserable with every word Jake had voiced, dismally aware of how very final he made them sound. "It really isn't any of your business. Don't blame Jake, he... I mean, he and I aren't...we aren't...um..."

We aren't what? she asked herself. We aren't in love? That wasn't true; she was more in love than she'd ever been in her life, and she was certain Jake loved her, too. We aren't ready for a commitment? she posed further. For Rebecca, that wasn't true, either—she would gladly jump in with both feet. For Jake, however, perhaps commitment was precisely the problem. Maybe he just needed to get used to the idea of including a woman seriously in his life again, she told herself optimistically. Maybe it would just take a little time for him. But maybe he would come around. Maybe...

Rebecca braved a glance in his direction and what she saw told her everything she needed to know. His jaw was set with anger and annoyance, his eyes were stormy blue and dangerously dark. It was the expression of a man who resented being put on the spot, and a man who was determined not to be moved in his conviction. She knew then without question that Jake would never come around.

He'd been hurt badly by his ex-wife and simply

would not risk being hurt again by marrying. He had told Rebecca that flat out at the beginning of their relationship and had never led her to believe he would change his mind. Jake Raglan had been completely honest with her from the start in attesting to the fact that he intended to stay single. But Rebecca, ever-optimistic and overcome by her love for the man, had tried to tell herself there might be a chance that she could change his mind.

Obviously she'd been terribly mistaken. And now she and Jake were embroiled in a very awkward situation, one she wasn't entirely sure they'd be able to escape unscathed. The Bellamy family were fiercely protective of their own. If they sensed that Jake Raglan was about to hurt the youngest and perhaps most vulnerable of their number, they would circle and pounce and do everything they could to prevent it.

"What I'm trying to say, Daddy," Rebecca tried again after screwing up enough courage to make her sound convincing, "is that Jake and I haven't discussed marriage because I've decided I don't want to marry again."

"*What?*"

All four members of Rebecca's family who were present stared at her in utter disbelief.

"Rebecca..." she heard Jake caution her. "You don't have to—"

"The fact of the matter is," she went on, trying to sound indeed matter-of-fact, "I realized recently that of the more than twenty weddings I've planned over the past five years, nine of the marriages have already ended in divorce."

"So what does that have to do with you?" her mother asked skeptically.

Rebecca lifted her chin defensively. "It's made me reevaluate my opinions on the subject of matrimony."

"And?"

"It's made me reconsider my desire to plunge into something that could wind up being a worse situation than my first marriage was. Statistically speaking, second marriages often end more quickly than the first."

Her mother gazed at her through narrowed eyes, then at Jake, then back to Rebecca again. "Kids today," she muttered softly under her breath. "What crazy notions."

The quiet that ensued stretched to an uncomfortable silence, until Rebecca mercifully ended it by announcing that she and Jake had to get back to the city by mid-morning. She felt like she was tiptoeing on the thinnest of ice as she gathered their things and bade goodbye to her relations. Certainly her revelation about her intentions to stay single must have come as a terrific surprise to them. They all considered Rebecca to be the most family-oriented member of the clan, the one who insisted the others get together on a regular basis. She was sure they were suspicious of what she had told them, but at least she and Jake had escaped with minimal fuss. She tried to reassure herself that such a victory was what was most important.

They made the drive back to town in complete silence. Jake seemed to be thoroughly wrapped up in his thoughts, and Rebecca wanted to draw as little attention to herself as possible. She seemed to do a very good job of it, because Jake didn't look at her once

during the forty-five-minute period. It wasn't until he
pulled up into the driveway of her little tollhouse that
he finally seemed to remember she was there.

For several minutes he studied the house that looked
like something from a fairy tale, all dusted with silver-
white snow, before he finally turned to look at Rebecca. She would have expected him to say a number
of things, but the question he posed was not included
on the list.

"Why did you buy this house?"

He couldn't have caught her more off guard had he
asked her to name the capital of Assyria.

"Because I liked it," she answered simply.

"What did you like about it?"

"It has an interesting history. It was built in the
middle 1800s and used to be the tollhouse for the rail-
road that runs alongside Frankfort Avenue. About
twenty years ago, the previous owners bought it and
moved it back to this lot before renovating it. I kind
of liked the idea of all the people who must have
passed through it over the years and maybe left a little
of themselves behind."

"What else did you like about it?"

Rebecca shrugged. "I don't know. I liked the size
of it. It's cozy, perfectly sized for one. And I figured
when I got married and moved out of it, I could still
hold on to it for a rental property or maybe use it for
my office if I could get it zoned for business use."

Jake nodded. "So even when you bought your
house, you were thinking about getting married someday."

"Yes," she told him honestly. She wasn't about to

lie to him, and she certainly wasn't going to let him make her feel as if she should defend her actions.

He nodded once more, gazing at her with an expression in his eyes she was helpless to understand. "I'll call you this weekend," he said softly, finally.

The words tore at Rebecca's heart as if it were nothing but paper, and she expelled a single breath of air that might have been a chuckle had there been something funny in her situation. "Sure you will," she replied coolly, hopelessly.

Before he could say anything more, Rebecca shoved open the car door with the ferocity of a Trojan, leapt out and rushed to her front door. She didn't look back, didn't want to see Jake driving out of her life forever. Instead, she went quickly inside, slamming the door behind her, gathering up her cats, and gazed solemnly at the cold, empty house she called her home.

She might as well get used to it, she told herself. What she had said to Jake was the truth. When she had purchased the house, it was with the intention that it would only be a temporary place of residence, that eventually she would marry and move out. Now, of course, she was sure she would be living here forever. Because the man she wanted to marry was a man who was determined not to. And he had spoiled any chance she might have for a life with someone else, because he had branded her his own. Jake Raglan had locked himself into the deepest part of Rebecca's heart, and she knew she would never meet another man who would rouse him from there.

Old Lady Bellamy, that's what she was destined to be. Just a little old spinster living with her cats in her cottage in Crescent Hill. Despite the whimsical over-tones, it wasn't a life-style Rebecca looked forward to pursuing.

All in all, she thought morosely, this hadn't been one of her better Christmas celebrations.

It's just another New Year's Eve, Jake told himself as he stared out his living room window at the last scattering of flakes left over from the afternoon's snowfall. The sky above was slate gray and thick with clouds promising more snow later, the dying rays of sunlight were dim and chalky and harsh. The day out-side reflected the way Jake was feeling inside. Cold and empty and barren.

It's just another New Year's Eve, he repeated si-lently, this time with a bit more fortitude. Then a little voice in the back of his head piped up unbidden, An-other New Year's Eve spent alone. Jake tried to assure the little voice that he was alone because he wanted to be. Unfortunately, he wasn't quite sure of that at all. Because more and more lately, Jake had begun to think that the reason he led such a solitary existence wasn't because he chose to be alone, but because he was afraid not to be.

Tonight was a night when other people would go out to have a wonderful time, reflecting on the changes the past twelve months had brought to their lives, and making plans for the year to come. It was a night to put old hurts and differences behind and look forward to new beginnings. A night to forget about the pain and focus on the pleasure.

Ever since his divorce, Jake had made it a point not

to go out on New Year's Eve. He hadn't wanted to
bear witness to people who were able to pick themselves up and begin again, hadn't wanted to risk becoming part of such potential renewal himself. Because he'd been afraid if he did, he would ultimately,
if inadvertently, open himself up to other things. Other
things like chances—specifically the chance to love
someone again. And in opening himself up to the
chance to love someone again, he knew he would also
be setting himself up to take another fall. A fall that
might just leave him too broken up to pull himself
back together again.

So Jake had always stayed home on New Year's
Eve, and was sure he hadn't missed out on a thing.
Certainly he hadn't felt as if his life was lacking anything. At least, not until lately he hadn't. But Rebecca
Bellamy had changed all that. She had not only provided him with the best Christmas he'd ever enjoyed,
she had also afforded him, if only temporarily, the
chance to see what a truly full life was like.

Rebecca. Jake hadn't been lying when he'd told her
he would call her last weekend. He truly had intended
to call her. But for some unknown reason, he'd never
picked up the phone. No, that wasn't true, he thought
now. He did know the reason. It all came back to the
same thing—his fear of not being alone.

For most people, loneliness was the worst thing life
could bring, something to be avoided at all cost. They
often resorted to drastic and dangerous measures to
make sure they were never alone. For Jake Raglan,
just the opposite was true. He went out of his way to
make certain no one entered his life beyond a super-

ficial, temporary presence. No attachments, no strings. That way he didn't have to worry if the other person had ulterior motives, didn't have to wonder how long it would be before he wound up alone and desolate again. Instead, he was the one who called the shots and kept the status quo. He was in charge of who came and went, and made sure people went before they became important. It was a system that had always served him well.

Until he met Rebecca.

Somehow, when she had entered his life, Jake had lost the upper hand. True, it was her job to organize things and take charge, but it was only his Christmas she was supposed to have taken control of, not his entire life. Yet she had done just that. Now there were reminders of her presence all over his home—in the holiday decorations that still adorned the rooms, in the piles of food left over from his party that she had wrapped up and put into his freezer for him to feast upon throughout the winter. Rebecca Bellamy was everywhere—in his house, in his head, in his heart. And Jake was beginning to think she would remain there forever, no matter what he did to try and chase her away.

She'd never spent more than a few hours at a time in his home, but it was as if she belonged here more than he did. Jake's house had been nothing but a collection of stones and tile and mortar filled with bits of wood and cloth before Rebecca had entered it. Now it looked warm and welcoming. It could *feel* warm and welcoming, too; he knew it could. But only if Rebecca were in it with him. Permanently.

Maybe it was about time he stopped being afraid, Jake thought. Maybe it was about time he took a chance. He was forty years old, soon to become a great-uncle. If he worked this out right, maybe he still had time to be a great father, too. But first he had to prove he could be a great husband. And for that, he was going to need a wife. Good thing there was someone he was already in love with.

He only hoped Rebecca didn't already have a date for New Year's Eve.

"Okay, so what's the big emergency?"

Rebecca still wasn't sure why she had agreed to come over to Jake's house. It had been surprising indeed to be interrupted during a leisurely bath and snatch up the phone on the sixth ring—having halfway decided not to bother—only to hear Jake's deeply intoned greeting at the other end of the line. He'd sounded almost as if he could actually see her standing in the middle of her living room wrapped in nothing but a damp towel, and his words had fairly dripped with the promise of pleasures never before experienced by any woman.

Reminding herself Jake had said he would call *last* weekend and hadn't, Rebecca had managed to collect her wits enough not to sound like a complete imbecile as she'd coolly responded to his numerous questions. No, she wasn't busy at the moment, but, yes, she *did* have a date for New Year's Eve. However, she had hastened to add, kicking herself mentally for doing so, they weren't plans that were etched in stone. In fact— although she didn't tell Jake, of course—she was sure

Marcus Tate had only asked her to join him in attending a string of parties that night out of pity for her, having heard through the legal grapevine that Jake had given the brush-off to the woman everyone had thought would surely snag him.

When Jake had asked her if she would come over to his house that evening, Rebecca had been skeptical, wanting to know why. He had then cited that he had a slight emergency for which she was responsible, and could she please come over and help him deal with it? Thinking it must be something to do with the remnants of the party she had planned for him—although thoroughly puzzled by what could possibly be causing an emergency two weeks after the fact—she had reluctantly agreed to come.

But not before making herself look presentable in an oversize amber sweater and brown wool trousers. Now she stood at Jake's front door damning herself for going to any trouble for this man who had turned her world upside down and tied her heart in knots, this man who clearly had no regard for his own appearance where she was concerned—although he did look rather...rather roguish and somewhat...sexy in his faded jeans and rumpled denim work shirt with the tails untucked. After all, she reminded herself, there was an emergency somewhere—whatever it might be—and she couldn't expect him to be as pressed and polished as a West Point cadet, could she?

"It's upstairs," Jake said simply, still leaning in the doorway as if weighing some very serious consideration, like whether or not he should allow her into his home.

"Upstairs?" she asked, now more confused than ever. "But I never did anything upstairs."

"Yes, you did."

"Well, I changed my clothes that one day, but that's all."

"Believe me, that was enough."

Rebecca sighed impatiently, doubling her fists and pressing them against her hips in challenge. "Look, Jake, I drove all the way over here because you said I caused some kind of emergency, and now you won't even tell me what I did. I have better things to occupy my time than to stand here trying to outguess you. Now, what's the problem?"

Instead of answering, he crooked his index finger upward, slowly curling and uncurling it in the "come hither" gesture men have perfected over the centuries. Rebecca was no more immune than any other woman who had fallen prey to it in the past, and quickly found herself following Jake up the stairs and down the hallway of his big house. She felt just as strange being in his private domain now as she had the first time she had invaded it, but for some reason, this part of the house was still every bit as inviting as the rooms where she had spent so much of her time óver the past few months. Jake's house was a nice house. It would be the perfect place to raise a large family.

Don't start, she warned herself. Just don't start again.

"In here."

Jake stood beside the door to a room Rebecca had never entered, a room she had never even braved a peep into, despite her constant curiosity about it—his bedroom. She had stopped walking when he had and now stood two feet beside him, well to the right of his bedroom door. Instead of taking the two steps necessary to bring her fully in front of it, Rebecca, still very confused, bent forward from the waist until she could peek around the corner of the door.

"It's your bedroom."

"Yes."

Biting her lip nervously, she straightened and met his gaze. For long moments neither of them spoke, until the silence became too much for Rebecca to bear.

"Although I wouldn't doubt that there have been a variety of...um...emergencies that may have taken place in this room over the several months you've lived here," she began, "I fail to detect the presence of one at the moment, particularly one for which I am responsible."

Jake smiled at her for the first time then, a wonderfully crooked, deliciously seductive smile that served to reveal a slash of a dimple in his left cheek that Rebecca had never noticed before. She was so intrigued by it that she was unaware she had raised her hand to trace a finger over it until it was too late. By then, Jake had captured her hand in his, and was placing a warm kiss at the center of her palm. Tiny shocks of electricity exploded throughout Rebecca's body, leaving tingling vibrations that shook her from head to toe.

"You don't see the emergency?" Jake asked her softly. "You don't *feel* it?"

He pushed the sleeve of her sweater up toward her elbow, trailing soft kisses behind it—first on the back of her hand, then on her wrist—then traced the tip of his tongue along the sensitive flesh of her inner arm until he reached the inside of her elbow, where he placed another tender kiss. Rebecca was helpless to stop the tremble of excitement that wound through her body like a mountain road, and couldn't prevent the little gasp of arousal that escaped past her lips.

"Well," she murmured quietly, drawing the word out as she fully considered the sensations heating every cell, every fiber of her being. "There is a certain…ah…insistence…but I don't know if I would call it an emergency…just yet."

With a gentle tug on her wrist, Jake pulled Rebecca into his arms, and all she could think about was how nice it felt to be there again. When he bent his head and took her lips with his, rubbing his mouth over hers in a kiss that was tender but still demanded response, she gladly obliged him. Circling her arms around his neck to pull him closer, she rose up on tiptoe to receive his kiss more fully.

Deeper and deeper Jake explored her mouth, tasting every inch of her he could reach. His hands on her back made reassuring up-and-down motions, moving lower and lower until he could spread his fingers open wide over her derriere. Only when he curled his fingers deep into her soft flesh and urged her hips forward to rub his hard length against her did Rebecca realize how intimately they had entwined themselves together, and only then did she force herself to put an end to what he had begun.

"Jake, stop it," she whispered raggedly when she finally tore her mouth away from his. "I didn't come over here for this.'' Doubling her fists against his chest, Rebecca pushed herself away from him, touching her fingers lightly to her lips in an attempt to dispel the lingering heat of his kiss. ''I'm not the kind of woman who's going to come running every time you get the urge, only to have you discard me when you're satisfied.''

Jake stared at her for a long time before replying to her suggestion that he only wanted her for sex and would tell her to go home as soon as he was through with her. With no small amount of guilt, he realized she had little reason to feel differently, because he had done just that both times they'd made love. Only then he had been running away because he was afraid to admit that he wanted to be with her. Now he wanted nothing else than to lose himself in Rebecca forever.

''I missed you,'' he told her softly, honestly.

Rebecca almost crumpled into a quivering heap on the floor at the sound of his voice—so full of emptiness and desolation and loneliness. ''I missed you, too,'' she managed to whisper in reply.

''Rebecca, I...'' His gaze was locked with hers, guileless, unflinching, and completely candid. ''I love you. And I want you to come home.''

''Home?'' she asked in a very quiet voice, still not allowing herself to believe he was saying what she so much wanted to hear.

''My home,'' he clarified. ''Our home. I want us to be together...here...forever. When I'm here alone, this house is just a building. But when you're here with me, it's...it's a home. I know that sounds corny, but there you have it. The minute you set foot in this place, you possessed it somehow. Just like you possessed me.'' He shrugged nervously, shoving his hands into his pockets, suddenly realizing how desperate he sounded, how desperate he felt. ''I think we should make it official,'' he finally concluded. ''I think we should get married.''

It was as if a two-ton weight she'd been unaware of carrying was suddenly lifted from her back. Rebecca felt all the air leave her lungs in a rush, to be replaced by a flood of warm laughter. Jake Raglan loved her. And he was finally admitting it, not only to her, but to himself.

''Well, it's about time,'' she said as she threw her arms around him once again. ''It's about damned time.''

His laughter joined hers as he scooped her into his arms and carried her over the threshold and into his bedroom. Gently, Jake set Rebecca down on her back at the center of his bed, leaning over her to gaze down into her eyes, amazed that he'd even tried to convince himself he could live without her. He'd been so blind for so long that he'd almost lost sight of the one thing that kept life bright—the love of another human being. He had been willing to deny himself the pinnacle of joy, because he had been afraid of being hurt again. Now Jake had found Rebecca. And now he feared nothing.

''I love you,'' he told her again, trying to make up for all the times he'd felt it and hadn't said it aloud. ''I love you.''

Rebecca threaded her fingers through his hair, pulling him close for a soft, chaste kiss. ''I love you, too,

Jake. And I won't hurt you. Just like I know you'll never hurt me.''

He nodded silently, and each knew those would be the final words spoken on the subjects of their past marriages. Now they had the future to look forward to, a future that was brighter than either would have ever anticipated. Rebecca kissed Jake again, this time on his neck, then lowered her head and murmured something unintelligible against his chest.

''What?'' he asked, smiling at what seemed to be a sudden, uncharacteristic bout of shyness on her part.

''I said this is an awfully big house for two people.''

Jake's smile broadened at her less-than-subtle hint. ''Well, your house is too small for two people.''

Her eyes met his briefly, then Rebecca dropped her gaze again. ''I wasn't suggesting that we live there instead of here. I love this house.''

Jake kissed the crown of her head, and laced his fingers with hers. ''Then what were you suggesting?''

When Rebecca lifted her head to face him boldly, her cheeks were tinged with pink. ''I was thinking maybe we'd be better off filling it with the pitter-patter of tiny feet.''

Jake feigned consternation. ''You want to bring your cats with you? Ohh, I don't know, Rebecca....''

''Jake!''

''Well, all right. I guess I can handle a couple of cats.''

''Jake!''

''But only if we can have a couple of kids, too.''

Rebecca smiled at him in smug satisfaction. ''There

are those cat lovers who would argue that they are one and the same.''

He grinned at her indulgently. ''Nonetheless, I think I'm going to have to insist that at least some of our children bear some resemblance to us. And that means no whiskers until they've survived puberty, and even then, only on the boys.''

''That sounds reasonable,'' Rebecca agreed. ''But, Jake.''

''Yes?''

''We're never going to have any children if we just sit here yammering all night.''

With an expression that almost mimicked shock, he replied, ''Aren't you planning on wearing white at our wedding?''

She shook her head resolutely. ''Nope. Ivory silk. I've already decided. Besides, it's too late to worry about my purity, anyway. You soiled me for life months ago. Or have you already forgotten?''

Jake's grin became lascivious as he purred, ''Remind me.''

This time Rebecca grinned, too. ''With pleasure.''

The pleasure began for Jake when Rebecca worked free the buttons of his shirt and pushed the softly worn fabric from his shoulders. She was fascinated by the warm ridges and hard planes she discovered beneath her fingertips as she skimmed them across the scattering of dark hair that spiraled across his chest and down his flat abdomen. Jake's body was truly a work of art, she mused, more perfect than anything found in a museum.

As she explored further, Jake went on a little expedition of his own, tugging Rebecca's sweater over her head to discover she was wearing a very revealing brassiere of the most transparent fabric he'd ever seen, in a color reminiscent of a desert sunset. Her full breasts strained against the garment as if begging to be set free, but instead of unfastening the clasp, Jake leaned his head down to taste her through the sheer voile.

Rebecca groaned when he drew her into his mouth and tongued the peak of her breast to life despite the barrier of her brassiere, then removed it herself to facilitate his ministrations. So focused was she on the mind-scrambling sensations his mouth wreaked on her body, that she never noticed when he removed the rest of her clothing. She only knew that suddenly Jake cupped his hand over the most feminine part of her, and was delving into her softness with one long finger as he continued to stroke his tongue over her breast.

Finally he ended the twin onslaught long enough to fully disrobe himself, and Rebecca wanted to cry out in joy at seeing his hard, sculpted form in its purest sense. He was without question the most beautiful man she could imagine, certainly the most beautiful she had ever seen. And he was hers. The knowledge warmed Rebecca to the depths of her soul, and made her want to give herself completely to him in return. Opening her arms wide, she welcomed him to her, sighing when she felt his strength against the soft core of her, crying out in triumph when he joined his body to hers with one mighty thrust.

Slowly he plunged deeper, until their bodies were virtually fused by the heat they created together. Up

and up they went, scaling every sensual peak, falling
ecstatically into every sweet chasm only to rise higher
than before. Again and again Jake thrust into Rebecca,
until each was branded by the other's love. Finally
they reached the point where they were made utterly
certain that things would remain this intense, this incandescent, for them forever, and their releases came
in a fury of emotion. Gradually the fires that had leapt
out of control were banked to a comfortable, tender
warmth, and then Jake and Rebecca held each other,
murmuring words of love and hope and promise.

Rebecca recalled then that it was New Year's Eve,
a time to reflect on the past and plan for the future, to
forget old wounds and sow for new growth. She
smiled in contentment as she cuddled closer to Jake,
who pulled the blanket up over both of them. Outside
the window, she saw that it had begun to snow once
again.

"Happy New Year, Jake," she whispered softly.

"Happy New Year, Rebecca," he replied in a quiet
voice. "And happy new life."

"Yeah," she agreed with a peaceful sigh. "Isn't it
just?"

Epilogue

"Gather 'round, everybody, Rebecca's going to throw her bouquet!"

Rebecca gazed over and smiled at a round-bellied Daphne, looking pert and very pregnant in her peach organdy dress. Along with Rebecca's sister, Catherine, she had been a bridal attendant, and had somehow taken it upon herself to completely run the wedding. Now she was corralling the other fifty people in attendance for the throwing of the bouquet, and Rebecca couldn't help but recall that a little less than a year ago, she herself had caught Daphne's.

What goes around comes around, Rebecca thought affectionately. With any luck at all, before the year was out, she'd follow her newly acquired niece down the road to maternity, too.

Rebecca glanced up to find Jake staring at her as he

had been all day, with an expression of pride, joy and promise. She knew exactly how he felt, embraced similar emotions for her new husband. She could scarcely wait until they left the reception and headed off for their honeymoon. They'd told everyone they were going to loll away the following week in the Caribbean. However, they were actually planning to spend the week at home alone with the phone unplugged.

Home alone, she thought. Now alone meant just the two of them, and now home meant the big yellow creek-stone house in Bonnycastle, filled with furniture and mementos that belonged to them both. Together, they would start a family, and together, they would establish traditions to be carried on by generations that followed them. Although it was still six months away, Rebecca couldn't wait for Christmas. Oh, the things she had planned for them. And as they filled their house with children, the holidays would only become more festive.

"Is everyone ready?" Rebecca called out from the top step overlooking her parents' living room.

All the single women present set their plates and glasses on whatever surfaces were convenient and assured Rebecca that, yes, they were. Turning her back, Rebecca silently counted to three, then tossed the collection of white flowers and holly bound with an ivory ribbon over one shoulder. In the living room below her, chaos resulted, and amid cheering and laughter and moaning, Rebecca turned to discern who would be the next bride.

"Who caught the bouquet?" she called out to Daphne.

"Oh, Rebecca, you'll never guess!" her niece replied with a laugh.

"Come on, who?"

But Daphne became so doubled up with laughter that all she could do was shake her head and brush the tears from her eyes.

"Jake?" Rebecca asked when she caught her husband's eye.

Jake, too, was smiling broadly, but he pointed his finger toward the opposite corner. When Rebecca allowed her gaze to follow, she saw that there beside her cousin, Denise—with whom he was no doubt trying to make time, she thought dryly—stood Marcus Tate with her bouquet cradled in his hands as if it were a newborn baby.

"Marcus, congratulations!" Rebecca cried with a chuckle as she hurried down the stairs. Then she added playfully for her cousin's benefit, "Run, Denise! Run while there's still time!"

Coming to a halt beside Jake, Rebecca looped her arm through his and pulled him close. "Remember when you offered me the same advice?"

Jake nodded, gazing down at his wife with unmistakable love and devotion. "Yeah, that was back when I was a coldhearted bastard. Good thing you warmed me up."

Giving his arm an affectionate squeeze, Rebecca eagerly agreed. "Gosh, I think this celebration has just about run its course, don't you?"

Jake looked around at the large group of people he now called his family. It felt nice to belong to such a gathering. It felt nice to know he was in this too deeply to get out. But what felt best was knowing he would be going home soon. Home with Rebecca.

"Yeah, I think you've got a point," he replied softly.

"What say we get home and start working on our next celebration?"

"And what might that be?" Jake wanted to know.

Rebecca smiled privately and said simply, "A baby shower."

Jake looked down quickly and whispered, "You're not…?"

"No," Rebecca told him regretfully. "Not yet. But you can never start planning these things too early, you know."

Jake nodded vigorously. "I see what you mean." As he wrapped his arm around his wife's waist and urged her toward the door, he said quietly, "You know, I suppose we could spend the rest of our lives planning celebrations and then celebrating. It's a good thing you do this for a living. You can get us all kinds of discounts."

Rebecca smiled as she cupped her palm under his chin. "Forget about the discounts, mister, and let's just focus on the celebrations themselves."

"Baby shower first," Jake agreed.

Rebecca's smile grew broader. "And maybe second and third."

And as their family and friends continued to revel well into the night, Jake and Rebecca went home to enjoy a little celebration of their own.

* * * * *

Dear Reader,

Few of my books have generated as much response from you as the story of an unscheduled "virgin" birth in the cab of a big rig on a snowbound interstate on Christmas Eve. Few characters I've created over the years have proved as enduring as bossy, opinionated Mirabella Waskowitz and her gentle knight, the quietly stalwart Jimmy Joe Starr. I certainly had no idea when I wrote this book that it was going to give birth to several more, including *One More Knight*, and the SISTERS WASKOWITZ books, as well as my current STARRS OF THE WEST miniseries. I'm so thrilled to have this opportunity to introduce Jimmy Joe and Mirabella and their warm and wonderfully imperfect families to a whole new audience. I hope you enjoy them as much as I have.

May you all enjoy a warm and happy holiday!

Kathleen Creighton

ONE CHRISTMAS KNIGHT
Kathleen Creighton

For America's long-haul truckers,
with thanks.

ACKNOWLEDGMENTS

As anyone who has traveled I-40 through
the Texas Panhandle knows, the towns of Adrian
and Vega do exist, approximately where I have
placed them. So does Santa Rosa, New Mexico.
Beyond that, any businesses, structures or individuals
described in this story are pure fiction.

During Thanksgiving week in 1992,
a blizzard swept down out of the Arctic and deep into
Texas, creating driving conditions on Interstate 40
exactly as I have described them. Since that time,
it is my understanding that the state of Texas has made
tremendous improvements in its preparedness for and
methods of handling such emergencies. I am certain
that I join countless long-haul truckers in a heartfelt
"'Preciate it."

Chapter 1

"Lord, I hate these California turnarounds."
I-40—Arizona

Like all well-brought-up Southern boys, Jimmy Joe Starr had been taught to respect both automobiles and good women. So when the lady in the shiny new silver-gray Lexus cut in front of him in the entrance to the Giant truck stop that was clearly marked Trucks Only, he didn't give her a blast from his airhorn or push his Kenworth's blue "anteater" nose up on her bumper to teach her a lesson, like some drivers he knew would have done.

But he did shake his head and smile to himself. Oh, yeah. She was a looker, no doubt about that. Just as sleek and fine and pretty a sight as you would ever want to see. And the woman behind the wheel wasn't bad, either.

Jimmy Joe wasn't generally all that attracted to red-
heads, but hers was a real nice color, a rich, glowing
auburn. And she had a self-confident, bordering-on-
arrogant tilt to her head that appealed to him—which
was something else that set him apart from most
Southern men of his acquaintance. Having been raised
by a mama with pure applejack running through her
veins, he was pretty well adjusted to uppity women.

There were a couple of other reasons why Jimmy
Joe was inclined to be in an easygoing and forgiving
mood. For one thing, that was just pretty much his
basic nature. For another, it was the 23rd of December
and he'd just dropped off a load of textiles in the garment district of downtown L.A. and picked up a shipment of piece goods destined for an after-holiday sale
in Little Rock, after which he was going to be headin'
for Georgia, where a little boy named J.J. was waiting
for his daddy to bring Christmas home with him. The
Good Lord willin' and the creek don't rise, Jimmy Joe
expected to be rolling into his mama's front yard just
in time for turkey and all the trimmings.

So that was why, when the redhead finally got herself sorted out and the silver Lexus pointed toward the
four-wheeler parking lot, he just chuckled to himself
and said, ''Well, Merry Christmas, darlin'.'' She
crossed right in front of him with a saucy little flip of
her sleek auburn head, and he caught a glimpse of a
California license plate.

''Figures,'' he muttered.

''You will never in a million years guess where I'm
calling you from,'' Mirabella Waskowitz said to her

friend Charly Phelps, in an ambiguous tone somewhere between chagrin and glee.

"Sounds like a truck stop," said Charly, much to Mirabella's disappointment. She loved Charly dearly, but the woman had no respect for a punchline.

"How did you know?"

"I can hear the loudspeaker in the background. They just called some driver for something-or-other up to the fuel desk."

"Oh," said Mirabella, who hadn't been paying attention. In her experience, voices on loudspeakers seldom had anything to say that concerned her.

"You would not believe this place," she continued after a moment, her enthusiasm undaunted. "For one thing, it's *huge*. Acres and acres of trucks. I've never seen anything like it. It's kind of awesome, actually. Oh—and they don't call them truck stops anymore. They're called 'travel stops' now—I guess so they'll appeal more to the Winnebago set. It's like a minimall in here. They have all sorts of stores, a post office, a couple of fast-food places, and a regular restaurant that actually has a salad bar, can you believe that? And get this—the phones are on the tables! At this very moment I am sitting in a comfy booth, one that actually has enough room to accommodate my stomach, with my decaf and a fairly decent turkey club on whole wheat in front of me."

"What?" said Charly drolly, "no sushi?"

"Mock if you must, but the rest rooms are clean. Oh—and Charly, you'd love the gift shop. What an eclectic mix. They have some lovely signed Acoma Indian pottery sitting right next to key chains made

out of honest-to-God rattlesnake heads and license-
plate holders that say Honk If You're Horny. Oh—and
my personal favorite—there's this little bald fat-guy
doll, and when you squeeze a bulb he drops his pants
and moons you. I think you're supposed to put him in
the back window of your car. I'm thinking of getting
one for my Lexus.''

Charly, who was originally from Alabama, laughed
and said, ''Get used to it. You know the place you're
heading for is the world capital of tacky.''

''I thought that was Venice Beach.''

''No, no, no, darlin'—Florida! Birthplace of the
pink plastic lawn flamingo. Need I say more?''

A gasp cut short Mirabella's chuckle of appreciation. She added, ''Ouch…damn,'' and as she leaned
abruptly back in the booth, her gaze collided with that
of a young man, obviously a trucker, who was sitting
in a booth identical to hers, just catercorner across the
dining room. He was on the phone, too, but not talking, and as he listened, for some reason he seemed to
be frowning right at Mirabella.

''What's the matter?'' Charly demanded. ''The little
tyke giving you problems?''

Hearing the alarm in her friend's voice and knowing
Charly wasn't above doing something rash, like putting in a call to the highway patrol, Mirabella hastened
to reassure her. And while she was at it, she put a
dazzling smile on her face for the benefit of the nosy
trucker across the way.

''Oh, you know,'' she said through the smile, ''it's
just these darn pressure pains. Seems like they've been
getting worse the last couple of days.'' She lost the

smile, though, as she shifted to find a comfortable position for her legs while a lump the size of a small grapefruit was slowly blossoming on the right side of her abdomen. She rested one hand on the lump and rubbed it with a gentle circling motion as she said through held breath and clenched teeth, "Right now it feels like the little rascal's doing push-ups on the nerves in my groin. I get these shooting pains that go all the way down to my toes. There wasn't anything about this in the books, I can tell you that."

"Bella, you're crazy to be doing this—you know that, don't you?"

"Hey, I'm fine." The young trucker had finished his phone call and was now drinking coffee and watching her intently through its steam.

Cute guy, said a voice way in the back of her mind. And then, *My God, he's young.*

It was a purely objective observation; Mirabella considered herself something of a connoisseur when it came to masculine physical attributes, having recently done some extensive research on that subject. This one was tall, lean, tan and blond—some of her very favorite flavors. In fact, if she could pick—

She gasped, gulped cold decaf and nearly choked on it.

"Bella?" said Charly's voice in her ear. "You okay?"

"Fine—I'm fine." Mirabella mopped her bulging front with her napkin. "Spilled my coffee, dammit. Look, of course I'd rather have flown—and I don't see why they make such a fuss about it, for God's sake, my due date's still four weeks off, and anyway you'd

think nobody'd ever had a baby in a plane before—
but on top of that, it's the holidays, and there just
wasn't anything available. It's not like I had much
choice.''

''That's not what I mean, and you know it.''

''Charly...''

The sigh that drifted across the wire was suddenly
contrite. ''I know, I know. I'm sorry. How's your dad
doing, by the way? Have you talked to your mom?''

''I talked to her this morning. He's doing better,
actually.'' She took a deep breath to calm the fear that
always rippled through her when she thought about
her father, and about the utterly unthinkable possibility
of his dying. Pop, die? No. Not for—oh, at least
twenty or thirty years, yet.

*Pop, you'd better get well, and stay that way. I need
you, dammit!* Because, aside from the fact that she
couldn't even begin to imagine a world without her
dad in it, she just hadn't counted on raising this child
without Pop Waskowitz for a grandpa.

Especially, she thought with a twinge of guilt she
tried to ignore, if he couldn't have a dad of his own.

And with some mysterious homing instinct, like
birds returning to a favorite nesting place, her eyes
found the long, slender form of the young trucker in
the booth across the way. *Incredible,* she thought. *Un-
canny.*

''They're calling this heart attack a warning,'' she
said to Charly in a tone bright with false optimism.
''Mom said it looks like they'll let him go home for
Christmas, but then after the holidays they're going to

want to run tests. You know how it goes—see if he's going to need surgery.''

"He'll be okay, Bella. Bypass surgery's not even a big deal nowadays.''

"Yeah,'' said Mirabella on an exhalation, not in the least convinced. "I know.''

"He know you're coming?''

"He doesn't know I'm driving. Mom didn't want to tell him. She's sure he'd only have another heart attack worrying about me.''

"So, you're gonna be his Christmas present.''

"Let's hope,'' said Mirabella. "So far I've only made it as far as New Mexico.''

"New Mexico! Is that all? My God, it's been two days.''

"I can't help it. The problem,'' said Mirabella defensively, "is that I keep having to stop all the time to go to the bathroom.''

"And you're still going to make it by Christmas?''

"Uh…Christmas Day, yeah, hopefully. I should be able to.'' But she had to shut out the little voices of self-doubt that were starting to kick up a fuss in the back of her mind, and her natural bent toward honesty made her add, "If I can make it as far as Texas by tonight. Which reminds me, if I'm going to do that, I'd better say goodbye and get on my way. What about it, Charly, shall I get you a souvenir? That Acoma pottery's nice.''

"You sure you've got room? If I know you, that Lexus is probably packed to the roof with presents already.''

"Just the trunk," said Mirabella with a guilty smile. "I did try to behave myself this year."

"Well, if you insist," said Charly, "I'd rather have the license-plate holder. Listen, you take it easy now, okay? Your mom and dad want you to get there in one piece. And I do mean one."

Mirabella laughed. "Oh, I'm taking it easy. Obviously."

She said her goodbyes, punched the Off button and returned the handset to its cradle on the wall next to the booth, then took a deep breath and picked up a triangle of her club sandwich. At last the baby had settled down. Maybe she could actually eat in peace.

She did notice that the young trucker across the way had picked up the phone again and was no longer paying any attention to her, thank God, but just looking out the window, watching the big trucks roll in off the interstate, one after another....

Jimmy Joe Starr was finally getting through to his mama's house in Georgia. He listened patiently to the rings, and on the third one the voice he wanted most in this world to hear said, "This is the Starr residence. How may I help you?"

He just had to chuckle, hearing all that coming out of his eight-year-old son's mouth. J.J.'s regular greeting up to now had been more along the lines of, "H'lo, who's this?"

"Gramma been workin' on you?"

"Dad!"

"Hey, J.J., whatcha up to?"

"Oh, nothin' much. Where are you? When are you comin' home?"

Those were J.J.'s two standard questions, and they never failed to wring a twinge of guilt and regret out of Jimmy Joe's insides. And of course, never more than at this time of year. "I'm in New Mexico," he said, hoping it sounded cheerful enough. "Got a load to drop in Little Rock tomorrow, and then like I told you, I'll be headin' for the barn. I'll most likely be there when you wake up Christmas morning."

"Promise?"

"Sure, I promise—long's the road don't open up and swallow me."

"Dad..."

"Come on, J.J., you know I'm gonna be fine."

"I know, but...you know what? There's supposed to be a big snowstorm in the Texas panhandle. What if you get stuck?"

"Hey, where'd you hear about this snowstorm, huh? Gramma tell you?" He was going to have to have a little talk with his mama, is what he was going to have to do—remind her what a worrywart J.J. was.

"I saw it on The Weather Channel. They called it the Arc-Arc-tic Express. It sounds really bad."

Jimmy Joe shook his head. What was he going to do with an eight-year-old kid who watched The Weather Channel? "Hey, what'd I tell you? The Big Blue Starr'll drive through anything, right? I'll be there on ol' Santa's heels, just like I said I would. Now, quit your worryin'—you're startin' to sound like an ol' lady, you know that?" He smiled at J.J.'s outraged denial. "So, tell me quick, what you been up to? I gotta get back on the road. Everybody gettin' ready for Christmas? Who was that had the phone tied up so long? Your Aunt Jess, I reckon. Am I right?''

"I guess. Dad?"

"Yeah, son?"

"When can I go back to school?"

"Back to—what kinda question is that? It's Christmas vacation!'' Just as Jimmy Joe was starting to think his kid had come down with some kind of bug or other, something in the boy's tone of voice got through to him. He let his breath out and said, "Okay, J.J., what's up? You in trouble with your grandma again?''

"It wasn't my fault, Dad, I swear! I mean, what else was I supposed to do? She *kissed* me!''

"What? Who kissed you? Gramma?''

"No! Sammi June."

"You don't mean your *cousin* Sammi June?"

"Yeah. Right smack on the lips, Dad. Yuck!''

Jimmy Joe was trying his best not to laugh—at least not enough so it would spill over into his voice. With deep seriousness he said, "What on earth do you suppose made her do a thing like that?''

A heartfelt sigh drifted over the wire. "Well, *she* said it's on account of the mistletoe.''

"Mistletoe?"

"Yeah, Aunt Jessica went and hung little bunches of it all over the house. Sammi June says if you catch somebody standing underneath one of the bunches, they have to kiss you, it's a rule. Is that true, Dad?''

Jimmy Joe coughed and said, "Well, I think it's more like a tradition than an out-and-out *rule*. So, anyway, she caught you and she kissed you. And then what did you do?''

''I socked her.'' He said it like, ''Well, of course—what do you think?''

''Oh, Lord. J.J.,'' said Jimmy Joe sternly, ''what do you know about hittin' girls? Come on, now, I don't have to tell you that. You tell me.''

There was another long sigh. ''Never, never, never hit a girl. *Ever.*''

''You got it. And that *is* a rule. And don't you forget it. You hear me?''

''Yes, sir…''

''So, what'd your grandma give you for punishment?''

That patented sigh again. ''No computer till after Christmas, and I have to do Sammi June's chores for a *week.*''

Jimmy Joe snorted. ''You got off lucky. Times have sure changed, you know that? I'd have got my butt paddled, but good.''

''I'd rather have a spankin' than no computer,'' J.J. said in a mournful tone. Then instantly he added, in a much perkier voice, ''Dad, can we get on-line?''

Oh, Lord, thought Jimmy Joe. ''Hey-hey,'' he said. ''Wait just a darn minute—what brought this on?'' Unnamed alarms were already spiking through his insides.

''Can we, Dad? It'd be so cool—there's all this neat stuff you can do—''

''Absolutely not!''

''But Da-ad…''

''Now, don't start with me, J.J. You're way too

young to go surfin' around the Internet, or whatever it is they do, unsupervised. Shoot, there's stuff on there'd make *me* blush. I'd sooner let you go to the downtown bus depot by yourself.''

''Dad, you would not. There's creeps and weirdos down there.''

''Yeah, well, there's creeps and weirdos on the Internet, too. What put this idea in your head, anyway?''

''My friend Rocky just got on-line. He gets E-mail. If I went on-line, we could send each other E-mail.''

''Yeah, and so could anybody else.'' What in the world, thought Jimmy Joe, was he going to have to protect his child from next? Television was bad enough, but there at least, he—or anyway, his mama—had some control over what came into the house. ''I can't believe his parents'd let him do something like this, J.J. You sure Rocky isn't just puttin' you on?''

''No, Dad, honest. It's like this, see. His parents are divorced, and his mom works, so she got Rocky on-line so she can keep track of him and help him with his homework from her office. Isn't that cool? And very ed-ja-cational, too.''

Jimmy Joe couldn't think of a reply to that, so he muttered something along the lines of, ''Yeah, well, we'll talk about it.'' And remembering the mistletoe incident, he pointedly added, ''*After* Christmas.''

This business of being a single parent, he thought, by no means for the first time, was getting harder and harder every day. He had a lot of sympathy for Rocky's mother, even if he didn't think much of her idea of a solution to her problem. It made him sad to think about a little kid doing his homework in front of a computer screen, all by himself in a big old empty house, instead of at the table in a nice warm kitchen with his mama cooking dinner a few feet away. That was the way it ought to be. That was the way it had been for him, and the way he tried to make sure it was for J.J. Of course, he had to admit, it did help to have a whole bunch of kinfolk around to help out.

"Hey," he said, "guess I'd better get back on the road if I'm gonna get there in time for Christmas turkey. You tell your grandma I called, and behave yourself, now, y'hear?"

J.J.'s sigh was resigned. "I will, Dad, I promise. But I wish you were here *now*."

"I wish that too, son."

"I miss you, Dad. And I miss Rocky, too. There's nothin' but *women* around here."

"Yeah?" Again, it was hard to keep laughter out of his voice. "Well, all I can tell you is, there's gonna come a time that won't seem at all a bad thing."

"Uh-*uh*, Dad—no way."

"Well, we'll see. Okay, you be good now." And he added the trucker's sign-off, like he always did when he was on the road: "Ten-four."

"Ten-four, Dad."

Jimmy Joe hung up the phone with a hollow belly and a heavy heart, which was about normal after talking to his son.

As he slid out of the booth he figured he could let himself look one more time at the woman across the way. The fact was, it had come as something of a shock to him when he'd realized that the pregnant woman squeezing her belly into that booth was none other than the driver of the silver-gray Lexus with the California plates. No doubt about that auburn hair, though. He decided he liked the way she wore it, shoulder-length and parted on the side, in a way that reminded him of the old 1940s movies Granny Calhoun liked to watch on her VCR. He thought it was kind of sexy, the way it showed her ear on one side, but dipped across her eyebrow and just barely grazed her cheek on the other. Sexy, with attitude; he hadn't been wrong about that little "So what?" tilt of her chin.

All in all, she was just plain nice to look at. She wasn't tall, which he thought might make her look further along than she was—not like his sister Jess, for instance, who was tall and big-boned and could hide a pretty good-size baby under a men's blue work shirt until the last minute if she wanted to. Obviously this lady wasn't interested in hiding anything, though, because the top she was wearing—a long-sleeved turtleneck in some kind of thick, silky stuff in a deep, dark plum that shimmered in the light—had a tendency to cling. Not in an embarrassing way; like the car she drove, the lady had class. Just enough to give a hint of the way her body might look under normal circumstances—all curves and sweet, giving softnesses, voluptuous as a Southern summer.

He would probably have looked at her a whole lot more, but he figured he'd already embarrassed himself enough, getting caught flat-footed staring at her like some kind of no-account Cracker without the manners his mama had taught him.

As it turned out, though, the booth where she'd been

sitting was empty and the waitress was clearing off the table. Just as well, he thought, and tried to put the lady and some vague feelings of disappointment out of his mind.

Which was easier said than done. It wasn't about her being such a looker, either, although she sure was that. But he wondered what in the world was she doing, a California girl, way out here in the middle of New Mexico, as far along as she was. And all by herself, by the looks of things.

One thing for sure, Jimmy Joe thought, if she wasn't single, her husband ought to be ashamed of himself. And if she was… Well, it was a shame. A real shame.

He just hoped she knew what she was getting herself into.

Mirabella emerged from a stall in the ladies' room feeling not much better than she had going in. She washed her hands and blotted her face with a wet paper towel and then, since there wasn't anyone to see her, paused a moment to study her reflection in the mirror above the sink. As usual, what she saw did not please her. Her hair was okay, and her complexion, though paler even than usual, didn't trouble her; but she didn't like the dark circles under her eyes and the deep grooves, like tiny parentheses, around her mouth. She hadn't been sleeping very well, that was the problem. Just lately it seemed as if the baby had changed position, or something, and it was almost impossible for her to find a position that was comfortable—or if she did, one that would stay that way for any length of time. Small wonder—she was just so *huge*. Like a bloated hippo, she thought, eyeing her enormous and slightly pendulous breasts and bulging belly with dismay. How would she *ever* get back to her normal size and shape? Was it even possible?

Then, as she always did when such thoughts overcame her, she felt terribly guilty. I didn't mean it, she hastily assured whatever powers might be listening. *It's what I wanted. No matter what, it's worth it.*

She knew what she needed more than anything was just to lie down for a little while, maybe put her feet up. She considered with longing the lounge she'd glimpsed during her earlier explorations—a nicely darkened room with a TV and several comfy-looking couches. But it had been in the section designated Professional Drivers Only, and she didn't think it very likely anyone would mistake her for a trucker—even though from what she'd seen, some of them had stomachs as big as hers. Bigger.

Oh, well. Mirabella hadn't gotten where she was by being a wimp or a crybaby, and she didn't believe in giving in to minor inconveniences or discomforts like backaches and leg cramps. She did, however, believe in extra-strength Tylenol. So before going back out to her car, she dug the bottle she always carried with her out of her purse and shook two of the white caplets into her hand.

She was looking around for a source of water with which to swallow them when she noticed a crowd of truckers gathered around a large lighted wall map over near the ATM and the machine that sold prepaid phone cards. She'd spotted it earlier but hadn't stopped to study it, having had more pressing needs on her mind at the time. Now she deduced that it was some kind of weather map—one that displayed all the time zones, major truck routes and temperature and weather conditions for the whole Northern Hemisphere. In addition to which there were up-to-the-minute weather bulletins constantly ticking across the top of the map, like the news headlines in Times Square. She noticed that most of the assembled truckers seemed to be watching the message like it was Michael Jordan going down the court for a layup, except they didn't look very happy about it.

Mirabella had more than her share of natural curiosity, so of course right away she wanted to know what was so interesting about that weather board. On the other hand, she wasn't crazy about the idea of venturing into a crowd of fairly scruffy and rough-looking men. She felt comfortable enough with men when she was in familiar territory and calling all the shots, but this wasn't L.A. None of the men she customarily dealt with wore parts of snakes as clothing accessories or clanked when they walked.

Plus, there was nothing she hated more than being stared at, and she wasn't exactly inconspicuous at the moment. Not that she ever had been.

So she was hanging around the outer edge of the crowd, trying her best to read the message from a distance and thinking maybe it was time to get her contact-lens prescription updated, when she happened to spot the cute blond trucker from the restaurant. Since he was also busy trying to get a closer look at the board and not paying attention to anything else, Mirabella was pretty much free to stare at him all she wanted.

She couldn't get over it. It was all there—tall and lean, blond hair with just the right amount of curl, and not even a hint of a freckle that she could see. Good facial bones, strong but not heavy; nice cheekbones, straight nose, firm chin. No eyeglasses—unless, of course, he wore contacts, too. But for some reason she just knew he didn't. God, he was perfect. Everything about him was just…perfect.

No doubt about it, she could have been looking at her baby's father, in the flesh.

Right then, almost as if he'd felt her staring at him, the trucker looked around and straight at her, and she had to turn her head away quickly and try to pretend she'd only happened to glance his way by accident. Then, while she was being careful not to look at him, she was certain she could feel him watching her. Only she didn't dare look to see if he was, because if he was, then he would know she was looking at *him*.

And she wondered, Is this what it's going to be like? Every time I see a tall, good-looking blond guy walking down the street, am I going to ask myself, Is it him? Is he the one?

It wasn't, of course. She knew that. No way. Her baby's father was a student, a music major. It didn't seem likely to her that a trucker would fall into either the music or student category, even if this one was wearing a University of Georgia sweatshirt. The shirt had a picture of a bulldog on the front, and looked faded and comfortable, like an old, well-washed favorite. Maybe, she thought, letting her gaze travel on down to slim hips encased in equally worn and comfy-looking blue jeans, he just happens to like big, ugly dogs....

"Excuse me, ma'am, is there somethin' I can help you with?"

If Mirabella had been the type to die of embarrassment, she surely would have then. Fortunately, however, she'd had lots of experience dealing with humiliation, and had learned that the best way was usually just to brazen it out. Caught flat-out staring, she raised her eyebrows and said, "I beg your pardon?" in a haughty tone, as if she wasn't the one who was being rude.

The young trucker was frowning at her, but looking more puzzled than hostile. "I was just wonderin'—do I know you from somewhere?"

God, he was cute. Brown eyes, interestingly enough, not blue. Mirabella gave him a small, tight smile that said, "Fat chance," and shook her head.

"I don't think so."

"Well, hey, I'm sorry I bothered you then. I just thought, the way you were lookin' at me, like you were tryin' to figure out where you knew me from..." He had a nice, easy smile—not cocky, more sweet. Like Robert Redford. And damned if that wasn't a dimple.

Mirabella's heart did a little skip, which she knew from experience meant she was attracted to this guy and consequently in imminent danger of making a fool of herself. So of course, right away her attitude got even more haughty. "I apologize for that," she said, drawing herself up like a grand duchess. "You re-

minded me of someone I used to know.'' Then, realizing she'd been given a golden opportunity, she
paused and allowed herself to melt a little. ''Actually,
I was trying to see that message board over there.
What's going on, do you know?''

The trucker's dimple disappeared along with his
smile. He sort of rubbed at the back of his neck and
looked uncomfortable, as if the weather was in some
way his fault. ''Ah…there's a blizzard, I guess. In
Texas.''

''A *blizzard?*'' Mirabella was a Californian, born
and bred; even the word sounded foreign to her.

''Yeah, guess so. They say it's snowin' as far south
as Dallas.''

Geography not having been one of her best subjects,
Mirabella wasn't sure precisely what that meant. She
did, however, know that Texas was where she was
heading. And furthermore, that she was going to have
to get through it in order to reach her final destination.
She drew a vexed breath and said, ''Texas. Lovely.''

''Yes, ma'am,'' muttered the trucker humbly. Then,
aiming his beautiful dark brown eyes right at her and
narrowing them into a frown of what looked like genuine concern, he ventured, ''Ma'am, it looks like the
Panhandle might be pretty rough goin'. You might
want to think about headin' south—take I-25 out of
Albuquerque, swing on down to ten. Whereabouts you
headed?''

''Florida,'' Mirabella told him without even thinking whether or not she should. ''Pensacola.'' Oh,
Lord, she thought, those eyes…

The trucker nodded and looked relieved. ''Oh, yeah.

That's what I'd do, if I were you. Look here—'' he touched her elbow in a deferential way, just enough to guide her closer to the map as he pointed ''—this here is I-25, see that? Goes right on down to I-10. You'd miss all the mess that way—be a lot safer.''

A lot longer, too. From what Mirabella could see, just doing a rough calculation in her head, it had to be four hundred miles longer that way, at least. A whole extra day. No way she would make it by Christmas, then. ''Which way are you going?'' she asked, angling a look at the trucker.

''Me?'' He shrugged. ''I don't have much choice. Got to stay on forty—got a load to deliver in Little Rock. But if I was you…''

''Thanks for the advice,'' said Mirabella, who wasn't in the habit of taking advice from anybody, especially men—not even cute ones with big brown eyes and dimples. *Especially* not really young cute ones with big brown eyes and dimples. ''But I think I'll just push on.''

She was thinking, Hey, guy, if *you* can make it through on I-40, so can I.

From the look on his face, the trucker obviously didn't think so, but Mirabella was used to seeing that look on men's faces and, if anything, it only made her more determined to prove him wrong.

''Well, good luck, ma'am.'' He was giving her his half-frowning, concerned look, but with more intensity this time. Enough to make Mirabella's heart do that little skip again, which she really wished it wouldn't. ''You have a safe trip now—drive carefully.''

''Thanks,'' said Mirabella crisply. ''I plan to.''

Chapter 2

"Westbound, what's it look like back your way?"
"Eastbound, your front door's lookin' dry and dusty
all way back to the Texas line. Hammer day-yown."
I-40—New Mexico

As she pulled out of the travel-stop parking lot and back onto I-40, Mirabella's thoughts didn't dwell on the cute blond trucker with the heart-stopping dimples. She was thinking about what lay ahead of her, and feeling not nearly as confident about it as she would have liked.

Not about the weather or the road conditions in Texas—the way she figured it, people must drive around in snowstorms all the time; otherwise, life would pretty much come to a screeching halt for half the year in the northern half of the country. Besides, she had more than enough confidence in her Lexus and in her own driving skills, and if worse came to worst, she could always pull into another truck stop and pick up a set of tire chains. No way was she going to let a little old blizzard keep her from getting to Pensacola in time for Pop's Christmas.

No, what was worrying Mirabella was something a lot smaller than a blizzard and probably a lot more common, too. Although she never liked to admit to being afraid of anything, lately she'd begun to notice a queasy feeling in her stomach whenever she thought—really thought—about this business of having a baby.

She'd had no doubts about it before. None at all. After all, she'd planned this pregnancy down to the last detail, and it wasn't in her nature to second-guess herself. Besides, it had been fun, at first. There'd been the exhilaration of knowing she'd succeeded—not that she was accustomed to settling for anything less, or had ever *really* doubted for a minute that she would; but still, she'd been warned that it could take as many as ten or twelve tries, and she'd managed it in only three.

For a while after that, she'd kept it her own delicious secret. Never much of a reader, she'd devoured every baby magazine in the doctor's-office waiting room, then had gone out and bought every book she could find on pregnancy and child care. Mirabella never did anything by halves. Thus informed and prepared, she'd been fascinated rather than dismayed by the sequence of changes taking place in her body, for once not minding when her breasts suddenly grew three cup sizes. Hey, this was great—suddenly it was okay to gain weight!

The night she first felt movement, she'd called up Charly and they'd gone out for frozen-yogurt sundaes at two in the morning to celebrate.

She'd really loved putting her talent and training as an architectural interior designer to work turning her guest room into a nursery and redesigning the rest of the house to make it absolutely babyproof. She'd delighted in having an excuse to dress for comfort, which she preferred anyway. She'd enthusiastically enrolled in natural childbirth classes, having coerced a somewhat less-than-enthusiastic Charly into being her coach. After that, she'd felt confident and ready for whatever came next.

Nothing to it, she remembered thinking. This was going to be a breeze.

But lately, in the past week or so, things had begun to...well, change. Radiantly healthy up to now, she'd suddenly become extremely uncomfortable. That was because the baby had "dropped," the doctor told her. Nothing to worry about; perfectly normal, she'd insisted. But to Mirabella it had an ominous sound. Plus, the pressure pains in her groin really did hurt. She wasn't sleeping well at night. And in the past couple of days she'd noticed, to her horror, that she'd developed a tendency to *waddle*.

It was very hard, she'd discovered, to maintain your dignity when you were shaped like a Weeble.

And dignity was important to Mirabella, which was something few people seemed able to understand. For most of her adult life, people—her female friends and sisters, mostly—had been telling her how beautiful she was, and, they were sure to add, how much more appealing she would be to men if she would only let her guard down and lighten up more. But they'd never understood about the dignity thing. How could they? Eve, Mirabella's younger sister, had been blessed with the face and body of Princess Grace, so who cared if she had all the dignity of Soupy Sales? And Sommer, the oldest, designed more along the lines of Princess Di, seemed to have been born with a shy and coltish awkwardness that somehow made the whole concept of dignity irrelevant.

How could they ever understand Mirabella, who had had the misfortune to be born short, stocky, red-haired, freckle-faced and nearsighted, or know that there had been times when she was sure pride and dignity were all that had kept her from dying of humiliation?

It was just beginning to occur to her that giving birth might be a difficult thing to accomplish with one's dignity intact.

It had also occurred to her recently that it wasn't something she cared to go through alone. But Charly was…well, she was a dear and loyal friend, but she just wasn't… For some reason she just didn't have what Mirabella needed right now. Neither did her sisters, preoccupied as they were with their own busy lives. So when her mom had announced plans to fly out for Christmas and stay until after the baby was born to help out for the first weeks and get acquainted with her new grandchild, she'd been profoundly and unexpectedly relieved.

But then Pop had had his heart attack.

"Of course, you can't leave him." Mirabella had been astonished her mother would even think of it. And with characteristic decisiveness had promptly added, "I'll go there instead."

It was only later that she'd acknowledged the squeezing sensation in her chest that had prompted her to say it, and to recognize it for what it was: pure panic.

And it was only now that she could admit to herself that the real reason she was so anxious to get to Pensacola had nothing to do with Christmas, or even her father's heart attack. She was having a baby, dammit. And like countless women before her, she wanted someone wise and nurturing to guide her through the experience. In short, she wanted her mother.

Jimmy Joe wasn't dwelling on the problems ahead, the blizzard in Texas, or even a little boy in Georgia sulking about missing his daddy. Although it didn't make him happy to have to admit it, he couldn't seem to get the uppity red-haired pregnant woman from California out of his mind.

She had to be crazy, that's what it was. Plumb crazy to think she could drive that pretty silver car of hers through a Panhandle blizzard all alone. And in her condition! What was she tryin' to do?

He thought then about that little boy waiting for him to come home, and he thought about the sweet little daughter he'd never even gotten a chance to know; and in the depths of his easygoing soul he felt the stirrings of unaccustomed anger.

What in the name of heaven is she thinking of? he

wondered as he pointed his big blue Kenworth down the I-40 on-ramp, pumping his way methodically through the gears. Didn't she know how precious a gift she was carrying?

He tried hard to be fair, figuring she must have thought she had good reason to be doing what she was doing. But he could have told her it wasn't worth it. As far as he was concerned, no reason was good enough to risk a child's life. He wished he had told her when he had the chance. Now it was too late.

Once he was rolling along with the asphalt ribbon unfolding nice and smooth in front of him, Jimmy Joe picked up his mike, thumbed the button and said in his growly CB drawl, "Westbound, what's it look like back your way? What'sa story on that Texas blizzard? Come on."

He listened to static for a moment or two before he got an answer. It sure wasn't what he wanted to hear.

"Uh...looks like they gonna be closin' 'er down, here, pretty soon."

Somebody else broke in with a groan. "Ah, hell, don't tell me that."

"That's what they're sayin'. Shuttin' 'er down at Tucumcari. Ain't lettin' nobody through."

"Oh, man..."

"What I hear, ain't nobody comin' through the Panhandle."

"I just come up twenty-five," somebody else said. "Dry and dusty down that way."

"Hell, that don't do me good. I gotta get to Nashville!"

"That's just a crime, you know it? Shuttin' down a whole damn interstate for a little bit a' snow."

"Shoot, Texas don't even know what a snowplow is."

"Ain't that the truth?"

The chatter went on, but Jimmy Joe didn't join in. He hung up his mike and listened to all the bitching and complaining, which he mostly agreed with. But he was still thinking about that redhead in the Lexus, wishing he had some way to warn her. Wishing she had a CB so he could talk to her, at least let her know what she was driving into.

Mirabella couldn't see what all the fuss was about. She'd rolled right through Albuquerque without any problems, if you didn't count a couple of idiots in pickup trucks driving like kamikazis, and some bewildering lane changes in a construction zone. She did see a little bit of snow going through the mountains on the other side of the city—just a light dusting on the junipers, not even enough to look pretty. And she did feel a twinge of indecision as she came up on the turnoff to I-25 south. *Last chance.* The thought flashed through her mind. Last chance to change your mind, Bella.

But the road was dry and the skies were clear, and she was moving along normally, which is to say well over the speed limit—Mirabella preferred to think of speed limits as "guidelines," anyway. So she sailed on past the turnoff, set her cruise control at seventy-five, and popped her favorite chamber-music tape into the deck. As part of her campaign to imprint her unborn child with a taste for good music, she turned the volume up high and settled back for the long haul.

At this rate, she told herself smugly, she would easily make it as far as Amarillo tonight—maybe farther. After that it was only another thousand miles or so to Pensacola. Okay, that did sound like a lot, but hey, she had two days. She could still make it by Christmas night. She *would* make it. She'd made up her mind. And when Mirabella made up her mind to do something, she did it.

Not long after that, everything came to a halt.

Now what? thought Mirabella. According to the last mile marker she'd paid any attention to, she was still at least a hundred miles from Texas, and, it looked to her, a lot farther than that from the nearest snowflake.

Right about now she should be approaching the town of Santa Rosa—barely a speck on the road atlas that lay open on the seat beside her—where she'd planned to make a quick potty-stop. Her back was aching and her legs had developed an alarming tendency to go numb, but she'd figured on pushing ahead another fifty miles to Tucumcari before taking a real break. Which she was never going to make if it kept going like this. What, she wondered irritably, was the holdup, anyway? It had to be an accident of some kind. Dammit, just her luck.

Then she noticed that trucks were beginning to pull over and park along the shoulder of the interstate, in a long, grumbling line that stretched back toward Arizona as far as she could see in her rearview mirrors. That struck her as a very bad sign.

The traffic lanes were moving, though, still creeping

slowly but steadily along. And now up ahead she
could see flashing lights, and state troopers waving
lighted batons like semaphores. It appeared the two
lanes of traffic were being merged into one, then directed toward the nearest exit ramp. Mirabella didn't
see any signs at all of an accident. She began to get a
queasy feeling in her stomach.

When she got to the first state trooper she stopped
and rolled down her window. Raising her voice above
the oboe solo in Albinoni's Adagio, which was issuing
full blast from her tape deck, she said in an imperious
tone, "Excuse me, officer, what's the problem? Why
is the highway closed?"

The young Native American trooper first gave her
an impatient look, then did a double take and came
ambling over. He leaned down to the window, started
to speak, then interrupted himself and instead said
loudly, "Ma'am, could you turn that down, please?"
Mirabella turned off the tape player. "Thank you.
Ma'am, since you haven't been listening to your radio,
I guess you probably don't know. The interstate's
closed at the Texas state line. They got blowing snow,
icy roads and zero visibility through the Texas Panhandle."

"But that's a hundred miles from here," Mirabella
protested. She couldn't believe he was serious. Snow?
Impossible. It was so *nice* here.

But the trooper was straightening with an air of finality and a shrug. "Got to close it somewhere,
ma'am—preferably somewhere people got a place to
stay. Tucumcari's full up. Santa Rosa's the next stop
down the line. Unless you have business between here

and the line, I'm gonna have to ask you to exit here, ma'am. Move along, now...thank you. Exit to your right, please.'' He pointed toward the off-ramp and waved her on with his lighted baton.

Mirabella did as she was told, which was something she never enjoyed, especially when she had no other choice.

At the stop sign at the bottom of the exit ramp she was faced with two choices: she could turn left onto what appeared to be the town's main drag, where at the moment there was a traffic snarl that resembled an Orange County shopping-mall parking lot the day before Christmas. Or, she could turn right, onto a two-lane numbered highway that curved past a truck stop and disappeared into the dry hills and arroyos to the south.

South. Mirabella was chewing on her lip and thinking about that when somebody behind her gave an impatient blast on his car horn. Being a seasoned L.A. driver, she flipped him an appropriate response, then put on her blinker and turned in a deliberate and leisurely fashion to the right.

The truck stop's huge truck parking lot was already filled to overflowing with idling eighteen-wheelers. More trucks were pulling in along all the side and frontage roads on both sides of the interstate. Fortunately, there seemed to be relatively fewer passenger cars entering the truck—oops, *travel*—stop's passenger-car parking lot, and she was able to find a spot not too far from the entrance.

She was engaged in the clumsy process of extricating her bulky body and numb legs from her car when a wickedly cold wind came skirling around the open door, whistled down her collar and blew freshly up her pant legs. As she got her jacket from the back seat, she found herself remembering early mornings on the California deserts of her childhood, waiting with her sisters for the school bus, stamping the ground and blowing on her fingers to keep warm; remembering a certain smell in the air, brought on the wind from the distant Sierra Nevadas.

For the first time, snow began to seem like a real possibility.

The travel-stop store was stuffy by comparison, overheated and jam-packed with stranded motorists and ticked-off truckers all milling around grumbling and griping about the situation they were in. After making her mandatory stop in the ladies' room, Mirabella pushed her way through the crowd around the fuel desk.

"Excuse me," she said to the girl behind the counter, who was busy with a customer, "could I just ask you a question?"

The cashier—young, Native American and obviously unflappable—nodded and went on with what she was doing, which was ringing up someone's assortment of snack foods.

"That road out there," Mirabella persisted, "the one right in front—eighty-four, I think it was—does it, by any chance, go to Texas?"

Again the cashier nodded. Mirabella was encouraged by that and about to ask for further details, such as how far was it to Texas, and were there any places to stop along the way, when one of the men waiting in line broke in with a snort and said, "Not today, it don't."

There was a general rumble of agreement. Somebody else said, "Ain't nothin' goin' to Texas today. They got the whole damn state shut down."

Another voice piped up, "I heard it was even snowin' in Dallas."

The first man who'd spoken reached past her to put his purchases—a paperback mystery, a package of Twinkies and a bottle of Rolaids—on the counter. As he did he gave her a look—down, then back up again—and said in a more kindly tone, "If I'z you, I'd get myself a motel room, ma'am, before it's too late. Might as well be comfortable. You ain't goin' any further tonight."

She stood very still and didn't reply. She was, quite simply, dumbstruck.

To Mirabella, "No" had always been a challenge; the word "impossible" a spur to action, and "You can't," a gauntlet, a dare. It was her belief that there was a way around almost any obstacle, if a person looked hard enough. Right now her mind was racing in high gear trying to find a way around this one, only it just kept coming back to where she was. *"You ain't goin' any further tonight."*

She couldn't believe it. It simply didn't compute.

But she was. She was stuck. In Santa Rosa, New Mexico, for God's sake, for who-knows-how-long. And no matter what, she wasn't going to get to Pensacola in time to spend Christmas with her parents. Instead she was going to spend Christmas somewhere on the road, alone, among strangers. She was suddenly struck by a horrifying urge to cry.

Except that Mirabella *never* cried. She took a deep breath, murmured, "Thanks," to no one in particular, and pushed her way back through the crowd. At the entrance to the dining room she paused, knowing she ought to eat something, at least. But she wasn't hungry. What she was, she realized suddenly, was exhausted. The trucker was right; she should get a motel room. Then at least she could lie down.

After the overheated store, the cold outside took her breath away. Mirabella tried to hurry across the windy parking lot, but the best she could manage was a slow, ungainly, roundabout kind of pace, which she thought must be like trying to walk with a basketball pressed between her thighs. Reaching her car at last, she unlocked it, heaved herself inside and sat, breathing hard and shivering, while she waited for the heater to warm up. She'd never felt so frustrated in her life.

"I don't believe this," she kept muttering furiously to herself. "I *don't* believe this."

Half an hour later she was still saying it as she drove slowly down the town's main drag, passing motel after motel, No Vacancy sign after No Vacancy sign. Other stranded motorists, equally frustrated, were zipping in and out of motel parking lots, tires squealing, engines roaring, as they raced each other in a frantic search for the last available rooms. Too late, some people shouted and banged their fists on countertops. Mirabella had banged on a few herself, and even played unabashedly on her "condition," hoping the sympathy factor might melt some adamant desk clerk's heart.

But to no avail. There simply wasn't a vacant room left in town.

"No room at the inn," thought Mirabella whimsically. And then felt vaguely blasphemous, even though she'd never considered herself a particularly religious person.

In the restaurant at the 76 Travel Stop, Jimmy Joe was trying his best to have a phone conversation with his son, J.J. It wasn't easy, being as how the decibel level in the dining room was about the same as the first turn at Indy at the start of the 500. He'd turned his back to the room and stuck his finger in the ear that wasn't pressed up against the receiver, but it wasn't doing much good, and he kept having to yell, "What?" every other sentence.

"I said, you don't have to shout, Dad, I can hear you fine," J.J. was saying.

"Well, *you* better shout then, 'cause I can't hear you worth beans," Jimmy Joe hollered back. "This place is a zoo."

"How come it's so noisy?"

"Ah, it's crowded, is all. Everybody's pretty much stuck here in New Mexico for a while, I guess." He took a deep breath and broke the news. "They up and closed the road—because of that snowstorm you told me about? Looks like they're not lettin' anybody through the Panhandle right now."

"Told you," J.J. said in a know-it-all tone of voice. But his father knew him pretty well, and heard the quiver in it anyway.

For J.J.'s sake he tried to make the best of it. "Hey,

don't worry, okay? They can't keep a whole interstate shut down for too long, can they? Soon as they open up the road, I'm on my way.'' And he would drive right on through, if he had to. The way he had it figured, it wasn't likely the weigh stations were going to be open on the holiday, so unless he got pulled over by the DOT, there wasn't going to be anybody checking his logbook. It wasn't something he would chance, ordinarily, but this was Christmas. And he'd promised J.J.

''It looks really bad, Dad. There's trucks and cars turned over and everything. I saw it on TV.''

''You watch too much TV,'' said Jimmy Joe, ''you know that? How come you're not outdoors playin' or somethin'?''

'''Cause we got rain. I gotta do something, Dad. I'm on restriction, so no computer, remember?''

Jimmy Joe chuckled. ''Yeah, so how are you and Sammi June gettin' along? You two kiss and make up yet?'' At that, J.J. muttered something his father couldn't quite catch. He hunched himself over the phone and yelled, ''What?''

Just then there was one of those little lulls that come over a noisy crowd sometimes, kind of like everybody in the room stopped to take a breath at the same moment. But whatever it was his son was telling him, Jimmy Joe missed it anyway, because in that quiet moment he heard a soft voice, practically at his elbow, say, ''Excuse me....''

He jerked around, thinking it was the waitress finally come to take his order. But it wasn't. It was about the last person he'd expected to see—none other than the redheaded pregnant woman he'd last seen a couple of hundred miles back, getting into a gray Lexus. And although she was trying her best to maintain that uppity lift of her chin, it was easy to see that it was costing her plenty to do it.

For a moment or two he just stared at her. Then he figured he must have made some kind of sound, because he heard J.J. say, "Dad? What did you say? I didn't hear you."

That snapped him out of it. He mumbled, "Hang on a minute, J.J.," then managed to gasp, "Ma'am?" as, being a well-brought-up Southern boy, he almost killed himself trying to mind his manners and stand in the confines of that booth.

She quickly put out her hand, motioning him to stay put, and said in a not-too-steady voice, "Please—don't get up. I was just wondering— I'm sorry to bother you, but would you mind if I shared this booth with you? There doesn't seem to be anyplace else...."

It occurred to Jimmy Joe while she was saying it that the way she looked, if she didn't sit down right soon, she was going to fall down. To put it mildly, she looked dead on her feet. Her face was so pale you could darn near see through it. There were dark smudges under her eyes, and although she kept wanting to smile, what she looked like to him was somebody trying real hard not to cry. And—he hadn't noticed it before, but those eyes of hers were enormous. Dark blue-gray, like the ocean when it rained. Looking into them, he began to feel a little bit dizzy, as if he was standing on the edge of a cliff, looking down....

"Dad?"

"Oh—sure! By all means…" His natural, ingrained reflex was to get up and help the lady to her seat. But before he could get himself untangled and out of the booth, she'd already slipped in across from him with a sigh and a whispered, "Thank you."

"Dad? Who's that you're talkin' to?"

"Uh…listen, J.J., I'm gonna have to call you back after a while, okay?"

"Oh, please," the woman inserted hastily, "don't— not on my account. I didn't want to intrude."

"That's okay, I was about done anyway," Jimmy Joe assured her as he was hanging up on J.J.'s wounded-sounding, *"Da-ad…"* Then for a minute or two he had a bad case of the fidgets, while he tried to adjust to her being there and at the same time figure out how he felt about that.

One thing he felt was nervous, which was understandable; he never had been real comfortable around beautiful women. Pretty, okay. He liked flirting with a pretty woman as much as the next guy. But knock-your-eyes-out, movie-star gorgeous? Uh-uh. Women like that made him feel like he'd forgotten how to breathe. With that dark red hair and pale-as-milk skin of hers, what she reminded him of more than anything was paintings he'd seen of the Madonna. Except the thoughts he'd been having about her… Well, he would have been ashamed to think them in church—put it that way.

On the other hand, beautiful or not, she was damn well ticking him off by the way she was acting, driving across the country all by herself, taking chances with that baby she was carrying. Which was also understandable; having lost one child because of a woman's pure selfishness and irresponsibility, he had a low tolerance level for that sort of behavior.

What had him confused, though, was that now that she was sitting right there across the table from him, and he could see in her eyes how tired and scared she was, it was real hard for him to stay mad at her. Although he did mean to try. For one thing, it made it a whole lot easier for him to overlook how beautiful she was.

"Hi," she said as she settled herself, in a kind of breathless and sheepish way that for some reason made her seem more likable than she had up to now. Then she stuck her hand out and, in a more forward and businesslike way than most of the Southern women he was used to, added, "I'm Mirabella Waskowitz."

And he decided he liked that, too.

"Jimmy Joe," he said, as he took the hand she offered.

Chapter 3

"Boy, I got heartburn so bad I'd give five
dollars for one Rolaid."
I-40—New Mexico

His hand felt nice. Firm and warm and strong. Just the kind of hand you hoped would be there to reach for if you really needed one.

Which was precisely why Mirabella let go of it as quickly as she possibly could without being rude about it. She didn't want a hand from anybody, especially a man. She was doing just fine without one, thank you.

But he was just so damned *adorable*. That Southern accent, that Robert Redford hair and smile, and that name...*Jimmy Joe?* Really, it was almost *too* cute.

"I can't thank you enough," she said, her relief so overwhelming she was unable to hold back a sigh. At least, thank God, she hadn't burst into tears. But it had been close. *Too* close.

He mumbled, "No problem...my pleasure."

Polite, thought Mirabella approvingly. Kind of distant, too, which she also happened to like; she despised men who presumed they'd earned the right to instant familiarity the minute they told you their names. Still, she found herself wondering about it; wondering if Jimmy Joe really was shy, or if this was an example of that Southern reserve she'd heard about, or if maybe the coolness she'd detected in his eyes was only the natural wariness of someone who wasn't about to get involved with the problems of a total stranger.

Which was fine with her and just as well, because after all, here she was just four weeks away from becoming a middle-aged, unmarried mother, and she ought to be ashamed of herself for even having such thoughts about a kid who probably couldn't even buy beer without getting carded.

It was just awkward, that's all. It was hard to get past the fact that she was sitting across from a man who was the walking-around-in-the-flesh spitting image of her unborn child.

And impossible to deny the secret delight she felt when she thought about the prospect of having a little towheaded toddler version of Jimmy Joe running around her house sometime soon—a version, of course, that would be possessed of both athletic and musical talent and an IQ in the "gifted" range. She was absolutely confident of that—those qualities having been even higher on her list of priorities than a tall, lean body and olive-toned skin. When Mirabella planned something, she left as little as possible to chance.

"You want somethin' to eat?" Jimmy Joe asked, stretching around to look for a waitress. "Let me see if I can get somebody—"

"No, that's okay," said Mirabella. "I'm not really hungry. I just needed…to sit down for a while." The miniature-genius version of Jimmy Joe in her belly chose that moment to execute an athletic maneuver closely resembling that of a frolicking dolphin, causing her to lean sharply backward in her seat and suck in air in an audible hiss.

"You okay, ma'am?"

Since she had her eyes closed, she couldn't be sure whether it was alarm or compassion she heard in Jimmy Joe's voice, although she thought it was probably a little of both.

She waited until the worst of the pains had gone shooting off down her legs, then nodded and let out along, slow breath. "Oh, yeah, it's just too much sitting, I guess." *If I could just lie down,* she thought. *God, please…just let me lie down.*

It suddenly occurred to her that she was teetering on the brink again. She recognized that weak, hollow feeling, the one she'd had earlier as she'd stood helplessly surveying the jam-packed restaurant dining room, just moments before she'd spotted Jimmy Joe sitting all alone in a booth big enough for two. She knew she was just one shaky step from the edge, one kind word away from tears.

Panic seized her. She couldn't humiliate herself in

front of him—she *couldn't*. "Well—better go—thanks for the breather," she chirped, not even caring how ungainly she looked, frantically hitching her beach-ball-shaped body along toward the edge of the bench. Or how crazy she sounded, leaving so abruptly when she'd only just sat down. All she could think about was getting out of there, away from people, away from *him*, before she made a complete fool of herself.

But before she could make good her escape, Jimmy Joe's hand shot out and snagged her elbow. And there was nothing shy or reserved about the way he held on to it, or the tone of his voice when he demanded, "Hey—wait a minute. Where're you off to?"

Ordinarily, Mirabella's tolerance for being manhandled or questioned was just about zero. However, at the moment she was operating on sheer bravado, and the best she could come up with was a superior smile and a toss of her head meant to convey the impression that she was just bursting with self-confidence.

"Listen—thanks very much. It was nice of you to let me, uh, share your table for a moment," she heard herself babble. All the while she was looking anywhere but at Jimmy Joe, at anything but the strong, masculine fingers curled around her arm, or the earnest young face leaning close, now, to hers. "But...I'm pretty tired. So I think I'm going to go out to my car and lie down for a while." *Yes—oh, yes, that would do it.* She could curl up on the back seat. That would be better than nothing. Or did the front seats recline? She had no idea; she'd never had occasion to test them. *Just...please, God, let me get out of here. Please let me lie down.*

She was standing now. So was he. Desperately, Mirabella focused her eyes on the picture of the ugly bulldog on his University of Georgia sweatshirt. She stuck out her hand, not an easy thing to do since he was still holding her elbow, and said, "Well. It was nice meeting you, Jimmy Joe." And she was thinking, Please, God, don't let me cry.

Jimmy Joe knew he was about to do something rash the minute he saw those big gray eyes of hers go wide and shiny, and realized she was about one blink away from spilling over. That panicked him; he never had been able to stand seeing a woman cry.

He coughed a little bit to loosen up the nervous knot in his chest, then said, "Look...ma'am, I've got a sleeper in my truck. It's pretty comfortable, and it'd be warm. I'm not usin' it, so if you want it, well... What I mean is, you're welcome to it."

Well. He could see he'd surprised her as much as he had himself, saying that. Because her eyes, which had been staring a hole in the middle of his chest, suddenly flew right up and smacked into his in a way he wasn't prepared to handle. Sort of made him wish he could have ducked.

Then she shook her head hard and said, "Oh, no, I couldn't. Thanks, but..."

Just like that, he didn't know why, but all of a sudden he was mad at her again. His voice got soft and polite, which, if she'd known him better, she would have known meant he was in no mood to be crossed.

"Excuse me, ma'am, but you're about out on your feet, far as I can see, and I got a perfectly good sleeper goin' wantin'. Now, I'm gonna take you out to my truck and get you settled, and then I'm gonna leave you to rest as long as you need to, y'understand? Come on, now—you need anything from your car? No? Okay, let's go, then. Come on…."

It was the tone of voice he mostly used to get J.J. to see things his way when the boy was feeling contrary and muleheaded about something, and he was glad to see it worked just as well on muleheaded pregnant women. Just when he thought he might have to tell her his personal views on women who were too selfish or too proud to do what was right for their babies, he felt her kind of relax and let out a shaky breath of surrender.

She whispered, "That's…really nice of you," then looked around like she'd maybe misplaced something, and mumbled, "I just…need to use the ladies' room first, okay? 'Scuse me…." He let her go, and she turned and headed off in the direction of the rest rooms.

As she went, Jimmy Joe saw her duck her head and brush at her eyes, and he suddenly knew she was doing her best to hold on to her pride, and hide from him how tired and grateful she really was. And he felt a softening inside, a slow melting around his heart.

He flagged down a waitress and gave her his order, along with five bucks to make sure she held his table for him until he got back. Then he got his coat and keys and went to stake out the ladies' room from a discreet distance, not really believing she would try to skip out on him, but not quite trusting that pride of hers, either. While he waited he fidgeted with his keys and paced a little, and tried to figure out why he was letting himself get so riled up over this woman.

Mirabella. What kind of name was that, anyway? Italian, that's what it sounded like. But with a last name like—what was it? He couldn't remember, except that it was hard to pronounce and definitely not Italian. Unless—well, of course, it was probably her married name. That would explain the last name, but not the Mirabella. If he'd had to guess he would have said she was Irish, with that red hair and those thick dark eyelashes, and pale as she was, in the good light in the restaurant he'd detected the faint ghosts of freckles.

Not that it was any of his business.

The fact that she wasn't wearing a wedding ring wasn't any of his business, either, but there was no use denying he'd noticed. Or that it bothered him a lot more than it should have. Jimmy Joe didn't like to think of himself as being a judgmental person, but along with everything else he'd observed so far about this woman, the fact that she'd let herself get pregnant out of wedlock couldn't help but have an effect on his opinion as to her basic good sense.

And it still wasn't any of his business.

Except that now, by offering her his sleeper to rest up in, what he was doing was butting in and *making* her his business, wasn't he? Which she hadn't asked for. And doing her a kindness didn't give him the right to pass judgment on her character. He hadn't been brought up to behave that way, and he didn't mean to start now. No, sir.

So here's what you do, Jimmy Joe, he said to himself as he made one more pass around the rack of paperback books, which by this time had been pretty well picked over, so there were mostly Louis Lamours and maybe a few John Grishams left. Sue Grafton's latest—but he'd already read that. *What you do is, you're gonna let the lady rest until they open up the road, and then you're gonna go on your way and forget about her. Ten-four.*

When he came around the rack, there she was, just coming out of the door marked Women. She looked as though she might have washed her face and taken a brush to her hair, but as far as Jimmy Joe could see, all it had done was make her look like a lost little girl.

That was when he knew the last part of that vow he'd just made might not be so easy to live up to.

To Mirabella, the walk through the truck parking lot felt like the longest of her life. It was just so damn *cold.* There wasn't any snow, but a bitter wind cut like a knife through her coat, which was a soft, lightweight leather designed for southern California winters. She wanted to hurry, but that was impossible, and for once she didn't mind that Jimmy Joe kept a firm grip on her elbow, or resent the way he patiently adjusted his long, lanky stride to match her slow, side-to-side waddle.

"Sorry I can't go any faster—I know I walk like an obese duck," she said at one point, characteristically trying to mask her embarrassment with laughter.

Jimmy Joe glanced at her and drawled, straight-faced, "Naw…more like you sat on a horse too long."

Mirabella gave a short, surprised laugh. Surprised, because he sounded so much less reserved when he said it, as if he really might have a sense of humor underneath all that politeness. And because all of a sudden she didn't feel self-conscious about the way she walked anymore. And she couldn't for the life of her figure out what it was about what he'd said or the way he'd said it that could have had that effect on her.

Then they were passing between the seemingly endless rows of idling trucks, hundreds of them, rumbling away with a sound like an oncoming stampede.

"They're so *big*," said Mirabella through her shivers, knowing it was an inane thing to say, which *didn't* surprise her, being right on a par with her usual snappy social repartee. Considered a clown in her family and a wit among her female friends, and at the very least, concise and articulate in professional situations, when it came to a conversational one-on-one with an attractive member of the opposite sex, Mirabella was generally about as eloquent as…well, a duck.

But they *were* big. Huge. Awe-inspiring, especially up close like this. Having a very literal mind, she rarely thought in poetic analogies, but the trucks made her think of great slumbering beasts—domesticated, pampered beasts, to be sure, many of whose owners had decked them out for the holidays in tinsel garlands and Christmas lights, with wreaths and red bows tied to their front grills.

"This here's the one," said Jimmy Joe, and let go of her arm while he took out his keys. When he stepped in between two of the massive machines and unlocked the door of one of them, she noticed that his truck didn't have any Christmas decorations on it. Then he pulled the door open and she could see the words Blue Starr Transport written in silver on shiny royal blue, along with a logo that looked like the star of Bethlehem, and she decided that with a name and a logo like that, he didn't really need anything more.

Shivering even harder, she said, "I can see where the Blue comes from, but Starr, with two *r*'s?"

"That's my name," he said in an offhand way as he rejoined her, pocketing his keys. "Jimmy Joe Starr. And my daddy's before me. Come on around here to the other side. That way you won't have the steering wheel to fool with."

"You sure you're not going to need a crane to get me up there?" she asked, laughing uneasily as she followed him to the passenger side. The truck had shiny chrome steps up to the cab, but it still looked like a climb, considering her limitations.

He didn't even chuckle, although she did catch a glimpse of that sweet grin before he turned away from her to open the door. "Naw, you'll do fine. Okay, here you go, now—upsy-daisy."

And before she had time to be worried about it he'd stepped around behind her and put his hands under her elbows and boosted her right up onto the first step. One more good boost and she was where she'd never in a million years thought she would ever be—sitting in the cab of an eighteen-wheeler.

"Wow," she said, looking around, "I'm impressed." She hoped he would know she wasn't just saying it, that she really meant it. She wasn't sure exactly what she'd thought he meant when Jimmy Joe mentioned a "sleeper," but she hadn't expected anything like this. The control panel just looked bewildering, complicated enough to operate a 747, but behind the seats it was like a tiny little RV, with a wide, comfortable-looking bed, no wasted space and a place for everything. Designing space for maximum use and efficiency was what Mirabella *did,* and she could appreciate a masterpiece when she saw it.

"It's comfortable," Jimmy Joe said with a diffident shrug. He showed her how to turn off the lights in the cab and where to turn them on in the sleeper, and how to adjust the heater in case she got too warm. Then he seemed to hesitate, as if he wasn't sure what to do next.

"I really appreciate this," Mirabella said with bemused sincerity. "Thanks."

He nodded and muttered, "Okay, then." He started to back out of the cab before pausing to add, "Might want to lock your doors." And then he was gone and the door slammed shut on the cold, mean wind.

Mirabella waited for a moment, then locked the doors and turned off the cab lights the way he'd told her to. She went into the sleeper and drew the curtain across the opening, then stood for a moment or two just looking, trying to orient herself to the strangeness of being in a man's private space.

She was surprised at how tidy it was. The bed was neatly made, and except for a pair of boots standing upright and together on the floor, everything seemed to be stowed away in its proper place. There was a tiny closet for hanging clothes, and drawers she didn't look in. An overnight bag, some folded towels and a baseball cap occupied a shelf above the bed; compartments at its head held paperback books, a pack of gum and a plastic bag with some change in it. He wasn't a smoker, thank God.

No bathroom, though; not even a potty. Which was too bad, because she already felt the need for one, although it had only been a few minutes since she'd left the truck-stop rest room. No way she was going back there now, though. It was just one more discomfort she would have to ignore.

She turned off the light and sank onto the bed with a sigh, curling carefully onto her side, which was the only position left that could even remotely be considered comfortable. And as the darkness and the vibration of several hundred truck engines folded in around her, it occurred to Mirabella that it felt a little like being in a womb herself...safe, warm, rocked by the throbbing of a massive diesel heartbeat.

Walking back to the restaurant, Jimmy Joe caught himself looking around to see if anybody had noticed what he'd just done, as if it was something he ought to be ashamed of. It was a first for him, no doubt about that. He'd had the Kenworth almost five years now, put more than half a million miles on her, and this was the first time a woman had ever set foot inside her sleeper.

It wasn't that he hadn't had those kinds of opportunities come knocking—sometimes literally—on his door. And he hadn't said no to them when they did because he was some kind of prude, or had a religious thing about it—nothing like that. He just didn't believe in mixing recreation with work, was all. Of course, nowadays most of the better truck stops, including this

one, had pretty much put a stop to the lot-lizard nonsense, which did cut down on the temptations
considerably.

Not that Mirabella was anywhere near being in the
same category. This was a different thing altogether.
But he still felt weird about it.

Back in the restaurant he found his booth still vacant and a mug of hot coffee waiting for him. He'd
just about sat down when his hot roast-beef sandwich
arrived, and he was hungry enough that he put off
calling J.J. while he gave his dinner his full attention.
After he'd gotten that put away and his coffee mug
refilled, he picked up the phone and punched in the
endless string of numbers it took to connect him via
calling card to his mama's house, then settled back to
listen to the rings.

That was when he looked up and felt a catch in his
chest as if a big bite of roast beef had gotten stuck
there. Darned if it wasn't her, standing there same as
before except maybe looking even more pale and
peaked. He wasn't glad to see her. He especially
wasn't glad about the way his stomach jumped up underneath his ribs and made his heart beat faster, kind
of like the way it did sitting on top of a forty-ton load
when he knew a four-wheeler was about to cut him
off and he had no place else to go.

He told himself he really had hoped to have seen
the last of the uppity woman with the red hair, Madonna eyes, Italian name and no good sense, except
maybe for helping her out of his truck tomorrow morning and into her own car and waving her on her way.
Lord, didn't he have enough to worry about, what with

the weather screwing up his schedule, and wondering how he was going to make it home for Christmas in time to keep from breaking a promise, not to mention J.J.'s heart?

He sure didn't need to be thinking about whether or not it was normal for a beautiful pregnant woman from California to have dark circles underneath her eyes, a little wrinkle of a frown in her forehead and a white look around her mouth even when she smiled.

"Hi," she said sort of shy and sheepishly, reminding him of J.J. when he was little and used to come pit-patting down the stairs on some excuse or other after he'd been all tucked in snug for the night.

Jimmy Joe put the phone up quickly—he *hoped* before anybody had picked it up on the other end, because he didn't want to have to hang up on his son twice in one evening. "Hey," he sang out, "how you doin'? Everything all right? Somethin' you need?"

She shook her head and mumbled, "Couldn't sleep," as she eased in across from him, moving like she was made of blown glass. She put her elbows on the tabletop and pushed her hair back from the sides of her face with both hands, then left them there and used them for props. "I had to come in to use the rest room anyway. Thought I might as well see if you wanted to take the bed. No sense in it going to waste."

It was a true mystery to Jimmy Joe why she couldn't sleep, because she looked and sounded to him like she was in danger of dozing off where she sat. A terrible thought occurred to him. Trying not to sound as worried as he felt, he said, "Ma'am, if you don't mind my askin', when's that baby of yours due?"

She made a vague waving motion with one hand and in the midst of a great big yawn, mumbled, "Oh, not for a month yet." Then she kind of straightened herself, making a real effort to lift up her chin. "No, I'm okay, really. It's just hard to get comfortable, you know? I get these pressure pains in my legs...."

Jimmy Joe nodded in sympathy. J.J.'s mama had had those pains, both times. He could remember times when she'd shot up out of bed like she'd been hit with a cattle prod, cussin' like nobody's mama should. He said with relief, "Maybe you ought to eat something. Might make you feel better."

She finished up another yawn, then shook her head. "I'm not hungry."

"You got other reasons to eat besides feelin' hungry," said Jimmy Joe sternly, nodding toward the part of her that was pushing up against the edge of the table. "Got to keep your strength up." He was fed up with the way she kept ignoring the needs of that baby of hers, so he didn't wait to see if she agreed with him, but just started looking around for a waitress.

Things having settled down some by that time, he was able to spot one right away. She came ambling on over and brought the coffeepot with her, probably assuming he was wanting a refill. The waitress was one he didn't know—a skinny woman with frizzy gray hair and deep lines on her face from smoking—but she looked cheerful and sort of motherly, so he checked the name tag pinned to her uniform blouse and turned on the charm.

"Hey, Dottie, what kind of soup you got today?"

Dottie looked up at the ceiling like she expected to

see the menu written up there and gave it some thought. "Let's see. Tonight we got...I b'lieve it's cream of broccoli and chicken noodle."

"Well, okay. You can bring the lady a bowl of that chicken noodle, if you would. And a big glass a' milk." He grinned, flirting just a little bit, and added, "And I'll take some of that coffee, since you brought it."

Looking pleased, Dottie sang out, "Chicken noodle, comin' right up." She splashed coffee into his mug and went on her way.

Jimmy Joe sat back in his seat prepared for an argument, but he could see right away he wasn't going to get one. He was glad to see the woman wasn't stubborn to the point of being plain stupid, and at least had the sense to recognize a lost fight when she saw it.

But...*now* what was she doing? She had her big pocketbook open on the seat beside her and was digging through it and dragging out bottle after bottle of some kind of pills.

He put his hands on the table and laced his fingers together and watched her, watched the slick, shiny red curtain of her hair swing back and forth across her face, catching the light, and tried to think whether he'd ever seen anything in his life before that was exactly that color.

Finally he cleared his throat, shifted around in his seat, and came out with, "I know it's none of my business, but..."

Her eyes flicked at him like a dog after a fly. "Vitamins,'' she explained shortly, and went back to rummaging.

"Ah,'' said Jimmy Joe, nodding. He felt unreasonably pleased. And at the same time, bothered by the notion that it did seem to matter to him whether or not this woman he wasn't ever going to see again after tonight did or did not care about her baby's well-being. It gave him a case of the restless fidgets, and after watching a moment or two longer, he reached out and snagged one of the bottles. "Vitamin K,'' he read off the label. "That's one I never heard of. What's it supposed to do?''

"That's for blood clotting,'' she said without looking up from what she was doing, which was making a neat little pile of the pills on the table in front of her. "That's to prevent excessive bleeding during childbirth.''

Jimmy Joe put the bottle down in a hurry. He hadn't been present during the actual births of either of his children, through no fault of his own, and there were some images associated with the whole process he preferred not to dwell on.

"How 'bout these?'' he asked, poking at some brown pills that looked big enough to choke a goat.

"Those? That's brewer's yeast. B vitamins and protein.''

"Uh-huh…and this one here?''

"Let's see. That's the antioxidant combo, I think. C, E and—what else? Shoot, I can't remember—''

"What in blue blazes are anti—what did you call 'em?''

She looked shocked. "I can't believe you've never heard of antioxidants."

Well, as a matter of fact he had, but he couldn't recall exactly what it was he'd read or heard about the blamed things, and it seemed as good a topic of conversation as anything he could think of right off the bat. So he shrugged and told her half a lie. "No, ma'am, can't say's I have."

"Okay," said Mirabella, taking a breath and squaring her shoulders as if it had just become her sacred duty to educate him on the subject. Then she launched herself into a detailed explanation of what antioxidants did, which as far as he could tell involved keeping her cells' neurons from flying off to look for mates somewhere else. "In other words, oxidizing," she concluded.

"Oxidizing... Well, now I know what that is," said Jimmy Joe humbly. "I reckon that's pretty much the same as rusting, isn't it?"

To his great surprise and extreme pleasure, she burst out laughing. "Doesn't seem to be working too well in my case," she remarked, fingering a strand of hair that had fallen across her face and having to make her eyes go crossed in order to focus on it.

"Well, now, ma'am, I wouldn't say that," Jimmy Joe murmured, studying her somberly. "Looks to me like it's workin' just fine."

He was thinking about what a powerful difference a little thing like laughter could make in the way one person looked at another. For such a beautiful woman to make fun of herself like that, even crossing her eyes... Well for one thing it made him ashamed of himself. Here, just because she had a face that would tie Don Juan up in knots and happened to drive a fancy new car, he'd been judging her to be just another spoiled rich airhead from La-la Land. And hadn't his mama taught him better than to judge people by their looks? Now he was beginning to see that there might be a lot more to this Mirabella than met the eye. That for starters, she wasn't just pretty; it was turning out that she was also intelligent, funny and, doggone it, nice.

And that made him wonder all the more what she was doing out here in the middle of New Mexico, pregnant and alone, and why she wasn't wearing a wedding ring. But he was a Southern boy, and way too well-brought-up to ask.

Chapter 4

*"Where'd you say that truck stop is? I'm so hungry
I'm chewin' on air."*

I-40—New Mexico

The bowlful of steaming chicken-noodle soup the
waitress set in front of Mirabella looked good and
smelled even better. Even so, she sat regarding it without enthusiasm until Jimmy Joe picked up her spoon
and held it out to her and said, "Eat," in a tone that
brooked no argument. Then with a sigh she took the
spoon from him, plunged it into the bowl, lifted it
laden with noodles and dripping broth, and blew on
it, more to forestall the moment when she would have
to put it in her mouth than because it actually needed
cooling.

Jimmy Joe, who wasn't fooled, said, "Come on,
quit stalling." Mirabella took a deep breath.

It wasn't that she wasn't hungry. That is, her *stomach* felt hungry—she just didn't seem to have any desire for food. Which was a state of affairs she would normally have relished, having spent most of her life fighting the inescapable effects of a disgustingly healthy and indiscriminating appetite. But the truth was, she simply felt too awful to eat.

She was so tired. And she had *such* a backache. Plus, she was worried about the weather, and feeling emotionally vulnerable about Christmas, just the thought of which made her throat constrict like a too-tight collar. And as if *that* wasn't enough, there was the distracting and disturbing presence of Jimmy Joe Starr.

As hard as she tried to ignore it, as determined as she was not to acknowledge it, to look somewhere else—anywhere else—and pretend a nonchalance she didn't in the least feel, she was acutely aware of him. She knew he was studying her, though trying his best not to be obvious and rude about it; watching her when he thought it was safe with a puzzled intensity she couldn't quite fathom. Why is he looking at me like that? she kept wondering. As if he had a question that was burning a hole in his tongue. If there's something he wants to know about me, she thought irritably, why doesn't he just ask? Or is he just too damn polite?

That was it. It had to be. He was so young, he probably hadn't had much experience with pregnant women, so naturally, Mirabella told herself, he would be curious. But it wasn't exactly the kind of thing you could just ask a stranger about—not without being rude—and if there was anything in the world this guy was, besides cute and young, it was polite.

Thinking about the man—boy, really—in those terms, while being careful not to actually *look* at him, Mirabella began to feel gratifyingly mature and maternal. Her confidence growing, she lifted her lashes, found Jimmy Joe's nice brown eyes and smiled.

And just like that, all the maternal feeling she'd managed to conjure up went right out the window, along with most of the maturity and confidence.

Oh, Lord, she thought, what does *this* mean? The particular intensity in that warm-as-mink gaze couldn't possibly be what it appeared to be. Of course not. *Oh, no.*

The truth was, one of the few things in life Mirabella had never learned how to handle was male admiration. Other than in a business context, of course; appreciation of her talent and capabilities from the male-dominated world she worked in was something she not only welcomed, but considered no more than her due. But let the soft glow of admiration in a man's eyes flare into something more personal, more primitive—like lust, say—and her instant reaction was apt to be, "Who, me? What, is he *nuts?*"

Catching a glimpse of something of the sort in Jimmy Joe's eyes, her first reaction was shock: *My God, how can he? I look like a whale!* That was closely followed by dismay: *What can he be thinking of?* After that came disappointment. She concluded sadly that he must be one of those men she'd heard about who actually found pregnant women sexy. Which she considered truly disgusting.

Thoroughly unnerved, compelled almost against her will to be sure, Mirabella braced herself, then stole another look. This one was more covert than the first, slanted upward through her lashes as she dipped her head to meet the laden spoon. But now the heavy-lidded gaze she encountered held nothing more than patient amusement.

"Eat," said Jimmy Joe sternly, tapping the tabletop with a forefinger.

Okay, I was wrong, she thought. *Oh, thank God.* Giddy with relief, she feigned resentment. "I'm eating. I'm *eating,* already. You don't have to watch me, you know."

"Yeah, I do," said Jimmy Joe. But his tone was teasing, and his smile wry.

Relaxing, Mirabella tossed back the wing of hair she'd been hiding behind and smiled across the table in a friendlier way. "Seriously—I don't need a baby-sitter. I know I intruded on whatever it was you were doing—making a phone call, weren't you?—so why don't you just go on, pretend I'm not here. I won't listen, I promise." Go ahead, she thought, pretending she didn't in the least care, call your…girlfriend? Wife?

He scooted back the sleeve of his sweatshirt in order to look at his watch, then shrugged and gave her a regretful little smile. "Ah, I was just tryin' to get ahold of my son, is all. Past his bedtime back there now, though. I'll catch him in the mornin'."

"You have a son?" For some reason, that jolted Mirabella, and she halted her spoon in surprise. It wasn't that he didn't look old enough; how old, after all, did a guy have to be to make a baby? But she'd just finished convincing herself that he was only a boy himself so she could feel comfortable with him, and now fatherhood made that image somewhat difficult to maintain.

"Yeah...his name's J.J." He said it with diffidence. But something about his voice, the smile that flitted across his face like a blinding flash of sunlight he hadn't been able to avoid, caused a sudden soft prickling in the area of Mirabella's heart, rather like a bad case of static electricity.

He's so proud of him, she thought. And hard on the heels of that realization came another, much more unexpected: *I'll bet he's a terrific father.* "Tell me about him," she said mistily. "How old is he?"

Jimmy Joe kind of stretched and rubbed a hand across the back of his neck while he thought about it—which she was almost certain he didn't need to do in order to tell her how old his own child was. What it did was add a touch of winsome modesty to his already considerable charm. "Ah, let's see.... He'd be eight."

"Eight months? Oh, that's a cute age." An image flashed into her mind—a softly lit picture of Jimmy Joe cuddling a baby against his manly pecs. Which produced another of those peculiar stirrings deep in her own chest.

He grinned. "Not so cute. That's eight *years*. They tend to get pretty ornery by that age."

"You're kidding." Mirabella's spoon, halted once more on its downward arc, clattered unnoticed to the table.

290 One Christmas Knight

His head bobbed in an affirming nod. "Be nine next July."

Lacking Jimmy Joe's Southern reserve and good manners, she went ahead and said it: "You don't look old enough."

He didn't exactly seem flattered by that, which, she thought, was in itself a measure of how young he was. Instead he shifted in an embarrassed sort of way and muttered, "Oh, I'm plenty old enough. Pushin' thirty."

Thirty. Mirabella couldn't think what to say. After a moment she picked up her spoon and calmly murmured, "Well, you don't look it." She was thinking, *Eight…almost nine years… My God.* The prickly feeling in her chest slowly dissipated.

"So," she said brightly, "where's your little boy now?" Being from California, she had none of Jimmy Joe's hesitation about asking questions when necessary, whether as a desperate attempt to make conversation, or because there was something she really wanted to know. Since the one she'd just asked fell more into the former category than the latter—just a variation on your basic "Where are you from?" gambit—the answer she got kind of took her by surprise.

"He's with his grandma—that's my mama—back in Georgia."

Mama? Well, after that there wasn't anything she could do but proceed to the next question, this one definitely in the "want to know" category. But as curious as she was, and even though tact had never been her strongest suit, she did try to make it as casual as she could.

"What about your wife?" she began confidently enough, before fumbling into stammering ineptitude. "Er…J.J.'s mother. She doesn't live… I mean, she's not…" She gestured hopefully with her empty spoon.

"His mama's dead," Jimmy Joe quietly answered, apparently taking pity on her.

Mirabella was thoroughly and sincerely aghast. For all her arrogance in business and thorny attitude toward men in general, she had a compassionate and sympathetic heart. It was, although she preferred to keep the fact a secret, a veritable marshmallow, especially where children were concerned. So it was that, forgetting her own discomforts and worries, she instantly and instinctively reached out to the motherless boy she'd never met through the only avenue available to her—his father.

Pushing her soup aside she lightly touched his hand—something she would never have dreamed of doing otherwise—and then, forgetting also the dangers inherent in such contact, let herself touch the deep sadness in his eyes, as well. "Oh, God, I'm so sorry," she whispered.

"It was a while ago. Five years." His voice seemed so matter-of-fact, for a moment Mirabella wondered if she'd mistaken the look of profound regret—as if, she thought, he somehow felt himself responsible. But then he took a breath and went on, and she thought she understood why his feelings might be a little bit complicated. "I didn't hear about it right away. Hadn't seen or heard from her in years—we'd been divorced since J.J. was just a baby. She was livin' in New Orleans at the time."

"How did she die?" Mirabella asked softly, thinking tragic thoughts about cancer and car accidents.

She was unprepared when he hitched a shoulder and angrily and impatiently growled the word, "Drugs."

"Oh, God." Suddenly chilled, she pulled her fingers from his and pressed them against her lips. She hadn't exactly led a sheltered life, having spent a large part of it—the most recent part—in downtown L.A., where the drug culture's human toll called to her daily from wretched alleyways and reached out to her from every street corner. *"Spare some change, lady? For food…?"* But nothing in her own experience had ever brought the reality as close to her as this.

In a low, horrified voice, she said, "You mean…an overdose?"

He shook his head, the brief boil of anger dissipating as quickly as it had risen. "Couldn't say. More'n likely it was a combination of things—malnutrition…pneumonia. Maybe she just plain ol' gave up." He shifted again in that restless way he had, as if talking about himself made him itch. "She'd had trouble with it since she was just a kid. I guess I was a fool, but I thought I could help her. I just didn't know…"

Mirabella watched him take a deep breath, the way people do when they need to make room for pain inside. "For a while I thought I had. Then, after J.J. was born… Well, I guess I wasn't strong enough. Or she wasn't. I had to give up tryin', or take chances with J.J.'s life I wasn't willin' to take. So…" He shrugged and looked away, making it clear that he'd said all he cared to say on the subject.

And Mirabella, having been in that position herself often enough to respect it, didn't pursue it.

"So," she said wonderingly after a moment, "you've raised your son on your own since he was just a baby."

The truth was, she felt humbled and chastened, and was looking at Jimmy Joe in a whole new light. He'd seemed so *young,* an impression that she now thought might have had more to do with his smile—that sweet, sleepy grin that reminded her of a tousled child just waking from a nap—than with smooth cheeks and buns that still looked good in jeans. And of course he *was* young—not even thirty!

But the impression she'd formed of carefree youth and unsullied innocence had vanished the moment she'd allowed herself to look into his eyes and recognized a certain quiet sadness in them. This was no callow, untested boy, she suddenly realized. Jimmy Joe Starr was a full-grown man—one who'd loved and married and struggled and lost; one who'd already known tragedy and failure as well as joy; one who'd unhesitatingly taken on the worries and responsibilities of fatherhood. In short, a man who'd experienced a whole lot more of life in his almost-a-decade-fewer years, than Mirabella had, by far.

A vague, indefinable sadness crept in around her heart—something like the feeling she sometimes got listening to the blues all alone late at night, or certain songs by John Lennon. If only, she thought. *If only…*

"Well, I wouldn't say alone." Jimmy Joe squirmed uncomfortably, trying to be honest about it. He wasn't sure what had just happened, but for all he'd been so disapproving of her, now that she'd handed him his chance to speak his mind on the subject of single parents raising babies, he didn't feel he had the right. The idea had come to him that maybe he ought to get to know her a little better first, find out how she felt about things, what made her tick.

It surprised him some, too, to realize how much he wanted to do that.

"My mama, you know…she helps out a lot. And my sister Jess is there, too. Lately she and her little girl have been livin' with Mama while her husband's gone overseas—he's in the military. Sammi June— let's see, I guess she'd be ten—she's company for J.J." He grinned. "Although if you were to ask him, I don't think he'd exactly agree with that right at the moment. He's feelin' just a mite outnumbered. Too many women."

Mirabella leaned her chin on her hand and smiled. "Yeah? Think how my dad felt—he had three daughters."

"No kiddin'?" Jimmy Joe blinked; one Mirabella was dazzling, but the idea of two more like her was enough to boggle the mind. He couldn't help it—he had to ask. "They all look like you?"

She made a face, and a sound that could only be described as a snort. "We don't even look like the same *species*. If you stand us up in order, we look like the letter *H*—I'm the little short piece in the middle." She sighed, then smiled in the way people do when they want you to think they aren't hurting inside. "My sisters are both tall, slim, blond and gorgeous. I'm the ugly duckling."

Well, he didn't even begin to know what to say to that. Figuring she had to be kidding, or was maybe fishing for compliments, which was a feminine ploy he did *not* admire, he just mumbled, "Come on…"

He felt a lot better when she laughed. "Oh, I don't mean *now*. I mean, well, I didn't exactly turn into a swan, but at least I think I'm…you know, an okay duck. But you should have seen me when I was a kid." Which was just what he'd been thinking, too, but he kept his mouth shut.

"Carroty-red hair," she elaborated, tweaking a rich mahogany strand across her eyes and again making a face at it. "Straight as a stick. Face as round as a Moon Pie and speckled as a turkey egg. And great big glasses. Now I wear contacts," she explained, flashing her luminous eyes at him and batting her thick dark lashes like the heroine of an old movie. "Oh—plus, I was fat. Well…plump. And short. Built like a fireplug. So naturally I was terrible at sports." She smiled the hurtin' smile again. This time Jimmy Joe felt it in his own gut. "All the necessary traits for a guaranteed miserable childhood."

"I find it real hard to believe that," he murmured, stunned.

She shrugged, still trying to make light of it. "I had the nicknames to prove it: Carrot Top…Freckle-Faced Freak…Four Eyes, to mention a few. Oh—and Firecracker. I also had one helluva temper."

And brains, he thought. And courage. And probably a great sense of humor. Hadn't anybody seen it?

"I was very popular, actually," said Mirabella, as if she'd heard his thought. "Lots of girlfriends. And the boys, well…'' She made the snorting sound again. ''I mean, boys just couldn't seem to leave me alone. Hey, who could blame them? I was just so darn much fun to tease. As you can probably imagine.''

Jimmy Joe didn't know what to say. He wanted to tell her he wished he'd known her back then, and that if he had, things would have been different. He wanted to believe that *he* would never have made fun of her, and that he would have busted any kid who dared to do so right in the chops.

He *did* believe it, because for one thing, he knew his mama would have busted his butt if she'd ever found out he'd been teasing someone, and in a town as small as the one he'd grown up in, she would for sure have gotten wind of it sooner or later. But more than that, he believed it because he felt as a certainty in his soul that he would have *liked* that little red-haired girl—freckles, glasses and all. He would have liked her spunk, for one thing. Maybe, in his little boy's heart, he would even have secretly thought she was cute, although he would never have had the gumption to say so. But he knew for sure he would have wanted to be her friend. He just wasn't so sure he would have had the courage.

''Must've been something wrong with those boys,'' he finally mumbled, shaking his head. ''That's all I can say. Must've been stone-blind.''

She kind of half smiled at him, obviously thinking he was just being polite. ''That's very sweet of you. But you weren't there. You didn't see me back then.''

''Well, I wish I had been,'' he said with feeling. It bothered him a lot that she didn't believe him, and he

knew he wasn't going to be able to make her believe
him, no matter what he said. Because he could now
see what he'd missed before—that the uppity tilt of
her chin was there mainly because of the chip on her
shoulder that had been there so long it had grown to
be part of her basic nature. And that made him sad.
More than that—it made him mad.

She was gazing at him now with her chin propped
in her hand and a shiny look in her eyes, still smiling
that little half-smile. "Jimmy Joe," she said softly,
"do you know that when I was in junior high, you
were barely out of diapers?"

"Come on." Shock jerked him against the brown
vinyl seat, his head moving back and forth in pure
disbelief. "No way!" She nodded, and he just kept
shaking his head. He couldn't believe it. He had put
her age at maybe twenty-six, twenty-seven, tops. "No
way you can be that much older than I am," he insisted, feeling vaguely betrayed and insulted without
having the last idea why. "You know, I'm older than
I look— Hey, did I mention I'm almost thirty?"

"You did," Mirabella said, laughing now, but
gently. She thought he looked so endearingly *af-
fronted,* with his hair mused and flopped down across
a thunderous frown, and dark eyes flashing lightning.
Like one of her sister Sommer's kids passionately arguing, "But I *am* big enough! I *am.*"

Passionate. Oops! Her heart gave a little flip-flop of
dismay and of warning. How had the conversation gotten so personal? What was this tension, this glow of
awareness that was all of a sudden zapping back and

forth across the table like a current between two electrodes?

Just then, as if in response to all the fuss and turmoil taking place one floor above, the tiny tenant who'd been peacefully snoozing beneath her ribs suddenly lurched into wakefulness. For Mirabella it was—literally—a kick from reality. The warm tingle of growing attraction vanished like campfire sparks in a cold night sky, and backache and pressure and overwhelming tiredness came to take its place.

To cover the source of her involuntary gasp, she looked at her watch and murmured, "Wow, look at the time—past midnight. I'm really sorry...I should let you go. You could be getting some rest, at least." And then she surprised herself by yawning.

Without a word, Jimmy Joe slid out of the booth, snagging the check on his way. Once upright, he pulled his wallet from a hip pocket, took out a couple of dollar bills and dropped them on the table. Then he reached over and touched Mirabella's arm. "Come on," he said in a husky voice, jerking his head for emphasis. "I'll walk you back out there. Put your coat on."

It was an order, not a subject for discussion, which ordinarily would have ticked her off royally and at the very least triggered immediate and total insurrection. But for some reason all she could summon up was a feeble and completely ineffective, "Oh, no, I insist—"

"Ma'am," said Jimmy Joe softly, leaning over and looking earnestly into her eyes as if she were a small child on the verge of misbehaving in public, "you and

that baby need it more'n I do. Now, we're gonna give
it one more shot, okay?''

Did he *have* to keep calling her *ma'am?*

And with that thought, suddenly Mirabella found
herself in the depths of depression, weary beyond all
reason and once more on the verge of tears—very
much, in fact, like that contrary child. Was that why
she allowed herself to be taken in hand like a helpless
wimp instead of proclaiming her right to be proudly
and independently miserable, as she normally would
have done? She didn't know. But she did know that
there was something indefinably comforting about
having the reins taken out of her hands, for once; and
that instead of resenting the one who'd wrested them
from her, she felt a profound sense of gratitude.

As before, Jimmy Joe waited patiently while she
made yet another potty stop and took her arm as they
crossed the cold, windy parking lot. This time, though,
there was no attempt at polite conversation. Mirabella
just waddled as fast as she could, teeth clenched, hugging herself and shivering in waves, far too miserable
to worry about how silly she looked or what anybody
might think of her. When she saw the royal blue truck
with its bright shiny star looming before her, she felt
an urge to laugh out loud with sheer joy and thanksgiving, like a half-frozen wanderer stumbling onto a
friendly campfire.

''Hold on, just a second...let me get 'er unlocked.''

Jimmy Joe had to let go of her arm while he stepped
up to the door, but he kept looking at her sideways
while he did, just in case she decided to fold up on
him. She reminded him of a poor little bird, standing

there all hunched up, with the wind whipping her hair across her face. Like that nursery rhyme—he remembered it from years and years ago—that started out, "The north wind doth blow,/And we shall have snow,/And what will the poor robin do then,/Poor thing?"

Okay, he was starting to worry about her. He knew what she'd told him—about her baby not being due for another month—but he also knew from personal experience that babies had a way of doing things their own way and in their own good time. Either way, it was a sure bet that all this stress and strain wasn't going to be good for her *or* the baby. What she needed, he thought, was to be safe at home where there were kinfolk to look after her, somebody to make sure she got enough rest, see that she put her feet up, and rub her back for her when she couldn't sleep.

And then he told himself all over again, Jimmy Joe Starr, she's not your concern.

He got the doors unlocked, then went around to help her into the passenger side, trying not to let out most of the warmth in the process. He had to almost lift her up the two high steps and into the cab, and once inside it seemed a natural thing to leave his arms where they were and just go on holding her. She didn't seem to mind, which surprised him some. Then again, he thought, maybe she was so cold she would have been willing to hug a grizzly bear for the heat. Shoot, that coat she was wearing was so thin it wasn't worth a nickel in weather like this. But then, what could he expect from somebody from California?

And again he told himself, Jimmy Joe, she's not your concern.

It was warm and close in the cab, and after a minute or two she pulled away from him, giving herself a little shake, like someone throwing off a blanket. Neither of them said anything, although Jimmy Joe did sort of cough and mutter, "'Scuse me," as he moved past her to turn on the light in the sleeper.

The light wasn't kind to her. He thought about what she'd told him, about how she'd been in junior high when he was still in diapers, and he still didn't believe it. He still thought she was the most beautiful woman he'd ever set eyes on in his life, but now for some reason it made his throat ache to look at her. Seeing her like this, so pale and drawn, and the glassy look of pain in her eyes, all he wanted to do was make her feel better.

And he told himself, Jimmy Joe, she's *still* none of your concern.

But this time from another part of his being a whole new voice answered back, *Yeah, she is.*

Although his overriding urge was to put his arms back around her and hug her some more, he didn't give in to it, limiting himself to a guiding touch on her elbow while he held back the partitioning curtain. "There you go," he said gruffly. "Climb right on up there, now. Pull back the covers if you want to. Be warmer that way."

"Thanks." She sat on the edge of the bed and looked up at him, and he could see she was beginning to feel uneasy about him being there. "I'll be fine."

He knew she was waiting for him to go. He knew he ought to. But that new voice inside him had other ideas, and he wasn't all that surprised to hear himself say, with a firm, no-nonsense shake of his head, "I'm gonna just stay and make sure you're settled before I go."

"You don't have to do that." Her voice sounded breathy. "I'll be all right now. Honest."

Honest... She sounded just like a little girl when she said that, which made him smile. "Ma'am," he said as he put his hands on her shoulders, "I don't intend on goin' anywhere until I know you're resting, y'hear? Just lie right on down there, now." And as gently as he knew how, he eased her over so she was lying on her side with her knees pulled up against her belly and her head resting on her folded-up arm. "That's the way. There you go. How's that?"

She flashed him one bright, angry look that cheered him considerably, then closed her eyes without answering. He could tell by the way she was breathing through her nose—in slow, deep breaths—that she was hurting.

It came to him suddenly, gleaned from memories of suffering through two pregnancies with J.J.'s mama, what her problem might be. "Your back achin'?" he asked, sitting beside her on the very edge of the bed. She nodded, just too plain miserable to talk. "Yeah..." he said softly. "That's what I thought."

He put his hand on her shoulder, overcoming a powerful urge to reach beyond it, just to smooth the hair back from her face. With that tenderness simmering inside him, he said, "Ma'am, why don't you turn over on your other side? What I'm gon' do is rub your back a little. Make you feel a whole lot better, help you relax. Okay? Come on, now.... Roll on over."

Instead of doing what he'd told her, she suddenly squinched up her face without opening her eyes, as if she'd felt a sharp pain, and said in a sulky voice, "Do you *have* to keep calling me *ma'am?*"

That made him grin, but her eyes were closed so he didn't have to worry about her seeing it, and thanks to all those phone conversations with J.J. he knew how to keep it from showing up in his voice. "Sorry about that," he said, solemn as a judge. "I don't mean anythin' personal by it. It's just a habit—shoot, it's probably in my genes."

"Well, it makes me feel really *old.*"

Now he did chuckle, resisting again the urge to touch her face, just to run his fingertips lightly across the ivory curve of her forehead, which, as far as he could see, in spite of her concern, was completely unmarred by any wrinkles. "You have to understand, it's got nothin' to do with how old you are, just the fact that you're female."

Opening her eyes about halfway, she studied him from under her lashes. "You call your mom ma'am?"

"Oh, you bet."

"Uh-hmm. Your sister?"

"Well, now…"

"Girlfriend?"

He wanted to laugh, now that he thought he knew where she was headed. "No, don't believe I would—if I had one."

She chewed on that for a moment or two, then said slowly, "The waitress in there—you called her ma'am. Would you have done that if she was nineteen?"

"Sure would. Yes, ma'am."

"So…it's a matter of respect." She said it like, "Aha!"

"That's right." But he was beginning to feel just a little uneasy, wondering if he knew after all what she was getting at.

"So…you don't respect your sister or your girlfriend?"

Well, she had him there. He rubbed the back of his neck while he thought about it, then said, "It's kind of hard to explain—especially since I don't believe I was ever called upon to try to before. You grow up in the South, it's just somethin' you take for granted, like grits for breakfast. But I guess what it is, it's respect. But it's more like—it's formal, you know? You don't use it when it's personal, like with your friends, or your close kin—" he paused to smile before he said it "—unless they're older."

"Let me get this straight." A little pleat of concentration puckered the skin between her eyebrows, but her voice had grown drowsy and he could see that the warmth in the truck, the lateness of the hour and her tiredness were beginning to have their way with her. "You can't stop calling me ma'am because you don't know me well enough."

"Yeah, I guess that'd be about right."

"But you know me well enough to rub my back?"

So that was it. Again that tenderness wafted through him like a warm breeze over damp skin, stirring shivers of laughter that felt like goose bumps inside. Keeping it soft so as not to rile her he murmured, "Okay, Marybell, I'll make you a deal—you quit arguin' and roll on over there, and I'll quit callin' you ma'am. How's that? Deal?''

"Deal," she whispered.

It was only after he'd helped her through the ponderous process of rolling over and she was once more settled on her side, this time facing away from him, that a tiny echo in her head said incredulously, *Marybell?*

But then she felt the warm weight of his hand on her lower back, on the exact spot that ached so awfully, and a firm, circling pressure that felt so wonderful she forgot everything else; so wonderful she almost wept with the sheer relief it brought her.

"Oh…God," she groaned, "how did you know?"

Jimmy Joe's voice was soft and oddly muffled, as if she were hearing him through a layer of fur. "Oh, I've done this for J.J.'s mama a time or two. It's been awhile, but I guess you don't forget how."

"Lucky," Mirabella muttered with a sigh. "How'd I get through eight months without you?"

A chuckle undulated along her auditory nerves like ripples in black velvet.

Chapter 5

"You got one of those new anteaters? Man,
that is one ugly truck."
"Bet you wish you had one as ugly."
I-40—New Mexico

Mirabella was hearing voices. Mostly men's voices, but now and then a woman's, too—strange voices, mumbly and scratchy at the same time, sometimes far away and crackly, other times loud and clear, as if whoever it was talking was standing right next to her. At first she ignored them, hearing but not really registering the sounds, the way you do when you fall asleep with the TV or radio on. Gradually, though, words began to filter into her consciousness, then string together in a way that made some kind of sense.

"East a' Tucumcari."

"Couple a' county mounties come through here

*'while ago with their lights on. Don' know where they
was goin', but they was hurryin'.''*

"Dry and dusty to the Texas line."

*"They gonna open 'er up sometime 'fore Christmas,
or what?"*

*"Uh...they're sayin' maybe noon, that's what I
heard."*

*"One helluva mess. Got more'n a hunnerd acci-
dents 'tween here and Amarillo. Got rigs off to the
side, four-wheelers ever'where...."*

"Where'n hell they keepin' the snowplows?"

*"Ah, hell, Texas don't waste snowplows on the Pan-
handle...."*

Along with a return of familiar discomforts, full
awareness brought the realization that, yes, she was in
a bed in an honest-to-God truck, a huge blue eighteen-
wheeler belonging to one Jimmy Joe Starr, a genuine
Georgia redneck who happened to have healing hands
and dimples and a smile like an angel's, assuming the
angel spoke with a Southern accent and looked like a
young Robert Redford.

And what she was listening to wasn't a TV, but a
CB radio. Which meant, since she hadn't heard a peep
out of it last night, that Jimmy Joe must have turned
it on. And since she couldn't imagine he would turn
it on without a reason, that meant he must be listening
to it. Out there, right now. He was here in the truck
with her, just beyond the curtain.

That thought zapped through her with a tingle that
must have been adrenaline, because she felt the way
you do when you've been jolted awake too suddenly—
weak and trembly, heart beating way too fast. She was

lying there blinking, thinking about that, trying to make sense of it and feeling scared and disoriented, when the reason for all her inner turmoil stuck his hand through the crack at the edge of the curtain and knocked on the side of the sleeper.

"Hey," he called softly, "you awake in there?"

"Yeah, I'm up," she called back in a husky, too-eager voice that betrayed that for the lie it was, struggling to get her feet around so she could at least make a stab at sitting up.

"Mornin'." The curtain was pulled back and Jimmy Joe's face appeared like a ray of sunshine. "How you doin'?"

"Okay," she responded airlessly; in her present position even sarcasm was beyond her.

He drew a small plastic bottle from a pocket in the sleeveless, down-filled nylon vest he was wearing over his Georgia Bulldogs sweatshirt and held it out to her. "Thought you could do with an eye-opener. Get your blood sugar pumpin'." He was wearing his heart-melting smile, which Mirabella, not being a morning person even at the best of times, was in no mood to appreciate.

"I don't know where I'd put it," she muttered, eyeing the orange juice with revulsion. She felt like a dead whale that had lain out in the sun too long—in other words just about ready to explode. Plus she'd slept with her contacts in, so her eyes felt like two tennis balls, and her tongue was so furry she knew she must have a horrendous case of morning breath. The last thing she wanted was a sexy, adorable guy anywhere within ten yards of her, so she was not thrilled when

Jimmy Joe plunked himself down beside her, completely ignoring warning signs that were usually sufficient to send close family members diving for the nearest cover.

"Just a sip," he said, as if he were addressing a three-year-old. "Then I'll walk you in so you can wash up, if you want. Come on, now—upsy-daisy."

How does he do it? she wondered as, groaning, she allowed him to hoist her upright. *Why do I let him do it—treat me like a contrary child, or worse, a helpless female?* In her former life she would have flayed alive any man, no matter how attractive and charming, who'd dared to try such tactics with her. She'd spent most of her life perfecting the defenses and signals to ensure that those who did try were few and far between. So what was it about this man?

She sipped orange juice on autopilot while her analytical mind chewed on that anomaly. She knew it couldn't just be his kind eyes and sleepy little-boy smile; she'd never been vulnerable to that sort of thing, and in fact usually found extremely handsome men to be pretty much of a turnoff. More likely, she thought, it had something to do with him being way too young for her, and therefore no threat to her sexually—rather like a lioness's tolerance of the immature males in her pride. That, combined with her own vulnerability in her present condition, and the uniqueness of the circumstances.

Yes, she thought, satisfied with her conclusions. That would explain it.

It did cross her mind that she just might have come up against a man with a will equal to her own, but she rejected that idea. As far as Mirabella was concerned, such a man did not exist.

How does she do it? Jimmy Joe wondered, gazing at her as she drank and then licked the juice glaze from her lips. *How can she look so doggone beautiful after the night she had?*

He'd sat and watched her long after she'd fallen asleep literally under his hands, finally free to marvel all he wanted to at the old-Burgundy shine of her hair, the delicacy of her bones, the way her skin seemed to glow from inside like his mama's good china when you held it up to the light. Free to touch, with a mettlesome finger and breathing temporarily forgotten, one strand of hair that lay along the curve of her jaw and pooled in the hollow of her neck, and daringly lift and stroke it behind the fragile sculpture of her ear.

She'd stirred, then, so that his fingers had brushed against her warm cheek and intersected the flow of her breath as it sighed from between her barely parted lips, and he'd been shocked by the stirring of response in his own body.

He'd squelched it immediately. It had seemed wrong to him; a violation not only of her trust in him, but of some indefinable quality—he wasn't sure what it was—something about the way she looked with one childlike hand pillowing her cheek and the other resting with maternal protectiveness on the side of her swollen belly. *Innocence?* How could that be? Or... *purity?* And yet, he thought he'd never in his life seen anyone so overwhelmingly, breathtakingly *female*.

Which was confusing, because while part of him

had been ashamed of his body's jolting acknowledgment of that femininity, something else in
him had found it downright exhilarating.

He'd pulled the comforter over her and left her then,
but hadn't gone back to the truck-stop café, although
he knew he would have been more comfortable there.
Instead, unable to bring himself to leave her, he'd
turned off the light in the sleeper and drawn the curtain
and settled into the passenger-side seat with a book
and a pillow. He'd made pretty good headway in the
new Tony Hillerman mystery he'd picked up in L.A.,
even dozed some off and on before full daylight and
the comings and goings of his neighbors had roused
him.

On a quick trip into the truck stop for a cup of
coffee and to use the john he'd heard rumblings about
the road opening up, so he'd made the coffee to go,
picked up the bottle of orange juice for Mirabella and
hurried back to his truck to see what he could find out
from the CB. He'd expected she would wake up, with
all the noise from the radio and slamming doors and
all, but she hadn't, and he'd listened for a good half
hour before he was convinced the news coming out of
Tucumcari was more than just wishful rumors, and he
knew it was time he was going have to wake her.
Wake her, say goodbye and send her on her way.

Now, sitting beside her, watching her drink the juice
he'd brought, he felt the same protective feelings welling up inside him that had kept him watching over her
all night. Last night those feelings had made a certain
sense to him—enough so that he hadn't thought to

question them, anyway. This morning, though, they were doggone confusing.

"No more," she said, shoving the juice bottle blindly in his direction. "I really have to go—*now.*" Her eyes had lost their unfocused, waking-up look and now held a bright glaze of distress.

"Okay, easy now, I'm gonna get you there," he said soothingly, reaching past her to set the bottle on the recessed shelf at the head of the bed. "What'd you do with your shoes?"

"I don't know. I kicked them off, I think."

He found them in the folds of the comforter and knelt to help her into them, noticing that they went on easily enough. He remembered that swollen feet at this stage of the game were not a good thing, so that eased his mind in one small way.

"There you go," he grunted as he got to his feet. "What else d'you need? Your pocketbook?" She was already wrestling with the sleeves of her coat. He helped her with that, found her purse and hooked the strap over his shoulder, then bent to get an arm around her and hoist her to her feet.

"It's okay, I can make it," she protested. "You don't have to help me." To Jimmy Joe her breathlessness sounded not so much cranky as desperate. Hearing it, he did as she asked and let go of her, and after hovering anxiously for a moment, went to open the door for her instead.

"I heard the CB," she said as she eased herself between the seats, moving like a rig backing into a loading bay. "Did I hear right? Did they say the road's going to be…opening soon?"

She'd paused, apparently to catch her breath, so he pulled the door closed again to save the heat. "That's what they're sayin'. 'Bout noon, looks like."

"What time is it now?"

"Goin' on eleven. Plenty a' time, if you want to wash up…have some breakfast." He pushed the door open, stepped onto the running board and held out his hand to help her down.

But she'd spotted his pillow and paperback on the seat; he could see her looking at them with that little pleat of frown wrinkles between her eyes as she squeezed by. She transferred the frown to him as she took the hand he'd offered and asked, not with gentle concern but in a sharp, accusing tone, "Did you get any sleep?"

Jimmy Joe couldn't help but grin, she sounded so much like his mama. "I dozed some," he said, easing her down to the ground. "Mostly I just read." Then he had to laugh; the way she glared at him, you would have thought he'd confessed to spending the night in a honky-tonk bar. "It's *okay*. Hey, I like to read."

"You do?" For some reason that seemed to surprise her. Then she shook herself—or maybe it was a shiver as the cold wind hit her—and said, "Oh, that's right— I saw your books."

They'd turned and started slowly walking together toward the truck-stop café, and since she seemed to have forgotten he still had her hand, he kept it and tucked it into the bend of his elbow and covered it with his to keep it warm. Looking down at her, he could see that her nose was turning pink and her face had a pinched look to it, and he knew she would go faster if there was any way in the world she could. That high-plateau wind cut like a razor—you could smell the snow in it. To keep her mind off it he picked up the thread of the conversation they'd been having about books, asking her in a polite way if she liked to read.

Her shoulder nudged against him as she shrugged. "I've never been much of a reader. It's not that I don't *like* to read—it just seems like I always have too many other things to do."

"Yeah? What do you do when you want to just... you know, relax?"

"Relax?" She made it sound like a word she'd never heard before. Glancing down at her, he saw that she was frowning again, thinking about it.

He didn't pursue it, just shook his head and said, "I guess I can't imagine not readin'. Probably because my mama used to read to me, from the time I was too little to remember. She read to all of us kids. You know...startin' with those little picture books with animals in 'em, then Mother Goose and Dr. Seuss, all the way through the Little House books and *Tom Sawyer* and *Treasure Island*. Seems like there never was a time we didn't have a book goin'."

The wind caught her hair suddenly, and unfurled it like bright red party streamers around her face. She grabbed at it, gathered it in one hand and held it while she looked up at him, squinted an eye shut and asked, "How many of you were there? You mentioned your sister...."

"Three sisters, three brothers."

She gasped. "Seven! My God, how did she find the time?"

"I don't know," said Jimmy Joe with a shrug. "She just did."

For a few moments she didn't say anything, just walked along with her head down, her hair caught up in her hand. He felt her take a deep breath. "My mom read to my sisters and me, too. I don't know why it didn't take with me." She let go of her hair then, and shook her head as if saying to the wind, *Go on, have your way with it, I don't care!* He saw her face light up with some intense emotion he didn't know the name of—something fierce and joyful and proud—and she said, "I'm going to read to my baby though. I've been buying books, all sorts of books. Mother Goose and Dr. Seuss and those little picture books with animals in them." And suddenly she laughed.

Jimmy Joe wondered if it was the first time he'd ever heard her laugh. He knew it was the first time he'd heard her laugh that way—a sound as merry and as good for the heart as sleigh bells on Christmas morning.

It also occurred to him that it was the first time he'd heard her talk about her baby like that—as if it was a real live person and not some kind of condition. He wanted to hear more, ask her some questions, like whether she wanted a boy or a girl, and what she planned to name it, and whether the kid's father was going to be around to help her walk the floor at two in the morning. But they'd reached the truck stop's double entrance, and there was nothing for him to do but hold the doors for her, first the outer, then the inner, and he had to really hop to it to get there before she did. And he was sorry.

Inside, she left him with a distracted wave and made a beeline for the bathroom. He watched her go, then went to see if he could find them a table in the café. As it turned out, he didn't have any trouble; with the word out about the road opening, the drivers' section was emptying out fast. There was a stirring in the air, a buzz of energy like the revving of diesel engines, all those drivers itching to be on the road again—most of them, like him, heading home. He felt it too, the restlessness, the building up of energy inside him, the pull of loved ones waiting and watching for him. But for him there was something else, too; kind of an uneasiness, as if he was leaving something unfinished, something undone. Something important.

While he waited for Mirabella to come out of the bathroom, he ordered coffee—regular for himself, decaf for her—then thought about calling J.J. He still had hopes of making it home by late Christmas Day if he drove straight through without stopping. But he didn't want to get the boy's hopes up until he was safely through the Panhandle, so he didn't make the call.

He was scowling at the menu when Mirabella joined him. It was starting to be a habit, he thought, the way she would show up at his elbow, taking possession of the space around him so that suddenly even the air he breathed seemed filled with her—her presence, her scent, her energy.

She looked different this morning. She'd scrubbed her face and pulled her hair back and fastened it on top with some kind of clip in a way that made her seem even younger than she had before. Not the old-fashioned movie star now; more like a high-school cheerleader. But it was more than that. It seemed to him there was a new kind of *quietness* about her....

But it wasn't until she was easing into the booth across from him that he finally put his finger on what was different. It was her arrogance, that uppity tilt to her chin that was missing. And that worried him.

The first thing she said to him was, "How come you're not on the phone? Aren't you going to call your son and let him know you're on your way?"

Which reassured him some, being the sort of bossiness that he'd already come to understand was just her basic nature. So he smiled and said, "Naw, I'll wait a bit. Like to make it through Texas, first. Then I'll know I've got a shot at gettin' home by Christmas."

She nodded and looked quickly down at her menu, but not before he caught a glimpse of shadows in her eyes. That and the tiny quiver of her mouth made him ask, even though it wasn't any of his business, "What about you? You got folks waitin' on you?" *Like a husband, maybe?* That would explain it, he thought, if she was tryin' so hard to get to him, to be with him for the holidays. He could almost understand that.

"My mom," she said, still looking down at the menu. She swallowed and added, "And my dad," in a whisper he could barely hear.

Then he wondered why talking about her daddy made her choke up so, but poking into people's business, getting them to spill their personal secrets wasn't something he'd had much experience in or felt comfortable doing. So all he said was, "They're in Pensacola, you said?"

She glanced up at him and cleared her throat, and he could tell she was back on steadier ground. "Yes— Pensacola Beach, actually."

"Oh, man." Feeling for her, he shook his head, picked up his coffee and took a cautious sip. "That's more 'n a thousand miles. You're not gonna make that by Christmas."

She looked at him and he could see the fury in her eyes, wanting to argue with him, not ready to accept it yet. Funny, how clear the workings of her mind were becoming to him, like words and pictures printed on the pages of a book, because somehow, as if he'd known her all his life, he knew what a careful planner she was and how she hated it when things didn't work out her way.

"I thought…if I can just get through Texas—"

Jimmy Joe put his coffee mug down and reached for her hands. He took them and held them gently, making his voice gentle, too, saving all his steel for his eyes the way he did when he needed to get something straight with J.J. once and for all, and no room for dispute. "Don't you even try it. You take it easy, now, y'hear? Your mama and daddy, they'll understand. You know they'd rather have you late a thousand times than have any harm come to you or that baby."

Oh, Lord, he could feel her fighting it. Feel it in the tension in those small-boned hands, see it in the anger burning dark in her eyes. How she did hate to give in!

But then he saw the fire in her eyes cool behind a glaze of tears he knew she would die rather than shed, and she took a breath with a quiver in it and let it out along with the words, "I know."

He waited a moment more before he released her hands. As soon as he let them go she straightened and used them to smooth invisible strands of hair away from her face, which he knew was just a way for her to get her poise back. It seemed to work, because her voice was steady when she went on, "I really wanted to spend this Christmas with my dad. He just had a heart attack—"

"Oh, Lord," said Jimmy Joe. "I am sorry." He was thinking of his own daddy, dead long before his time, and the second heart attack that had been his last. It was not an uncommon way for a man raised on Southern cooking to go.

"He's going to be okay," said Mirabella firmly. "But he can't travel, obviously. My mom was going to come and stay with me until after the baby…but she can't leave my dad, so that's why I thought I'd go there instead. But I couldn't get a flight on such short notice, so then I figured I'd just drive. Plenty of time, right? Or so I thought. And now…here we are." She held out her hands, gamely smiling. "Looks like it'll just be me and Junior this Christmas."

Jimmy Joe laughed, although his heart was hurting for her. "Hey, you know, this kinda reminds me of a movie I saw once—funny as the dickens—about this guy tryin' to get home for…Thanksgiving, I b'lieve it was." He kept on talking—glib as a traveling preacher, telling her about all the crazy things that happened to the poor guy in the movie, wanting only to make her feel better somehow—until the waitress came to take their order.

While they waited for the food to arrive they tried talking about movies some more, but it was hard to find enough common ground to base a good discussion on. Jimmy Joe liked action movies and slapstick comedies, the kind Mirabella called "brainless." She went for the type of films critics cooed over and nobody else had even heard of, until somebody in one of them got nominated for an Academy Award. That, and movies based on Shakespeare's plays and Jane Austen's novels, which always put Jimmy Joe straight to sleep. Then they found out they'd both seen every Walt Disney film ever made, and got into an argument about which was the greatest cartoon feature of all time that lasted all the way through breakfast.

The waitress came and refilled their coffee cups, slapped down the check and hurried away with a distracted, "You folks have a safe trip, now." Silence fell. Jimmy Joe reached for the check, but Mirabella got there first.

"Let me buy you breakfast," she said, although she didn't sound nearly as bossy as he'd grown accustomed to. "It's the least I can do, after all you've done for me." She watched him with quiet, unreadable eyes.

Every Southern-bred instinct in him wanted to refuse, but he could see it was important to her, so even though it caused him embarrassment to do it he gave in and let her take the check. He sipped his coffee in uncomfortable silence while he watched her fish in her pocketbook for her wallet, then haul out a bottle of Tylenol and shake a couple into her hand. She swallowed them down without looking at him, but she didn't have to, or say a word, either, for him to know she was hurting again. He was starting to recognize the signs.

She opened up her wallet and took out a couple of dollar bills and tucked them neatly under her coffee cup, then gave him a bright look and said, "Ready?"

Jimmy Joe said, "Let's roll," and scooted out of the booth ahead of her so he would be ready to give her a hand—if she would let him. He had a funny feeling in his chest as if he'd gotten a wad of food stuck way down deep in his esophagus, right under his breastbone. It was the kind of lump he got when J.J. was sick and he had to leave him anyway; the same lump that had been there when he'd left the hospital after visiting his daddy for the last time. He told himself the lady really wasn't any of his business, that she was just a passing stranger he'd happened to lend a helping hand to, and now it was time to go his way and let her go hers.

He was a little surprised when she took the hand he offered her and let him help her out of the booth. She let go of it in a hurry, though, and tugged the silky sweater down over her belly and fooled with her hair and her pocketbook in nervous little gestures as she said in a voice as bright and false as her smile, "Well, I guess this is goodbye."

He shook his head. "I want to see you to your car."

"I, uh, have to make a stop first."

"That's okay, I'll wait."

He tried to avoid it, but she pressed some money into his hand and went off to the rest room one more time, leaving him no choice but to wait in line at the cash register. In a way, though, he was glad to have something to do so he wouldn't have to watch her walk away from him, moving as if every bone in her body hurt.

When she came out he was waiting for her near the main entrance. He gave her her change, then held her pocketbook for her while he helped her on with her coat. He thought how natural it was beginning to feel to help her like that, and how she seemed to be getting used to having him do it.

They made the slow walk to her car without saying anything. It was still cold, with a slate-gray overcast that looked like snow. But the wind smelled of fuel and the air vibrated not with thunder but with the indescribable roar of several hundred big diesel engines growling through their gears as they headed out onto the highway like giant beasts joining a vast migration. Hearing that sound, seeing the rigs moving slowly past him, Jimmy Joe could feel his heart begin to beat faster.

She unlocked her car with a little gadget on her key chain that chirped like a cricket when she pressed on it. He reached past her and opened the door for her and then stood so he was shielding her as well as he could from the wind while she eased in under the wheel, stuck the key in the ignition and fired it up. All this, while he was being careful not to touch her and she was being just as careful not to look at him, and both of them were wondering who was going to be the first to say it.

"Well," she said, her voice sounding dry and breathless, "at least it started, huh?" She looked up at him then, with dark, fierce eyes, almost as if she was angry with him about something. Funny how he knew that wasn't it at all.

"You got enough gas?" he asked, dragging it out even though he was restless and anxious to be on his way.

She glanced at her gauge. "Half a tank. I thought I'd fill up in Amarillo."

He nodded and straightened, looking out across the roof of her car. "Well, then. Guess you're all set to go." He took a deep breath and ducked back down like somebody bobbing for apples in a barrel of water. "You take care now, y'hear? Drive safely." His voice sounded garbled to him, as if maybe it *was* coming from under water.

"I will." She sounded impatient, a little annoyed with him for doubting her. Then she gripped the wheel with both hands, and as if it was the hardest thing she'd ever done, looked up at him and croaked, "Ah...thanks. For everything. For...you know, letting me use your sleeper, and...everything. It was really nice of you."

"No problem." He cleared his throat. "My pleasure..." And he could tell by the ghost of a smile that quivered the corner of her mouth that she knew how close he'd come to saying "ma'am."

She squinted up at him, still thinking about smiling

but not quite doing it. "I hope you make it home to your little boy in time for Christmas."

"Yeah," said Jimmy Joe. "Me, too. And I hope your daddy gets to feelin' better real soon."

She laughed on a shaky breath. "Yeah, me, too." Then, reaching out for the door handle, she said, "Well...okay. Thanks. Again. See ya. Oh—and Merry Christmas."

"Yeah, you have a Merry Christmas, too." After that there wasn't anything to do but stand back out of the way and let her shut the door. He hung around while she fiddled with the radio and heater controls, then gave him a wave through the window to show him she was on her way. He waved back and watched her head out across the parking lot toward the four-wheeler exit and the highway beyond.

It was when he'd turned to walk back to his truck that it occurred to him that after all that, neither one of them had said it. Neither of them had said goodbye.

Chapter 6

"I got me four big boxes a' tapes here, and there's not a one of 'em I feel like listenin' to. I'm just runnin' through the radio, lookin' for a station."
I-40—New Mexico

One radio station on the whole dial, and it had to be playing Christmas music. Then Mirabella remembered it was the day before Christmas—Christmas Eve. What else would they be playing?

She just didn't want to believe it was Christmas Eve. How could it be? It didn't *feel* like Christmas Eve. On the day before Christmas people were supposed to be snugged up in their houses frantically wrapping presents and stuffing themselves with popcorn and eggnog, or at the very least fighting their way through the mall for some forgotten-till-the-last-minute gift or other, half-deafened by the din of the crowds, canned Christmas carols on the loudspeakers, and those Salvation Army Santas jingling away in every doorway. Who had ever heard of a Christmas Eve spent slogging across a cold, lonely desert along with a lot of other poor hapless pilgrims....?

A shiver went skittering down her spine. Okay, she thought, this is just a *little* weird.

But there *was* something almost biblical about the vastness of the landscape, where the Rockies melted gradually into juniper-studded plateaus and twisting arroyos before disappearing completely in the flat, treeless prairie. Out here the horizons seemed to stretch forever and the leaden sky came down to touch them, and somewhere out there in the deep lavender haze where they met she could almost imagine a pyramid or two, and yes, perhaps even a caravan of camels plodding slowly eastward.

'''We three kings of Orient are;/Bearing gifts we traverse afar,''' Mirabella sang lustily in her off-key baritone, attempting with sheer volume to dispel the loneliness and depression that was slowly but surely creeping in around her heart. '''Field and fountain, moor and mou-oun-tain,/Following yonder star./*OO*, star of wonder, star...''' *Starr...Jimmy Joe.* Her voice fizzled into silence just as the music critic in her belly began expressing his outrage.

"Sorry, sweetheart," she said with a soft and rueful laugh, rubbing at the mushrooming bulge just below the right side of her rib cage. "Bad idea, I know. Wish I'd brought along some James Galway or Pavarotti tapes, but I didn't think about it. So I guess the best I can do is..." She pushed a button and the radio's automatic tuner settled on the only available station, which blared forth a lush and throaty, "Blu-blu-blue Chriss-mas." She settled back in her seat and sighed. "Elvis."

Although really, she told herself, things could be a lot worse. After all the fuss, the road was "dry and dusty," as she'd heard the truckers on Jimmy Joe's CB radio call it, with not so much as a flake of snow or a smidgen of ice that she could see. Traffic was heavy but moving right along, and she was sure that whatever problems they'd been having through Texas—well, they must have gotten them cleared up or they wouldn't have opened the road, would they? Of course not. Plus, she was feeling much better after Jimmy Joe's back rub and a good night's rest, and the Tylenol seemed to be helping because her back didn't ache nearly as much.

At this rate, she told herself optimistically, she would be in Amarillo in three hours, and maybe, just maybe, she could find a flight going...anywhere. Somewhere *south*. She wouldn't even have to tell them she was pregnant—if she kept her coat on maybe they would just think she was fat. She would fly standby, if she had to. Then, if she could get to some-place even *close* to Pensacola, she could rent a car, and... *Yes,* she could still do it, by God. She could still get there on Christmas Day. And she *would*.

When Mirabella put her mind to something, she didn't give up easily.

Jimmy Joe was glad to be back on the road. It felt good, even knowing what he was heading into, watching those miles roll by, knowing every mile marker he passed put him that much closer to J.J. and home.

Home. He thought about that, focusing his mind on what it felt like to be there, walking himself one by one through the rooms of the big old white frame, two-story house he'd grown up in. Remembering what it smelled like—the smell of canning tomatoes in his mama's kitchen in the summertime, the wet-dog odor of the back porch when it rained, the sweet, warm fragrance of honeysuckle. He thought of the pantry door where his growth and that of all his brothers and sisters had been charted from the time they were big enough to stand straight and tall, and rooms filled with shabby furniture and cluttered with books and magazines and children's artwork in crayon and poster paints. He thought of the old tree house, and the silk spider that had spun her web in its doorway.

And he thought about his own house—a real nice house about a mile down the road, solidly built of red brick, with a big front porch and white trim and a nice big sunny kitchen, and great old oaks and pine trees for shade. He'd done a pretty good job with it, too; made it nice and homey for J.J., filling up the rooms with books and pictures and things he'd brought back from his trips, interesting things from all over the country. Navajo rugs and Acoma pottery, and a big old bed he'd found up in the Blue Ridge Mountains, hand-carved from four-hundred-year-old walnut trees.

He was happy there, and so was J.J. And when he had to leave, well, there was the old place and a grand-mama right down the road, and you couldn't ask for better than that. No, sir.

He said to himself, Jimmy Joe Starr, you're a lucky man. Couldn't ask for more than you've got, and that's a fact.

When it came to families, he'd always thought it was too bad everybody couldn't have one like his. They weren't perfect, nowhere near it, with his daddy dying so young; and his mama could be tough as nails sometimes. And there was his sister Joy Lynn's two divorces, which was something of a family record, and brother Roy who liked his beer a little bit too much, and his youngest brother Calvin who'd dropped out of high school and never had learned how to work a lick or hold on to a job.

But there was a lot of love in the family in spite of nobody being perfect. And when the holidays rolled around, or somebody's birthday, and the whole bunch got together—and there would be babies crying and kids running underfoot, and the womenfolk gathered in the kitchen all talking at once, and the men outside arguing politics or throwing a ball around if the weather was good, and the older kids playing hide-and-seek or hunting turtles in the woods behind the house—then he knew how good he had it.

Then he knew—oh, how he knew—that he was lonely.

Much as he hated to admit it, it was the truth. No matter how much he loved his kid, or how great his mama was, or how much he enjoyed his brothers' and sisters' company, there were times when it wasn't enough. Times when he would come in off the road and walk into his house and hear his footsteps echo in a kitchen that smelled of nothing but "empty," and his big old hand-carved bed seemed cold, and way too roomy for one person. Times he would even feel envious watching his brothers and sisters bicker and squabble with their mates. It had been a long time since he'd had anybody to argue with over breakfast about something as foolish as Walt Disney movies.

I'm going to read to my baby....

Suddenly, clear as a bell, he could hear Mirabella saying that, hear the fierceness in her voice, the joy in her laughter. He could see her face, too, the sparkle in her gray eyes, her nose turning pink, and the wind in her hair....

His heart went *bump* against his ribs. He muttered, "Christmas," under his breath and reached over and turned on the radio to see if he could find some music to take his mind off things he had no business thinking about.

He was lucky. On the only clear station in that part of New Mexico he caught Brenda Lee just finishing up "Rockin' Around the Christmas Tree," and right after that Elvis started in with "Blue Christmas." He left it there and turned the volume up loud so he wouldn't have to listen to all the talk coming in on the CB about the mess waiting for him up ahead in Texas.

For one of the few—the very few—times in her life, Mirabella was feeling uncertain; she would never admit to being afraid. But as she clung to the wheel of her Lexus and doggedly followed the taillights of the big rig in front of her, she felt a chill that had nothing to do with the snow blowing past her windshield.

Everything had been fine until about ten miles into Texas, when all of a sudden both lanes of traffic on the interstate had slowed to a crawl. A few miles farther on she'd come to know why. Snow—not from the threatening black clouds overhead, but blown by the wind across that flat, unbroken plain—had reduced visibility to nearly zero. Packed down by the tires of hundreds of eighteen-wheelers, it had turned the road surface into a narrow track of bumpy, rutted ice. The double line of trucks became one, an endless train creeping fitfully eastward at a pace slower than a man could walk. With very good reason. If Mirabella needed more dramatic evidence of the need for caution, there were the dozens of cars stuck in roadside drifts and even a few big rigs jackknifed on the median to remind her.

Oh, God, she thought as she crept past yet another disabled vehicle, what if I...

No. Ice trickled down her spine, and she shivered. No, she wouldn't even think of such a possibility. It wouldn't happen to her; she wouldn't let it. She wasn't an idiot; she knew enough not to make stupid mistakes. She knew the rules: *Don't brake or accelerate suddenly. Always turn* into *a skid.* She would be okay if she kept her head. She wouldn't panic. Of course not—Mirabella never panicked.

Oh, but how long could this go on? It was only fifty miles to Amarillo, but at this rate, that would take hours. *Ten hours.* It would be dark in three. And—oh, God, she had to go to the bathroom *now.* How was she ever going to be able to wait that long?

She knew the answer, of course. She would simply

have to. Because there was absolutely no way she could stop, even if there had been a place to do so in that vast, unending whiteness.

To make matters worse, the Tylenol she'd taken this morning at breakfast had worn off, and now she couldn't even reach for her purse to get some more. She didn't dare take a hand from the wheel, not for an instant. But, oh, how her back hurt. The pressure was worse than ever, too. She felt as if she were being squeezed in a giant vise.

In fact, Mirabella was absolutely certain she had never been so miserable in her life, and that things couldn't get much worse than they were right now.

A few minutes later she knew how wrong she was.

Suddenly there was a soft *pop,* and she felt a flood of warmth and wetness, a simultaneous release of pressure. She gasped. No—she felt as if the air were being sucked from her lungs.

For the first time in her life her mind went completely blank, as if someone had pushed a button and instantly wiped her data banks clean of every rational thought and all common sense. In short, she panicked.

And then she hit the brakes.

The next thing she knew she was clinging uselessly to the steering wheel while the world outside her windows passed by in a dizzying white blur. There were horrifying lurches and teeth-jarring crunches and explosive popping sounds and things flying at her from all sides. *Air bags!* Thank God—she was engulfed—all but smothered—in air bags. Then there was stillness...and silence, except for a soft whimpering, which Mirabella realized with utter horror was coming from her.

She was no longer uncertain. Nor was she afraid. Now she was positively terrified.

She knew what had happened. The impossible. The unthinkable. *Her water had broken.* And it had shocked her so badly she'd done just what she knew she shouldn't have, which was tromp on the brake, and as a result her car had skidded off the icy road and was now stuck in a snowbank, like those of all the other poor souls she'd passed and pitied. And now she and her baby were in big trouble. *Desperate trouble.*

Oh, God, she thought, what am I going to do?
Get ahold of yourself, Bella. Don't panic.

All right, it was a little late for that last bit of advice. But she did need to get ahold of herself, stay calm, and *think.*

Okay. The first thing she had to do was get help. *Please—somebody help me!*

But she couldn't just sit here and wait for someone to come along. There was no telling how long that might be, and she had to get to a hospital *now.* So there wasn't any way around it; she was going to have to get out of the car and try to flag someone down. Someone…someone in one of the endless caravan of trucks that continued to growl slowly by, only a few yards and a whole world away.

Jimmy Joe had lost the New Mexico radio station, which was just as well. He had no business listening to the likes of ''Grandma Got Run Over By a Rein-

deer'' when he had enough to do just to keep his rig
on the road. The CB was really cracklin', too, what
with a few hundred drivers all stuck in the same place
and all trying their best to relieve the tedium and tension.

"*Eastbound, you got a four-wheeler on the side at
mile marker…*"

"*Yeah, you got two more down here.…*"

"*Hell, you got 'em everywhere! I quit countin'.*"

"*Federated, you okay down there?*"

"*Yeah…think I got me a little problem.…*"

"*Man, I mean, this is criminal.*"

"*Can you believe an interstate in this condition?*"

"*Anybody got any idea what it's like in Amarillo?*"

"*S'pose it's like this all the way to Oklahoma?*"

"*Oh, man, I sure do need to pee.*"

"*Well, you better open up the door, then, 'cause you
ain't gonna find no bushes out here!*"

"*Uh…eastbound, on that four-wheeler on the
side…looks like you got somebody out of the car, trying to wave somebody down. Ah, hell…looks like a
lady—you believe that? What's she doin' out here,
anyway?*"

When he heard those words Jimmy Joe felt a jolt
that went right through his insides. *What's she doing
out here?* Wasn't that just what he'd said to himself
the first time he'd set eyes on that crazy red-haired
pregnant lady from California? The one he hadn't been
able to get his mind off since.

A four-wheeler on the side and a woman trying to
flag somebody down—he sure didn't like the sound of
that. How many women could there be, out here all

alone in conditions like this? He picked up his mike, thumbed the Talk button and growled, ''Uh, what's the twenty on that four-wheeler with the lady wavin'? Come on...''

He waited through some crackling and muttering, counting his own heartbeats, before the answer came back. ''Uh...cain't see the mile sticks.... Make it 'bout a mile past the grain elevators at the Adrian exit. That'd be...what, twenny-two?''

Jimmy Joe watched the grain elevators at the Adrian exit crawl past his windows and swore out loud, which was something he didn't do often, having had his mouth washed out with soap more than once in years past for that offense. He did so now because he knew it was a good twelve miles to the next exit, which at this pace was going to take him more than two hours, and that meant there wasn't going to be any way he could get off the interstate. And there sure wasn't any place to pull over to the side. So it looked like, if he was going to stop and pick the lady up, he was going to have to do it the hard way, which was to stop the whole blamed line of traffic.

Picking up his mike again, he thumbed it on and growled, ''Breaker...this is the Big Blue Starr. I'm gonna be slowin' down here in a little bit. Gon' try an' pick up the lady. Just don't want anybody crawlin' up my back door....''

From all up and down the line the responses and assurances came crackling back at him. And then, loud and clear, one that made his blood run cold:

''Oh, Lordy, looks like she's got one in the oven,

and from the looks of 'er, she's 'bout to pop, too. *Somebody* better get 'er, quick.''

''I'm on it,'' Jimmy Joe said grimly into the mike as he checked his mirrors once more and then turned on his four-way flashers. ''Hey, yellow truck—J.B. Hunt, that you on mah back door?''

The answer came back—a woman's voice, calm and confident. ''I got you, Big Blue. You got lotsa room… go for it. Ten-foh.''

''Thank ya kindly… 'Preciate it.'' He hung up the mike as the word was being passed back up the line.

A strange calm settled over him, the way it did sometimes when his way, though difficult, seemed clear and certain. Outside his windows the white crept by, yard by yard, while inside the cab he counted off the seconds with his own heartbeat and the chatter on the radio faded into a tense and waiting silence. In his mirrors he could see the J.B. Hunt truck's headlights dropping back. How much longer? he wondered. A mile past Adrian—that would make it ten, maybe fifteen minutes. Seemed like an hour already….

At last he saw her, a tiny figure standing hunched and forlorn beside her disabled car, too dispirited now to even wave. There was no mistaking the silver Lexus or that red hair, either, although the rest of her didn't bear much resemblance to the Mirabella he'd come to know. Nothing very uppity about her now, that was for sure. Not a trace left of that know-it-all tilt to her chin. She looked cold and scared, plumb done in and all alone. *''And what will the poor robin do then, poor thing?''*

Carefully manipulating brakes and gears, he eased

his truck to a gentle stop. Behind him, in an unbroken line that stretched clear back to New Mexico, one by one the other drivers did the same. Then, while a thousand rigs sat idling on the icy interstate, Jimmy Joe set his brake, opened the door and stepped out into the teeth of that freezing wind. It just about took his breath away.

He made his way around the front of the Kenworth, holding on to the bumper and slipping and sliding on the unevenly packed ice. When he got around to the other side, Mirabella was just struggling through the ridge of filthy black snow thrown off by all the truck tires. She was bent over, half crouching, with both hands held out to keep her balanced, and through the wind-whipped ribbons of her hair her eyes reached for him like prayers. In all that whiteness, the palest thing he could see was her face.

"Jimmy...Joe," she gasped, clutching at him. "I have to...get to..." And now he could hear what he couldn't before. She was sobbing.

"Easy...easy, now," he said, soothing her the way he did J.J. when he'd had a bad dream. "It's okay...I gotcha. You just hold on now.... Here, put your arms around my neck."

She did as she was told, her big, scared eyes never leaving his face, and somehow he got his arms under her and lifted her up like a baby. Praying that the Lord would guide his feet because he sure couldn't see where to put 'em, he carried her through the rocklike frozen sludge to his truck, set her down on the first step while he got the door open, then braced himself and levered her up and into the cab.

"Stay there," he told her—unnecessarily, for sure—as he slammed the door shut. Plowing back through the snow to the Lexus, he got the keys out of the ignition and her pocketbook from the front seat, then popped the trunk. After he'd locked up the car again, he grabbed what looked to him like an over-night case out of the trunk, slammed it shut on a mountain of Christmas presents and ran for his truck, thinking he might just about make it there before he plumb froze to death.

Back in the Kenworth's nice warm cab, he found Mirabella still sitting in the passenger seat where he'd left her, shivering so hard he could just about hear her bones rattle. "Hey there, Marybell," he said with forced cheerfulness as he heaved her luggage into the sleeper, "aren't you s'posed to be in Florida?"

Her big, terrified eyes followed him. "I have...to get...to the...ha-ha—" But the shudders racked her and she couldn't get the words out.

"Come on back here—let's get you warm." He took her by the shoulders and gently eased her around and then to her feet, guiding her like a sleepwalker.

He knew he didn't have much time, that he had to get the rig rolling again, but he couldn't very well leave her the way she was, either. Silently asking his brother and sister drivers for patience, he began to talk to her in an easy, soothing voice while he shucked off her worthless coat and sat her down on the bed, then knelt down and took off her ruined shoes. The thin, calf-high stockings she was wearing were soaking wet too, so he hiked up her pant legs and peeled them off.

Then he opened up his locker and got out a pair of his nice thick winter socks.

"Here ya go," he said gruffly. "Put these on—get those feet warmed up." But she just looked at him.

After a moment it became clear to him that she wasn't up to putting the socks on alone, so once again he skinned up her damp pant legs and did it himself. He couldn't help but notice how cold her feet were, and how small and defenseless they looked. The socks came clear up to her knees. He told himself it wasn't all that different from helping J.J. get dressed on those winter mornings when the boy didn't feel like waking up and going out in the cold to catch the school bus. But as small as her feet were, they weren't a little boy's feet. They were a woman's. And the way he felt when he touched them wasn't anything at all like he felt when he was dressing J.J.

He got her eased down on the bed and the blankets tucked in nice and snug around her, then left her and slipped back into the driver's seat. For a moment he sat and listened to the living, breathing, waiting silence coming over the CB radio. Then he picked up the mike, thumbed it on and drawled, "Uh…this potty stop was brought to you by the Big Blue Starr. Hope y'all enjoyed it…. Ten-foh."

He grinned as the radio erupted with whoops and hollers and crackling static, with everybody within earshot trying to talk at once. A few nearby drivers cut loose with blasts from their airhorns. Then he hung up his mike and put the Kenworth in gear, and slowly, slowly the line began to move again.

When he was pretty sure things were going along

okay, nobody taking any unscheduled side trips into
the median, he glanced around and called hopefully,
"Hey, you doin' okay back there?"

He thought he heard her whisper, "Fine…" But
through the open door of the sleeper he could see that
she was still curled up on her side with the blankets
cuddled close, and that her eyes were closed. She was
still shivering, too. He turned up the heat another notch
and went back to concentrating on keeping his rig on
the road, but worry was beginning to gnaw at his insides.

The channel 19 airwaves were pretty much back to
the normal chatter, drivers bitching and moaning and
looking out for one another, just generally doing what
they could to keep their spirits up. Jimmy Joe listened
to it while another couple of miles crawled by, then
once again picked up his mike. He thought a minute,
then thumbed it on.

"Uh…anybody seen any bears lately? Come on…"

That got him some guffaws and some rude remarks.

*"Hell, there ain't no bears out here. Ain't no place
for 'em to hide."*

*"I ain't seen a smoky since yesterday. Cain't say's
I miss 'em."*

"Westbound…anybody out there?"

*"Ain't no bears gonna be movin' westbound. They
do, they ain't gonna get back to Amarillo, not unless
they can fly."*

*"How come there's never a bear around when you
need one?"*

Jimmy Joe let a breath out, taking his time about it.
It was pretty much what he'd expected, but he didn't

like it. After thinking about it another minute or two, he punched the mike button again. "Breaker…this is Big Blue Starr again. I'm gon' be switchin' channels here for a while, gon' try and raise somebody over on nine. Uh…I could use a little help. Got a lady here in need of transportation right quick, that's 'bout the… twenty-four-mile yardstick. If you got any bears in your neighborhood, I'd appreciate it if somebody'd flag 'em down. Ten-foh.''

He didn't wait for a reply. When he had channel 9, the emergency channel, tuned in, he listened to nothing for a few seconds, then thumbed on his mike once more. He spoke in a low voice with only a trace of his trucker's drawl.

"Mayday…Mayday… This is Blue Starr Transport. I'm eastbound on I-40, about three miles east of Adrian…got an emergency situation here. Repeat— this is an emergency. Come back…" He listened hopefully, then tried once more. "Mayday, Mayday…anybody out there listenin'?''

There was only silence.

"Jimmy Joe?''

Oh, Lord. He held the mike against his thumping heart while he cleared his throat, then sang out, "Well, g'mornin', sunshine. You feelin' better?''

She crept in between the seats, wrapped like an Indian in the comforter from the bed—an old quilt he'd borrowed from his mama's house—and eased herself into the passenger seat. He knew he ought to tell her to fasten her seat belt, but a quick look over at her, the way she was holding herself, made him think… maybe not.

"Jimmy Joe..." She took a deep breath and pulled herself up straighter, and he could see that she was trying hard to recover some of the dignity she'd lost back there in the snowbank. "I think you should know.... My, uh, my water broke."

Oh, Lord, he thought. Lord, no.

But she took another breath, shakier than the first, and went on with it like somebody scared silly but determined to make a full confession. "Back there. It...startled me. That's why I lost control of my car." Her voice, which had started off calm and strong, got gradually fainter until she finished in a whisper, "I have to get...to a hospital. I think I'm going to have my baby...now."

Chapter 7

"Eastbound, you got your ears on?"

I-40—Texas

Well, Lord, Jimmy Joe thought, if you're listenin', this would be a real good time for a miracle....

Because he knew that all the "Maydays" and all the prayers in the world weren't going to get an ambulance out on that track of rutted black ice, and if one did manage to get here, there wasn't any way in the world for it to get back to Amarillo with Mirabella—not with a solid line of trucks plugging up the road. Not unless it could fly. And until the wind died down and the snow quit blowing, there wasn't much chance of that, either.

The best he could hope for was to keep going, keep heading for Amarillo, and hope he got there before the baby did. Amarillo…no more than fifty miles, now. At this rate that was ten hours. *Ten hours.*

He didn't know why he wasn't more surprised. Scared, yes, but not surprised. Icy sweat filmed his upper lip and ran in a trickling trail from his armpits and on down his ribs. Maybe we'll make it, he thought. Sure, we will. Babies, especially the first one, can take a long time.

"Jimmy Joe?" Her eyes were dark, beseeching.

"Yeah," he said, and cleared his throat, wondering how long he'd been sitting there in frozen silence. "I heard what you said." He realized he was still holding his CB mike pressed against his chest and reached out to hang it up, stretching his arm slowly…stalling.

"I'm sorry."

I'm sorry. He glanced at her, then transferred his scowl to the left-hand mirror instead, where beyond the endless line of headlights he could see streaks of red in between the layers of black and purple clouds. Somewhere out there behind him the sun was going down. It was going to get dark soon.

"Hey," he said, "let me ask you something."

Hearing the hoarseness and the edge in his voice, Mirabella caught her breath and waited. She wanted him to look at her with the calm, reassuring eyes she remembered—eyes the warm, comforting brown of teddy bears and chocolate. But he kept his face turned away from her, and the angle of his head and the set of his jaw had a tense, angry look.

"You said your back's been hurtin' you. That a steady kinda hurt, or more off and on?"

She closed her eyes and leaned her head against the

back of the seat. "Off and on, I guess. I just thought it was the Tylenol taking effect. I thought I was aching because of too much sitting. I thought I was just tired. I never thought—"

Jimmy Joe was muttering under his breath. He broke off to ask, "How long has this been goin' on?"

Wretchedly, Mirabella whispered, "Since yesterday, I think."

Then he did finally look at her, with eyes that were more black than brown and in no way comforting, and exclaimed, "Good *night,* woman, what's the matter with you? Don't you know enough to know when you're in *labor?*"

She flinched at the word—an appalling thing to do, but she couldn't help it. Even though she knew she'd earned his anger, it seemed so unexpected, so incomprehensible, more frightening than anything that had happened to her so far. To her utter dismay she began to tremble, and then to cry. "It wasn't supposed to *be* now!" she wailed. "It's not supposed to be for another month. I just thought…I was, you know… uncomfortable. I never dreamed… It's not supposed to…"

Another month. Oh, Lord. He remembered now; she'd told him that. Lord help us, he thought. A month early—a preemie. Oh, hell. Oh, damn. Anything but that. He felt himself go icy cold, then numb.

But not too numb for it to occur to him he'd forgotten who he was dealing with, to know he'd lost control of himself, and as a result now he had a very upset woman on his hands. Not too numb to feel like a bully, and thoroughly ashamed of himself.

He took a deep breath and stretched his arm slowly across the space between them, gripping the back of the seat, near enough to her to touch the quilt she'd wrapped herself in. "Easy... You just take it easy, now," he muttered. A tremor went through him as he felt the slippery warmth of her hair against his fingertips. "It's gonna be okay...it's gonna be okay."

She bowed her head so that her hair pulled through his fingers like a shuttle full of silk floss through a loom. It slithered forward across her cheeks and his hand found her neck instead. In a voice he could barely hear she whispered, "Jimmy Joe, I'm scared."

Scared? He wanted to tell her he was scared, too; as scared as he'd ever been in his life before. *Lord,* how scared he was. He wanted to tell her—and God, too—that he didn't want any part of this.

No, Lord, I don't want ever again to hold a too-tiny baby in my hands and watch it slip away before it even has a chance to live. Not again, Lord. Not again.

"It's gonna be okay," he said for the third time, trying to make himself believe it. His voice sounded like the scratched 78-rpm records Great-granddaddy Joe Doyle used to play on his windup phonograph. "We're only fifty miles from Amarillo."

He could feel her turn to look at him, with a gaze both direct and solemn. "How many hours?"

Since he never had been any good at telling lies, instead of trying to think one up he gave her neck a little squeeze and then took his hand away. In his scratchy gramophone voice he said, "I put a call out on the emergency radio channel. We'll get you some help out here, don't you worry."

Then he had an inspiration. Taking his mike down from its hook, he held it out to her and showed her with his thumb how to work the speaker button.

"Here," he said, "why don't you give 'em another call right now? You just mash on this right here when you want to say somethin', then let 'er go so you can listen. See there? Go on, give 'er a try." If nothing else, he thought, it would give her something to do, make her feel, if not better, at least maybe not so helpless.

One of her hands crept from the folds of the quilt and took the mike from him. It came as a shock to him to feel how cold her fingers were. He heard a soft sniff, a throat-clearing cough, and then in a low voice, "What do I say?"

"You probably oughta start with 'Mayday,'" he said dryly, trying out a grin to see if it had any effect on his spirits. It didn't, and his words came out with an impatient edge. "Then, I don't know. Tell 'em it's an emergency. Tell 'em where you are. Then…shoot, just tell 'em what the problem is."

"I've never done this before." She gave a nervous, hiccuping laugh. "I feel funny."

He looked over at her, saw her trying to smile, and the sheen of fear in her eyes. His voice gentled. "No trick to it," he said softly, dragging his eyes back to the road. "Just hold it up to your mouth, mash the button and talk. Nothin' to be bashful about."

"Okay, here goes…." He heard her take a breath, clear her throat. "Okay… Mayday, Mayday. This is an emergency. Uh…I'm in a truck—Blue Starr Transport—on I-40. Let's see, that's about fifty miles west of Amarillo. We're stuck in traffic, and I'm, uh, well, I'm in labor. And, uh, we need help. So…please send someone. Please. Help…

"What now?" she whispered after a tense little silence. "Nobody's answering."

"Did you remember to let go of the button?"

"Oh…shoot." She swore under her breath. Another few minutes of silence went by. "Still nothing. Shall I try again?"

"Sure, might as well." Then he had to smile as this time she jumped right in with a self-confident singsong. He had to hand it to her—the lady did learn fast. Sounded just like a born trucker.

"Mayday, Mayday, this is an emergency. Repeat, this is an emergency. I am in a big rig owned by Blue Starr Transport, stuck in westbound traffic on I-40 about fifty miles west of Amarillo. I am in labor and in need of assistance. Please respond. Mayday."

Together they listened to crackling static and breathing sounds. Then in a flat, expressionless voice she said, "Well. So much for that." From the corner of his eye he could see her hand reaching toward him.

Wordlessly he took the mike from her and hung it back up, wishing he could have taken her hand instead, just because sometimes when there wasn't anything to say, it was kinda good to have a hand to hold on to. But the mike was there in the way, and by the time he had it taken care of, the moment had gone by. So all he could do was try and find some words.

"We'll keep 'er on that channel," he said gruffly. "Just keep on tryin'. Sooner or later we're bound to raise somebody. Meanwhile, maybe you oughta go on back there and lie down for a while. Seems to me if you keep quiet, things might slow down some. Get out of those wet things, too, while you're at it. I know I've got some clothes back there you can wear. Couple of sweatshirts, some long johns…''

"Jimmy Joe…'' Just that.

The way she said it, the way she was breathing, got his attention real quick. He looked over at her, his heart jumping right out of his chest. "You havin' a contraction?''

She nodded rapidly, clinging to him with eyes suddenly gone dark and scared. "I guess it must be.''

"Okay…okay.'' He gripped the wheel and stared a hole in the windshield, hoping he didn't sound as scared as he felt, hoping he didn't drive right up the tailgate of the reefer truck in front of him. "Now…''

What now? It had been a long time since he'd attended those childbirth classes with Patti—J.J.'s mama. All he could remember about them was a lot about relaxation, and something called "cleansing breaths.'' Which, judging from the sounds she was making, Mirabella already had down pat.

Finally getting up enough courage to look over at her, he saw that she had her eyes closed now and was concentrating on those breaths for all she was worth. It gave him an odd, lonely feeling to watch her, as if she'd gone away somewhere, to some place he could never follow. Nothing for him to do but keep his mouth shut and drive, until finally she let out her breath in a long, slow hiss and finished it up with, "Oh, boy.''

"Bad one?'' he asked awkwardly, fully aware of

the fact that no matter how she answered him, he would never really understand. Nothing like childbirth to make a man feel totally useless, he thought. Probably why in ages past at times like this the womenfolk were always sending the men out to chop wood or boil water or hunt buffalo, just to make 'em feel like they were good for something.

"Not so bad." She said it with a relieved chuckle, like a kid finding out that the punishment he'd been dreading wasn't so terrible after all. "If they don't get any worse than that, I can handle it."

"How often you havin' 'em?"

"I don't know." She shifted restlessly. "I guess we'd better start keeping track."

"Okay, say we start—" he pulled back the sleeve of his sweatshirt and got a good look at his watch, adding a couple of minutes for the time they'd been talking "—now. Okay, now, you tell me the minute you feel the next one comin' on, y'hear? And right now before it does, you best get on back there and lie down." He jerked his head in the direction of the sleeper. "Get some rest."

Then he caught a replay of himself. He shook his head and made a sound that was full of all the self-disgust and helplessness he felt. "I beg your pardon—don't mean to be givin' out orders. I just do it so I'll feel like I'm doin' somethin'." He gave her about half a grin, which was the best he could muster.

"That's okay." After a moment she gave a soft laugh and added dryly, "You probably ought to get in some practice while you can. Looks like you're going to be my childbirth coach."

With that she got up and eased herself between the seats. The quilt got hung up on the gearshift and he reached automatically to unhook it for her, taking more time than he needed, fussing with the dragging end like a bridesmaid with a bridal train while he tried to get some spit flowing in his mouth again. He'd never known his mouth to be so dry. Fear. That's what it was.

But he couldn't let Mirabella know. That was why he scraped up a little laughter and kind of a confident, know-it-all tilt to his head and drawled, "Childbirth coach... Oh, yeah, I sure do remember that. Those classes, now... I reckon that's what they're for, don't you? Make the father feel like he's actually doing something worthwhile, even if all it is is propping his wife up and yelling at her to do what she's already doing anyway."

"You went to childbirth classes?" He heard the surprise in her voice along with the soft grunts and scuffles she made as she settled herself back in the sleeper. "Really?"

"Sure did. Went with my wife when we were expectin' J.J. It was a while ago, though—don't know how much of it I remember." Traffic having stopped for the moment, he twisted around to look at her and then had to laugh out loud at the pure disbelief on her face. "Why, what's that for?"

"What's what?"

"That look. What'sa matter? You don't think I've been to childbirthin' class?"

"Well...it's kind of hard to imagine."

"Yeah?" His eyes were bright, teasing. As uncom-

fortable as she was with the way the conversation had
turned, Mirabella was glad to see his smile again.
''Why's that?''

''Oh…well, uh…'' she faltered, realizing that as
usual she'd put her foot in her mouth, and there wasn't
going to be any way she could answer that without it
sounding like a put-down. And the galling thing was,
she had the feeling he knew it, and didn't mind.

''Doesn't fit my image, huh?''

''I guess it just seems like a Yupppie thing,'' Mirabella hedged lamely. *Not a truck-driver thing.* How
awful it was, to discover that she was a snob.

''What, you don't think we got Yuppies in Georgia?'' His eyes were attentive, his smile gentle and
off-center.

''Oh, I'm sure.'' Shame made her snappish. ''But
you're not.''

''Now, how do you know what I am?''

The two things Mirabella hated most were, number
one, being teased, and number two, being bested in a
verbal battle. The first of those usually brought on an
urge to stamp her foot and scream. Fortunately, determination not to succumb to the second almost always
gave her a strong enough incentive to resist that urge
and hold on to her temper.

''I'm from L.A.,'' she said dryly. ''If there's anything I know, it's Yuppies, and believe me, you're not
one. Anyway—'' She broke it off, suddenly both furious and panic-stricken, because she'd just discovered
that the last thing she wanted to do was try to define
Jimmy Joe—even to herself, much less to his face. ''I
didn't mean anything by what I said. It's just—I never

would have thought Southern men were into that kind
of stuff, that's all.''

''Now, there you go,'' Jimmy Joe said, overdoing
the vexation just enough so she knew he was kidding.
''Where do you get your ideas about Southern men?
I bet every single thing you know about us Southerners you got from redneck jokes and country music.''

''I don't listen to country music,'' she said stiffly;
she considered the very term an oxymoron. ''And I
think redneck jokes are...'' His sudden laughter and
her own latent sense of good manners stopped her.

''Hey—not all of us Southern men are rednecks.''

''I never thought you were!'' But she could feel her
face warming. There it was—the *R*-word, the one
she'd been trying to shut completely out of her mind.
She didn't want to admit to herself that she'd ever
thought of him that way. But she had, at first—okay,
sure, cute as the dickens, but a redneck nonetheless.
And now she felt ashamed of that.

''Now, what do you think a redneck is?'' he persisted, his eyes bright and teasing, his drawl exagger-
ated. ''Pert' near anybody that talks with a Southern
accent, right?'' He shook his head, making a ''Shame
on you'' sound with his mouth. ''That's prejudice, you
know that? You Northerners think anybody talks with
a Southern accent has got to be ignorant, otherwise
we'd a' learned to talk 'right.'''

''I do not,'' said Mirabella stiffly. But she'd already
begun to perk up, stimulated by the promise of a good
argument, by which was about anything that didn't
touch her on a personal level.

''Sure you do. Take 'ain't.' You Northerners think

sayin' 'ain't' is bad grammar, but I'll tell you somethin' I bet you didn't know. 'Ain't' was considered
perfectly fine grammar in Shakespeare's time. That's
right. That's the thing about Southern grammar—you
Northerners might think it's bad grammar, but that's
not necessarily true, see? What it is, it's just Southern,
is all.''

Mirabella could never, but never pass up a chance
to be right. So she couldn't resist reminding him, ''*You*
don't say ain't.''

Jimmy Joe let her see his grin before he shifted
gears and turned to face the front again. ''Yeah, but
that's because my mama was a schoolteacher. She'd
skin me alive if I ever did.''

''Aha!''

''Aha, nothin'. She never did let me take the Lord's
name in vain, either, and lots of educated folks do
that—includin' Northerners.''

''Including me,'' she had to admit.

Jimmy Joe was plainly on a roll. ''You want to
know what's ignorant?'' he said, smacking the steering wheel with an open palm. ''I'll tell you what, you
get these people tryin' to talk like Southerners, sayin'
'y'all' when they're only talkin' to one person—now
that's ignorant.''

Mirabella suddenly realized that she was smiling.
And that she wasn't afraid anymore. And that she no
longer knew whether this discussion had a point to be
made, or cared whether she won or lost it. It was
just…fun. Fun to be with him. Fun to listen to him.
Arguing with him was less a matter of winning than
stoking a fire, just so she could bask in the stimulating

warmth of his voice. It was a totally new experience for her, and one that for the moment, at least, seemed to have taken her mind completely off the *other* new experience she was caught up in.

"Hey—I'll tell you what a redneck is, if you want me to." Jimmy Joe's accent was suddenly thick as molasses. He looked back at her and she saw that although his face was perfectly straight, his eyes were liquid with laughter. She held her breath, keeping back her own.

"Now, you know, what rednecks enjoy doin' more'n anything in this world is to lay around in the woods amongst a bunch a' hounddawgs, old washin' machines and cars that don't run, and drink Red Dog beer and shoot at things...occasionally one another."

Mirabella let out a snort of laughter. Jimmy Joe held up a finger, paused as if to give it some thought, then continued in a nasal singsong. "Then, one step up from there you got yer good ol' boys. Now a good ol' boy reveres his dogs. In his esteem, his dog ranks above his wife and kids, but probably somewheres below a good huntin' rifle and his pickup truck, which he likes to decorate with replicas of the Confederate battle flag. Don't laugh—" Mirabella, who was trying not to wet herself more than she already was, made a strangled sound. "Miss Marybell, I swear to you—" he solemnly made a crisscross on his chest and held up his right hand in a "Scout's honor" sign "—I am not a redneck. Never in my life have I used an old tire for a planter or called anybody 'bubba'—oh, well, except for Bubba Johnson back in junior high school, but you can't hardly count that, bein's how Bubba was his given name.''

I know what he's doing, she thought. Somehow, in spite of her desperate snorts and giggles, he must know about the quivery, achy, tear-filled reservoir inside her that was ready to overflow without warning. And obviously he was no more eager than she was to have that happen—although whether it was a matter of gallantry on his part, or whether like most men he was simply chickenhearted when it came to a woman's tears, she couldn't decide.

Either way, she was grateful to him. Grateful for the arguing and the laughter, grateful for the distraction, for the opportunity to recover some of the dignity she'd left back in that snowdrift. Grateful for the chance to forget, for a little while at least, what lay ahead of her, and how grave her situation was. It wasn't easy to do under the circumstances, but since he seemed to be trying so hard to help her, she did her best.

''Speaking of given names,'' she said after the laughter had run its course, making a poor job of smothering a yawn as she curled on her side on the sleeper's wide bed and snuggled the quilt around her—discovering that through the curtain of her lashes the back of his head and neck looked surprisingly mature, the spread of his shoulders broad and powerful. ''Jimmy Joe—is that really yours? Or is it a nickname, like…short for James Joseph?''

His chuckle seemed to stroke her auditory nerves, soothing as a caress. ''Just Jimmy Joe—that's it.''

''Huh. Nobody ever calls you Jim?''

"Jim was my daddy's name. *His* daddy was James, and I think the Joseph came from another grand-daddy—that'd be Joe Doyle. To avoid confusion, I got Jimmy Joe. Does beat the heck out of Junior. Hey," he said with another of those caressing chuckles, "it was good enough for the president of the United States."

She murmured, "Jimmy just seems—" *Right.* That came to her balanced on the edge of sleep, and she felt an odd little flare of surprise. And then a flutter near her heart.

"Hey, you know, you can call me anything you want to." For some reason his voice had grown husky. "Shoot, call me Jim if you want to."

She smiled and murmured, "Too late—I've gotten used to Jimmy Joe, now." She would have a hard time calling him anything else. *Jimmy Joe.* What a sweet, gentle sound...

"How 'bout Mirabella? How'd you ever get a name like that? Especially with a last name like—"

"Waskowitz? Yeah, I know—awful, isn't it? My dad's family was Polish—I think they shortened the name somewhere along the line. My mom—she was a teacher, too, by the way—she's just kind of this unique person—part English, part Irish, but I think she picked our names based on whatever her kick happened to be at the time. My sisters are Sommer and Eve. Don't ask me how I got Mirabella." She yawned unbashedly. "I looked it up one time. It means—"

The word evaporated in a puff of air that blew every last vestige of sleep fog from her brain and left her senses blasted and cringing. The nagging ache in her

back, which up to now she'd been able to ignore, sort
of like a radio turned down low, had suddenly intensified as if someone had given the volume knob
marked Pain a wrenching twist to the right.

"Mirabella...that's a mouthful. Everybody always
call you that? Your family...friends?"

When he didn't get an answer, the first thing Jimmy
Joe thought was maybe she'd finally dozed off. He
wasn't sure what made him look back, but when he
did he could see that even though she had her eyes
shut, she definitely wasn't sleeping.

"Focus," he barked, which was the first thing that
popped into his head as his heart gave another one of
those bad leaps, banging against the wall of his chest.
"Breathe."

Damnation, he thought. *Damn.* He could hear her
begin to whimper, making a sound like a hurt puppy
that had to be about the worst thing he'd ever heard
in his life.

He just did remember to check his watch. "Nine
minutes," he yelled. Was that a good thing? He wasn't
sure, but he thought it must be good, because didn't
the pains have to be a whole lot closer together before
things really got serious? Maybe they had more time
than he'd thought. Maybe the road would improve.
What he ought to do was get back on the radio again
and find out what was going on up ahead. Maybe they
would make it to Amarillo, after all.

But then, he thought, what if they didn't? It was
almost dark now. At the rate they were going, it was
still a good many hours to Amarillo. And then, what
if somebody jackknifed and blocked the road? Mean-

while, Mirabella was back there all by herself, having those pains, which were only going to get worse. She needed somebody to be with her; somebody to make her do those breathing things she was supposed to do. Dammit, he couldn't very well help her and drive at the same time!

What should he do? If he was going to help her, he was going to have to pull off somewhere. But if he did that... Everything inside him went cold and quiet. Because he knew that if he did get off, he wasn't going to get back on again. He would be committed. Unless by some miracle help did arrive in time, whatever happened, it was going to be just him and Mirabella. Him, Mirabella, and a baby that was bound and determined to show up four weeks ahead of schedule.

Oh, Lord, help me, he thought. *What should I do?*

It was right then that his headlights picked up the sign for a rest area that was coming up, next exit, just one mile ahead. A rest stop—that was a whole lot better than one of the crossroads, with their overpasses and uphill off-ramps, where he would stand a good chance of jackknifing his rig. And there would be a rest room, water, maybe even a phone. He let out a breath that was almost relief, figuring if that wasn't a sign of some kind, he didn't know what was. Almost as if the decision had been taken out of his hands.

"Bella..." It came from the sleeper on a soft cushion of air, much like a sigh.

Jimmy Joe, who was busy changing radio channels, glanced back and said, "I beg your pardon?"

She was sitting up straight, rocking back and forth slightly. Her face was pale, her eyes dark and calm.

She gathered her hair away from her face with one hand and took a quick breath, then smiled. "Bella. That's what my family calls me. And most of my friends. You want to hear a joke? It means—"

Channel 19 came crackling in, drowning out the rest. He unhooked the mike and held it while he waited for a lull in the chatter, but when one came he didn't hit the Talk button right away. Instead he looked back at Mirabella and got her eyes for just a moment, and he said softly, "Means 'beautiful'—I know that much Italian. And I never heard a more fittin' name."

He grinned at the stunned silence he got in reply as he thumbed on the mike and intoned, "Breaker, one-nine... This is Big Blue Starr. I'm gon' try an' get off here at this rest stop east of Adrian. Uh...I got a lady havin' a baby here, so if any a' you drivers happen to run across any help out there, I'd 'preciate it if you'd send it my way. I'm gon' be listenin' to channel 9 for a while.... Anybody knows anything about delivering babies, I'd sure like to hear from you over there... Ten-four.'

He hung up the mike and got the channel changed just as the rest-stop exit sign was picking up the glow of his headlights. He flashed his running lights and switched on his turn signals and sent up a prayer.

"Hang on," he muttered to Mirabella as he turned the Kenworth's nose onto the snow—and ice-choked ramp.

Chapter 8

"Gotta make a change here. Got a'
alligator in the road."

I-40—Texas

While the big truck churned slowly along the exit ramp, carving its own tracks in the frozen, unblemished white, Mirabella focused on its driver's hands. They looked so strong and sure, so steady on the wheel. And she thought, We'll be okay in those hands, my baby and I.... Everything will be all right.

The truck came to a lumbering stop. There was an explosive hiss of air through the brake lines and then, except for the quiet grumble of the idling diesel engine, silence. Jimmy Joe set the brakes and flipped switches, then turned in his seat to grin at her. "Well," he said with a little half-shrug, "here we are."

She arranged her own lips into a smile for his benefit, although there was still a hollow feeling in her chest, and asked, "Where, exactly, are we?" It looked pretty much like nowhere to her—eerie in its emptiness, without so much as a light showing in the distance.

"We're at a rest stop." He let out a breath and stood, leaning across the passenger seat to peer out the side window into the darkness. "Not much of one—pretty much just picnic tables and potties. I expect the rest rooms're gonna be a mite chilly—"

"Rest rooms! Seriously?" That right there was enough to pick up her morale. "Oh, God—where?"

He gave her a doubtful look. "You sure you want to go out there? I was thinkin' maybe I could rig up somethin'…you know…" He paused, coloring a little. "Portable, or somethin'."

"Over my dead body," said Mirabella through her teeth. At some point, modesty was probably going to become optional, even for her. But not yet. Not yet. "I can walk. Let me out of here—now. Open the door."

He made an exasperated noise as she looked ready to bowl right over him, but he managed to get a good firm grip on both of her arms. "Okay, now hold on, wait a minute," he said as he steered her backward into the sleeper. "At least put a coat on first, okay? One of mine—that one a'yours isn't worth a darn.…" As he spoke he was opening a door, at the same time taking the precaution of maintaining a hold on one of her elbows as if he expected her to make a break for it as soon as he let go. "Here," he said, pulling out a

Levi's jacket lined with sheepskin, "this oughta do it—put this on."

"It's my bottom half that's wet," she told him as he held the jacket for her and guided her hands into the sleeves as if she were a three-year-old.

And suddenly hearing herself, she thought, I can't believe I told him that. A man and a stranger, and I told him as easily as if we were best friends and I'd known him forever.

It just didn't seem real to her. None of this did. The world she lived in—her carefully planned, controllable universe—had vanished. Everything was different. All the rules had changed.

"What's the matter?" Jimmy Joe's body had gone tense and still. "You havin' another one?"

She shook her head rapidly and tried to explain. "I just...don't believe this is happening. It's not... Nothing's the way I planned...."

"Hey."

He turned her toward him, his brow furrowing as he watched his hands tug the two halves of the jacket together just below her chin, slip inside the collar and under her hair and carefully lift it free, then return to fuss unnecessarily with the lay of the collar and lapels. Only when he had them smoothed to his satisfaction did his eyes finally move upward to her face, while his fingers, left on their own, slipped back into the warm places along the sides of her neck as if they belonged there.

The warmth, the feel of them there, made her want to close her eyes, but he cradled her head as if it was something precious and tilted it slightly so that she had nowhere to look except into his eyes.

"Now, you listen," he said, his voice gone soft and growly. "Everything's gonna be okay, you hear?"

She nodded, but the gentle movement of his sensitive fingers along the cords of her neck made her shiver. So he repeated it: "Everything's going to be okay." Then he closed his eyes and pulled her gently forward. She felt the tickle of his exhaled breath in her hair as his arms came around her, and then her eyes were closing, too, and she was leaning into him, holding on to his strong, hard body as she accepted with a sigh the support and comfort he offered.

How wonderful this feels, she thought, her skin, her cells, her being soaking up the unfamiliar sensation of masculine hands drawing gentle patterns on her back. As if even they knew...

I wish I could stay like this...forever.

Knew that for her, forever would be counted in minutes...seconds...fetal heartbeats. And measured in the tolerance of a tiny but independent creature for being squashed between two large and inconsiderate bodies.

They both felt the kick at the same time and drew apart, laughing. Jimmy Joe coughed and said, "That's some little slugger you got there," and hooked a thumb in his pocket and shifted his feet in endearing awkwardness.

"Tell me about it," said Mirabella, gasping at the continuing convulsions taking place in her belly.

"Well," he said, "I reckon that's a good sign."

She gave a short, soft laugh. "Yeah, I guess..."

And then, frowning: "Jimmy Joe?" As it often did, unguided by thought, her hand had come to rest on the quivering bulge just above her navel, where it moved in gentle, circling strokes. Emotion crept up on her, stealing the words, but still somehow she managed, "I, uh...thanks. For stopping...for picking me up. For...you know. Being here." And although she didn't want it to, the wobble in her voice added, *And for everything we both know is still to come.*

As clumsy as it was, he seemed to understand, murmuring huskily, "Shh...no problem." And all the while his eyes followed the movement of her hand on her belly, his own hand hovering in the space between them as if he very much wanted, but wasn't sure he had the right, to touch.

Seeing that, all at once Mirabella's heart felt swollen, and something very much like grief stung the backs of her eyes and throat. Why couldn't it have been? she thought. Oh, *why* couldn't I have found someone like this *before?* I wouldn't have given up! It wouldn't have had to be like this! *Dammit, where were you?*

She forced a laugh to explain the unexplainable tears, then sniffed, drew a breath and in a high, distressed voice, said, "Uh...can we go to the bathroom now? *Please?*"

He jumped as if she'd startled him out of a doze, lifting the errant hand and using it to push a fallen lock of blond hair back from his brow, letting out a breath with a sound not unlike the truck's air brakes. "Oh—sure. Just let me get a flashlight...."

From yet another of the sleeper's storage compart-

ments he produced a battery-powered lantern, the kind
you can either carry or set down on its base. He kept
a light hold on her arm as he edged past her and
reached across the passenger seat to open the door.
Then, guiding her carefully after him, he backed out
into the darkness.

The wind was brutal. The instant it touched her, she
swore and began to shake uncontrollably. All she
could say was, "Oh, God. Oh…God."

Jimmy Joe switched on the flashlight and set his
teeth and concentrated on not shivering so much himself, and also on resisting the strong temptation to lift
Mirabella into his arms and carry her. It probably
would have been faster and easier, and a darn sight
warmer for both of them if he had. But a lot of stuff
from those childbirthing classes was coming back to
him, and one of the things he remembered was that
laboring women were apt to be funny about being han-
dled; that sometimes they liked to be touched and
sometimes they didn't, and that it wasn't always easy
to know what kind of mood they were in. He figured
he and Mirabella had lots of time ahead of them to
get to know each other's ways, and he didn't want to
take a chance on messing things up before they'd gotten started.

Hugging her, now. Holding her. That had been nice.
He thought about it as he crunched beside her through
the frozen snow, supporting her with one arm hooked
across her back and under her arm while she hung on
to his hand with a grip like a vise. Yes…she'd seemed
to like that. He'd liked it, too. Probably a lot more
than he should have, considering the circumstances.

The fact was, he didn't know quite what to do with the thoughts and feelings that kept coming over him where Mirabella was concerned. He kept thinking—and telling himself—that he ought to be ashamed. But he wasn't. For one thing, what he felt for her wasn't the usual kind of lust or desire for a beautiful woman's body, which likely *would* have been shameful. It seemed to him it was more a kind of "connectedness" that had been growing on him for a while now, ever since he'd put her to bed in his truck and sat beside her and rubbed her back and watched over her while she slept.

Maybe even before that. When he'd ordered chicken-noodle soup for her. Or when he'd first offered her his bunk.

But whenever it had started, what it had grown into was a sense of closeness, a degree of familiarity he couldn't remember having had with any woman since J.J.'s mama. Not even then. It was probably something to do with the drugs and alcohol and all that, but there had been a big part of Patti he'd felt closed off from; a part—maybe the most important part—that he could never reach.

What was even stranger to him was that in the years since their divorce he hadn't met a woman he'd even wanted to get that close to. And he couldn't for the life of him figure out why, when he finally did, he'd picked one about as different from himself as it was possible for two humans to be.

It didn't make much sense to him. He didn't know what it all meant or where it was going, and to be honest, he didn't even want to think about it. Tonight, whatever happened, it looked as if it would be just the two of them, and a baby to be brought safely into the world. Right now he had to concentrate on that.

The rest-room building was dark and as cold as he'd thought it would be. If there was any power in the place it was evidently out—lines were down somewhere, probably. Any ideas he'd had about calling for help from here were fleeting; the phone was dead, too.

It made him think maybe it was time he got one of those cellular phones for his truck, which up to now hadn't seemed like a high-priority expense to him. Between the radio and the table phones in truck stops, it just hadn't been necessary—plus, he had a real strong dislike of people, mostly four-wheel drivers, he'd seen goin' down the road with phones in their ears instead of payin' attention to their driving.

Against her wishes, he helped Mirabella into the ladies' side of the cinder-block building and got her situated in a stall. Then, although it made him uneasy to do it, he put the flashlight down on the cold concrete floor for her and left her there.

There was enough reflected light from the snow for him to see by as he made his way around to the men's room, although inside it was so dark he had to take care of his own necessities pretty much by feel. The water in the lavatory was flowing, but the way it felt to him, it wasn't much more than a degree or two above freezing. That made him think about that porta potty and microwave oven he'd decided not to have installed in the truck when he'd had the cab customized, but he'd figured he would never have much oc-

casion to use 'em and it was just going to be a waste
of money and space, so why bother?

Goes to show you, he thought. You just can't predict where life's gonna take you.

He had plenty of time to think about that while he
huddled in the lee of the rest-room building shivering
and stamping his feet and trying his best not to freeze
to death while he waited for Mirabella to come out.
You can't predict life.

"I can't believe this is happening," she'd said,
which was her way of saying the same thing, he supposed.

Except that in his life so far, he figured he'd seen
just about everything, and what he hadn't seen he'd
probably heard about, and the fact was, there wasn't
much about life that surprised him anymore.

He did still have a sense of wonder, though, which
was a whole lot different than surprise or disbelief.
And it was definitely wonder he felt as he stood there
in the snow with a Panhandle wind blowing right
through him and all around him a black sky full of
cold, bright stars coming down to touch the edges of
the whirling snow. There was a strange, desolate
beauty about the night, and something more than that.
A shivery kind of feeling. A sense of excitement. Anticipation, maybe.

He wondered if it had more to do with it being
Christmas Eve, or the fact that just inside those cinder-
block walls there was a woman about to give birth to
a baby. What an incredible thing that was, when he
really thought about it. And what a strange way to
spend Christmas.

He thought about how it would have been, how it usually was: his family all gathered together—Mama, J.J., Jess and Sammi June, Granny Calhoun and his other sisters and their husbands and kids, and his brothers and probably a few odd aunts and cousins and neighborhood strays. Right now they would most likely be gathered around the old upright piano, Mama bangin' out the accompaniment while everybody sang carols out of the hymnbook—"O Little Town of Bethlehem," "Away in a Manger" and "Silent Night."

"Away in a manger,/No crib for a bed…"

That was when it occurred to him that maybe this Christmas Eve wasn't so strange after all. And he wondered if this was how Joseph must have felt, pacin' up and down outside that stable, all those years ago. And whether Joseph had felt the same kind of awe, excitement and fear.

It had been a long time since he'd thought much about praying. He'd been about Sunday-schooled to death when he was a kid, and through all the troubles and bad times with Patti he'd given up on the whole notion of religion; these days he left that aspect of J.J.'s education pretty much up to the boy's grandmama.

Now, though, standing there all alone in the cold looking up at those stars, thinking about the woman and child who were depending on him, he suddenly felt more than a little bit overwhelmed. He figured what he needed now was some help, and it wasn't the kind that was going to come in a chopper or with flashing lights and a siren. He also knew there wasn't any way he was ever going to find the words to say what he wanted to say, or to ask what he needed to ask. So in the end he just stood real still and quiet and prayed that the Good Lord would know without being told.

With that taken care of, it began to seem to him like Mirabella had been in the rest room a long time. He was just thinking maybe he'd better chance it and go and see if she was okay, when he saw the shadows shift and the lantern light come splashing out onto the snowy walkway. He went to her and put his arms around her and hustled her back to the truck as fast as he could, neither of them saying anything until they were back inside, and shivering and shaking and rubbing themselves warm.

"I'm...sorry...I took...so long," she said as soon as she could get the words out. "I had...a contraction...in there."

It was pretty much what he'd thought, and concern made his voice harsh. "You okay?" She nodded, and he drew a big breath.

"Okay, let's see...." He looked at his watch and tried to figure how long it had been between that one and the one before, but with everything that had been going through his mind, he'd lost track. Near as he could tell, though, the interval seemed shorter.

"It was really strong," Mirabella said with a shudder. "Stronger than the others. I think..." She paused, hiccuped, and finished thoughtfully, "It might have something to do with gravity."

"Gravity?"

"Yeah, because I was standing up. You know...the weight of the baby...more pressure."

372   *One Christmas Knight*

"Yeah, well, maybe you ought to be lyin' down," said Jimmy Joe uneasily.

"What for? I was thinking, maybe if I walk around—well, move around anyway, just in here, like this—it'll go faster."

"Faster?" His voice rose to a squeak he'd never heard before. "Don't you think we ought to be tryin' to slow things down? I was thinkin', if we can hold off until daylight, maybe the wind'll die down enough by then, they can get a chopper out here...."

But he realized as the words were coming out of his mouth how selfish of him it was, to want her in pain that much longer, and that it was pure-and-simple panic making him say that.

So he wasn't surprised when she gave him a dirty look and said with a snort, "That's easy for you to say—you're not the one in labor."

Then, in spite of everything, he just had to grin. It was such a Mirabella thing to say—the old Mirabella, the one with the uppity chin and the California brass. The cold had put color in her cheeks and the wind had played havoc with her hair, and she looked wild and sort of magnificent sitting there glaring at him with that spark of anger in her eyes.

"Yes, ma'am," he said contritely, and was rewarded with another dirty look. Only this time he could see by the quiver at the corners of her mouth that she knew he was teasing her, and he had an idea she'd already forgiven him.

After that an odd little silence fell, a moment of comfortable friendliness of the kind that happens between people who know each other well, just sitting there in the truck's front seat with the armrests folded up, knees almost but not quite touching, facing but not looking at one another, heads turned instead toward the dark windshield. They both drew breath to speak at exactly the same moment, then laughed.

Mirabella said, "Go ahead," and Jimmy Joe gestured toward the radio and muttered, "Ah, I was just thinkin' maybe I ought to try callin' again."

She nodded. "Good idea. I was thinking I should go and put on some dry clothes while I've got the chance."

But while she knew her voice was gratifyingly brisk and businesslike, she also knew her actions definitely weren't. Getting up was a slow and ponderous process—in her view, much like an elephant rising from a mud wallow. Jimmy Joe, of course, was instantly there trying to help her, but she waved him off, saying through clenched teeth, "It's okay, I got it," as she finished the job herself. A small victory, but she felt immeasurably stronger for it.

The fact was, she'd had some time to think, sitting alone in that frigid toilet stall, counting her way through a contraction bad enough to make her sure she didn't want to experience very many more like it. And what she'd decided was that she didn't like feeling lost and scared and helpless. She wasn't used to it. It wasn't *her*. What she wanted was to feel like herself again—strong, capable and in control.

She'd reminded herself that she'd planned this thing from the very beginning, every aspect of it, and just because fate had decided to step in at the last minute didn't mean everything had to fall apart. So this was the way it was going to be? Fine. So she was having her baby in a truck? Big deal. People had babies in worse places—like taxicabs, for instance—all the time. So nobody was coming to help? At least she'd been through the whole course of childbirth classes, so she knew what to expect.

And she wasn't alone. She had Jimmy Joe. There was no reason why things shouldn't be fine. Of course not. All she had to do was stay strong and keep a clear head.

She was running all that through her head, making her way between the seats when she felt it—first the tension in her back, then radiating pain that coiled around and under her belly like a saddle girth, stopping her in her tracks. She clutched at the seats for support and her right hand found Jimmy Joe's shoulder instead.

He didn't say a word, but was suddenly there behind her, his body warm and solid against her back.

"Easy, now…I got you." His voice was a calming murmur, a soft vibration against her temple as his arms gently encouraged her to lean into him. "You just relax now. *Relax.* Don't hold your breath. Breathe easy, now…. Let 'er go…let 'er go."

Relax…yes. I'd forgotten. That's what I have to do. Relax.

But it was easier said than done. "I *can't*," she gasped, and was instantly furious with herself. Ordinarily, "can't" was simply not a word she allowed in her vocabulary.

"Sure, you can. Close your eyes, now, and lay your head back. 'Atta girl, just like that. Think about something else. Water, now... Yeah, water's good. Just float...."

She did as he told her. The words blew softly past her ear, tickling. She smiled, and the pain seemed to grow smaller, as if she were drifting away from it.

The humming in her ear became singing. "'Row, row, row your boat/Gently down the stream....'"

That struck her as funny. She giggled, and seemed to drift even further away from the pain, leaving it behind....

Then it was gone. And it felt so good. "It's over," she announced on a long exhalation, almost trembling with euphoria, as if she'd just won a tremendous battle. She didn't want to open her eyes; it would be so nice, she thought, to stay right here and float like this forever.

But Jimmy Joe was saying something to her, shifting her weight, easing her back into her own axis. Her legs and body felt odd, as if she really had been on a boat and was now having to accustom herself to solid ground again.

"That was much better that time." A tremor crept into her voice as she felt the shock of separation, the chill of air where his body had been. "It really helped. Thanks." And suddenly she was laughing. "'Row, row, row your boat'?"

"Well, shoot," Jimmy Joe said with a shrug and an abashed grin, "it was the only water song I could think of. Tell you what, I'll try an' see if I can come up with somethin' better next time." He looked at his watch and frowned, fiddled with it for a moment, then flashed her his smile again. "Okay, we'll see how that does. Supposed to be a stopwatch—don't think I've ever had occasion to use it before. If it works right, we're gonna know just how far apart those pains are coming.''

"Right," said Mirabella staunchly.

She realized she liked the way he kept saying "we."

Which was a new and strange feeing for her, accepting a partnership when she was so accustomed to going it alone. And even more strange to feel so overwhelmingly grateful for someone's presence. She, who had always valued her privacy above all else and guarded her independence so jealously. But right now, standing close to this man who should have been a stranger still, so close her belly almost brushed his belt buckle, she found that she wanted nothing but to lean against him and lay her head on his chest and feel his arms around her and his warm breath in her hair. And she wondered how it could feel so comfortable and right.

"You aren't havin' another one already, are you?"

She blinked Jimmy Joe's face into focus and found that he was frowning at her in alarm, and realized only then that she'd been gazing at him—with God only knew what sort of dopey expression on her face.

"No," she said quickly, looking away. Swallowing hard. Telling herself, *It's just the circumstances. As soon as this is over he'll be gone. And I'll be glad, won't I?*

"That's good." His frown eased into something else—something she couldn't read. Then he reached unexpectedly to touch her face, rubbing his thumb over the place between her brows where tension gathered. "We want to be ready for the next one so it doesn't sneak up on us again. Get you relaxin'… breathin' right."

"Right," Mirabella whispered. His eyes were so dark and warm…as bracing as coffee on a cold morning. She wanted to hold on to them, wrap herself around them and drink in their strength and certainty.

His smile blossomed slowly, almost without her noticing…until, like a finger of sunlight reaching into a dark corner, it touched something deep within her, and she felt stirrings like the fine tremblings of a moth's wings—like the first tiny movements of the new life inside her.

"We're gonna do okay, you and me," he said in a husky voice, drawing a feathery line across her forehead with his fingertips like someone leaving stroke marks in velvet. "Don't you worry now, y'hear? Everything's gonna be just fine."

She nodded, and her hand rose unguided to touch his where it cradled her cheek—touch, then catch and hold it there. She made what was for her an unprecedented sound, a laugh so saturated with emotion it sounded almost like a sob. Embarrassed by it, she closed her eyes…and felt the soft brush of his mouth on hers. Just that, there and then gone, so quickly she might have imagined it, if his next words hadn't blown like a whisper of breath across her lips.

"You'd best go now…get outta those clothes while you can."

Dazed and disoriented, she let him turn her and guide her into the sleeper.

"I got that out of your car for you," he said, pointing to the navy blue overnighter that she'd somehow
failed to notice sitting in the far corner of the bed
compartment. "Don't know what all you got in
there—hope it's somethin' you can use. If you need
anything of mine, just go on and help yourself."

She murmured her thanks, and heard the curtain
slide across the opening. A moment later she heard the
crackle of radio static, and his growly CB drawl saying, "Mayday, Mayday, we got us an emergency
here…anybody out there listenin'? Come on…"

My overnight bag. She reached for it and pulled it
toward her, smiling mistily and shaking her head even
though she knew she ought to be used to Jimmy Joe's
ways by now. But she wasn't, and she didn't think she
would ever get over being a little bit awed by him—
and grateful. At least she hoped not. People like him
shouldn't ever be taken for granted, she thought. Like
roses and robins, and the Grand Canyon.

Mostly her overnight case held cosmetics and toi-
letries, her hair dryer and changes of underwear, none
of which she was likely to be needing anytime soon.
This trip, however, she had thrown in a nightgown,
for convenience during one-night motel stops. It was
her favorite, an enormous T-shirt with a picture of a
glowering cat on the front and the words, I Don't Do
Mornings. Made for comfort rather than modesty or
style, it did absolutely nothing to camouflage her swollen breasts and bulging belly. It wasn't very warm,
either, but it was long enough to cover her legs to mid-
calf, and since she wasn't going to be wearing any
bottoms, that seemed a big plus. For warmth and mod-

esty she could always wear one of Jimmy Joe's shirts on top of it.

No bottoms… A little spasm of queasiness gripped her. I feel like a virgin preparing for my wedding night, she thought. And then the irony of that struck her and she had to sit down, holding her stomach and hiccuping with silent laughter.

"How you doin' in there?" Jimmy Joe called from the front.

She jumped guiltily and began to shuck off clothing as fast as she could, managing to answer with a muffled, "Fine…just about done."

After a pause, his voice rode in on a ripple of laughter. "Hey, I thought of a good water song."

"Yeah?"

"Yeah…how 'bout 'The River'? Garth Brooks."

Preoccupied with peeling off her wet pants, she had to confess she'd never heard of either the song or, "Garth…*who?*"

Which clearly appalled Jimmy Joe. "Come on, now. You don't mean to tell me you never heard of Garth Brooks? One of the biggest country singers the last couple years. Songs've been at the tops of the charts— Where you been, woman?"

Mirabella sniffed. "Oh…well. I told you, I don't listen to much country music."

"Huh." There was a little silence, then, on a note of curiosity, "What've you got against country music, anyway?"

"I don't have anything against country music. I just consider it a contradiction in terms, is all." But she was smiling, exhilarated by the prospect of a new battle. Arguing with Jimmy Joe was such *fun*.

He gave a loud disdainful snort and to her delight countered with, "Don't know why that surprises me, comin' from a woman who thinks *Pinocchio* was Walt Disney's best movie."

"What?" She swept back the curtain with a grand gesture. "Oh, not again. How can you even argue that? It's common knowledge Pinocchio was Disney's masterpiece. All you have to do is look at the artistry, the animation, the characterizations, the themes.... What?" Jimmy Joe was solemnly shaking his head. "Okay, why not? Just give me one good reason."

"One's all I need," he said, watching her with his soft, unreadable eyes, smiling a quirky half-embarrassed smile she'd never seen before. "And I'll tell you what it is. It hasn't got a romance in it."

"What?" Mirabella blinked, then laughed. "*Romance?* What's that got to do with anything?"

He shrugged, then got up and came around the seat. Disconcerted, she took a step backward. "It has to do with everything, that's what. Don't you know that? Pretty near every great story's about love. You notice every other Disney movie has one? *Cinderella* has one, *Snow White* has one—even *Bambi* has one. Only *Pinocchio* doesn't. Shoot, the only female in it's that fairy."

She sat on the edge of the bed and stared at him. "I can't believe it. You're a romantic."

He accepted that with that same half-serious, half-embarrassed little smile. "And you're not," he said thoughtfully.

The sleeper felt crowded and too warm, and she didn't know whether it was because of his presence in it, or the subject under discussion. "As far as I'm concerned," she said tightly, "the whole business is overrated. I've never met anybody in love who was happy about it. It just seems to make everybody miserable."

"You ever been in love?"

She just looked at him; opened her mouth to answer, then closed it again and gripped the edge of the mattress with both hands.

Another one. He'd been half expecting it. He was puzzled, though, and a little disappointed because now he didn't know whether it had been the contraction coming on or the mention of love and romance—particularly the question he'd asked—that had made her tense up like that.

If it had been the latter, that might explain a lot, he thought as he thumbed his stopwatch, glanced at it, then set it again. Say she'd got her heart broken, the baby's father had run out on her—now that was a possibility that hadn't even occurred to him, but it sure would explain her being where she was and the situation she was in. Not to mention the attitude.

Hard to imagine any man doing that, though. Especially to her. If she'd been his...

He squelched the thought, but it lingered in his voice as he coached her with a fierce kind of tenderness. "Don't tense up on me, now. Breathe..."

Chapter 9

"How you doin' back there?"
"I'm droppin' back a little, but I'll make it."
                    I-40—New Mexico

"Why do you always say that?" she asked in a strained and testy voice. "You and Charly—always the same thing: *Breathe*. I *am* breathing, dammit. Otherwise I'd be dead. Oh—*ow*. That hurts."

"It hurts," Jimmy Joe scolded, "because you're not breathin' right. And you're all tensed up. Look at you." Although he couldn't exactly blame her, considering the knot his own insides were in. "You gotta relax, now."

He peeled one of her hands off the mattress and sat down beside her. Holding it with both of his, he began to delicately manipulate the small bones in her palm, gently bending each finger, lightly stroking along the tendons in the back of her hand as if he were fine-tuning a musical instrument or an intricate piece of machinery.

And all the while his jaw was clenched tight and his mind was screaming, *Charlie? Who's Charlie?*

"Charlie—that your husband?" he casually asked as he watched his fingers work their way from the base of her palm to the incredibly fragile bones of her wrist. He told himself it was to get her mind chewing on something else besides the pain she was in.

But it was hard to overlook the way he felt when she replied, with a funny little snort of laughter, "She's my coach." He felt light-headed and sort of goofy, like he wanted to smile but knew he shouldn't.

"Well, she's right. You should listen to your coach." He crooned the words with a perfectly straight face. But inside, his heart was singing like a set of jakes on a downhill grade. *She. Not a husband. Not even a boyfriend. She.* "Here, why don't you lie over there, now. Let me rub your back...get that breathin' goin' right."

She shook her head rapidly, emphatically. Her eyes were closed and he could see that she was in that other place now, the place he couldn't go, concentrating hard on the breath she was taking. The hand he was holding had gone limp and boneless and the other appeared to have relaxed its grip on the edge of the mattress, so he kept his mouth shut and rode it out with her. Which was all he could do.

"It's going," she whispered on a long exhalation, slowly rocking herself back and forth. And finally,

''There.'' And she smiled and opened her eyes. ''Gone.'' She looked triumphant.

He noticed then the nightgown she was wearing, the outlines of her body clearly visible beneath the cartoon character on the thin T-shirt material—the fullness of her breasts, the pert little button of her turned-out navel. Her bare arms and her feet swathed in his thick white socks looked oddly defenseless, almost childlike.

''You warm enough?'' he asked her, lightly brushing her arm with the backs of his fingers, frowning when her skin suddenly roughened with goose bumps. ''Let me get you somethin' to put on....'' His voice thickened in his throat.

He loosened his hand from hers in a hurry, heart thumping, and got up to rummage through his closet. He found a plaid flannel shirt, one of his favorites, nice and soft with some blue and green in it that he thought would look nice with her hair.

''Here you go,'' he muttered, the words crowding his chest, getting mixed up with air he seemed to have forgotten to exhale. ''Put your arm in here.''

It smells like him, she thought as she pulled the shirt around her. She inhaled deeply, closing her eyes as she took in his scent, letting her mind drift, free to follow paths and currents of its own choosing. She saw—no, *felt*—a beautiful shimmering spring, its water warm and clear and life-giving; felt it surrounding her, bathing her in comfort and security. And then somehow the water wasn't there anymore and instead it was Jimmy Joe, and for a moment it was he who held her, safe and comforted, in his arms.

"That's good," she heard him say softly. "You're relaxin' better already."

She felt his fingers on her forehead, on the spot between her brows where the tension knot would be. And for some reason his touch made her face ache and her sinuses burn with an overpowering urge to cry. She let the breath out abruptly and pushed herself erect, compelled by a confusing combination of fear and birthing instincts to stand, to move, to flee.

"Let me out—I want to go to the bathroom," she said, querulous and demanding, knowing she was being unreasonable. And not caring.

A chuckle came from close behind her, near enough to stir the hair behind her ear. "You'd freeze to death out there, dressed like that. Come on, now...settle back down here."

His hands brushed her upper arms. She pulled away from him like a contrary child, insisting, "But I have to *go*."

"No, you don't. You just think you do. You just went not ten minutes ago, you know that?" His voice was gentle, patient. "Wait a little bit. Then if you want, I'll wrap you up in a quilt and take you."

"You're not going to carry me!" Mirabella rounded on him, raw and furious. "I'll walk, or I won't go at all."

"Suit yourself," he said with a shrug. And to her added fury, she caught a fleeting glimpse of a dimple.

Suddenly she felt smothered, as if she was being buried beneath an avalanche of emotions. Confusing, conflicting, overwhelming emotions. "How am I supposed to do this?" she demanded, gesturing wildly. "I can't do this!"

"What is it you can't do?" Jimmy Joe's eyes were soft, his voice tender. She wanted to hit him.

"*This!* I can't have a baby here. There isn't any room. I can't even walk around. How am I supposed to have a baby if I can't walk around?"

She hardly heard her own words, but it didn't matter. They weren't what she wanted to say anyway. She didn't know the words for what she was feeling— frightened beyond imagination, utterly overwhelmed by what was happening to her; and not just to her body, but to her heart and soul. And the most incredible thing was that Jimmy Joe seemed to understand it all.

"Shh," he said. And again, "Shh...hush, now."

And she felt his arms come around her, wrapping her in his own special scent, his warmth and comfort, just as in her vision. She felt his heartbeat thumping against her cheek and his hand stroking her hair, and the trembling and fury inside her cleared away like storm clouds before a fresh spring wind. She felt her breathing calm and time itself to his...she felt warm again, and safe.

"I'm sorry," she whispered. "I'm sorry."

"I know...I know. It's okay."

"I'm not really... This isn't your fault. I know it isn't. I'm just being..." She paused and gave a small, liquid laugh. "I suppose this is normal, isn't it?"

His chuckle rumbled softly against her ear. "I imagine it is."

"I guess you've been through all this."

"How's that?"

"With your wife."

"Oh." He coughed, and she felt him jerk slightly; his hands moved restlessly over her back. "Yeah... well. To tell you the truth...."

It was coming again. She could feel it. Feel it lurking like something dark and terrifying just beyond the reaches of her consciousness. It was coming, and there was nothing she could do to stop it.

"Jimmy Joe, it's starting again."

How calm her voice was. But he knew. He could tell by the way her muscles went rigid beneath his hands and her breathing suddenly seemed to drag as if even her lungs had stiffened.

"Don't tense up on me now.... *Relax.*" His voice growled in his throat. Calm... Stay calm, he thought. How you gonna keep her calm if you're not?

He clicked his stopwatch, then cleared his throat and asked, "You want to lie down?"

She shook her head, too busy coping with the pain now to answer. He took a breath. Closed his eyes. "Okay." He heard himself sigh. "Hold on to me now. Let it come...let it come." And he felt her weight come against him and her breathing time itself to his, while he held her and rode it with her, all the way up the long, dark climb...and down the other side.

All the time he was thinking, Oh God, how am I gonna tell her? Here she was depending on him, counting on his knowledge and experience. How was he going to tell her he was as much a novice at this as she was? God knows, he didn't want to tell her; she was scared enough as it was. But he knew he had to,

because sooner or later he was going to let her down.
Better now, he figured, than later, when she was apt
to be going to pieces anyway.

"It's going," she said on an exhalation, telling him
what he already knew.

Then for a while neither of them spoke. He felt her
skin quiver beneath his hands and her breath flow
warm and easy against his throat, and he thought how
much like the aftermath of sex it was; the sweet, fragile time when bodies grow quiet and whispers of secret
fears, drowned out by the drums of passion, are heard
from again.

Presently she stirred and said, "They're coming faster, aren't they?"

He nodded without looking at his watch. Faster,
longer, harder. Just like it was supposed to. He wondered how much time they had—half of him wanting
things to hold off as long as possible, preferably until
help arrived; half wanting it to be over so she wouldn't
have to hurt anymore. He just wished they had some
way of knowing. In a hospital, he knew, they would
have ways of telling how far along she was. But he
didn't, and all he could do was stay with her and try
to make her as comfortable as he knew how, and when
the time came, pray to the Good Lord to help them
both.

"You know what?" she said, straightening and
pulling away from him, restless again. She pushed into
the space between the seats, stared for a moment
through the windshield, then turned and came back
again. He could see the tension between her brows,
like the pleats in a tiny accordion. "Is there anything

to eat in here? I'm hungry. And thirsty. Really thirsty.''

"Shoot," he said under his breath, thinking hard. The truth was, he'd never been one to carry much with him in the way of food and drink. Truck stops being as plentiful and convenient as they were these days, if he had his druthers, he preferred to do his eating in something that didn't vibrate. And as far as fluids were concerned, well…he'd learned the hard way that whatever he took in, sooner or later he was going to have to find a place to get rid of it, so unless the weather was hot and dry and he had to be careful about dehydration, he was apt to go real easy in that department.

Then he remembered the orange juice he'd brought her—was it just this morning? Yes, it was still there in the little alcove at the head of his bed where she'd set it down. She hadn't drunk much of it. He reached for it and at the same time grabbed the plastic bag he kept his pocket change in.

He gave the orange-juice bottle a shake and held it out to her, smiling as her face lit up and she came for it like a hungry lamb. "There you go," he murmured, guiding her until she was sitting on the bed again, "you stay here and sip on that. I'm gonna go see if I can find us some vending machines."

Eyes closed, already drinking, she made wordless sounds of acquiescence and gratitude while he found the lantern, checked the beam, then braced himself, opened the door and stepped once more into that strange, unearthly night.

He was struck at once by the stillness. The quiet

growl of the big diesel engine behind him, the constant rumbling of the trucks passing in endless procession just beyond seemed to have no connection with the land or the scene spread out before him. The wind had died down, leaving a quiet cold that burned like fire in his lungs. In the east there were clouds, lit to shades of indigo and silver and milky white by the rising moon, while under the light of the shrouded moon and brilliant stars the snow lay like a pale blue blanket across an empty land.

"Silent night! Holy night!/All is calm, all is bright...."

To take his mind off how cold the night was and how alone he felt in it, he sang the words of the carol in his mind as he made his way to the cinder-block shelter that housed the vending machines, keeping time with the crunch of his footsteps in the frozen snow.

"O little town of Bethlehem,/How still we see thee lie...."

He fed coins into the machines until he couldn't feel his fingers, stuffing the pockets of his vest with packets of cheese and peanut-butter crackers, Oreo cookies and cans of 7-Up.

"Above thy deep and dreamless sleep/The silent stars go by...."

The coins were gone. Breathless with cold, hugging his goodies-filled vest and feeling like Santa Claus, he retraced his steps to where his truck sat patiently grumbling, giving off welcoming plumes of vapor like smoke from a farmhouse chimney. Halfway there he slipped on an icy patch and almost fell on his butt, interrupting his silent singing to utter aloud a cussword so inappropriate in that context it made him whoop with laughter.

He was still chuckling, singing, ''Here comes Santy Claus,/Here comes Santy Claus,'' under his breath as he climbed into the cab, but the song and the laughter both fizzled out when he saw Mirabella sitting in the front seat, looking wide-eyed and clutching the CB mike in both hands as if it were a wild bird she'd just captured.

''Someone was there,'' she said in a hushed and excited voice. ''I was going to turn on the radio. I thought I'd try to find some music. Then I heard crackling, and I think…a voice. But it was so faint. So far away. I tried to answer, but I don't think they heard me. Oh…'' She broke off to wipe a furious hand across her eyes and nose, and he took the mike from her gently, ever mindful of emotions so perilously near the surface. Well aware that some of them were his.

He slid into the driver's seat and shut the door behind him, then eased on over into the space between the seats, pulling cellophane packages out of his vest pockets with one hand while he thumbed the mike on with the other. Mirabella watched him hungrily until he grinned and handed her a packet of cheese crackers.

''Mayday, channel 9, Mayday… Come on.'' He listened to silence broken only by rustling paper and munching sounds, then fiddled with the tuner and tried again. ''Mayday, Mayday, anybody out there listenin'?'' He heard a faint crackling and caught and held his breath while he listened with every nerve cell in his body. But whoever it was trying to reach him, the signal was too weak and too far away.

"Jimmy Joe..."

He felt something lightly touch his face and realized only then that he'd been listening with his eyes shut. When he opened them he felt as if his heart was turning clear over inside his chest, because he could see then that it was her hand that lay along his beard-stubbled jaw, her fingers stroking back the hair just above his ear. He couldn't remember exactly but he thought it was the first time she'd touched him like that, of her own accord. And when he looked at her he knew everything he was feeling must be right there in his face for her to see.

"Jimmy Joe, it's all right," she said, and stopped a tiny, silent burp with her hand. She shook her head and went earnestly on, smelling rather touchingly of Ritz crackers. "Even if nobody comes, I know everything's going to be okay. You're here...."

He shook his head and had to look away from her, the back of his hand, clutching the CB mike, pressed hard against his lips.

"I mean it," she whispered earnestly, "I'd rather have you for my coach than anybody. Promise you won't leave me."

"Lord help us, I ain't goin' anywhere!" he exclaimed, his voice raspy and full of bumpy laughter.

"Um, shame on you, you said 'ain't.' What would your mama say?" She was laughing, now, too, but stopped when she picked up her own thread again. "I mean...even if somebody comes. Please don't leave me. Promise you'll stay with me until my baby is born. Please, Jimmy Joe.''

He grabbed at her hand, but it was going to be a little while before he could bring the words up out of the jumble inside him. He waited, head bowed, holding her hand while he worked at it, and when he was pretty sure he had his own voice back he cleared his throat and said, "Marybell, there's something you've gotta know." He lifted his head and looked straight at her then, facing up to the truth like a man, like his daddy had always taught him. And because he knew he was going to let her down, it was one of the hardest things he'd ever done. Especially with those big trusting eyes of hers gazing into his.

He took a breath. "I didn't lie to you. I did go to those childbirthing classes with Patti—my wife. I just… See, I never got to go through the actual birth with her. It was just the way it happened. Both times I was out on the road. The first time—"

"Contraction," she gasped, and then went right on breathing like that, way too hard and too fast.

He yelled, "Slow down!" just to get her attention, but she stared at him and didn't ease up on the breathing even a little bit, and he knew she was caught up in it and didn't know how to stop. He took her face in his hands and felt her skin growing clammy to the touch.

"Breathe with me, dammit," he said between clenched teeth, hoping he wasn't going to start hyperventilating himself.

She shook her head frantically. He could feel that her jaw had gone rigid, see her eyes darken with panic.

Lord, he thought, forgive me. He took a deep breath.
And then he kissed her.

As kisses went, he supposed it wasn't much. On a
thrill scale, he would have had to rank it somewhere
below an electric toothbrush and a fresh stick of cinnamon chewing gum. But it did what it was supposed
to do, which was to stop her breathing long enough
for her to get control of it again. To shock her enough
to break the grip of her panic, like a slap in the face
or a bucket of cold water. That was the way he meant
it, and he hoped she would know that and forgive him
for it.

The trouble was, his *body* didn't know it. All his
mouth knew was the shape and texture of hers, and
the messages that got sent along his nerves to his brain
were all about how sweet and good it tasted, how
warm and soft it felt. And so of course his brain—not
the thinking part of it—had to go and put the word
out to other parts of his body: happy, joyful, excited
messages, clanging Christmas bells and choruses singing "Hallelujah."

It might not have been so hard if she'd stiffened up
and pulled away from him like he'd expected she
would. But instead, after the first frozen moment, the
first shocked gasp, she leaned into his mouth—hard,
and then harder, as if she couldn't help herself, as if
in some strange way there was a connection between
the kiss and the cataclysm that was taking place in her
body. It almost made a kind of sense to him, although
he couldn't have explained why or how. He only knew
it affected him deeply—more profoundly than any kiss
ever in his life before.

It ended when the contraction did, but for both of them the shock of it seemed to linger, so that their first words were whispered across an airless space of only inches.

"What did you do that for?"

"You were hyperventilating."

"Oh."

"I'm sorry."

"No—that's okay."

"I didn't mean—"

"I know."

He felt her grip on his forearms ease; until then he hadn't noticed how her fingers were digging into his muscles. She sat back, widening the space between them. He watched her draw in a breath, long and deep, then slowly let it out, at the same time lifting both hands to sweep and hold the hair back from her face. He noticed that she still looked horribly pale—almost greenish. The residual effects of the carbon-dioxide imbalance, he was sure.

He smiled at her and lightly touched her cheek. "You gotta watch that, you know? Next time, you keep your eyes on me, you hear? Breathe with me. That's assumin' *I'm* not hyperventilating."

She didn't smile back; her eyes had a glazed, distant look. But as he watched, he saw them darken and focus on his face, and she nodded gravely. "I will. I'll try. You have to help me, Jimmy Joe." He nodded, and she took his hand and held it in both of hers. "We didn't have much time to practice this, did we? We barely had time to get to know each other."

"We still got time," he said, his voice husky. But she shook her head.

"I didn't tell you—I had two contractions while you were out there. *Two,* Jimmy Joe. Hard ones. It seems like there's hardly any time between them. I just feel like one big raw nerve." She said the last words with a kind of breathy desperation, then paused as for a moment or two she struggled to regain control. She cleared her throat and continued in a low voice, clinging to his hand. "So, I guess it's getting serious. Isn't it?"

There had been a couple of other times in his life when he'd wished and prayed for something to be different from the way it was, and he'd never wished or prayed any harder than he was doing right now. But he knew from past experience that in the end all a person could do was accept what was. So he nodded and said, "Yeah, it is."

And now she did smile, a little crookedly, with her head tilted to one side. "So, it's true? You've never done this before, either?"

He ducked his head and made a rueful clicking sound with his tongue. "It's the truth. Missed the big event completely." Lifting his eyes back to hers, he forced himself to smile. "So I guess I'm as much a novice as you are."

"I kinda doubt that," she said dryly. Then after a moment, "Jimmy Joe? A while ago you said—" she frowned, and his heart began to beat faster "—both times. What did you mean? You told me about your son—J.J., right? So, what…"

Impulsively he lifted his hand, the one she was

holding, and added his free hand, enfolding both of hers in the process. Closing his eyes, he pressed them, his and her hands together, against his lips. His throat had locked up tight, but she waited in patient silence, not rushing him but not letting him off the hook, either. And presently he swallowed past the pain and began to push words against their tightly clasped fingers. Eventually they came more easily, and to make room for them he let their hands fall to the space between his knees—though he didn't let go even then, and neither did she.

"J.J. was my second baby," he said. "My first was a little girl. Patti—my wife—was pretty heavy into drugs and alcohol then. She'd promised me she'd quit, you know, but she lied about it, and I was gone so much, what with tryin' to get my business goin'—my daddy had just passed away not long before, and I was out there on my own for the first time... Ah, hell." He stopped, shaking his head. He'd made the same excuses for himself so many times. "The fact is," he said, exhaling in a rush of guilt, "I didn't keep as close a watch on her as I should have. She had the baby early...way too early." He heard Mirabella's soft sound of distress—he'd been waiting for it—and pushed past it before she could say anything.

"My little girl was born so tiny and sick, I reckon she never had a chance. I was out on the road. When I got there, they had her on life support—just this tiny little scrap of life, all hooked up to tubes and wires. Patti, she didn't want to have anything to do with her, wouldn't touch her, wouldn't even come to see her. I guess I couldn't blame her, really. They told me my little girl couldn't live without those machines, wasn't ever going to have a chance for a normal life. And they asked me if I wanted to hold her. So they unhooked her and wrapped her in a little pink blanket and put her in my hands. It seemed like she hardly weighed anything at all. They had this rocking chair…and I sat there and rocked her and sang to her until she left me.…''

His words became whispers, then nothing. It hurt too much. His chest, his throat, his whole body, like an old wound torn open again, raw and fresh as if it had happened yesterday. But how could he tell her about that when she was in so much pain herself? He had no right!

His face was wet. He knew some of the moisture and warmth he felt was his own tears, but there was something else there, too. Something miraculous. Somehow there was the soft flow of breath, *her* breath, issuing from her lips as they gently brushed his cheeks, his eyelids, his brows. And her fingers, stroking through his hair.

''I'm sorry.…'' It was a whisper of sound—no more—breathed against his temple. ''Another contraction… Please hold me.''

Nothing had ever seemed more natural to him than to do as she asked. He pushed his fingers through her hair and cradled her head in his palm and drew it gently down, tucking it into the hollow beneath his chin. And it felt to him as if he'd been keeping that place for her for all of his life; a special nest, just for her head. Her arms came around his neck, not frantically clutching, but holding fast with complete and unquestioning trust. His hands stroked down her sides and around to her back to find the place where the pain was sharpest and the tension lurked, and as he began a kneading, circling pressure, he felt the breath gush through her in a sigh of sheer relief.

They rode it out that way, facing each other across the space between the seats, arms wrapped around each other, legs comfortably sandwiched, breathing almost as one being.... Entwined like lovers.

How natural it seemed. How sweet and easy.

Chapter 10

*"I'm gonna start noddin' off, here, pretty soon.
Talk to me…talk to me."*

I-40—Texas

"What was her name?" Mirabella asked, her voice muffled and dreamy.

Still dazed, Jimmy Joe mumbled, "Pardon?" and she lifted her head from his chest and gazed at him with an earnest-but-unfocused smile.

"Your baby girl. Did you name her?"

"Oh." He coughed and cleared his throat as he straightened. At the same time she took her arms from around his neck and let them slide through his hands, until that was the only part of them still touching. "Amy," he said, without taking his eyes from their clasped hands. "We named her Amy."

"Amy… That's pretty." She said it absently, then

rose abruptly, breaking even that small physical contact.

He watched as she moved away from him, rubbing at her back, distracted and restless again, and was conscious of a sense of loss and regret. He had an idea it was the way she would be from now on, becoming more and more introspective and closed off from him as her time grew nearer and she concentrated all her energy, mind and body, on the job ahead of her. She would be focused on that, wrapped up in it, consumed by it, deaf and blind to everything else, including him.

Which was normal, he told himself. Just as it should be. And which made what had just happened between them—her compassion and concern for *his* pain—seem so miraculous to him.

He hadn't meant to get in her way. The way he saw it, his job was just to be there for her even when she didn't know he was, to lead and guide her like a blind person through a swamp, to keep her safe from harm, to keep her from feeling lost or scared. Thinking about the responsibility of it all made him feel awed and humble. He just hoped he was up to it.

"You got a name picked out for your baby?" he asked.

"Hmm?" She turned like a sleepwalker, frowning. Already it was becoming harder to distract her. "Oh—yeah." A smile flickered across her face, sure and confident, for an instant a touch of the old Mirabella. "Eric. His name is Eric. It means, 'all-powerful.'"

He nodded. "Nice. How 'bout if it's a girl?"

She shook her head emphatically. "It won't be. It's a boy."

It had been so long since he'd seen that little lift of her chin, he couldn't help but smile. "You know that for a fact? I mean, did they do the tests and all?"

"I've seen the ultrasound. The doctor says he's sure it's a boy. Anyway, I hope…it is." She hiccuped, and distress flitted briefly across her face.

Automatically, he reached behind him, found one of the cans of soda he'd brought back from the vending machines and popped it open. "Why's that?" he asked as he handed it to her.

"Why do I want a boy?" She lashed him with a dark and furious look, snatched the soda from him and gulped heedlessly. "How can you even ask?" She waved the can like someone who's maybe getting tipsy. "Because it's still a man's world, dammit. And I don't want my child…to have to *struggle*…like I did. Ow…*dammit.*"

He rescued the soda can and found a safe place for it on the floor in front of the driver's seat, then turned his attention back to Mirabella. But when he reached for her, she squirmed away from him with a furiously hissed, "Don't touch me!"

And then, before he could even decide whether it was okay to ignore that or not, she cut loose with a belly-deep wail, a growl, almost, that seemed to come from the depths of her soul.

"Noooh!" Shaking her head. Fighting it. Denying it. "No. Not now. It's too soon. I'm not ready. I want to rest. I can't…*do this!*"

Somehow he got his arms around her. Somehow he managed to still her thrashing and get her leaning against him, get her to breathe with him, slow and steady, the way she was supposed to. And all the time he was crooning to her, telling her yes, she *could* do it. Telling her how strong and brave and beautiful she was. Meaning every word.

By the time it was done she was sobbing, "I'm sorry, I'm sorry," over and over, and he was stroking her temple with his chin and growling, "It's okay, it's okay.... Nothing to be sorry about..."

He felt lost...helpless.

He wanted to tell her it was happening too fast for him, too. That he wasn't ready, either. He wanted to tell her he wished he'd had more time with her, time to get to know her better. A lifetime of time. Time to get to know her ways, her body's tender secrets—where she hurt and how she liked to be touched, and the mysterious feminine noises she uttered when she made love. There was so much about her he wanted to know. So many things he wished he'd asked her when he'd had the chance.

Mostly, he wanted to know why. Why, on Christmas Eve, was she here with him, a stranger, having her precious baby in a snowbound truck when she should have been in a warm, comfortable place with people to take care of her, and a husband to hold her and stroke her and tell her how much he loved her—the baby's father, sharing it all, the whole wonderful miracle of it, with her? *Why?* He thought it had to be a tragedy of some sort—he couldn't imagine any other explanation. He really wanted to know.

But she'd moved beyond him now. She was out of his reach, and he thought it was too late to ask her.

She'd pulled herself together and moved back a little, lifting her eyes to his, eyes that were filled with questions of their own. "Jimmy Joe?"

"Yeah, I'm here," he murmured, pretending he knew the answers.

She drew a bright and hopeful breath. "I really do need to go to the bathroom. I know I'd feel better if I could just—"

But he stopped her there, firmly shaking his head, wishing he didn't have to see the entreaty in her face. "I can't let you go out," he said as gently as he could. "It's not just cold, it's icy and dangerous. What if you hurt yourself—or your baby?"

He brushed her cheek with the backs of his fingers, wiping away a tear she probably didn't even know about. "Tell you what, though. I'm gonna find you something, so you can go...." Now she was shaking her head—wildly, frantically. He saw the fear in her eyes and somehow knew that what she was most in dread of at that moment was the thought of losing her privacy—her dignity.

Mindful of that, he caught her chin and held it still, and leaning close, whispered his instructions in her ear as if they were in a room full of strangers and it was the most intimate of confidences he was sharing with her. So softly she had to catch her breath, still her breathing in order to hear him. When he was finished, she shivered like a child with a secret and whispered an airless and mollified, "Okay."

He guided her into the sleeper compartment with a deferential touch, as if he were escorting a duchess to the dinner table, reached up to take down the pile of towels from the shelf above the bed and presented them to her without a word.

From another compartment he took out a plastic trash bag with a drawstring top and his first-aid kit. He left the bag on the bed, tucked the first-aid kit under his arm and backed out of the sleeper, pulling the curtain closed as he went. Then he slid into the driver's seat, dialed in channel 19 on his CB radio and turned the volume up loud. Static and chatter filled the cab, drowning out all other sound, even the sigh of his own exhalation and the drumming of his rapidly beating heart.

For a while he just sat and listened to it. He felt curiously drained, felt a need to rest and rebuild his store of energy, not so much from what he'd already been through, but for what was still to come. Because this was only the beginning. He knew that, just as he knew she was going to need everything he had to give her.

The radio blared suddenly with a crackly, tinny rendition of Tennessee Ernie Ford bawling, "O Come, All Ye Faithful," somebody evidently trying to share his own particular brand of Christmas cheer through his open mike. Takes all kinds, Jimmy Joe thought as he picked up his own mike and thumbed it on, grinning. Even among truckers.

"This is the Big Blue Starr— Hey, shut that thing off, will ya? I got a lady havin' a baby over here. Need to talk to somebody.... Come on."

"Hey, Big Blue!" The voice was nearby, loud and excited. "'Bout time you put your ears back on. Good to hear from you, buddy. How you doin' over there?"

Jimmy Joe chuckled. Already the sound of other drivers' voices had lifted his spirits, made him feel hopeful, not quite so alone. "Doin' okay, so far. Could use a little help, though. Anybody seen any smokies lately?"

"Hell, no— 'Twas the night before Christmas and not a bear stirrin'—"

"Hey, Big Blue, they're talkin' 'bout you all way back to New Mexico. How's the little lady doin'?"

"Hangin' in there," said Jimmy Joe. "Listen, we'd sure 'preciate it if you'd pass the word along to Amarillo. Tell 'em we need some help out here."

"Already been done, Big Blue."

And from farther away: "Uh...that's affirmative. Word got there—oh, been a while ago. Word now is, they're, uh, tryin' to set somethin' up, tryin' to patch through a relay, or somethin'. Got a buncha phone lines down, so it's takin' awhile, but they're workin' on it. You'd best go on over there to channel 9 and wait for 'em...."

"Thank ya kindly, 'preciate it," said Jimmy Joe. He was about to turn the dial when a woman's voice broke in.

"You tell the lady we're all prayin' for her."

And from all up and down the line the voices of lonely, snowbound drivers chimed in.

"Yeah, you hang in there, now."

"We're pullin' for ya...."

"Y'all have a Merry Christmas!"

"Take care..."

"We're with you, Big Blue!"

"God Bless..."

"Thanks," said Jimmy Joe. "I sure do 'preciate it. Y'all have a Merry Christmas, now. Safe trip... Ten-four." He signed off with a lump in his throat and tears in his eyes.

For a moment he just sat there holding the mike while all that flood of emotions and feelings just sort of rolled over him like a great big wave, and when it receded, he felt calm again. Peaceful. As if somebody had put out a hand and touched him and said to him, "Son, everything's gonna be okay."

He took a big breath and huffed it out, then dialed in channel 9 and went through his "Mayday, Mayday!" thing once more. He thought he heard some faint mumbles and crackles in response, but since it wasn't clear enough to be any use to him, he hung the mike back on its hook and left the channel open with the volume turned up loud.

There wasn't any sound coming from his sleeper, so he turned on the regular radio and found a pretty clear station playing Christmas music, which he left on low just to provide some cover noise in case Mirabella still needed the privacy.

Then he started going over in his mind what she and the baby were going to need, making sure he had everything ready. Thank God, he thought, for his comfortable sleeper and for the reliability of his good ol' diesel engine. They had the most important things—warmth and shelter and a comfortable bed. Towels and bedding for her; soft, clean flannel shirts to wrap the baby in. The first-aid kit, with scissors and disinfectant and all kinds of stuff to tie off the cord. Even a plastic squeeze bottle that held eyewash—which he dumped out—in case he needed something to suction out the baby's nose and mouth.

As far as he could see he had everything except water for boiling, but what the heck—he always had wondered what all that hot water was supposed to be for. So it looked like he was ready. Ready as he was ever going to be.

On the radio Garth Brooks was singing "Silent Night." Jimmy Joe smiled a little, remembering what Mirabella had said about never having heard of him, and turned it up some more so she could hear it.

"All is calm, all is bright...."

This is the calm before the storm, he thought, rubbing his eyes.

Then for some reason he remembered that Mirabella had mentioned she wore contacts. He wondered if she'd thought about them, and whether she might want to take them out and put them away for safekeeping. He wondered just how blind she was without them. There was so much about her he didn't know.

He reached through the curtain and knocked lightly on the side of the closet. "Hey, how you doin' in there?" He listened, and when he didn't hear any urgent orders to keep out, went ahead and pulled back the curtain.

She was lying on her side with her back to him, knees drawn up slightly and her head resting on her arm. He could see the pale curve of her cheek, and her hair pooling like spilled wine on the pillow behind her. He thought for a moment she might be sleeping, until he saw that her hand was moving over her belly in slow, caressing circles. He went to sit on the mattress beside her, being careful not to jostle her too much, and reached over to smooth back the wisps of hair from her face. He felt dampness, but didn't know whether it was sweat or tears. Either way, he felt his throat tighten.

"Everything okay?" he asked huskily. "Feelin' better now?"

She sniffed and nodded, moving her head slightly so he could see she had her eyes closed. Then she whispered something, and he had to lean closer to hear. "Make a mess..." was all he caught. He didn't know whether to laugh or to strangle her.

"Marybell," he said with an incredulous snort, "you really are the limit, you know that?"

The exasperation in his voice startled her enough so she opened her eyes and craned her head around so she could look at him, frowning. "Why?"

"You always this hard on yourself?"

The frown turned into uncertainty; she looked as vulnerable as a scolded child. "What...do you mean?"

With restraint and tenderness he brushed his knuckles across her eyebrows, using his thumb to smooth out the worry-creases between them. "Look at you— here you are, doing probably the most fantastic and wonderful thing it's possible for any human being to do, and you're worried about makin' a *mess?* Woman, what am I gonna do with you?" She drew a quivering sniff and didn't say anything. He cocked his head to one side and teasingly asked, "Tell me the truth—did you seriously think you were gonna have a baby without makin' a mess?"

"I sure did mean to try," she muttered.

It felt good to laugh.

While he was doing that, he also had a strong desire to gather her into his arms and kiss her, but he was pretty sure it was the last thing she would have welcomed. Instead, he remembered to ask her about her contacts.

"I already took them out," she told him, struggling to sit up. "They're in my overnight bag." She paused to glare at him. "And don't you dare lose them."

"Yes, ma'am," he said humbly, and was delighted when she socked him right smartly in the arm.

By the time he'd helped her get herself turned around so her legs were dangling off the edge of the bed, though, he could see the shine of sweat on her skin. He watched her as she sat gripping the edge of the mattress and breathing hard, slowly rocking herself, and then he reached out and gently wiped her forehead with the palm of his hand.

His throat ached when she sighed and murmured, "That feels good."

"Wish I had some cool water," he mumbled.

She took a breath and then surprised him with a soft laugh. "Do you know…that I planned to have this baby in a tub full of water?"

"A *what?*"

"It's called a birthing tub. It's the latest thing. It's supposed to make it a lot easier for…both them the mother and the baby. I had it all…planned. Oh…*damn.*" Her breathing had gotten faster and her voice more guttural, until it ended in one of those belly-deep groans. He could see her teeth clench as she tried to stifle it.

''Why don't you go ahead and holler?'' he grunted when he'd gotten his arms around her and her weight settled against his chest. ''I don't mind, and it might make you feel better.'' He doubted she even heard him.

Later when the crisis had passed, though still in pain, she tried again to tell him—almost, it seemed to him, as if she were compelled. As if it was terribly important to her, as if he wouldn't know she hadn't meant it to be like this.

''I had it planned,'' she whispered. ''I did… everything right. Everything.''

Not everything, he thought. And because it had been making so much noise in his head for so long, and because he didn't think she was really going to hear him anyway, he went ahead and asked it, in a harsh and raspy voice that wasn't even his.

''What about the father? He have any part in this plan of yours?''

Her head pumped wildly back and forth. ''No—he's not supposed to. That's not the way it works—'' Her breath gushed from her in a cleansing torrent. ''Oh…God. They're starting again. They…sort of slowed down for a while, when I was lying down. Now it's like…there's no time in between. I can't rest. It doesn't stop. I can't…do this!''

What could he do then but soothe her and calm her and get her settled down and focused again? But he was left feeling confused and guilty, and his questions were still unanswered.

He lost track of time. Or rather, to be more precise, he stopped letting himself think in terms of time. Instead, he started thinking about what they were doing as sort of like climbing a mountain, a great big mountain that was made up of a lot of little mountains. All he had to do was keep climbing the little mountains, one at a time, all the time keeping his eye on the big one, which a lot of the time seemed like it wasn't getting any closer. But he knew if he just kept climbing the little ones, sooner or later he was gonna get to the top.

He tried sharing his mountain image with Mirabella, but she wasn't in any frame of mind to appreciate it. She was having about all she could handle just getting over the "little hills"—although when he used that phrase to describe one of her contractions, for some reason, she tried to hit him.

He did his best to keep her relaxed, touched her when she would let him, massaging her back or her legs, rubbing her neck or her feet, depending on the mood she was in. He tried telling her not to think about the contractions, but to think instead about nice things, like good smells and bright colors and her favorite food, which she told him was chocolate-covered cherries. He told her his was macaroni and cheese, but didn't think she was listening.

When she got cranky and fed up he told her to cuss him if she wanted to, and she took him up on it a time or two. Again he told her to yell, really cut loose and holler, but as much as he knew she wanted to, he couldn't get her to do it. He didn't know if it was because she didn't want to upset him, or because she was afraid of making a spectacle of herself. Maybe, he thought as he began to know some of her ways, a little of both.

He was sorry about that, because he had an idea it would have made it easier for her. It seemed like such a natural thing to do. Like making noise during sex, he thought. And then he wondered why that idea didn't shame him. But the truth was, he'd been thinking for quite a while about how sometimes it seemed what was happening here and now—this birthing business—was a lot like making love. Only more so. Bigger. A whole lot bigger. Lovemaking to the ultimate degree. It made so much sense to him, because after all, this was what sex was supposed to be about, wasn't it? Two people in love makin' a baby.

Yes, it seemed right. Right that he should be holding this woman between his thighs, cradled against his body, her breathing so perfectly timed to his, her breasts heavy against his arms, and feel the tightening, the pulsing, the cataclysmic tremors deep within her body.

So profoundly right.

"Yeah…" he growled as he felt the pressure and the need inside her build. "Yeah, let it go. That's the way, darlin'. It's okay…let it go.…"

His eyes closed, his lips brushed her ear, his heartbeat rocked him like a boat caught in the ripples of a wake.

"Don't be afraid," he whispered hoarsely, wanting so badly to break through her barriers that he hurt inside. "It's just like loving…like making love when there's nobody to hear you. Think about it. Makin' love on a warm summer night in a cabin way out in the woods…with the frogs chirpin' and the whippoorwill callin' and the air so soft and sweet…and nobody in the world to hear you but the man who loves you more than life. Let him hear you love him. Come on, darlin'…let me hear it.''

She was so close…so close. He could feel her body arching, feel it building inside her like a cresting tidal wave. He heard the first sounds, like a rusty gate opening—and then suddenly it burst from her in an anguished, gut-wrenching wail: *''I ca-a-an't!''*

His chuckle was sympathetic but insistent. ''Sure, you can…sure, you can.''

But he'd already broken the dam, and the vocalizations he'd wanted came pouring out, complete with words. ''I don't know…I don't know…. I've never… made love before.…''

He laughed softly, thinking how funny she was, how sweetly confused. Stroking her damp hair back from her forehead, he murmured tenderly, ''Darlin', what in the world are you talkin' about?''

''I mean,'' she growled, ''I've never made love before. Can't you understand English?''

Sweating and muttering furiously, she subsided, leaving him bewildered, to ponder what she could possibly have meant by such a statement. He could think of a couple of possible explanations, none of which made him feel good. The unanswered questions sat in his chest like an anvil.

After that, when the contractions got to be too much for her, he told her to think of her baby. Her sweet, precious baby boy, and how good it was going to be to hold him in her arms soon. Think of that, he told her. Don't think about the contraction. Think of your baby.

Himself he told to think of nothing at all.

It seemed to Mirabella as though she'd been existing in a nightmare—or rather, in a sort of twilight world between wide-awake and dreaming. What it reminded her of was a time long ago in her childhood—the last and possibly the only time in her life that she'd been sick. Really sick. She remembered being in bed, having a terrible, terrible headache that seemed to go on and on. A second had seemed like an hour when it was happening, but then she would find that hours had passed in what she'd thought were only seconds. She remembered hearing people talk to her, hearing herself answer, knowing she was doing things—drinking water, taking medicine, eating soup, and getting up, trembling, to go to the bathroom—but having no real control over anything that happened to her. Right up until the moment when she'd opened her eyes, gazed into her parents' worried faces and said in a loud, clear voice, "I want *waffles.*"

She was in the waning moments of a contraction, coming down the back side of the mountain—that had been Jimmy Joe's idea, those mountains. How many more of them were there, she wondered, before she reached the top? Hundreds, probably. Hundreds and hundreds.

She felt an urge to hiccup, or perhaps to burp. But when she gave in to it, the ripples in her stomach seemed to want to go down toward her pelvis, rather than up toward her throat. "Oh," she said, startled.

"I want to push," she announced.

Jimmy Joe's face hovered above her. He looked exhausted. "Well, that's good," he said huskily, smoothing back her hair. "Real good. Looks like you're gonna be havin' a baby pretty soon."

For some reason he looked much older than she remembered—at least ten years older. She reached up to touch his face, trying to rub away a deep crease that had appeared near the corner of his mouth. With deep pity she said, "Oh, no, not yet. I still have all those mountains to climb. Lots and lots of mountains…"

There it was again—that strange, upside-down hiccup.

"No more mountains, Marybell."

She opened her mouth to argue, but instead of words, what came out was a low, growling sound. Was that *her?*

"That's it, you just go right ahead and push."

"I'm not…pushing," she gasped stubbornly. "Can't have this baby yet. Still…have…mountains… *oh!*"

"No more mountains." She felt Jimmy Joe's body behind her, lifting and supporting her. "Just a great big sheer rock cliff. Now you gotta pull yourself up to the top, you hear? Pull yourself up, hand over hand, one pull at a time…. Way to go…good girl. Now you rest a minute…just rest…."

Rest? That's easy for *you* to say, she thought resentfully. First all those mountains, and now he wanted her to pull herself up a cliff? What kind of a superwoman did he think she was? Here, her body was trying its best to turn itself wrongside out, and on top of that, now somebody—some strange man with a Texas accent—was yelling at her to, "Come in...*come in!*"

Jimmy Joe jumped up like he'd sat on a pinecone. Laying Mirabella back against the pillows as gently as he could, he lunged for the CB mike and got his thumb on the button.

"I'm readin' you loud and clear!" he shouted. "Come on back."

"Ah...this the fella with the lady havin' a baby, out there on the interstate?"

"That's me!" yelled Jimmy Joe. "Sure am glad to hear from you." And that, he thought, had to be the biggest understatement he'd ever uttered in his life. He was so relieved, his insides felt like jelly. "Hey, where are you? Baby's on its way. Right now. We could sure use some help!"

"Ah...well, we're gon' try our best. Listen, I got me a gas station over here, just west of Vega—my power and phone's been out pert' near all day, just come back on a little while ago, an' looks like it's a good thing it did. Didn't have my radio on, it bein' Christmas Eve, an' all. Anyways, I got a telephone call from the state police. They got a chopper standin' by, but they not gonna be able to get it in the air until the weather clears. So what they done is, they got me patched through to the hospital in Amarillo. Got a doctor here on the line right now. Wants to know how far along she is."

With the realization that that excited voice on the

radio was all the help he was going to get, Jimmy Joe
felt the terrifying sense of responsibility settle once
more onto his shoulders. He closed his eyes briefly,
then shrugged it off and spoke into the mike with a
calm and confidence he was a long way from feeling.
"She's wantin' to push. Ask the doc if it's okay to let
her, or if she ought to be pantin', or something."

There was a pause, then, "Doc says don't let 'er
pant, it'll just wear her out. Says, let her push, but not
too hard. Don't let 'er hold her breath, or turn purple,
he says. Just little pushes, if, ah…if that's what her
body wants to do."

"Gotcha," said Jimmy Joe, with a glance over at
Mirabella, who looked as if she was trying to lift the
back end of a truck. He was about to put the mike
down and get over to her when the voice spoke again.
"Uh…the doc here's got a couple questions for ya.
Wants to know, can you see the baby's head yet?"

Jimmy Joe's stomach gave a lurch and nearly
jumped into his throat. He broke out in a cold sweat
and just did manage to mumble, "Don't know…. I'm
gonna have to get back to you on that."

"Okay…he says check and tell him what you see.
Then he wants to know if you've got somethin' to
catch the baby with."

"Yeah," said Jimmy Joe, "I got that." He took a
deep breath and felt better. "Tell him I think I've got
everything ready. Got plenty of clean towels. Got a
pretty good first-aid kit—antiseptic and bandages, scissors, stuff like that. Ask him if there's anything else I
oughta have." Besides an ambulance and a couple of
experienced paramedics, he thought.

There was another pause. "Doc says sounds like you got it pretty well covered. Wants you to check her and get back to him."

"Right... Ten-four." He pulled the mike cord out as far as it would go and draped it over the back of the seat so he would have it within arm's reach when he needed it, then eased himself back into the sleeper and sat down on the bed beside Mirabella. "How you doin'?" he asked, his throat husky.

She rested, propped on both elbows, and glared at him. "How do you *think* I'm doing?"

"Guess you heard all that." She nodded, watching him. "I'm gonna have to look." And again she nodded.

And then she closed her eyes and groaned, "Well...be quick about it, dammit!" as another powerful contraction overtook her.

Funny, he'd been dreading that moment so. But she didn't seem to mind it when he gently and carefully drew her nightgown up and eased her legs apart— barely seemed aware of him at all, in fact. Instincts a lot more compelling than modesty were driving her now.

A moment later he was back on the radio, his heart beating like a jackhammer. "Can't see anything yet," he panted. Behind him, all inhibitions apparently forgotten, Mirabella was making all the noise he could ever have wanted, and more.

Pause. "Okay, doc says get back to him when you see the head. Oh—and he says, don't let her lie on her back. Says you should get her as upright as possible— get gravity workin' for you."

"Right." Back to Mirabella. He settled himself behind her, supporting her with his body, and whispered in her ear, "You're doin' fine, darlin'. Just got a little bit more work to do.... That's right...just a little bit more."

How much more could she do? he wondered. He'd never in his life seen anybody work so hard. Her hair was soaking wet with sweat, and he knew his arms would bear the imprint of her fingers for a long time to come. He began to get scared again. It seemed such an impossible thing she was trying to do, and it didn't do any good at all to remind himself that it had been done a few billion times before. What if she couldn't do it? What if...

And then...there it was.

"I see it!" he shouted into the mike. "I can see the head." He was laughing, crying a little, too, maybe. Trying to hold on to the mike and Mirabella at the same time.

"Doc says, you sure it's the head?"

"Yes, I'm sure... Hey, darlin', you hear that? We got a head!"

"I...hear...you!"

"Doc wants to know, is it facin' up or down?"

"Can't tell yet.... One more push, darlin'...one more...one more..."

"If you...say that...one more time...I'll kill you!"

"Down! It's facing down!"

"Doc says—"

"No, wait—it's turning! It's turning to one side!"

"Doc says that's okay—that's good."

"One more..."

I will kill him, Mirabella thought. If I survive this. She was on fire. Burning. Splitting in half.

And then—suddenly there was relief.

"The head's out! Darlin', you hear that? The head's out!"

I know....

"Just a little bit more—let's get the shoulders out—come on, now, one more good one..."

One more...one more...

"Doc says you gotta clear the airways!"

Silence.

"Hey—what's happenin' out there? Talk to me... talk to me!"

What's happening? Jimmy Joe? Oh, God...my baby...

And then she heard it. A faint gurgling, then a tiny, rasping cry. As the cry grew louder and stronger, a sob struggled up through her exhausted body. More sobs...laughter and sobs. She struggled to sit up, reaching for the purplish, squirming thing in Jimmy Joe's hands.

It was so tiny, slippery wet, all waving arms and frantic wails. He held it for a moment, then laid it carefully, almost reverently on her belly. She touched it—oh, God, what an incredible thing! Soothed and cradled it with her hands. And the wails quieted to soft mewings.

Jimmy Joe knelt beside her, and she felt his body quaking as his arms came around her, helping her, holding her up so she could see better.

"Merry Christmas," he whispered brokenly. "Say hello to your baby girl."

Chapter 11

"Okay, big truck, ya missed me.... Come on back."
"Thank ya kindly... Think I'll stay out here awhile."
I-40—Texas

"I can't believe it," Mirabella whispered as she gazed down at her daughter's tiny head, dwarfed by the breast she was so eagerly nuzzling—so tiny and yet, so utterly perfect. "A girl..."

She thought of the waiting nursery she'd decorated in primary colors and Disney characters. Thank God she didn't believe in genderizing, and had always hated pastels. But still...

She shook her head and laughed softly. "Here, all this time I'd been planning on a boy—"

"Yeah, well, my daddy had a saying," Jimmy Joe murmured, lightly stroking the baby's head with a wondering finger. "You want to make God laugh?"

He glanced up at her and for the first time in a long time she saw his dimple. ''Just make a plan.''

''Huh,'' said Mirabella absently, and smiled. She wondered briefly that it didn't seem at all strange to her, that juxtaposition of her baby's head, her naked breast, and Jimmy Joe's hand, or even that it had been he who'd shown her how to get the baby to nurse. But then it was a night for wonders.

She didn't remember very much about the immediate aftermath of her baby's birth. In a fog of exhaustion, exhilaration and awe, she'd been only dimly aware of Jimmy Joe...tying and cutting the cord, wrapping the baby in one of his own shirts, following instructions shouted over the radio. She thought there'd been some bad moments when he'd worried about bleeding, and it seemed to her that was when the voice on the radio had told him to try to start the baby nursing. And he'd shown her how, by tickling one tiny cheek so that the baby had turned her mouth instinctively, like a baby bird, toward the waiting nipple.

Then Mirabella had felt the most amazing, excruciating tingling sensations, tingles that radiated from her nipples outward and through her entire body. There had been more contractions, but not too terrible or lasting too long. The placenta had been delivered, the bleeding stopped, and soon after that the voice on the radio had gone away. She'd been vaguely aware of someone wrapping her in clean towels and warm blankets, of her sweat-damp nightshirt being pulled gently over her head, and her arms being guided into the sleeves of a warm flannel shirt. How strange and wonderful it had felt to be fussed over and coddled.

She remembered saying, "Look at us—we match," gazing at the incredibly beautiful, absolutely perfect little face nestled in a bunting of farmer's plaid and laughing tearfully, and that Jimmy Joe had laughed too, the same way, and had kissed her on the tip of her nose.

But she'd begun to shiver uncontrollably then, in spite of the warm shirt and all the quilts and blankets he'd been able to pile on her. So he'd stretched out on the bed and wrapped his arms around her and held her until the shivering quieted.

"Rest," he'd crooned to her, as if *she* were a baby. "Rest now."

Exhausted as she was, she'd been too full of fear and wonder to rest, afraid to take her eyes from her tiny daughter even for a moment. "I can't believe it," she'd said, and was still saying. "I can't believe it."

"Yeah," said Jimmy Joe in a groggy drawl, "I don't think Eric is gonna suit 'er. Guess you're gonna have to call her Erica."

Mirabella glanced at him, but he was still gazing down at his finger, watching it brush back and forth across the baby's downy head. She could see his wavy, dark-blond hair and matching eyebrows, his thoughtfully furrowed brow and dark cresents of eyelashes, the strong, straight bridge of his nose. Lips that were curved in an utterly besotted smile. And suddenly her chest seemed to swell, and for the first time in her life she understood what the phrase, "a full heart" meant. Her heart was so full she felt as if it would burst. So full it had to overflow—with the tears she'd been saving all her life and now seemed to have in endless supply.

"No." She paused and drew a quivering breath. "Her name is Amy." There was a moment of utter stillness, and then through a rainbow shimmer she watched his lips tighten and his lashes quickly drop in a vain attempt to hide the shine of moisture that had caught him unawares. Shaking with emotion, she leaned across the tiny bundle in her arms to kiss his temple, and then with her lips against his hair, to finish in a choked whisper, "Amy...Jo."

It was, finally, too much for Jimmy Joe. Unlike most Southern-raised boys, he'd never been indoctrinated with the taboos against men's tears; his uppity mama's opinions had been every bit as radical on the subject of rights and privileges for the male of the species as they were for her own sex. But he'd grown up in the real word, after all, and while he wasn't ashamed to shed a tear in private if the occasion warranted, breaking down and crying like a baby wasn't something he enjoyed, or felt comfortable doing in front of other people. The events of the night had already stretched the limits of his self-control just about to the breaking point; dazed and raw, he'd been sagging on the ropes trying to catch his second wind. And now this. He felt as if he'd suddenly been stripped naked. Enough! he wanted to cry. *Enough!*

For a few moments he couldn't move, couldn't speak, just sat rigid and vibrating with his arms locked in a protective circle around Mirabella and her baby, with Mirabella's cheek pressed tight against his forehead. But no male animal tolerates such vulnerability for long. Self-preservation messages sang along his nerves and shouted in his brain: *Protect yourself! Take cover! Flee!*

Heart hammering, muscles surging, he "fled" to the limits of available space, which in his case was only as far as the front of the cab—to his own realm, his domain, where he'd always been in supreme control—to his driver's seat. But it was enough. In that familiar space he felt his heartbeat slow and his panicked breathing ease, and a sense of humility and calm settled warm and soft around his shoulders. He looked over at Mirabella, propped upon the pillows, eyes shining in her pale face like silver stars as she gazed back at him, then down at the baby cradled against her breast. He thought he'd never seen such a beautiful sight in all his life. The Madonna herself couldn't have looked so lovely.

He huffed out air, smiled sheepishly and rubbed at the back of his neck. "Wow," he said. "Amy, huh?" And then again, "Wow."

"Would you like to hold her?" she asked softly.

His heart stumbled; his chest quaked. He nodded.

She leaned forward, holding the baby toward him in her outstretched arms, swaddled in his own favorite, his very softest blue plaid flannel shirt. He took her like the precious gift she was, with suspended breath, with gratitude and awe, and held her up so he could see her face-to-face…eye-to-eye. "Hello, Amy Jo," he whispered. *Welcome.*

She gazed back at him with her unfocused newborn's stare, one tiny fist curling and uncurling against one perfect, petal-like cheek. And suddenly it seemed to Jimmy Joe that he heard tiny, silvery tinklings and loud, rumbling crashes, the sounds of things falling and breaking all around him. Soft and miraculous as the sound of raindrops falling on flower petals—the sound of a heart falling in love. Mighty and powerful as an avalanche—the sound of the earth shifting beneath his feet, of his life changing forever.

My God, he thought. *My God.*

He thought how different this was from the way he'd felt when he'd first set eyes on his son, J.J. He'd been so proud, of course. Sorry he hadn't been there to see him born. And relieved the baby was healthy and strong, glad his own long vigil was finally over, hopeful Patti would stay off the dope this time, and sad because deep in his heart he'd known she wouldn't. It was only later that he'd come to love that little boy more than his own life.

But this—he'd never felt anything like this before. He felt awed and humbled, yes, but also strong and powerful, invincible and mighty. For this little girl he would slay dragons, move mountains, swim oceans. He would guard and protect her, lay down his life for her, and love her without condition until the day he died.

Behind him, the CB radio gave a little belch of static. He'd forgotten—he'd left the channel open in case the doctor in Amarillo or the state troopers needed to get ahold of him. Now, though, it reminded him of something.

"Somethin' I need to do," he muttered. And it pleased him, as he tucked the bundled baby neatly into the crook of one arm, that it felt so natural and easy, and how quickly it all came back to him.

He reached to unhook the mike he'd left dangling across the passenger seat and looked over at Mirabella. She smiled sleepily back at him and nodded. He glanced down once more at the baby nestled against his heart and then, using the hand with the mike in it, he tuned in channel 19.

Only the rush of the open channel filled the cab; in the lonely hours of Christmas morning, it seemed, even the tired truckers had run out of something to say.

Elation filled him. He was grinning from ear to ear as he mashed the button and calmly intoned, "Breaker, one-nine… Merry Christmas, all you drivers out there on I-40… This is the Big Blue maternity ward. Thought you'd like to know…we got us a little Christmas present here. Mama and new baby daughter are both doin' just fine. Folks…say hello to Amy Jo.…"

Well, the minute he said that, he knew it was a mistake. The radio just about exploded with whoopin' and hollerin' and everybody trying to talk at once. He got the volume turned down as quick as he could, but it didn't help much. From the sound of things, every driver within hearing distance of his broadcast was cutting loose with his airhorn. At the unaccustomed noise, Amy Jo's eyes, instead of staring with searching intensity at his face, squinched up tight, and her fists started waving and she began to make unhappy squeaking noises.

"Uh…sure do 'preciate all your good wishes," he

said as soon as he could reclaim the channel again.
"Let me tell you, it's been a long night, and I think
mama and baby could both do with a little peace and
quiet, so, uh, we'd 'preciate it if you'd use your lights
instead of your horns to say hello while you're passin'
us by.... Thank ya kindly, an'...y'all have a Merry
Christmas, now. Ten-four."

After that things got quiet, except for an exuberant
toot busting loose now and then. Jimmy Joe put away
the mike and gave his full attention to the baby, who
by this time was getting warmed up pretty good. Out
of the corner of his eye he could see Mirabella, riled
and worried as a mama bear hearing her cub squall,
but instead of handing the baby over to her, he cuddled
her closer and gently joggled her while he crooned,
"Shh...it's okay, sweetheart. Hush, now...hush."
And he began to sing to her the way he always used
to sing to J.J., and just once in her too-short life, to
another precious little girl.

"Bye baby bunting,
Daddy's gone a-hunting,
Gone to get a rabbit skin
To wrap the baby bunting in.

From the nest he'd made for her in his sleeper bed,
Mirabella watched him rock and sing to her newborn
baby and didn't once think about how politically in-
correct the lullaby was. Strange shivers and tingles ran
about beneath her skin like pulses of electricity; a
lump she couldn't identify sat in her chest—was it
panic? was it fear?—and no matter how many cleans-

ing breaths she took, she couldn't ease it. She wanted
to cry—what else was new? She wanted to laugh.

Oh, God, what is this? she wondered. Could it possibly be normal? Something she'd missed in all those
books she'd read, some kind of postpartum high, perhaps. It would certainly explain why she seemed to
see him as a blur in a wash of shimmery golden light.

But it wouldn't explain the desolation and longing
she felt, seeing him over there in his seat, so far away
from her. *So far away.* The emptiness in her arms
where her baby should be—that she understood. But
what was this chill all around her where *his* arms had
been? Why did she feel so lost without him near her,
so lonely without his body next to hers? *Come back!*
she wanted to cry. *Please come and hold me again.*
Her face ached with the pressure of her longing.

He must have seen something in her expression, because he rose slowly and came to lean over her, crooning as he settled the once-again-peacefully-sleeping
baby in her arms. Crooning to *her,* not the baby.
"There now…it's okay. Here she is…here she is.
Yeah…see there? Everything's okay now."

And as she gazed down at her daughter's face—so
perfect, so lovely—a sob shuddered through her. *No,
it's not okay. We're not enough, Amy and me. We need
you. Please stay. We're not complete without you!*

"Hey, now," he said huskily, sitting on the edge of
the bed. She felt his fingers under her chin, gently
lifting it. Felt his thumb brush at the wetness on her
cheek. "What's all this, hmm? Come on, now, Marybell, don't cry."

She raised her eyes to his face, able to see it clearly

now that he was close to her again, even without her contacts. She could see his kind, warm eyes, his sweet, familiar smile.

Oh, God, what am I doing? she thought. *What am I thinking of? After everything he's done for me. After everything I've put him through...*

She sniffed and said in a low voice, "I'm okay. It's just...I think I'm just really tired."

"Sure you are." He stroked the hair back from her temples, and she tried, really tried not to find anything but his own natural compassion in the tenderness. "You just lie back there and sleep. I'm not gonna let anything happen to your baby."

She nodded, but couldn't tell him how she felt inside—trembly and wired, her nerves jumping around inside her like popcorn in a popper. "You must be exhausted, too," she said huskily. "Jimmy Joe, I don't know how I'm ever going to be able to thank you—"

"Oh, hey—" he began, but she put her fingers to his lips.

"For everything you've done. I know I must have put you through hell."

He kissed her fingertips, then shook his head, eluding them. "Naw, you were great," he said in a gravelly voice. "You were fantastic. Beautiful."

She smiled ruefully at him. "I don't think so. I seem to remember I hit you a couple of times."

"'S okay...I had it comin'." His dimples flickered on and off, like signal lights.

"I know I yelled mean things at you."

"Hey, I told you to, remember?"

She allowed herself a brief ripple of laughter,

throaty and precarious. "Well, anyway...I just want
to apologize, okay? For the god-awful mess I've made
of your truck, for any really weird and embarrassing
things I might have said or done..."

He winced as if she'd poked him and made an exasperated clicking sound. "Now there you go again.
You worry about the doggonedest things, you know
that? Woman, you just brought a brand-new life into
this world! You got nothin' to apologize for, understand?"

"Yes, sir," she said meekly, and he laughed and
leaned over and kissed her. So naturally, so easily, as
though he'd done it many times before. And her heart
stood still.

"Although..." he said thoughtfully as he drew
away from her. She blinked and struggled to focus on
the teasing glint in his eyes. "Now that you mention
it..."

"Oh, no," she groaned, closing her eyes. "I knew
it. What did I do?"

"Well, now, there was one thing you said was kinda
cute—really had me goin' there for a while." He
paused for dramatic effect, showing his dimples.

"Tell me," she breathed. "I can take it."

"You told me you'd never made love before, and
since that's not very likely to be true, I was kinda
wonderin' if you could tell me what you mighta meant
by that."

"Oh, God." Heat flooded through her, rose from
her belly and chest and rushed up into her cheeks. She
tried to cover her face with her one free hand, desperately wishing she had something bigger—like a

grocery sack, maybe. "I can't believe I told you that," she whispered. "I never tell anybody that. *Ever.*" Her deepest, most closely guarded secret. Oh, God. Oh... damn.

"Yeah? Why not?" His voice was light, and she didn't notice, then, how still he'd gotten.

She took her hand from across her eyes and glared at him. "Well, how would *you* feel?" she asked hotly. "If you were pushing forty years old and still a virgin, would you go around admitting it? It's not like I planned it that way, you know. It's not like that's what I wanted. It just *happened.*"

"Are you tryin' to tell me...it's *true?*"

Humiliated beyond bearing, she couldn't look at him, could only hear the shock and utter disbelief in his voice. "Well, technically, I don't suppose I am anymore. But...yeah, it's true. I've never made love before. Ever."

There was a gust of incredulous laughter. "Marybell, I don't know how to tell you this, but unless I just witnessed the Second Coming, that just ain't possible."

She flicked him a pitying glance, then fastened her mortified glare on the front windshield. "What century are you living in? Of course, it's possible. Didn't you ever hear of artificial insemination?"

After a stunned silence, he repeated it. "Artificial...insemination?" The words seemed to hang in the air like an accusation. He rose from her side, moving slowly and stiffly, and paced the two careful steps to the front of the cab. Standing there facing the windshield, rubbing mechanically at the back of his neck, he said hoarsely, "Are you telling me...you did this by yourself? You went and had this baby...and you've never— Oh, man. I mean...I don't believe this."

"It's not what you think," Mirabella said in a low voice. He was looking at her now, and in his blanched face, his eyes seemed almost as black and cold as the night outside the windows. Looking into them she suddenly felt desolate and afraid. Words tumbled urgently from her. "I'm not...gay, or anything. I just always wanted children. I always took it for granted I'd have them someday—the usual way—you know, meet somebody, fall in love, get married. But that didn't happen. I never met the right one." *Until it was too late. Until...tonight.*

She took a deep breath and went on, looking down, now, at her baby's face. Her voice grew calm and soft. "I thought, maybe it was never going to happen. And meanwhile, the years were going by, and I was getting older. I didn't have forever, you know? Maybe I could have settled for something less. Settled for *anything*. Anyone. Just so long as he gave me children. But..." She shrugged, and her lips curved into a smile that ached all through her tired body. Mirabella had never "settled" in her life. "I thought this way was better."

And it was. *It was.* She'd seen enough of her friends suffer in bad relationships to know that. Her way was better. She was right. She knew she was right. *Don't you dare judge me,* her heart cried. *I have my baby, and it was worth it. It's worth it.*

Jimmy Joe suddenly realized that she was waiting for him to say something, watching him with a wry and weary smile that was going to haunt him from

now on. Not the smile so much as the pride and disappointment he could see in her eyes. But he didn't
have any words to give her. He never had been one
to spend them freely, and the ones he did, especially
at important moments like this one, he generally liked
to think about first, to make sure they were the right
ones and a true indicator of what he was feeling. Right
now he didn't know what he was feeling, and he
couldn't think. So he stayed silent.

He'd taken a deep breath, then didn't seem to know
what to do with it. The air in the cab already seemed
too dense, charged with tension and cluttered with
emotions. He thought suddenly that he was going to
suffocate if he didn't get out of there and get some
fresh, uncrowded air.

"I, uh, think I'm gon' go use the rest room," he
mumbled, and grabbing up his sleeveless, down-filled
vest, yanked open the door and dived out into the
night.

The door slammed. Mirabella winced involuntarily
and closed her eyes.

She felt bewildered and abandoned, but at the same
time vindicated, never more sure of the rightness of
her decision than at this moment. Relationships were
just too hard. Men and women never really understood
one another. They were like alien species, struggling
to cohabit on the same planet, each believing they'd
figured out how to speak the other's language when
in reality neither of them had a clue. And while it was
true that some people did seem to find ways to make
it work, those relationships always seemed wonderful
and miraculous to her, like stories of scientists cohab-

iting with chimps, or gorilla mothers rescuing human children. As far as she could see, most marriages—even seemingly happy ones like her own parents'—were quiet daily struggles just to understand and be understood.

I don't understand, she thought. What did I do to make him look at me like that?

It couldn't be the fact that she'd had a baby—a moment ago he'd told her, with glowing softness in his eyes and tenderness in his touch, what a wonderful thing she'd done. And if he didn't particularly approve of the way she'd done it, why on earth should it matter so much to him? What could possibly make him look at her with such pain and disappointment in his eyes? As if, in some indefinable way, she'd betrayed him.

It was one of the few times in Jimmy Joe's life he wished he'd had the courage to go against his mama and take up smoking. Then at least he would have an explainable excuse for what he was doing, stomping up and down in the bitter cold, trying to keep his extremities from freezing. Funny how nobody ever seemed to think it was crazy to risk a case of frostbite just to grab a few puffs of a cigarette.

But he couldn't think of any kind of reasonable explanation for not wanting to go back inside his nice warm truck just yet. He was just so…well, *hell*. He didn't know what he was, that was the problem. He didn't know if he was mad, or disappointed, or what. He for sure didn't know why it mattered so much.

Well, yeah, he did, too. He just didn't know what to do about it.

He thought about how he'd felt when he'd first run into Mirabella back there in New Mexico; how he'd judged her selfish and irresponsible for doing what she was doing, making a trip like that all alone; how angry it had made him to see her putting her child at risk. He hadn't known what to do with those feelings then, when she'd been no more than a stranger to him. And he sure didn't know what to do with them now that there was so much more at stake.

And that was the crux of his problem. Because somewhere along the way he'd gotten to know her, even thought he was beginning to understand her.

Somewhere along the way he'd fallen in love with her, even though she was as different from him—with her sophisticated big-city ways—as night was from day. And not only with her, but with her baby, too. And now he just couldn't figure out how in the name of heaven he could have done such a thing. How could he love a woman when her beliefs and her whole way of thinking and living were completely different from his?

You just do.

The answer didn't come to him like a revelation or anything, with beckoning stars and singing angels. It had been in his heart all along, and what he was doing out there freezing his butt off in the Panhandle wind was trying to get used to having it there. Trying to get used to the pain it brought him. Because yeah, he loved the woman, in spite of all the ways she was different from him. No doubt in his mind about that at all. And even if she loved him back—which was by no means a given—there wasn't any way in the world it was ever going to work out between them.

So, what was he going to do? What *could* he do?

Well, he knew the answer to that one, too. What he was going to do was go back there to his truck and keep the woman he loved and her new baby girl warm and safe until somebody came to take them away from him forever. And while he was doing that, he would be trying his best to understand how a beautiful, bright, funny woman could think it was okay to have a baby without ever knowing what it was like to make love to a man, and how she could do something so selfish as to deliberately deny her child the chance to grow up in a home with both a mom and a dad in it.

And, he thought, remembering the pain and disappointment in her eyes when he'd left her, if that didn't work, he would do his best to pretend it didn't matter.

An apology was sitting primed and ready on his tongue when he climbed back into his truck, but he never got a chance to give it to her. She'd gone to sleep at last, with the baby snuggled on her bosom, cozy as a bunny in a nest. And again he thought he'd never seen a more beautiful sight.

He went and knelt beside the bed, feasting his eyes on the two of them, mother and child. He picked up a strand of Mirabella's hair and let it run like silken strands through his fingers. "Ah…Marybell," he whispered. He'd never felt such a fullness inside. He touched the baby's head with a single finger, wondering at the incredible softness of it, like the velvet fuzz on a butterfly's wing. *Amy Jo…* He'd never felt such sadness. He wondered why it was he seemed destined to hold his sweet baby girls only once—just long enough to fall in love with them—and then lose them forever.

Mirabella awoke to the loveliest sound. Someone was singing "Greensleeves"—or rather the Christmas version, "What Child Is This?"—in a very nice tenor voice. Could it possibly be Jimmy Joe? No—the radio, of course. But what were such a nice voice and such a beautiful song doing on a country-music station? It had to be a country-music station, there wasn't anything else out here in the middle of the Texas Panhandle.

Then she realized that she *was* hearing something else. Something amazing. For the first time in her life she was awakening to the sound of a man snoring in her ear. She listened to it in sleepy bemusement, finding it oddly pleasant, thinking how surprising that was. She'd always thought she would hate sleeping with a man who snored. She turned her head slightly...and felt the tickle of hair on her lips. Her heart lurched and warmth burst inside her. Oh, God, she thought. *Oh, God...it's true. I do love him.*

And her logical mind quickly responded, *Nonsense! It's the circumstances. You only think you do because you were in trouble and he came to your rescue, dummy. Like a knight on a big blue charger. In fact, wasn't that what they used to call truckers? The Knights of the Road...?*

The baby nestled below her breast stirred, arching her tiny body and shooting out one fist like a miniature pugilist. So that's what she's been doing, her mother thought, gazing down in teary adoration. No wonder her legs had been going numb.

She moved her legs experimentally and was pleased to find that they seemed to be in working order, although they felt as though they each weighed several hundred pounds. Conversely, the middle part of her seemed light as a feather, if a little loose and jiggly, like half-set gelatin. And, when she laid an exploratory hand on it, it was not nearly as flat as she'd hoped. The lower part of her torso, the part diapered in thick layers of towels, it seemed wisest not to disturb.

Soon, she thought. It was getting light. Help would be coming soon.

She watched the light turn from blue-gray to mauve, and to a beautiful shade of rose…and then to gold. And suddenly streaks of blinding radiance shot across the sky and frozen landscape, splashed like molten fire over the dashboard and front seats and onto the bed where she lay with her baby in a sleeping man's arms.

She gasped at the sheer glory of it, and Jimmy Joe's snoring instantly stopped. He lifted his head from the pillow beside hers, his eyes going first to the baby then to her face. Reassured, he propped himself on one elbow and frowned at the light.

"Wha' time is it?"

"Morning," said Mirabella huskily. "That's all I know. Christmas morning."

"Everything okay?"

She nodded, unable to take her eyes from his face. For a long, seemingly endless time he gazed back at her without speaking. Then he leaned down slowly and kissed her.

She'd never been kissed like that—never. His mouth was so firm and warm and soft; strength and sensitivity wrapped in satin. It felt so wonderful. It made her feel like crying—like a beautiful sunset, a touching movie, a sad song, tiny children singing. It was nourishment—food and drink—and warmth and shelter and loving arms all rolled into one incredibly sweet, impossibly lovely touch. She wanted it to last forever.

But of course it couldn't. Her cheeks and eyelashes were wet when he lifted his head. She gazed at him through a silvery blur, trying to read the messages in his glowing brown eyes, finding tenderness and puzzlement and wonder and fear, knowing they must be reflections of hers. Her lips trembled as she waited for him to say something. Anything.

Her heart was hammering so loudly she could hear it. Or was it his?

But he'd suddenly gone still, listening as she was. And she knew it wasn't thundering pulses she heard. They both closed their eyes and their bodies relaxed together as the silent beauty of the morning, and that fragile and precious moment, were shattered forever by the clatter of a helicopter's rotors.

Chapter 12

*"Attention, K mart shoppers, there's a blue-light
special at mile marker..."*
*"We got a bear convention goin' on—bears in the
bushes, bears ever'where!"*
                                                        I-40—Tennessee

The helicopter threw a long blue shadow across a
sheet of unblemished white as it hovered above the
rest-stop parking lot. The snow was frozen so solid
even the chopper's rotors couldn't stir it up, and it set
down like a dragonfly alighting on a sheet of frosted
crystal.

Jimmy Joe watched it from the wind-sheltered side
of his truck, squinting into the just-risen sun and puff-
ing out clouds of vapor. Being a Southern boy through
and through, he was convinced air that cold could kill
you, and he was trying his best to figure out how to

extract enough oxygen from it to live on without actually letting it into his lungs.

When the chopper's rotors had slowed to a lazy thunk-thunk beat, the door opened. Two men—one of them the pilot, wearing orange coveralls and a knit ski cap and carrying a paramedic's kit, and the other an older guy in a fur-lined parka, a Stetson hat and ear-muffs—jumped out and headed for the truck with their heads down, walking fast, half jogging. Both were wearing sunglasses. Jimmy Joe stepped forward to meet them, wishing he'd thought to put his on. The cold and the glare were making his eyes water.

The guy in the parka stuck out a mittened hand. He had a large cold-reddened nose and a thick brown mustache that seemed to spread across his face when he grinned. "Howdy. Mr. Starr—it sure is a pleasure to talk to you face-to-face for a change." He laughed at the "Beg your pardon?" look on Jimmy Joe's face. "Dr. Austin—I was on the other end of that phone relay last night. How's ever'body doin' this mornin'?"

"Good—doin' just fine," Jimmy Joe mumbled. He nodded at the paramedic, who told him his name was Travis, shook his hand, then gestured toward his truck. "Been waitin' for ya."

He went to the passenger side and opened the door, stepped up and called softly, "Marybell? You ready for company?"

She was sitting up, swaddled from the waist down in his mother's old quilt, the baby cradled in her arms. He saw that she'd brushed her hair and fastened the top and sides back from her face with a clip of some kind. She looked about sixteen years old, radiant and a little apprehensive, like a little girl getting ready to take her first trip on an airplane.

"Okay," she said breathlessly. But her eyes clung to him as if for reassurance, pleading with him—for what, he didn't know.

He stepped down and gestured for the doc and the EMT to go on in, wondering as he politely held the door for them why it was resentment he felt more than relief. As if they weren't rescuers, but intruders. He felt like there was a primitive being inside him that wanted to be standing in front of that door snapping and snarling. Like a wolf, guarding his mate and their young in his den. *His mate. His woman.*

He heard the doctor sing out, "Well, hello there, little lady, how are you doin' this mornin'? Let's have a look at this pretty girl, here. You two all ready to go for a ride?" Then he slammed the door shut and turned away with his chest aching and his heart pounding.

He was pacing up and down alongside his truck, grinding his teeth and swinging his arms, too cold to think about anything except how to keep from freezing to death, when the door opened up again and Travis, the EMT, hopped out.

"You wanna give me a hand with the stretcher?" he called out as he loped off toward the chopper.

Jimmy Joe grunted, "Sure thing," and took off after him.

"That's one tough little ol' gal," Travis said as they were wrestling the basket stretcher out of the helicopter. "Sure is pretty, too."

Jimmy Joe grunted. "Yeah, she is."

"This your first baby?"

Jimmy Joe didn't know quite how to answer that. He stammered around and finally decided it wasn't worth explaining, so he mumbled, "Uh...no, I got a little boy—"

"No, I mean first one you ever delivered."

Then he felt a little sheepish and had to grin. "Oh. Yeah, it sure is."

"Yeah, well...it's always a thrill. Always a miracle." Travis bent down and picked up one end of the stretcher and Jimmy Joe got a grip on the other and they headed back to the truck at a jog-trot. Travis threw a look over his shoulder. "Must've been quite a night for you."

"Yeah," Jimmy Joe panted, "it sure was." *Quite a night.* One he wondered if he was ever going to be able to get over. One he sure as heck knew he would never forget.

The cab of Jimmy Joe's truck had suddenly gotten terribly crowded—full of noise and way too many strangers. Mirabella felt lost in all the confusion. She longed for the soft sounds of Christmas songs on the radio, Jimmy Joe's snoring, the tiny squeaks Amy made when she nursed. She wished they could go back to the way it had been; just the three of them together, cocooned in the truck, isolated from the world and swaddled in intimacy and warmth, magic and—daringly her heart whispered it—*love*.

Now all of that had been lost, the peace shattered, the cocoon stripped away. She felt jangled and panicky, lonely and unprepared. The world seemed to be spinning too fast, out of her control. She was bundled and lifted and settled and strapped, more like a parcel than a person. People talked around her and over and about her, never *to* her. She found herself retreating into dazed isolation, cloaked and protected by the paranoia of her newly awakened maternal instincts, clinging to her baby with primal ferocity, her eyes daring anyone to take her from her. Perhaps understanding, no one tried.

She looked for Jimmy Joe, desperately needing the reassurance of his sweet smile and kind eyes, his soft Georgia drawl saying, "There now…everything's gonna be fine." He was there, or at least his body was, helping to wrap her in layers of blankets and tuck her into the stretcher, bustling around collecting her belongings, making sure she had everything—her purse, her clothes, her shoes and overnight bag. She followed him with her eyes, silently begging him to look at her, to touch her, to reach out to her in some way that would let her know that the bond that had grown between them through that long, miraculous night was still there.

But he wouldn't look at her. She couldn't find him—the Jimmy Joe who'd held and stroked her, guided and sustained her, laughed and cried with her as he'd placed her newborn daughter in her arms. Where was he? Oh, God. *Please, Jimmy Joe, I need you.*

They were taking her to the waiting helicopter, Jimmy Joe at her head where she couldn't see him, the man in the orange coveralls at her feet, the big man in the cowboy hat alongside. It was cold, so cold, but Mirabella hardly felt it. Amy was safe and warm, snug in her arms in a thick nest of blankets, and Jimmy Joe was there with her. She knew as long as he was there, she and her baby would be safe.

She felt the stretcher tilt as it was lifted into the helicopter. The doctor climbed in beside her, the man in the coveralls moved up to the pilot's seat, and the air filled with wind and noise. Jimmy Joe was backing out of the open doorway.

Panic seized her. Struggling frantically, she managed to free a hand from the straps and blankets and fastenings and grab his shirtsleeve. *"Jimmy Joe—"*

"Yeah, I'm right here." He wrapped her hand in both of his and she held on to him with all the strength in her body, as if she were dangling over a void and he was the rope. "Everything's gonna be fine. You'll be in Amarillo in a little bit."

"Please—" she gasped. "You're coming with me, aren't you?"

His inverted face hovered above hers, lined with strain and pinched and reddened with cold. But for the eyes, with their familiar glow of kindness, she would hardly have recognized it. His fogged breath mingled with hers as he smiled. "Sorry...wish I could. Gotta stay with my truck. I'm gonna be along in a little while. Listen, you're gonna be just fine. You just take good care a'that baby, now, y'hear?"

"Jimmy Joe—" *Don't leave me!*

"Safe trip." He leaned down and kissed her, quick and hard. She felt his hand slip from her grasp.

The helicopter door clanged shut. A mittened hand patted her shoulder and a kindly Texas voice said,

"You just hold tight, now, honey. We'll be there soon."

Mirabella closed her eyes as her stomach gave a dreadful lurch. *Don't…leave…me….*

Jimmy Joe stood and watched the helicopter lift off. Watched it until it was just a speck in the sky. He felt as if a great big piece of himself had just been ripped off him and was flying away from him. And if he lived to be a hundred, he wasn't ever going to be able to forget the look in Mirabella's eyes when he'd left her alone in that chopper.

A truck crawling by on the interstate saw him standing there and blasted an airhorn greeting. Jimmy Joe lifted his hand and waved, then started walking back toward his big blue Kenworth, still idling faithfully away as it had through that long, cold night. She looked a mite road-weary, he thought, covered with grime and snow sludge, mud flaps crusted with frozen mud. He promised himself the first truck wash he came to after he got out of this mess, he was going to pull in and give her a nice bath. Himself, too, while he was at it.

And they were both going to be needing some fuel pretty soon; the Kenworth's tanks might have a few more miles left in them, but he was running on empty. The snacks he'd gotten from the vending machines were all gone, except for a half-eaten package of peanut-butter crackers. He ate those and washed them down with warm 7-Up, then tidied the sleeper as best he could and disposed of the trash. After a safety check of his rig and a last visit to the rest stop's freezing-cold toilet facilities, he was finally ready to roll.

First, though, he turned up the volume on his CB radio and took down the mike, then waited until he got a lull in the conversation. "Uh…this is the Big Blue Starr," he drawled. "I'm over here at the rest stop at the twenty-eight-mile stick.… Gon' be joinin' you here in a minute. I'd 'preciate it if you'd give me some room.… Come on."

As it seemed to be more and more often these days, it was a female voice that came back to him. "You got it, Big Blue. Sure am happy to hear from ya again. How's the lady and her baby doin'? Ever'body okay?"

"Doin' just fine. Chopper picked 'em up this mornin'. They're headin' for Amarillo as we speak."

"We sure are glad to hear that. We been prayin' for ya. My husband Tom, here, and me, we're drivin' team. Got two little babies ourselves, over there in Enid, Oklahoma. We're still hopin' to get home in time to hug 'em and tell 'em Merry Christmas, but…I don' know. If this don't clear up pretty soon…"

"How's it lookin' over that way?"

"Uh…pickin' up a little, they tell me. Looks like they finally got the overpasses sanded, anyways. Sun's gettin' up there now, though. Gon' start gettin' slick, here, pretty soon."

"Thanks," said Jimmy Joe. "I'll watch it."

"You do that. Pass on our good wishes for us, if you see the lady and that little baby again, would ya? 'Preciate it."

"I'll do that. Y'all have a safe trip, now."

"Back at ya. Ten-four."

Jimmy Joe hung up the mike and put his rig in gear,

sending up a little prayer as the first of eighteen wheels bit into unbroken snow. He churned down the on-ramp and a hole opened up for him. He eased the blue Kenworth into it and once more became part of the long caravan of trucks ploughing steadily eastward.

It felt real good to be on the road again, and heading for home at last. But for some reason, without Mirabella and the baby in it the cab seemed awfully quiet to him. And empty.

It was past midday by the time Jimmy Joe rolled into Amarillo. He'd made one stop, at a gas station on old Route 66 just west of Vega, where he'd bought a few gallons of diesel and shaken the hand of the man whose voice, coming through on the radio emergency channel, had guided him through the long night just past.

Turned out the fellow, whose name was Riggs, had a pretty good garage and a tow truck besides, so he'd given him some money and Mirabella's car keys and asked him to go pick up the silver Lexus as soon as the roads cleared up enough. Riggs had wanted him to stay and have a bite of breakfast, but hungry as he was, he was even more anxious to be on his way. So he'd settled for a cup of coffee and a quart of chocolate milk, and then he was on the road again.

On the outskirts of Amarillo, the going got a little easier. The bright sunshine hadn't warmed things up much—just enough to melt a thin coat of water on top of the ice that made it about as slick as grease. But at least the overpasses and the on- and off-ramps had been sanded. And the streets leading to the hospital had been well plowed. It looked like about half of the parking lot had been scraped clear, too, and the snow pushed up in a pile over to one side.

He parked his rig next to the pile and set the brakes, and was indulging in a good stretch when he noticed that the parking lot seemed to be an awfully busy place, considering it was Christmas Day. He noticed several TV-news trucks and vans with satellite antennas sticking out all over them.

"Wonder what's goin' on?" he muttered to himself as he climbed out of the cab. He hoped it wasn't some sort of disaster or other. Happening on Christmas— that sure would be a shame.

The hospital's front entrance and main waiting area were all a-tangle with people, quite a few of them carrying video cameras, the rest standing around drinking coffee out of plastic cups and looking out-of-sorts. Several of them kind of stared at Jimmy Joe when he walked in, which was a reminder to him that it had been a couple of days since he'd showered and shaved. He was glad he'd put on a clean shirt and his good boots and changed his trucker's vest for his fleece-lined Levi's jacket, but he knew from the glimpse he'd caught of himself in the glass doors coming in, with his two-day beard and bloodshot eyes, that he was no prize. On the other hand, it was Mirabella he'd come to see, not a bunch of strangers, and he had an idea she would forgive him if he looked a little rough around the edges.

He eased his way through the crowd with a few "Beg your pardons" and "'Scuse me, ma'ams" and made it up to the reception desk, where a sweet-faced, gray-haired lady wearing a pink pinafore was trying her best to ignore all the hustle and bustle.

She flicked him a glance and said, "May I help you?" in a tone of voice that warned him she would rather not.

He cleared his throat and leaned as close to her as he could across the countertop so he wouldn't have to shout his business to the whole world over the noise. "Uh...yes, ma'am, I'm lookin' for the maternity department?"

The lady in pink folded her hands together as if she was about to say her prayers and gave him a look that wasn't much warmer than the temperature outside. "Of course you are. And the patient's name?"

"Uh...yes, ma'am. That'd be Mirabella..." Damnation, what was it? "Uh, Waskowitz. She and her baby were brought in this morning."

"Yes, sir, and are you a member of the family?"

Whew, thought Jimmy Joe, if that voice had been any colder it would have given him frostbite. A moment later, when he thought about it, he knew what he should have done was lie—just say, "Yes, ma'am, I'm her brother," or something like that, and be done with it. But the habit of honesty was so ingrained in him, by the time the inspiration came to him, he'd already blurted out the truth.

"No, ma'am, I'm not. I guess you could say I'm a friend." He saw right away that wasn't going to get him anywhere, so he shuffled around and cleared his throat some more, and then jumped back in with, "But I know she'll want to see me. My name's Jimmy Joe Starr, and, uh,... Well, see, I was with her when she had her baby. In fact, she, uh, had it in my truck. And…well, I promised her I'd come by and see her, soon as I could. Just to say hi, you know, make sure she's okay…''

Somewhere along in there, it came to him that the people around him had gotten real quiet. In fact, he figured he could have heard a pin drop. He kept lowering his voice and leaning closer to the lady in pink, trying his best to keep his business private, but when he did that, it seemed to him that everyone in the place sort of leaned with him.

Then all of a sudden it was like a dam had burst. The whole roomful of people surged in around him, everybody trying to push everybody else out of the way, people shoving microphones and video cameras in his face and shouting questions at him, all talking at once.

''Mr. Starr—Mr. Starr!''

''Over here—''

''How did it feel—''

''Are you the trucker—''

''What do you think about being called a Good Samaritan?''

''When did you know you were going to—''

''Had you ever delivered a baby before, Mr. Starr?''

''Mr. Starr—Mr. Starr!''

''How does it feel to be a hero, Mr. Starr?''

Oh, man. Once when he was a kid, Jimmy Joe remembered, he and his oldest brother Troy had hooked a hornets' nest while they were fishing. That was pretty much the way he felt right now, like he wanted to cover his head and make for deep water.

But they had him cornered, and it looked like there wasn't much hope he was going to be able to make a run for it. Out of the corner of his eye he spotted the lady in pink making her escape; all he could hope was that maybe she'd gone for reinforcements.

In the meantime, he had to try and make the best of it. And one thing he wasn't going to try to do was outshout everybody. Neither was he going to shuffle his feet and look like some dumb Cracker—his mama had taught him better than that. In fact, it was his mama's methods he called on, particularly the one she used to always use to get the attention of a classroom—or a kitchen—full of kids all squabbling and hollering at once. He raised one hand, bowed his head, closed his eyes, and then…just waited. He waited until everybody got quiet again, which didn't take as long as a person might think. When he wasn't hearing anything except some rustling around and nervous coughing, he opened his eyes. And it seemed like everybody drew in a big breath and held it.

He pointed to a woman standing right in front of him, with sleek dark hair pulled back in a French twist and a familiar look about her, although he couldn't place her. He took a breath, hesitated a moment, then let it out in a rush and said, "Who *are* you people?"

Then everybody laughed, and it seemed like he'd made a whole roomful of new friends.

The woman he'd pointed to waved her microphone but this time remembered her manners and didn't poke it in his face. She said, "I guess you've been a little out of touch, Mr. Starr. This is a great story—Good Samaritan trucker delivering a baby on a snowbound interstate, on Christmas Day. It's a wonderful story. The whole country's been following it, ever since word started coming in last night. It seems you've become quite a hero. What do you think of that?''

Jimmy Joe looked at all those microphones and video cameras pointed at him—at a respectful distance, now—and for a few moments he didn't say anything. He was thinking about Mirabella. Remembering…so many things. Like the images in a kaleidoscope, fragmented and rearranged into images of unimaginable beauty.

Terrified eyes, shivering voice… "I think I'm having my baby…."

"I'm sorry…I'm sorry…."

"Can't…make a mess!"

Furiously… "Can't you understand English?"

"I ca-an't!"

The imprint of her fingers on his arm…the feel of her mouth.

"Too many mountains…more mountains…"

"If you say that one more time, I'll kill you!"

"Amy…her name is Amy."

"I've never made love before…."

"Please…come with me!"

"Don't leave me…."

He had to cough, clear his throat and take a couple of deep breaths before he could speak, and when he did his voice was still so raspy it didn't even sound like him.

"Well, first off, I'm no Good Samaritan, and, uh…I'm sure not a hero. What I did wasn't any more'n any other person I know of woulda done, under the same circumstances. The only hero here is that lady lying up there in that hospital bed. She's—'' And then he had to stop and cough some more. ''Well, she's just about the bravest person I ever saw, is all. And, uh…well, that's all I've got to say. Now, if y'all will excuse me…''

He turned blindly, thinking he knew how a trapped wolf felt just before he started gnawing his leg off, and there was a big burly fellow in a rent-a-cop uniform reaching out to him and saying in that quiet, no-argument cop way, ''Sir, you want to come with me, please? Right this way.''

Beyond the security guard Jimmy Joe could see the lady in the pink pinafore hovering, holding open a door marked, Hospital Personnel Only. From the pink in her cheeks and the smile on her lips, it looked like she might have warmed toward him quite a bit since she'd spoken to him last.

The security guard touched Jimmy Joe's elbow and raised his voice and said, ''Okay, folks, that's all. You want to step aside and let us through, please?'' He ushered Jimmy Joe through the door and the pink-pinafore lady closed it smartly after them. Jimmy Joe could just imagine her glaring in frosty triumph at the thwarted reporters left on the other side.

Left alone with the security guard, he didn't know exactly what to expect—whether he was about to be hustled out the nearest exit, or what. It sure wasn't to have the guy clap him on the shoulder and say, ''Son, I'd sure like to shake your hand. That was a wonderful thing you did. God bless ya.''

Feeling too dazed and confused to argue, Jimmy Joe

muttered some sort of thank-you and shook the guy's hand, which was about the size and texture of an old fielder's mitt. For some reason that made him think of his dad, and that brought a lump into his throat.

Maybe it's just being in a hospital again, he thought as the guard whisked him past offices and through storerooms and up an echoing concrete stairway, through clanging steel doors and then down polished corridors that smelled the way hospitals always do. Like most normal healthy people who don't actually work in one, Jimmy Joe wasn't fond of hospitals. Which wasn't surprising, considering that with one exception, his associations with them, starting with having his tonsils taken out when he was seven, were all pretty bad. The arm he'd broken playing football hadn't been serious enough to get him past the emergency room, but then there had been his dad's first heart attack, and then the last one. He remembered the long night in the waiting room, he and his brothers and sisters sprawled and draped over every available piece of furniture, and at dawn, the doctors coming with headshakes and expressionless faces. And the worst shock of all had been watching his mama's face turn old before his eyes.

Not very long after that, there had been Amy—the first Amy. And then, for a while, regular visits to a different kind of hospital, where patients shuffled aimlessly through the corridors or sat and looked out the windows with blank faces and empty eyes. Then there had been the exception—J.J.'s birth. But even that hadn't exactly been a happy time in his life. That had been almost eight years ago, and he'd done his best to avoid hospitals ever since.

"She's been askin' for ya," the security guard told him as they turned down a corridor painted in cheery shades of rose pink and aqua green. Jimmy Joe could hear trays clanking and people laughing. And mixed in with the regular old hospital smell was a new one, one he remembered well—diapers. "We've been tryin' to keep that horde downstairs away from her until she's had a chance to rest up a bit. Here ya go— you can go on in."

And suddenly there he was, standing outside a closed door that he knew Mirabella was on the other side of, and he didn't have a single idea in the world what he was going to say to her once he opened it. He felt like it had been days, maybe even years, since he'd seen her, instead of just a few hours. In his truck, it had seemed as if they were the only two people in the whole world, and that somehow the two of them and Amy Jo and everything they'd been through together had gotten woven into one whole cloth, like a beautiful tapestry, or one of those Navajo rugs he'd brought back from his trips. For some reason he'd thought they would be that way forever.

But from the instant that helicopter had set down in the rest-stop parking lot, he'd known it hadn't been real, and that the world didn't belong to just the three of them, after all. This was somebody else's world, and he, for one, didn't feel real comfortable in it. In this world, Mirabella and her baby girl were a media event, and everybody was trying to make him out to be some kind of hero. Well, he sure didn't feel like a hero. What he felt like was a man who'd just lost something precious to him—something so rare and beautiful he was afraid he wasn't ever going to come across it in his life again.

The security guard waved to him and moseyed off down the corridor, nodding to a couple of nurses along the way. A nurse bustling by did a sort of double take when she saw Jimmy Joe, and smiled, her face lighting up like a Christmas tree.

"It's okay," she chirped. "You can go on in. She's been waiting for you."

He nodded his head, took a big breath, and tapped on the door. A voice—like Mirabella's, and yet not quite hers—said breathlessly, "Yes—come in!"

The wide hospital-room door swung open and a woman he didn't know stood there beaming at him. She had shiny brown hair cut short but in a way that nicely suited her features, and greenish-blue eyes that crinkled at the corners. And although the two didn't have one single feature in common that he could see, he knew this woman was Mirabella's mother. In some strange way he couldn't put a finger on, she just reminded him of her.

In a hushed and excited voice, like someone trying not to wake a sleeper, she said, "Hello—you must be Jimmy Joe. The front desk phoned to let us know you were on your way. Oh, I'm just *so* happy to meet you. Bella," she called softly over her shoulder toward a partly drawn curtain, "you have a visitor." And then back to Jimmy Joe again, taking his hand and towing him inside. "Please, come in. I'm Ginger, by the way—Bella's mom."

"Ma'am," Jimmy Joe mumbled politely. As the door whisked shut behind him it occurred to him that he'd never felt so awkward in his life, or more conscious of the quarter-inch of stubble he was wearing on his face. Why hadn't he thought to bring something—flowers, maybe, or a baby gift?

And then Ginger was pulling back the curtain, and there she was. And he suddenly remembered how he'd thought her the most beautiful woman he'd ever seen in his life before. And forgot he'd ever held her naked body in his arms, massaged her feet or whispered love words into her sweat-damp hair. It was all he could do to unstick his tongue from the roof of his mouth long enough to mutter, "Hey, there, Marybell, how're you doin'?"

Chapter 13

"Man, that is a sight for sore eyes."
                                    I-40—Texas

"Other than the fact that my insides feel like jelly, I'm fine," snapped Mirabella, and she could just see her mother's eyebrows arching at the way she sounded, so brusque and cranky. So typically Mirabella.

She didn't mean it, of course; she almost never did. No one knew that sometimes it was simply the only way she could get a word out without her voice shaking, or how important it was to her pride and self-esteem that she always appear calm and completely in control.

Even more so now, considering the state of near panic she'd been in the last time she'd seen Jimmy Joe. And considering that not ten minutes ago she'd

been in a similar state just because she couldn't
shower and wash her hair.

"What am I going to do? I look like hell!" she'd
hissed in a burst of tearful hysteria that was completely
foreign—and consequently utterly bewildering to her.
"Mom—quick—let me have your brush! Do you have
any lipstick? Oh, no…I've lost my hair thingy. I look
like a wet cat. Oh, God, I can't let him see me like
this!"

"Bella," her mother had said, laughing in amazement, "since when do you *care?* Besides," she'd
added dryly, "I imagine the man has just seen you
looking a lot worse."

"That was *different,*" Mirabella had snapped, feeling free to behave like an unreasonable and obstinate
child as long as there was no one but her mother to
witness it.

It was only now, looking up at Jimmy Joe's face,
that she knew how right she'd been. It *was* different.
Unavoidably and inevitably, everything had changed.

He hadn't, of course; he still looked like a young
Robert Redford—an unshaven one, to be sure—lean
and blond, dimpled and adorable. His eyes were just
as kind and his smile every bit as sweet as she remembered. It wasn't he who had changed, she realized; or her, either, for that matter. What was so different was the way things were between them.

They were like…strangers. It was hard even to remember now, the closeness, the incredible bond they'd
shared. She hadn't imagined it—she knew she'd been
pretty much out of it for a lot of the time, but she
wasn't wrong about that. It had been real. Never in

her life before had she known, or even imagined she
could know, such a sense of *oneness* with another human being. It was as if she'd found a part of herself
she hadn't even realized was missing. But now the
piece was lost once more, and how would she ever
again be able to delude herself into believing she was
whole?

They were like strangers, but worse than that—
strangers with memories in common of time spent together in abnormal intimacy, both physical and emotional; of things said that could not be unsaid; of
secrets revealed that would never be forgotten. It was
only natural that there should be awkwardness between them, Mirabella told herself sadly. She should
have expected it.

What she couldn't have expected was that it would
hurt so much. She ached inside in places that didn't
have anything to do with having just given birth to a
child. She ached as though her heart had been torn in
two.

"What's all this?" he asked with a frown, waving
a hand at the plastic bag dangling above the head of
her bed, at the tube leading from it to a needle stuck
into the back of her hand and held in place with a
crisscross of white tape.

She glanced down at it and dismissed it with a
shrug. "Nothing—some fluids and antibiotics. I guess
I was a little bit dehydrated. The antibiotics are just
as a precaution."

"Where's the baby? She doin' okay?"

Mirabella smiled; it had become a reflex, automatically triggered by any mention of her daughter.

"Amy's fine. They've got her in the nursery, doing all the tests they usually do on newborns. But yeah…she's fine. Weighs five pounds six ounces. In another month, she'd a'been a chunky little seven-pounder."

"Like her mother," Ginger added, smiling smugly. "All my babies were seven pounds plus."

"Well," said Jimmy Joe. "I sure am glad to hear that." He shifted and cleared his throat, looking even more uncomfortable, if that was possible, rubbing at the back of his neck in that embarrassed way he had. "Uh…hey, listen, I'm sorry I didn't bring anything. I meant to get you some flowers, but…"

"Oh, that's okay," Mirabella murmured, feeling her face grow warm. God, how awkward this was. "You didn't have to do that."

Then for a moment there was silence, as both of them struggled to find something else to say. She felt as if she was suffocating.

"They say how long they're gonna keep you here?"

She lifted the hand with the needle in it. "I don't know. I guess until this is done. I think they might want to keep Amy overnight, just to be on the safe side. I don't know what I'm going to do, though. I mean—"

Her mother interrupted with, "Now, honey, I told you not to worry about that."

"Mom flew in this morning," Mirabella explained. "So I guess Amy and I'll just go back with her, as soon as the doctors say it's all right. But I don't know what I'm going to do about my car…all the Christmas presents…. Everything's still out there in that damn snowbank.'' She gave a strangled gurgle of laughter; she was damned if she was going to shed another tear—not while *he* was here.

Jimmy Joe was rubbing his neck again, looking ashamed of himself the way he always did, she was beginning to realize, when he'd done something to be particularly proud of. ''Don't need to be worrying about that. Got it all taken care of.'' He lapsed into hopeful silence. When he saw he was going to have to do a little more explaining, he coughed and looked pained.

''You maybe don't remember it, but the fella helped us out on the radio last night? Guy's name is Riggs. Anyway, he said he had a service station. I figured I'd stop in, you know, just to say thank-you to him for everything he did. Turns out he's got a nice little garage out there on old 66 just west of Vega—has a wrecker, too. Anyway, I gave him your keys and told him to go pick up your car, soon's the road clears up some more. He'll keep it for you until you can get back here for it, no problem.'' He patted his pockets, reached into one and pulled out a business card, which he handed to her with another of those embarrassed little coughs of his. ''So—you can just give him a call when you feel like it. It's all taken care of.''

Mirabella usually hated it when people—men especially—tried to take charge of her life. But instead of feeling resentful, she felt a curious melting sensation inside. Fighting against an urge to weep and sniffle, ''Oh, Jimmy Joe...'' like a swooning belle, instead she scowled fiercely and demanded, ''What about all my stuff? All my Christmas presents are in the trunk of my car."

"Oh, for heaven's sake, Bella!" her mother exclaimed, throwing up her hands. "You and that new granddaughter are all the Christmas presents your dad and I need! What is the matter with you?"

It was a question people asked her a lot, for some reason. But now it brought her even more dangerously close to tears. What *was* the matter with her? She should be just about the happiest woman in the world. She'd just had a baby; a beautiful, healthy baby, the baby she'd always wanted—she'd already convinced herself she'd really wanted a girl all along. So why was she still wishing for something she *didn't* have? Especially when it was something she'd come to terms with long ago.

Thoroughly ashamed of herself now, she made a gallant effort to brighten up, although faking cheeriness wasn't something she excelled at. "Thanks... 'Preciate it," she said grudgingly, and felt her heart bump when Jimmy Joe grinned at her use of the favorite truckers' acknowledgment, as if it was a private joke they'd shared.

She took a deep breath and pushed herself up on the pillows. "You going to see Amy before you leave?"

His smile grew tender. "Sure am. Yeah...thought I'd stop by on the way out."

Her world darkened, as if a cloud had drifted across the sun. "So...I guess you're anxious to be on your way."

"Yeah… J.J.'s waitin' for me. Still got a load to deliver, too. You know how it is.…"

"Yeah…" Her smile flickered, then went out like a snuffed candle when she met his eyes. She grabbed a desperate gulp of air and said, "You talked to J.J.?"

Jimmy Joe suddenly frowned. "Haven't had a chance. I'm gonna call him after I get out of here, I guess. That's *if* I get out— Did you know there's a whole crowd of reporters downstairs? They tell you about that? TV, newspapers, I don't know what all."

He sounded so incredulous, she had to laugh. "That's what I heard. So…I guess you're a hero, huh? Did you talk to them?"

"Hero…" he muttered under his breath, then gave a disgusted-sounding snort. "Didn't have much choice. They pretty much had me surrounded. Those media people sure are somethin' else. Damn—oh, 'scuse me, ma'am—darned if I didn't feel 'bout like General Custer at Little Big Horn. Course…" He smiled and reached out as if he meant to touch her, and her heart skipped a beat. But he let the hand drop to his side and then made sure it stayed there by hooking the thumb in his jeans pocket. "They only talked to me because they couldn't get at you. You know that, don't you?"

"Me?" She tried to laugh at the absurdity of it, at the same time shrinking back against the pillows. Because having lived most of her life in a media-crazy town like Los Angeles, she knew exactly how an ordinary, unremarkable story could catch fire in the public's imagination, especially when fueled by a hungry media trying to fill a slow news day. *This* story—

Christmas Day, lady stranded on snowy interstate, giving birth in a truck, handsome trucker-driver hero—
oh, God, it would be like manna sent from heaven!

Oh, God. Everything in her cringed at the thought.
How stupid she felt. How humiliating it was. To have
everyone know…the people she worked with… And
worse than the humiliation was the thought that the
specialness of her time with Jimmy Joe, the beautiful
intimacy they'd shared, might be taken away from her
to become just more fodder for the newsmagazine
shows.

"Oh, God," she whispered "Oh, no…"

"Marybell, I'm afraid you are about the biggest
thing to come along since Madonna had her baby,"
said Jimmy Joe, smiling crookedly down at her. There
was a look in her eyes she couldn't quite fathom, a
certain sadness, perhaps. Could he possibly regret the
loss of what they'd had together as much as she did?
Her throat filled. "The hospital's doin' a pretty good
job of keepin' 'em away, so far," he went on, "but
soon as you leave here, you know they're gonna be
waitin' to jump you. Probably be best if you just faced
the music. Hold a press conference, or something, get
it over with right here."

"I'd hate that," Mirabella snapped. She felt like a
cornered animal. I don't want to deal with this, she
thought furiously. Not now. Now when I feel so vulnerable, so not myself. So alone. "I can't do it."

She saw her mother and Jimmy Joe exchange looks.
Then he shrugged and touched her cheek with the
backs of his fingers, lightly, as if brushing away tears.
"Well, now…" he said in a soft, soothing tone, "you

sure don't have to, not if you don't want to. Hey—I'll just go talk to 'em for you, how's that? Sure…listen, I'm gonna take care of it, don't you worry about a thing.''

Okay, great, she thought resentfully. Now what does he think I am—a helpless wimp? Just because he saved my life, just because I needed him last night, does he now think I can't get along without him?

''You don't have to do that,'' she muttered, shifting around against the pillows. *I don't need you, Jimmy Joe Starr. You, or anybody else. Amy and I will be just fine!* She glowered first at Jimmy Joe, then at her mother. ''Okay—okay. Tell the hospital I'll talk to them. Just once, though. *After* I've had a chance to shower and wash my hair!''

''Marybell, are you sure you want to do this?'' Jimmy Joe asked, bending over her, his eyes dark and concerned.

''Of course I am,'' she snapped. ''I'm not a child.''

''Well, okay then.'' He ducked his head and planted a kiss on her forehead, then straightened and looked across at her mother. She heard her mother give a tiny gasp, quickly stifled, then a laugh that sounded both surprised and pleased.

''What?'' she demanded, her paranoia prickling.

''I think I'd better be rollin','' said Jimmy Joe in a husky voice as he leaned down to kiss her again. Not on the forehead this time, but on the lips, and with such tenderness she instantly forgot all her suspicions, forgot she'd just vowed she didn't need him. Maybe she didn't need him, but she wanted him. Oh, yes, she wanted him. Wanted him kissing her like this again—often—for all the rest of her life.

Then he straightened and she felt his fingers, briefly, in her hair. "I'll stop by the nursery, see if they'll let me say goodbye to Amy Jo. You take care a' yourself, now, you hear? Ma'am—sure was nice meetin' you."

And just like that, he was gone.

Mirabella stared after him, feeling stunned…like a hollow, aching shell. I can't believe it, she thought. *He's gone. I'm never going to see him again.*

"Well," her mother said when the door had closed silently behind him, letting her breath out in a rush of laughter. "I certainly can see why you feel about him the way you do."

"Oh? And what is that supposed to mean?" Mirabella's voice was light and breathy, cheery and fragile as a soap bubble.

"Oh, honey, anyone can see you're crazy about him."

"That's ridiculous," said Mirabella with a snort. "Just *look* at him, Mom."

Her mother's eyebrows rose. "I did. He's an absolute joy to look at. I also saw the way he looked at you, my dear. Those eyes…"

Mirabella rolled hers in exasperation and leaned back against the pillows. "Oh, brother. Don't read anything into it, okay? He just has kind eyes, that's all. And cute little dimples and a sweet, sexy smile. So what? He's not even thirty. That's eight years younger than I am, Mom. *Eight years.* So, forget it." She sniffed and threw an arm across her eyes. "Just forget it, okay?"

There was silence for a moment, and then Ginger said with a soft laugh, "Well, all I can say is, for somebody so young, he's awfully wise. He certainly managed to figure *you* out in a hurry."

Mirabella uncovered one eye. "What are you talking about?"

Her mother was wearing that arch, Moms-know-everything look that always annoyed her so. "I'm talking about that nifty little piece of reverse psychology he just pulled on you. Boy, how did he get your number so fast? That's what I want to know."

"Reverse—that was no such thing!" said Mirabella hotly. "I simply—"

"Bella, he *winked* at me."

"He what?"

"He winked at me—right after you'd 'knuckled under' to his demand for a press conference."

"He didn't."

"Yes, dear, he did. He saw you crumbling like a wet cookie, and somehow he already knows you well enough to realize that the best way to get you to do something you don't want to do is to tell you you can't do it, or offer to do it for you."

"Yeah, well, if he knows me so well," Mirabella sobbed angrily, "how come he didn't stay, huh? Tell me that!"

"Oh, for heaven's sake, the man had things to do! Besides, with all those prickles of yours, how was he supposed to know you wanted him to? Oh, my dear," her mother said huskily, "you have so much pride. But I'll tell you this—if you let that beautiful young man get away, you are absolutely crazy. Do you hear me? *Crazy.*"

And she said no more. Because like the terrific mother she was and always had been, she knew when it was time to ignore all the prickles, and simply…hug.

A nurse bustled in, strewing cheer before her like flower petals. "Oh—having a little cry, are we? We certainly know how that is! Well, I have someone here who's going to make you feel a lot better!" She held back the door and wheeled in a tiny plastic bassinet with a practiced flourish. "Here you go—this pretty little girl wants her mama, don't you, sweetie pie? Yes, you do.…"

Mirabella sat up straight, sniffling, and wiped her eyes on her hospital gown as she searched avidly through her tears. "Oh," she cried, laughing when she saw the tiny bundle tucked in a bright red Christmas stocking, a tiny red stockinette cap on her fuzzy pink head. "She looks just like an elf!"

"That's just what she is," cooed the nurse. "A li'l ol' Christmas elf. And she's all nice an' clean an' sweet, an' she's even had a visit from her handsome daddy, and now she's *hungry,* aren't you, darlin'? Here you go, mama."

And she scooped up the baby, red stocking and all. Mirabella held out her arms, and as the nurse placed her daughter into them, she wondered again in utter awe how something so tiny could rouse such enormous feelings in her.

"Oh…" she whispered, and a moment later she wasn't even astonished to hear herself doing something she'd vowed she would never, ever do. But she was. She—intelligent, sensible, no-nonsense Mirabella—was talking baby talk. Cooing like a besotted dove. ''Hi, there… How's my widdle girl? How's my sweetie—little-lov'ums, huh?''

Oh, it was awful. It was glorious. It was…Amy. Her baby. Her miracle.

The nurse hovered, ready to help with the breast-feeding, until she saw that Mirabella didn't seem to need any help. She laughed and said, ''Well, I see somebody's taught you right. I'll just leave you to it, then. Y'all just give me a buzz, now, if you need anything.'' She parked the bassinet beside the bed and went away.

''Who was it?'' Ginger asked softly. ''Jimmy Joe?''

Mirabella nodded, her head bowed as she gazed intently at her hungrily nursing daughter. She rocked herself slowly back and forth, awash in prickles and weighed down by an ache deep, deep inside her.

''Oh, look—Bella, look! She has *red hair!*'' her mother cried, just as a tear rolled off the end of Mirabella's nose and dropped onto the baby's downy head.

It took Jimmy Joe another four hours just to get out of Texas, and he was never so glad to see anything in his life as he was that Welcome to Oklahoma sign, or the smooth, dry blacktop beyond it. Something in him sure did want to put the old hammer down and not ease up until he hit Little Rock, but he knew that was just plain stupid, considering he hadn't had much sleep in more than two days and was already running on raw nerves. So the first Motel 6 sign he saw, he pulled off. His sleeper was going to need some clean bedding before he would be able to use it again, but it was a hot shower he wanted more than anything. He didn't stop to eat—he'd filled his belly before he'd left Amarillo, anyway—just got his rig buttoned down and himself checked in, then headed for his room, and a shower so long and hot it made his pulse pound. He didn't even remember falling into bed.

He woke up to early-morning light pouring in through the window he'd forgotten to draw the curtain across twelve hours before. He showered again, and shaved this time, then dropped off his key and hit the road. First truck stop he came to he pulled off again, this time to fill up the Kenworth's fuel tanks, and his own, too, while he was at it.

He thought about calling J.J. again, but decided there wasn't much point in it, since he'd already told everybody at home he was on his way. He'd made the call from the hospital, right after he'd left Mirabella and said his goodbye to Amy Jo. The pink-pinafore lady had been real nice about letting him use a phone in one of the administrative offices, out of sight of the pack of newshounds out in the front lobby.

He remembered how he'd worried about it, thinking it was worse than getting a tooth pulled, having to explain to an eight-year-old boy why he'd broken his promise to him. He remembered the way his stomach had tied itself in knots as he'd stood there with the receiver mashed up against his ear, listening to the rings.

It was picked up on the fifth ring, and he'd had to shout to be heard over the racket in the background.

And a moment later he'd heard his son's excited voice yelling, "Dad! Hey, guess what, I saw you on TV!"

"Naw," said Jimmy Joe. "No kiddin'?"

"No kiddin', Dad. It's on CNN—we all saw you. Is it true? Did you really deliver that lady's baby? Just like on *Emergency 911?*"

"Well, yeah…sorta. Hey, listen, how're you all doin'? What's all that racket I hear? Everybody havin' a good time?"

Before J.J. could answer, there was a click and his mother's voice said, "Hello, son. Merry Christmas."

"Merry Christmas, Mama. What's everybody doin'? Sounds like you got a houseful, as usual."

"Oh, yes, everybody was here for dinner. Al and Tracy left a little while ago—they had to get back, Al's on duty tonight. Pretty much everybody else is here, though, just relaxing—you know how it is. They've got the football game on now, I think. The girls are still cleaning up in the kitchen…,"

"Hey, Dad," J.J. interrupted. "You know that new computer game you got me? It is so cool. Oh, yeah—and I like the remote-control truck, too, only I haven't had a chance to play with it yet, hardly. Uncle Roy's been playin' with it all day, and he won't give it back."

Jimmy Joe was laughing when his mama said quietly, "Well, son, I guess you've had quite a time of it this Christmas."

His laughter turned soft, and he took a breath and said, "Yeah, Mama, I sure have."

"Well, you can tell us all about it when you get here. Where are you now? You headin' home?"

"I'm 'bout to. I got this load to drop off in Little Rock tomorrow, so it's gonna be late—sometime the next mornin', probably—before I get there. Don't you wait up, now, y'hear? You can save me some of that turkey and sweet-potato pie, though."

J.J. yelled, "We will, Dad!" while his mama was laughing in a way that told him she was probably wiping away some tears, too. Then she called out, "Hey, it's your brother—come and wish him Merry Christmas!" And then there was so much yelling and hootin' and hollerin' Jimmy Joe could hardly hear himself think, so he wished everybody a Merry Christmas and said his goodbyes laughing.

When he was hanging up the phone, he found that there was a lump in his throat, and a few tears in his eyes, too. And since there wasn't anyone around to see them, he figured this was one of those times he didn't mind letting them fall.

After that, he hadn't been able to think about very much except how badly he wanted to be home with his family, which made it easier than he'd thought it was going to be to leave Texas and everything that had happened there behind him. What with Christmas homesickness and road conditions that required all his skill and concentration just to keep his rig on the road, he thought he managed pretty well to keep his mind from dwelling on Mirabella and her baby. But that was yesterday.

This was another day, and after a good night's rest, it seemed like his mind just wanted to gnaw on the situation like a dog on a fresh bone. He went over everything that had happened—every minute, every word, from the first moment he'd set eyes on the lady in the silver Lexus, way back there in that New Mexico truck stop. And the conclusion he came to was that he was making way too much out of the whole thing.

It was something his son had said to him, about it being like the TV show *Emergency 911,* that had really pulled him up short. Shoot, it happened all the time—people delivering babies in taxicabs and snowstorms, saving people's lives and all that stuff—cops, firemen, EMTs, and sometimes even plain old ordinary guys like him. It stood to reason a man might feel some sort of bond between himself and a woman whose baby he'd helped deliver, or somebody whose life he'd saved, and that she might feel grateful and tender toward him, too. Sure, that would just be natural. But did these people go around falling in love with the ones they'd helped, or getting all involved in their lives? Uh-uh. That just didn't happen, except maybe for remembering birthdays, cards at Christmas, things like that. Mostly, though, their worlds were separate, and once all the excitement died down, everybody went back to their own world and got on with their lives. That was the way it was supposed to be.

And all for the best, too. At least that was what he told himself over and over again on that long drive home. He told himself he had J.J. to think of, a family that loved him and a trucking company to build, and that ought to be enough to keep him happy and occupied. He told himself just about the last thing he needed in his life was a headstrong and independent career woman from L.A. who hated country music and thought it was perfectly reasonable to go and have a baby without even knowing what it was like to make love with a man. It took him close to a thousand miles, but by the time he got home, he almost believed it.

Two days after Christmas, at four o'clock in the morning, Jimmy Joe's mama came downstairs and found him sitting in her living room in his daddy's old favorite chair, watching television in the dark. She stood in the doorway with her glass of antacid fizzing in her hand and watched with him for a while, then said, "Son, you're gonna wear out that remote."

He looked over at her. "H'lo, Mama, sorry I woke you up."

She shrugged and waved the glass. "Oh, I was up anyway. Always eat too much of that rich food over the holidays, then I have to take a few days and get my stomach straightened out." She came and sat on the couch and put her feet, which were clad in slippers that looked like a pair of pink lapdogs, up on the coffee table. "How long ago'd you get in? I didn't hear your rig."

"It's down at my place. I parked it and drove the car over. Didn't want to rouse everybody." He spoke absently, his eyes following the images on the screen. Images of a mother with burgundy hair with her newborn baby. The baby was dressed up in a Christmas stocking like a little bitty elf.

"Which one is that?" his mother asked, then answered herself. "Oh—*The Today Show.* I think CNN's after that one."

"Yeah, I know. I've already been through 'em once." Actually, he was on his third go-round, but he didn't tell her that. Or that he hadn't been able to bring himself to turn the tape off. Or what a shock it had been to him to see Mirabella's face, hear her voice again, and how turning it off had seemed worse than leaving her all over again, and how lonely he'd felt in the silent darkness of that cozy and familiar living room.

"Son," his mama said quietly, "are you in love with this woman?" ·

A laugh burst from him. "Trust you, Mama." But he knew from long experience she wasn't going to leave it alone, so he tried to joke her out of it, which was a tactic that never had worked with her very well. "Do you know how ridiculous that is? Now, how in the world am I gonna fall in love, huh? I got a child to raise, a trucking company to build, a house to take care of—"

His mother interrupted him with a sigh. "Yeah...sometimes I forget you're not my oldest child. Son, you're not even thirty, and you're older than any of them, you know that? I don't think you ever were a kid—you've been saddled with so many responsibilities all your life. There you were, taking on the responsibility for Patti when you were just in high school, then your daddy dying and you taking over the business, and trying to raise J.J. all alone. Tell me something—are you ever gonna think about yourself sometime in your life? Do what makes *you* happy?"

Jimmy Joe pressed the Pause button, freezing Mirabella's face just as she was looking down at the baby in her arms. Pain punched him in the gut. "I am happy, Mama."

"Yeah," Betty Starr said with a snort. "A happy man sits all alone in the dark watching a tape of a beautiful woman over and over."

His thumb moved on the remote and the image sprang to radiant life. His heart lifted. "Yeah," he breathed. "She is beautiful, isn't she?"

His mother chuckled softly. "So, I'll ask you again. Are you in love with her?"

He sighed and scrunched down farther on his tailbone. "I don't know. Sometimes I think I am, and sometimes I'm sure, and then other times...I'm sure I'm crazy."

"Well, good, you're confused. That's a good sign you are in love."

Jimmy Joe snorted. "I'm not confused, Mama. I know right well when a woman is out of my league."

The lapdog slippers hit the floor and the empty glass hit the top of the coffee table. "Now, you just stop that right there. I know I raised you to be humble, but I sure never raised you to be ashamed of who and what you are."

He sat up straight and raised a calming hand; grown-up or not, all of Betty Starr's kids knew to steer clear of her temper. "Now, simmer down, Mama. It's not a case of being ashamed of who I am. You know me better'n that. It's a case of knowin' who *she* is. We're from two different worlds. We're just—" he took a deep breath to ease the ache in his chest "—too different."

"Well, now," said his mother thoughtfully, "you know that's not necessarily a bad thing."

With one savage gesture Jimmy Joe shut off the VCR and slapped the remote down, then got up to pace in the restrictive area in front of the coffee table. He felt restless and jangled, overloaded with feelings he didn't know what to do with, and like any overloaded child needing to blow off some steam, he knew he was safe with his mama. "I'm not just talking likes and dislikes," he said with controlled fury. "Different politics and opinions, things like that—that's nothin'. What I mean is, we don't even think alike. We don't believe in the same things."

"You know this for a fact?" his mother said mildly. "That's an awful lot to know about somebody in just two days."

"She's a Californian, Mama, through and through." He paused to put up a hand, holding off what he knew she was going to say next. "I'm not judging—I'm not. But I've been around those people out there enough to know they don't think like anybody else in this world." He shook his head and blew out air in a breathy whistle. "She's got some strange ideas." *You don't know the half of it, Mama. She's a virgin at thirty-eight—a virgin! And she's just had a baby—a baby she made herself from a damn test tube. What kind of woman does that?*

Betty Starr watched him for a moment, then settled back on the sofa cushions, once more installing the lapdogs in comfort on the coffee table. "I don't know. I saw her on that interview, and she sounds like a real nice woman to me."

"Well—" he lifted his arms and blew out another exasperated gust of air "—sure, she's *nice*. She's intelligent and funny and fiesty and opinionated, and she can be a real pain in the butt sometimes." *And a whole lot of fun to argue with.* He looked sideways at his mama and grinned. *A lot like somebody else I know who's near and dear to my heart.* He leaned over to kiss her.

She patted his cheek and smiled at him. "Well, then?"

He pulled away, exasperated again. "Okay. So, say I do love her. Say I love her enough to get past all the differences—what about *her?* What's a woman like that gonna do out here? She's a city girl. She's got a career, friends, family…."

"If I heard right, she said her parents live in Pensacola."

"Yeah, yeah, they do, but she's got a couple sisters, some friends out there in L.A. The point is, she's got a life there. You think somebody like that's ever going to be happy living in a place like this, a hick Georgia town—"

With a sly smile, she finished it for him. "With a bunch of Crackers and rednecks?"

"You said it, I didn't."

They both laughed, and his mama sighed and said, "Oh, Jimmy Joe…"

After a forgiving silence, she said gently, "Let me ask you this, son. Who do you think you are to make that decision for her? Did you even ask her how she feels about it?"

He went back to his daddy's old chair, sat in it, and

leaning earnestly forward with his elbows on his knees, began to shape pictures for her with his hands, the way he sometimes did when he had something complicated to explain.

"It's like this," he said patiently, ignoring his mother's broad smile. "There's ducks, and then there's chickens. Ducks live in the water, and chickens live on dry land, and there's no way they're ever gonna find a way to live happily together. Now you take the chicken—that's me—and throw him in the water—that's the big city—and he's just gonna sink like a stone. The duck, on the other hand, she can go and live in the chicken yard, all right, but is she gonna be happy there?" He sat back with a fat sense of satisfaction, figuring he'd made his point about as well as anybody could make one. "Now, I ask you, can you think of anything in this world sadder than a duck who's never going to see a pond again?" He couldn't understand why his mama was just sitting there laughing.

"Oh, Jimmy Joe—" she chuckled, reaching over to pat him on the knee "—you know, I think you read too much." She paused to wipe her eyes, then gave a deep, amused sigh. "Son, I don't know how to tell you this, but people aren't chickens or ducks. People can live anywhere, adapt to anything, if they want to. Depends on their priorities, what they want out of life, what's important to them." She paused again, this time to let the seriousness in her voice settle in around them, and then continued, "And the only way you're ever going to find that out about a person is to ask."

Jimmy Joe stared at the floor and said nothing. He

was suddenly aware of how tired he was. Out of the corner of his eye he saw his mother's lapdog slippers slide off the coffee table as she stood and gathered up her antacid glass. He felt a lump settle into his throat as she leaned down to kiss him.

"I'm just so glad you're home safe and sound, son," she said huskily. She gave his shoulder a squeeze and shuffled off toward the kitchen. In the doorway she paused and turned. "You know," she said. And he thought, Uh-oh. He knew that sly tone of voice. "J.J.'s still got a week's vacation left. Why don't the two of you go on down to Florida, spend some time together? I'll bet Pensacola Beach'd be pretty nice this time of year."

He cleared his throat and waved his hand and tried his best not to sound like he was making excuses. "Ah, well...you know I sorta promised J.J. I'd take him to Six Flags. It's open just for the holidays. And then I got to service my truck...get ready to make another run out to California...."

"Son," his mama said sternly, "I never raised you to be a coward."

Chapter 14

"Westbound, you got a smoky comin' your way with his lights on—don' know where he's goin', but he's in a hurry."
"'Preciate it."

I-40—Oklahoma

The way Jimmy Joe saw it, it wasn't a case of being a coward. There was a difference between being a coward and being sensible. And he didn't think he was being stubborn and muleheaded, which his sister Jessie accused him of, either. What he was, he told himself, was patient. Patient and sensible.

All he needed was time. Time to forget. Time to forget everything that had happened to him out there in that Panhandle blizzard, and all but the haziest memories of a selfish and uppity redhead from California and her tiny pink scrap of a baby girl.

If only, he thought, she hadn't gone and named her Amy.

Still, he was sure it was just a matter of keeping busy and letting enough time go by so that the memories would start to fade. So he wouldn't keep thinking he heard Mirabella's voice talking to him above the highway hum and the growl of a big diesel engine. So he wouldn't keep waking up alone in his hand-carved walnut bed remembering the way her body had felt in his arms. Then, if he could get those memories out of his head, maybe the feelings that went with them would go, too—the aching sense of longing, and loss.

The problem was, it didn't seem to be working. Instead, it seemed the more time that went by, the more vivid the memories got. And the stronger the feelings. Sometimes he would tiptoe downstairs in the dead of night and plug the interview tapes into the VCR and run them over and over until his eyes smarted; the feel of her skin, wet and slick against his cheek, the smell of her hair, the salt taste of her sweat vivid in his mind, and every nerve in his body feeling as if it had been rubbed with sandpaper.

He couldn't even remember anymore how he'd felt about her back then, when he'd been handcuffed and hog-tied by the knowledge that she was a pregnant woman, a woman in labor, and almost certainly someone else's woman besides. All he knew was the way he'd come to feel about her since; the way he felt about her *now,* which was a way he hadn't felt in so long he was astounded to discover he still could.

The last time he'd felt like that he'd been—oh, about sixteen, grappling and groping with Patti in the back of his oldest brother's car, unable to think about anything in the world but how good her breasts felt in his hand, and how if he didn't get himself inside her he was about to blow apart into a million pieces. She'd been a virgin, too. They both had been—he, too randy and dumb to know that she'd lied to him about the bruises he'd found on her body, or that because of them there were blacker ones on her soul, and that he was about to make the biggest mistake of his life.

That was what those kinds of feelings did to a man, he thought. Made him forget everything he'd been taught about what was right and what was wrong, everything he knew about common sense, everything he believed in. He might have had some kind of excuse back then, being just sixteen. But he wasn't sixteen anymore. He was a grown man with a child of his own, and a future to make for him. And no matter what his mama had told him, going after something just because it would make *him* happy was a luxury he couldn't afford. If, in his longing for Mirabella, he sometimes felt like an addict at the end of his tether, well...too bad. He'd gotten over worse. He would get over this, too.

I'll get over you, Marybell.

No. Marybell had been *his* name for her, *his* fantasy. But that was just what it was...fantasy. Mirabella...that was who she really was—a woman as exotic and foreign to him as her name.

But...why did she have to go and name her baby Amy?

The week after J.J.'s Christmas vacation ended, Jimmy Joe hit the road again. It was a pretty good trip—a long one, which was okay with him—another load of textiles headed for L.A., after which he was supposed to go out to San Pedro to pick up a bunch of electronics components just come in off a boat from Taiwan and run them up to Boise. He planned it so he would take the southern route out and the northern route back, and that way avoid I-40 and the Texas Panhandle altogether.

But when he called in from Boise, his broker told him there was a load of designer-label beer down in Denver, if he wanted it, headed for Fort Worth, so he wouldn't have to deadhead it all the way home. He couldn't very well pass up an opportunity like that, could he? So much for well-laid plans.

The weather was downright balmy for January as he dropped down out of Denver and headed into New Mexico. He hit a little rain in Albuquerque, but none of the frozen stuff. In fact he couldn't see any traces at all left of the blizzard that had paralyzed the whole midsection of the country just a few short weeks ago.

Butterflies began to stir in his belly when he rolled past the Santa Rosa truck stop where Mirabella had spent the night in his sleeper, and he remembered how he'd rubbed her back and fed her chicken soup, and that they'd argued about Walt Disney movies.

From there, with the road dry and dusty, it was only two hours to the rest stop east of Adrian. It seemed incredible to him now, rolling along with his tires singing and the radio placidly droning on about the whereabouts of any bears in the vicinity, to recall that the last time he'd driven through there it had been in a single-file convoy creeping along at no more than walking speed.

The pounding of his heart didn't ease up after he passed the rest stop, either. Still to come was Vega, and Riggs's gas station where he'd left the keys to Mirabella's car. He wondered if she'd picked it up yet, or if it was still there, waiting for her.

He wasn't going to pull off and see. He'd sworn to himself he wouldn't. But suddenly there was old Route 66 and the sign that said Riggs's RoadSide Service, and the next thing he knew the Kenworth was heading up the exit ramp, and he was turning left onto the overpass, all the while cussing himself and calling himself several kinds of fool.

Riggs was tickled to death to see him; had to tell him all about how he'd seen Jimmy Joe on TV, and how he'd become something of a hero himself around those parts, and asked half-jokingly for his autograph. He took Jimmy Joe out to his garage and showed him the Lexus, all washed and polished and covered up with a nylon tarp to keep the dust off.

"Don't know how long she plans on leavin' it here," said Riggs. "Guess she's gonna be stayin' with her folks down there in Pensacola for a few more weeks, anyways."

"You talked to her?" Jimmy Joe asked, his heart flapping against his ribs like a tire going bad.

"Oh, yeah, she called me here, couple weeks ago, now. Right after New Year's, I guess it was. Wanted to know if I'd send her stuff to her, UPS. She had all her Christmas presents for her folks in the trunk, you know. She said she'd send me some money to do it, but, ah, you know, I went on ahead and sent 'em for her. I knew she'd be good for it, and she was—the money come just a few days later. Say, you know, she is just the nicest little ol' gal—sure am glad everything turned out okay for her.''

"Yeah," said Jimmy Joe. Funny thing—it seemed like all of a sudden he couldn't get enough air to breathe. "You, uh, you say you shipped her things to her UPS? You, uh…" He gulped oxygen and plunged. "You wouldn't happen to still have her address, would you?"

"Well, now, I sure do." Riggs looked at him sideways, kind of sly. "You thinkin' about gettin' in touch with her? Saw her on TV—my, she sure is pretty, ain't she?"

"Aw, you know," said Jimmy Joe, shuffling his feet like a teenager facing down his prom date's daddy, "I just thought I'd maybe drop her a note, or something. Find out how she and that little baby are doin'…"

"Well, sure 'nuff—I would," said Riggs, and added casually, "You can give her a call, if you want to. I got her phone number, down there in Pensacola where she's stayin' at her folks' place. Come on in where it's warm and let me find it for ya."

Ten minutes later Jimmy Joe was back on the interstate, heading east with a trailer-load of beer and a grin on his face, as his daddy would have said, "Like a possum with his paws full a' paw-paws." He felt jangled and so weak in the knees he didn't know how he was going to shift gears. "You're an idiot," he said to himself. "You know that, don't you?"

He did. But that didn't keep him from wanting to blast everybody he met with his airhorn and shout to the heavens, "Hallelujah!"

In Amarillo he left I-40 and headed down to Fort Worth on Highway 287, which was a long, straight shot, and once he'd left the little Panhandle towns and their speed traps behind, about as fast a one as a driver could ask for, for not being an interstate. He drove most of the night, pulling over on the outskirts of Fort Worth to catch a few hours' sleep, then slipped on into the city ahead of morning rush-hour traffic. When the wholesaler's warehouse opened up, he was there at the loading dock, waiting.

He unloaded, then pushed on down to I-20, to a truck stop he liked where he knew he could always find clean towels and plenty of hot water, plus a fairly decent cup of coffee. After a shower and a shave, and with a good hot breakfast under his belt, he screwed up all his courage and made a phone call.

Not long after that he was on his way again, heading east on I-20 in a cold, misty rain.

"I have this theory," Mirabella said, on the phone to her friend Charly Phelps in Los Angeles. "What I think is, that it's all just a matter of chemistry."

"No kiddin'," said Charly in her dry Alabama drawl.

"No—I mean actual brain chemistry. To be more specific, oxytocin."

Laughter bubbled against her ear. "Oxytocin?"

"Yeah, remember? They talked about it in child-birth class, It's this chemical that's released naturally during pregnancy, also during touching and during nursing. They call it the bonding chemical. It's what triggers contractions—also triggers orgasm, by the way.''

"Oh, that's good to know."

"Yeah, well, I've been reading up on it in my child-birth books since I got my stuff back last week—did I tell you the man with the service station shipped them to me UPS? The one that talked us through the delivery, and then Jimmy Joe gave him my keys and had him pick up my car? Turns out he's the nicest guy. Anyway, when you consider all that oxytocin oozing around inside me, then all that close physical contact—he was always touching me, Charly, rubbing my back, my legs, my feet, even my face…'' *And he kissed me—don't forget that. I'll never forget that.* "Then you throw in a whole bunch of endorphins on top of it, and I must have been a walking chemical love potion. It's no wonder my emotions were so susceptible.''

"So what you're saying is, it wasn't that this Jimmy Joe guy was so wonderful, just that he was *there?*''

"Charly, at that point I'd have probably bonded with a BarcaLounger."

This time Charly's hoot of laughter held the derision that is completely permissible between old and trusted friends. "Bella," she said fondly, "you are such an idiot." And then, after a brief pause to see if she would deny it: "So that's your theory, huh? Tell me this—are you buyin' it? Because I'm not."

"I'm working on it." Mirabella sighed and kissed the top of the downy head nestled like a sun-ripened peach against her heart, then leaned her head back against the crocheted afghan that lay draped, as it had for as long as she could remember, across the back of her mother's old rocking chair. "Right now it's too soon to tell. I mean, I'm nursing, you know? And that oxytocin is still flowing, so...it stands to reason I'd still have all those feelings and memories."

Just as strong and clear as if it had been yesterday we were together in that truck...Christmas carols playing on the radio, and Jimmy Joe's arms holding me and his voice yelling in my ear, "One more...one more!" And his face when he laid Amy on my stomach and said, "Marybell, say hello to your new baby girl..." so vivid in my mind I feel sometimes he's just in the next room, and if I call to him, in the very next moment he'll be here beside me, smiling his sweet, Jimmy Joe smile....

On her chest, Amy stirred and uttered a tiny squeaking sound, and Mirabella's hand began a slow stroking and patting rhythm to counteract the effects of her own rueful laughter. "Anyway, I'm hoping it will all go away once I get my body back to normal—like a bad dream, you know?"

"How's that coming, by the way? I know you, you're probably thinkin' you ought to already be wearing your regular clothes by now, and driving yourself nuts if you're not. Are you working out?"

It was Mirabella's turn to snort—but softly, so as not to disturb Amy. "I'm not *that* compulsive." But she smiled when she said it, because she knew full well that a few months ago she *had* been, about her physical self, anyway, and especially about her weight.

But now...she didn't think she could have explained it, certainly not to Charly, but since Amy's birth she'd noticed, well, a distinct *difference* in the way she viewed her own body. Where once she'd focused on and criticized its every flaw, now when she looked at her body she felt what could only be described as pride. *Yes,* the feelings seemed to say, *what a wonderful, marvelous body you are, to have done this miraculous thing!* Instead of her usual restless dissatisfaction, her constant drive to improve herself, she felt a kind of complacency that was almost catlike, bordering on smugness.

And something else—something she'd never known before, and so couldn't begin to explain. It was as if something sleeping deep inside her had been awakened, like jillions of tiny seeds sprouting where everything had been barren before. As if all those tiny new shoots and buds were pushing, straining, reaching for warmth and light, because like all newborn things, they demanded nourishment. She felt a new restlessness now—not of dissatisfaction, but of longing; an itch not of compulsion, but of desire. Having a child had fulfilled her, as she'd known it would; fulfilled the caring, giving, loving and nurturing woman she'd always known herself to be. But at the same time it seemed to have awakened a strange new woman, one she'd never met before. One who *needed* nurturing. One who needed, one who yearned, one who deserved to be cared for...given to...touched...loved.

"It's coming pretty well," she said, drawing a shaken breath. "I feel really good—I think the nursing's helping me get back in shape, if you don't count my chest, which of course is still enormous. I've been walking—not today, though. It's raining, and it's cold.''

"It's beautiful here," said Charly with typical California smugness. "Just your basic January in L.A. After all the lousy weather in December, suddenly the sun's shining and the hills are green. So, when are you coming home? I miss you, and I'm dyin' to see Amy.''

Home? Mirabella gazed at the rain-drenched Mandevilla vine growing up the trellis beside her parents' patio door and wondered how she was ever going to tell her best friend that Los Angeles didn't seem like home to her anymore. It seemed as far away to her as the moon, and about as hospitable. Sometimes her life there seemed like a rapidly fading dream.

But *if my home isn't there anymore,* she thought with a vague sense of bewilderment and sadness, then *where is it?*

"I'm not sure—" she began, just as a truck's air brakes hissed explosively out in the street. Her heart jumped and the hand holding the phone jerked so violently it startled Amy, making her tiny body jerk, as well. *What is this?* Mirabella thought. *Am I going to leap out of my skin every time I hear that sound for rest of my life?* Suddenly furious, she swore under her breath.

"What's the matter?"

"Nothing—just some truck making noise out in the street. One of my mom's neighbors is probably having something delivered, repaired or hauled away. This is a retirement community—there's a lot of that going around. Listen—I'll be home soon, I promise. I'm planning on it. Pop's doing a lot better. I think they're going to schedule him for a bypass in a month or two, and Mom would probably have an easier time of it taking care of him if Amy and I are out of her hair.''

She paused to chuckle. ''She made him go grocery shopping this morning, can you believe that? Said he needed to get out and get some exercise. They've been gone quite a while— Oh, now what? *Damn.* Someone's at the door. Looks like I'm going to have to get that. Hold on a minute while I get out of this chair—''

Supporting the sleeping baby with one hand and juggling the cordless phone with the other, she pushed herself awkwardly upright.

''Uh, Bella, maybe I should let you go.''

''No, no, that's okay, it'll just take me a minute to get rid of whoever it is. It's probably just somebody collecting for the Heart Association—there's a lot of that around here, too. Hold on—'' She had to use the hand with the phone in it to open the door.

''Yes? I'm sorry, but the Wasko—'' The words flew away on an exhaled breath, like whispers in the wind. The cordless phone fell to the floor with a clatter as, in a purely instinctive reaction, her hand flew to cover her baby's head. Her lips moved, soundlessly forming his name: ''Jimmy Joe.''

No smile, no dimples, although one corner of his mouth twitched slightly upward, obviously trying. The light in his eyes was uncertain and brooding as he stood with one thumb hooked in the pocket of his Levi's, one hip and shoulder canted higher than the other, raindrops sparkling on his skin and beginning to drip from the spiky-wet ends of his hair. Dangling from the other hand as if forgotten was a bouquet of pink roses wrapped in cellophane.

"Hey, there, Marybell," he said with a rueful sniff. "Guess your mama must not a' told you I was comin'."

She looks like she's seen a ghost, he thought, which was about the way he felt. Her hair was even brighter and her skin more translucent than he remembered, and she seemed tinier, too, somehow. She was wearing white cotton pants and a long-sleeved button-up-the-front shirt in some sort of gauzy material that draped gently over her voluptuous breasts and nested the sleeping baby's cheek like thistledown. The soft, sea colors of the shirt made him realize something he hadn't before—that in certain lights and moods, her eyes were more green than gray. Standing there in the rain and gloom of January, she seemed to him all sunlight and flower-scented freshness, like a spring breeze that had come without warning to snatch his breath away.

"Mom knew you were coming?" Her voice was an airless whisper of disbelief.

His heart was pounding so hard he couldn't think straight, but he managed a little half-smile of apology. "Yeah, I called yesterday from Dallas. Tried to again, a little while ago when I got into town, but your line was busy."

He stepped up onto the doorstep, and she sucked in air in a startled gulp. Cautiously, with a light touch on her arm and a raised eyebrow to ask permission, he leaned past her to pick up the telephone she'd dropped. Without taking his eyes from her face, as if she were

some rare wild creature that might vanish in a blink
if he did, he mumbled into the phone, "'Scuse me,
but can she call you back? 'Preciate it," then laid it
carefully, along with the roses he'd brought, on the
little table that was there in the entryway behind her.

Even with the rain coming down, he could hear the
small, sticky sound she made when she swallowed. As
dry as his own mouth was, he wasn't surprised that
her voice would still only come in a whisper. "Jimmy
Joe…what are you doing here?"

Ah, you know, I was just passin' through— That
was what he started to say, until somewhere in the
back of his mind he heard his mama's voice saying,
"Son, I never raised you to be a coward." So he took
the deepest breath he could and in an adolescent's
cracked and terrified voice, told her the truth.

"I came to see you. And because…there's something I've been wantin' to do."

In a world gone suddenly silent, Mirabella watched
his hand float across the space between them and come
to rest on Amy's head, a touch as sweet and reverent
as a benediction. She didn't breathe; her heartbeat
rocked her as the hand rose and she felt that same
touch on her own cheek. The warmth of it flowed like
oil into her neck, and when his other hand came to
cradle her head she gave a sigh of gratitude, for it had
grown too heavy for her own muscles to bear. The
warmth poured downward into her shoulders and
chest, into her belly and farther yet—deep, deep down.
Her breasts tingled and her legs grew weak, and all
the hungry new shoots inside her lifted and swelled
with joy.

"Oxytocin…" she murmured.

"Pardon?" His breath misted her lips.

"It's just…chemistry."

"You got that right," he growled, and brought his mouth the last sweet distance.

Their lips met like lovers who have traveled a lifetime and ten thousand miles to find each other—with yearning and gladness and thanksgiving and joy; with breathless awe and trembling disbelief.

"I *can't*," gasped Mirabella.

"Why not?" His mouth hovered a suspenseful whisper above hers.

"I can't do this—I can't," she breathed, moving her head back and forth just slightly, as if fighting a hypnotist's powers. "It won't work. I'm much too old for you. It's not—"

"Hush." With one word and a gentle shake of her head he silenced her. Then he pulled back, but only far enough so she could see his eyes. And there was no gentleness in them now; they were brooding and dark, with a fire in their depths she'd seen once before. When he spoke, the tone of his voice was familiar to her, too—the same firm, unyielding voice she'd clung to through a long, dark night, and that had calmed her fears and brought her safely through the birth of her child.

"I'm gonna ask you one question, and I want you to answer me truthfully, and then we're gonna be done with this, you understand? I want you tell me—in all that time we spent together in my truck, did it even once enter your mind to think about how old or how young either one of us was?"

"But that was—"

His mouth stopped her there. Then once again he drew back to gaze down at her, the fire in his eyes banked to a tender glow. "Marybell, I do enjoy arguing with you, and I expect we're gonna be doin' a lot of it, about a lot of things. But this ain't one of 'em. We're done with this now, y'hear?"

She was conscious only of mild astonishment as she heard herself answer meekly, "Yes, sir."

Overriding every other thought and feeling was the most intense hunger she'd ever known. She watched his mouth descend to hers as though it were the only drop of water, the last crumb of bread, the only blade of grass in a barren and thirsty world, feeling as though she would die if she couldn't taste it again— just once more. She actually felt a sharp pain when he suddenly halted, still a tantalizing, tormenting hairsbreadth away.

"Oh—" she cried, a sound somewhere between a laugh and a whimper. On her chest Amy was stirring and making impatient snuffling noises.

"Looks like she's wakin' up," said Jimmy Joe, one hand dropping, lightly as a falling leaf, to the baby's bobbing head. He looked at Mirabella and his eyebrows rose. "May I?"

"Oh—of course."

She watched, breath suspended, an aching knot of warmth growing inside her as she recalled the last time those strong, sensitive hands had cradled her daughter's tiny body—slippery wet with gunk and warm from her own body, attached to her still by a pulsing cord, kicking, punching and squalling with outrage at the shock of cold on her skin and the intrusion of air in her brand-new lungs. How gently he'd held her, then placed her on Mirabella's belly and guided her frantically searching hands to take the place of his.

"She sure has grown," he said huskily. In response to his voice, Amy's head turned slowly from side to side like a radar scanner as she searched for the face that went with it. Homing in and locking on, she studied it with infant intensity, her mouth pursing and stretching as she ran through her entire repertoire of facial expressions for this new and fascinated audience.

"Red hair?" He touched it with a fingertip and smiled. "She looks just like you."

And suddenly as if in response to his words, Amy's eyes crinkled up and her mouth popped open and then stretched wide, and the corners tilted upward. "She's smilin'," he said, looking up at her mama, all but thunderstruck. He felt as if his heart was going to burst.

"She sure is," Mirabella murmured, moving closer so she could see it, too. "That's a first." She looked oddly misty to him, like a flower in the rain.

"That's no gas pain, either. Look at her—she just won't quit." He thought he could have drowned in that smile. Then he felt like maybe he *was* drowning, the way his chest hurt and it was so hard to breathe.

"Okay, now she's got her priorities straight," Mirabella said with a tender snort, as one of the baby's waving fists found its way to her mouth and she began to suck avidly on it.

Jimmy Joe chuckled. "Looks like she's hungry."

"She's *always* hungry. Which is another way she's just like her mother. Yeah...funny, isn't it?" Her smile was blurred and soft as she gazed down at her daughter and tickled her cheek with a finger. Mirabella's eyes flicked up at him and her smile grew wry. "If you want to make God laugh, just make a plan—isn't that what you told me? All I can say is, He must really be holding his sides right now. I mean, here I had it all planned, picked out the perfect set of genes. I was going to have a tall, slim, blond little boy with a sweet, beautiful smile and..." Her voice caught, and she looked quickly back down at her baby with her face so full of adoration, watching her was like looking into the sun. "Look what I got—a round, roly-poly redhead with an appetite like Pac-Man...."

"And just as pretty as a little wild rose," said Jimmy Joe, in a voice so fierce and raspy he felt as if he might have swallowed a whole bush's worth of those rose thorns himself. "And I wouldn't mind..."

His breath ran dry, and he stared at her, realizing he was on the verge of blurting it all out, everything he'd come to say to her—that he not only wanted her and Amy to come and live with him and share the rest of his life with him, but that he would be tickled to death to have several more just like her, eventually, Lord willing. Just like that, without any warning or leading up to it, without telling her all the reasons he thought he could make her happy, without presenting any of the arguments he'd thought up to answer the doubts she was sure to have. Just clobber her with it, before he'd even had a chance to woo her— Lord, he hadn't even given her the flowers yet! And then if she said no, *then* what?

He was staring down at her, with the baby held between them like a vow and his heart hammering in his throat, feeling as scared and helpless as he had the night Amy was born, and Mirabella was staring back at him, looking so beautiful he wondered if maybe he ought to chuck his whole game plan and just kiss her again, and go on kissing her until she didn't have any breath left to say no.

He was about to embark on that new strategy when a voice behind him sang out, "Oops, home too soon!"

He turned, heart pounding like a guilty teenager's, while Mirabella said, "Hi, Mom...Pop," in a breathy, little-girl voice he didn't recognize.

"Pete," her mama was scolding as she bustled up the walk with her hands full of plastic grocery bags and a plastic rain-bonnet on her head, "I *told* you we should have eaten lunch first."

"The hell with that," growled the barrel-chested man beside her, waving around the umbrella he was holding so it wasn't doing much to keep the rain off anybody. "I told you I want to meet the man—shake his hand. And that's what I'm gonna do."

He heaved himself up the steps, furling the umbrella as he came, his chin jutting out ahead of him in a way that reminded Jimmy Joe so much of Mirabella, he almost forgot his manners completely. He had to fight hard to contain his smile when he saw the traces of rust mixed in with the thick, straight, iron-gray hair.

Mirabella gamely murmured introductions, which her father mostly drowned out with his crisp and authoritative, "G'mornin', son. I sure am glad to meet you…glad to meet the man that brought my grand-daughter into the world. Come on in here, now. No sense in lettin' all the warm air out." He dragged Jimmy Joe into the house, pumping his hand.

Behind her husband's back, Ginger caught Jimmy Joe's eye and winked. "Ohh, look—roses!" she cried, spotting the bouquet he'd left on the table. "Aren't they gorgeous? They need to go in some water. I'll just take these groceries into the kitchen—"

"Let me carry those for you, ma'am."

"Now, let me see, how's my little ol' baby girl?"

"She just woke up, Dad. She needs her diaper changed. She's hungry again, too. I was just going to—I better go feed her.…"

"You do that, honey. Son, you're plannin' on stayin' and havin' lunch with us, aren't you?"

"Well, sir, ah…" With his hands already full of grocery bags, there wasn't much Jimmy Joe could do but follow Mirabella with his eyes as she fled down the hallway with Amy in her arms.

In the kitchen with her parents, he had an attack of claustrophobia. The cheery room seemed too crowded with just the three of them in it, and yet he felt Mirabella's absence so profoundly, it almost bordered on panic. He couldn't shake the feeling he was losing her, that he was about to let everything he'd hoped for slip through his fingers, just when he'd had it in his grasp. Because he *knew* her. He knew exactly what she was doing right now, in there alone with her baby and her thoughts. Right now her rational, reasonable planner's mind was telling her all the reasons why things wouldn't ever work out between them; and in another minute, her stubborn, muleheaded, opinionated mind was going to set it all in concrete. And he knew that once Mirabella had made up her mind, there wasn't anything on earth, short of a force of nature, that was going to change it. So if he was ever going to try to do it, he had better do it now.

He set the bags of groceries on the kitchen table as gently as he could, and with a muttered, "'Scuse me, sir…ma'am," dived through the doorway and headed off down the hall in the direction Mirabella had taken.

He found her in a back bedroom—the guest room, by the look of it, since he didn't think Pete Waskowitz would have tolerated all those flowers, or the white priscilla curtains at the windows. There were a few of Mirabella's clothes and lots of baby things lying around, a white bassinet beside the bed, and a baby blanket spread out on the comforter. The room smelled of baby powder and a just-changed diaper, which brought back all kinds of memories for him.

She was sitting in a chair near the windows, so engrossed in the baby at her breast, she didn't notice him for a minute or two. He watched her—watched the play of rain shadows in her hair, the creamy-soft curve of her cheek as she bent over her child, the gentle smile no one else would ever see—and knew that he'd been right, and that he would love this woman and this child until he drew his last breath…and beyond that, until the end of time. It strengthened his resolve for what he had to do.

She gave a gasp of outraged modesty when she saw him, and yelped, "Jimmy Joe—go away!"

But he ignored her, and instead went to sit on the edge of the bed right opposite her, and leaned forward to watch her somberly with his hands clasped between his knees. Her eyes followed him, darkening with wariness, at first. But once she knew he wasn't going to run blushing at the sight of her naked breast, she relaxed and accepted his presence, it seemed to him, with a kind of quiet pride. They sat like that in silence for a while, listening to Amy's squeaky gulps and the whisper of the rain on the windowpane.

Then she shook her head, just slightly, and he saw her eyes fill with tears. "Jimmy Joe," she said in a broken whisper, "what are you doing here?"

He'd had a thousand miles to prepare for this. He'd probably thought of a thousand different ways to say what he wanted to say—clever, intelligent ways. Every one of them went right out the window. With his heart in his throat and in his eyes, he finally looked at her and said it: "Marybell, I've come to take you home with me."

Chapter 15

"That home cookin's smellin' awful good right now."
                                        I-40—Texas

He knew from her silence and sadness that she'd probably expected it, that she'd already guessed what he wanted to ask her. And that the tears in her eyes were there because she'd already convinced herself it wasn't going to work.

Funny thing—he never once thought it had anything to do with her maybe just not feeling the same way about him that he did about her. Somehow, he knew she did. It was just a feeling he had, something to do with the way she looked at him, the way her lips clung to his when he kissed her, the way she trembled when he touched her. And then, she'd named her baby Amy.

"Jimmy Joe," Mirabella whispered, "I can't." The ache inside her was so vast that she wondered as she gazed down at her daughter's fat, contented little cheek, how she could not feel it, too.

"You say that a lot," he said matter-of-factly. "So far you've been wrong every time."

Since normally there was nothing Mirabella hated more than being told she was wrong, that should have been enough to launch her headlong into an argument with no holds barred. But now, since deep in her heart she wanted nothing more than to be wrong, all she could do was snap, "It wouldn't work," then clamp her mouth shut again and glare at him in stubbornness and confusion.

He took a deep breath and for a moment didn't say anything, while she watched his eyes roam the room, touching briefly on her, on the baby at her breast, the rain-streaked window, the bassinet, as if searching for something that lay just...*there*—so near but always beyond his grasp.

Then his gaze came back to his hands, clasped between his knees, and he cleared his throat, lifted his eyes to hers and smiled his sweet, Jimmy Joe smile and said, "I've never been much good with words. I mean, I *know* a lot of words. I read—my mama tells me too much—and the words are all up there in my head, and I hear them sometimes when I'm drivin' and I don't feel like listenin' to the radio or one of my books-on-tape. Words just flow along so easy, then, like a river. But when there's something important I want to say, I don't know, it's like somebody throws up a dam, or somethin', and all those words back up inside me, and the only ones that come through is just my usual trickle."

He paused to grin, then shake his head and look down at his hands again. "See, I knew you'd have to argue with me. And I had about a thousand miles to think how I'd answer you. All the good reasons why, different as we are and crazy as it seems, I think I could make you happy. Now that I'm here, though…" He looked up at her, his smile slipping awry. "The minute I saw you, I knew I wasn't gonna have the words. So I figure the best way is just to show you. So…Marybell, that's why I'm askin' you to come home with me to Georgia. So you can see for yourself who I am and what I've got to offer you. And then you can decide if it's anything you want, or not. It's up to you. So…what do you say? Will you come with me?"

Come with me…. It's up to you. Oh, God, what was happening to her nice, controllable, well-planned world? It was as if he'd suddenly come to her and said, "Hey, you want to fly to the moon? Here are the tickets—we leave in an hour!" The wild, the crazy, the impossible, was suddenly there within her reach— and she felt confused, terrified, paralyzed, her heart racing and her mouth as dry as sandpaper. She opened it, but no sound came out. The silence grew tense and viscous. And then…

"Oh, for heaven's sake, Bella," her mother said, "don't be an idiot."

They both turned to see her standing there, Amy's infant carrier car-seat in one hand, the diaper bag slung over her shoulder. Jimmy Joe rose instantly, mumbling, "Ma'am," as good manners dictated. Mirabella simply sat, dumbstruck, as Ginger dumped the bag-

gage onto the rug and advanced with arms outstretched.

"Here—I'll take that baby. You go get your coat."

"But...she hasn't been burped—"

"I'll do it. Go and get yourself ready—now. This
instant."

Mirabella drew a sharp, reflexive breath as she saw
her baby lifted from her arms, an instinctive preparation for battle. Then she caught Jimmy Joe's quiet
gaze and the exhalation sighed softly from her lips.
"Yes, ma'am," she murmured humbly.

They rolled into the front yard of Jimmy Joe's
mama's place late in the evening, long past the usual
suppertime. He'd thought about whether he should
take her home, first, but then he'd figured that might
not be fair to her, and that he couldn't really expect
her to make a decision until she'd had a chance to see
what she was getting into. And that meant his whole
family—at least the part of it he lived with on a regular
basis, which was to say, Mama and Granny Calhoun,
Jess and Sammi June, and of course, J.J.

His heart did a little double-skip when he thought
about Mirabella and his son meeting for the first time.
He wasn't worried so much about J.J. liking Mirabella
right off the bat—how could he not?—and even growing to love her like the mama he'd never had.

On the other hand, he had to face the fact that his
son had pretty much outgrown the cute-and-adorable
stage, and that he could be a real pistol, sometimes.
He knew it was asking a lot of a woman with a brand-

new baby of her own to take on someone else's eight-year-old kid, besides.

But whichever way it was going to go, he knew he wouldn't have to be in suspense for long, because the minute J.J. heard the rumble of his diesel and the hiss of those air brakes, he would be out that front door like a shot, just like he always was.

With one ear tuned to the slamming of the door and the familiar cry, "Hey, Dad!" he turned to Mirabella, who'd come quietly to stand between the seats and was peering through the cab windows at the house, which for some reason was all lit up like Christmas. "We'll stop here a minute, if that's okay," he said, just a little out of breath. "Just want to pick up J.J., have you meet my mama. My place is just down the road."

She didn't say anything, but nodded and began to unbuckle the belt that held Amy's infant carrier securely in place in the passenger seat. He got out and went around to open the door and lift the carrier down for her. Then he offered her his hand to help her down the steps, remembering what a climb it had been for her before, wondering if her independent nature would let her accept. When she gave him a look but took his hand anyway, he thought it was a good sign.

They were standing together beside the truck, sort of straightening themselves out and shaking the road stiffness out of their legs, when he finally heard the door. Not a slam, though, and without the exuberant shout of welcome that usually went with it. He turned and saw that his son had come onto the porch. But instead of running on out to meet him as he always did, he was just standing there with the light from the windows behind him shining in his hair, so he looked like he was wearing a halo.

Jimmy Joe touched Mirabella's elbow and they started across the yard, last fall's dead leaves crackling and crunching underfoot. When they reached the front walk, J.J. started slowly down the steps and came toward them, holding himself straight and tall, as if he was walking down the aisle of a church, fixing to light the candles on the altar. Wondering what had gotten into his son, Jimmy Joe set the baby carrier carefully on the ground, cleared his throat and said, "Hey, son, there's somebody here I'd like you to meet."

That was when he got his first look at Mirabella, who had stopped dead-still in the middle of the walk. He didn't know how to describe her expression, except to say she looked…stunned. Then as he watched, her face began to take on a kind of glow, as if she was witnessing a miracle. She glanced up at him, and her eyes—again there was only one way to say it—her eyes were *dancing*.

"God does have a sense of humor," she murmured as she moved up beside him, her hand going out toward the boy standing so tall and stiff before her. Thinking she meant to ruffle his hair, Jimmy Joe held his breath, knowing how J.J. hated that sort of thing, but she stopped just short of it and instead said briskly, "Hey, how are you doing? I'm Mirabella."

Then, while J.J. solemnly shook her hand, his father let his breath out in silent thanksgiving, knowing it was going to be all right. He'd seen that look on Mirabella's face before, as she watched her baby while she slept.

"You're a lot prettier in person than you are on TV," J.J. said, studying her with his head cocked to one side.

"Thanks—I think," said Mirabella, laughing shakily. She still felt jangled after the shock of seeing her fantasy child in the flesh, right there before her eyes.

In the boneless way of all eight-year-olds, J.J. dropped to his knees beside Amy's carrier. "Boy," he said in an awed voice, "she sure is little."

"Can I hold her?" asked a tall, slender girl with long blond hair pulled back in a ponytail, who had just joined them.

"This is J.J.'s cousin, Sammi June," Jimmy Joe said. "Sammi June, say hey to Mirabella."

"Hey," said Sammi June dutifully. "Can I hold the baby?"

"Well—" Mirabella looked over at Jimmy Joe and caught his reassuring nod "—sure, you can. As soon as we get inside."

"I get to hold her first," J.J. hissed, glowering possessively.

"Uh-uh. I'm the oldest, so *I* get to hold her—"

"Uh-uh, do not! I saw her first!"

"Sammi June!" yelled a tall, slim, dark-blond woman from the doorway. "You get in here, now, and help Gramma put the food on the table."

"That's my sister Jess—Sammi June's mother," said Jimmy Joe, then muttered under his breath as he bent to pick up Amy's carrier, "Sure am glad everybody's just bein' their usual selves."

They went up the steps together, Mirabella thinking, Oh, God, is *everybody* in this family tall, thin and blond? Then she saw the woman standing behind Jimmy Joe's sister, waiting for the confusion to clear. A small woman, shorter even than Mirabella, with a neat cap of hair in a rich, natural-looking shade of brown, and a body that was still youthful, though definitely on the voluptuous side.

"Mama," said Jimmy Joe, sounding slightly breathless, "this is Mirabella."

"Betty," his mother said firmly, as she held out her hand.

She doesn't look anything at all like Jimmy Joe. That was the first thing to sort itself out of the mess in Mirabella's mind. Then she saw his mother's eyes—warm, brown eyes, with a golden gleam of fire lurking in their depths. And she thought, with a sense of familiarity that was almost like a homecoming, *Yes…*

"I'm just so happy to finally meet you," Betty Starr exclaimed, dragging them all through the doorway and into her house with the sheer force, it seemed to Mirabella, of her personality. "Let me see this little one, now. Oh, she's sound asleep, isn't she? Well, that's good. Just bring her on in, we'll set her right down beside the table. Y'all come on, now, food's on the table. We waited supper for you. Would you like to freshen up? No? Well then… *Mama…?*" Her voice rose to a melodic bellow. "Supper's ready, Mama. Company's here and food's gettin' cold."

In a kind of daze, Mirabella followed her into the large, informal dining room that adjoined a rather old-fashioned kitchen, with appliances that probably dated at least from the sixties. She was reassured by the light pressure of Jimmy Joe's hand on her back, and in a strange way by the children, fidgeting and hissing at each other as they came along behind. Children, at least, were the same everywhere.

While Jimmy Joe's mother directed everyone to their places and his sister Jess bustled off to the kitchen to see to last-minute preparations, they were joined by a tiny wraith of a woman, no taller than the two children and bent and gnarled as a tree root with osteoporosis.

"Hey, there, gorgeous," said Jimmy Joe, bending over to kiss and hug her, handling her as though she were made of blown glass.

The old woman beamed and reached up to pat his cheek, then clutched his arms and peered around him like a child playing hide-and-seek. "Where is she?" she croaked, her old eyes gleaming, and Mirabella knew that, frail though she might be, here was a woman who still held the reins of life firmly in her hands.

"Granny," said Jimmy Joe, "this is Mirabella."

"Yes…yes…it's nice to meet you." She peered intently up at Mirabella, who felt her hand clutched in a grip of surprising strength. Then Granny Calhoun announced to nobody in particular, "She's a lot prettier than she looks on TV."

My family… Jimmy Joe watched them assemble around the table, squabbling and bickering and bossing one another as they always did and always would, and felt the familiar feeling that always came over him when he'd just gotten home after being gone awhile. A sense of thankfulness for them all, a rueful acceptance that they weren't perfect, and acknowlegment that he loved them in spite of—maybe even because of—that.

He wanted to look at Mirabella and smile at her with his eyes in a way that said, Yes, I know, but they're part of me. A big part. And a big part of what I brought you here to see. So what about it? Do you think...?

But he couldn't look at her then, too afraid of what he might see.

They all took their places—Mirabella, with Amy in her carrier at her feet, at the end closest to the living room in case, she was told, she needed to get up and tend to the baby during dinner. Jimmy Joe was down at the other end—miles away, it seemed—at the head of the table, with Granny Calhoun and the two children on one side and Betty and Jess on the other. The food—roast chicken and mashed potatoes and gravy, and boiled greens and corn bread—all smelled delicious, even to a semivegetarian like Mirabella, but she didn't know if the twinges she felt in her stomach were hunger pangs or butterflies.

On her right, Jimmy Joe's mother held out her hand. After a moment's uncertainty, Mirabella placed hers into it. Then she noticed that everybody was joining hands all around the table, so she looked over to her left and sure enough, there was Jess holding out her hand, too. *Oh, God,* she thought, not even aware of the propriety of that as everybody bowed their heads for the blessing.

She felt cold, suddenly. Lost and alienated. Not unusual, surely, for somebody thrust abruptly and unexpectedly into the bosom of a strange family. But this was Jimmy Joe's family. He'd brought her here in the hopes that she might want to become a part of it, too. *Could she?* Maybe she wanted to. But how would she ever make it work, when everything was so... different?

She felt so...*lonely.*

Then, while Sammi June did the honors in a singsong, recitative voice, Jimmy Joe suddenly lifted his head and looked down the length of the table at Mirabella and smiled his sweet, special smile. And she felt a strange stirring, like the rustling of the wind through the pine trees outside....

Later, when supper was finished and they'd collected J.J. and everybody had said all their goodbyes and y'all-come-backs and they'd gone on home, Jimmy Joe got J.J. settled down and then went looking for Mirabella. He found her out on his front porch, wearing his Levi's jacket and hugging herself against the cold, just standing and listening to the sounds of the night.

He went to her cautiously, not knowing quite what to make of her stillness. He felt calm and confident now, as he mostly did when he was here in his own place, but wired and restless, too, in a way he couldn't remember ever feeling before. With J.J. all tucked in for the night in his bedroom upstairs, and Amy Jo sound asleep again in her carrier, suddenly it was just the two of them—him and Mirabella, alone in the quiet of the night for the first time since that Christmas, more than three weeks ago. It seemed like a whole lot longer—another time, another place.

"Chilly out here," he said.

And she nodded and murmured, "Yes."

And then after a moment she went on, drawing a deep, quick breath, "I like it, though. It feels so crisp...so fresh. Reminds me of when I was growing up. We lived in the desert, then. I don't think we ever had snow, but it could get cold, and I remember the sky being like this, so black and clear and full of stars."

Hope filled his throat. He coughed and said, "Yeah, it's real nice in the summertime." He made a little gesture toward the two rocking chairs he kept there, side by side. "Sometimes I like to sit out here in the evenings and watch the night come in—you know, the air feels soft on your skin and the honeysuckle smells so sweet, and the fireflies twinkle on and off in the trees...."

"I've never seen fireflies," said Mirabella wistfully. And then he could hear a smile in her voice as she added, "Except at Disneyland—fake ones."

"I've seen those. They look awful darn close to the real thing." He went and sat in one of the rockers, and after a moment, she took the other. "If you sit here long enough," he said after a while, "the whippoorwill'll start to sing, somewhere out there in the trees. Just sings his little ol' heart out."

"I've never heard a whippoorwill." Her voice sounded far away. "What do they sound like?" She caught her breath and flicked him a quick, delighted smile when he cleared his throat, pursed his lips and whistled the three-note song. Then she turned her head away again, but not before he saw her smile go soft and wry. ''I remember…you told me about the whippoorwill. The night Amy was born.''

Warmth rose in his cheeks, and he laughed. ''I'm kind of surprised you remembered that.''

''Oh, I remember everything about that night.'' She sounded wistful again. Almost sad, he thought. ''I remember you held me, and you told me it was like making love. And then…''

''And then, you told me…''

''I'd never made love before.''

''I didn't believe you,'' he said softly.

She gave a dry snort of irony. ''*You* didn't—I couldn't believe I'd said it. It's not something I go around telling people, ordinarily.''

''I didn't believe you,'' he said again in a muffled voice, talking to the boards between his feet. ''How could I? There you were, havin' a baby.''

''And then…'' Her breath sighed and the rocker creaked softly as she leaned back. ''I told you I'd been artificially inseminated.''

His short, dry laugh was an echo of hers. ''*Then* I believed you. I figured nobody would make up somethin' like that.''

''You were so shocked.'' Her voice was gentle; not accusing, just stating a fact. ''I know it…changed things. Between us. The way you felt about me.'' He shifted uncomfortably, wishing he could deny it, knowing he owed her the truth. Knowing she wouldn't let him deny it, even if he'd tried to. Her eyes were steady on him now, the light from the living-room windows shining in them like moonlight on water. "I know it did, Jimmy Joe. I felt it. What I couldn't understand was *why?*"

He looked at her for a long time without answering, trying to pick apart the knots of feeling inside him. He was discovering that knowing something in your gut was one thing; trying to reason it out so you could explain it was something else. Finally he shook his head and began, "I never meant to judge—"

"But you *did.*"

He looked down at his clasped hands. "Yes, I guess I did, for a while." He paused, then went on in a voice he kept low to hide the intensity of the emotions inside him. "I *know* what it's like, you know, raising a child all alone—I've been doin' it for eight years, now. And dammit all—I can't help it if I have strong feelings about a kid needin' *two* parents. Me, I know I'm one of the lucky ones, because of Mama and Jess bein' so close by, so even when I'm gone I know J.J.'s always got somebody around to love him and care for him. But I've seen what happens to kids, left alone with the TV or some computer for a baby-sitter."

He left the rocking chair, propelled by the tension he couldn't keep to himself any longer, paced to the railing and stopped. Leaning his hands on it, he stared into the darkness and said quietly, "I know things happen to people they can't help, and when they do they've got no choice but to make the best of things. But I thought, for somebody to do that to a child on purpose, that it was kind of…" He looked over at her, hating to say it to her now, because of the way he felt about her, but knowing it was best to get it said and over with right up front, too. So he took a breath and murmured, "Selfish."

She sat hunched forward in the chair, rocking it slightly, making faint creaking sounds, not saying anything. He watched the way her hair shone warm in the light, like polished cherry-wood, and thought again of the nursery rhyme about the robin.

"Selfish..." She whispered it, then shook her head and said slowly, "And yet, you brought me here."

His feelings burned inside him like fire. He wanted so much for her to understand. "But that's just it," he said with gravel in his throat. "I know you're not selfish."

"No—maybe I *am* selfish." She left the chair rocking, empty, and came to the railing, her chin lifted in that uppity way she had. And he caught his breath, filled with a sudden burst of pride and delight in her, so it was all he could do to keep himself from bursting out in smiles and dragging her into his arms then and there.

"I wanted to be a mother," she said, roused and angry. "That's pretty selfish, I know. And I had a good job, plenty of money, a really nice home, and all this love and warmth and security—everything a child could want or need, right? Except for one thing—oops, no father! Bummer. But then I thought, so what? The important thing is the *love,* not who it comes from, or how many. I know lots of kids with two parents who'd be a helluva lot better off with one—or none at all, if you want to know the truth. So I thought, I've got enough love for two people, and I knew I'd make one

522 *One Christmas Knight*

terrific parent, so I decided to do it. I planned to try it this way first, and if that didn't work, I'd adopt. But it did work. And if you want me to say I'm sorry I did it—well, I'm *not*."

He listened to the angry rhythm of her breathing and felt his own pulses quicken in response, and his body heat with a passion to match hers, although he knew it was a different kind. He meant to change that as soon as he could. He didn't move toward her, though, but said in a slow, soft drawl, "Well, Marybell, like I said, I know you're not selfish. And I won't say you're wrong about anything you just said, especially the part about the love bein' what's important, and you bein' a terrific mama. Which I guess just leaves me with one question." He turned his head to look at her. "Why? Why did you have to do it this way? I mean, look at you—you're smart, funny, warm, a whole lotta fun to argue with, and probably the most beautiful, the sexiest woman I've ever seen in my life!"

Her breath caught, and surprise flashed like summer lightning in her eyes. His own heart stumbled, then began to pound like answering thunder. He whirled away from her, not trusting himself so near her, heat pumping through his body. Struggling with it, searching for a way to say it without being crude, he finally burst out with, "Woman, there must have been men fallin' over themselves to be the father of your child!"

Behind him, she laughed softly and unevenly, as if someone had taken her by the shoulders and shaken her. "Maybe so. But not the *right* one." Silence pulsed between them.

Then she said in her brisk, businesslike Mirabella voice, ''I guess you want to know how come I'm a virgin at thirty-eight. Well, like I said, I didn't exactly plan it that way. My problem has always been, you see, that I don't look anything like who I really am. I told you what I was like as a child. Well, there was a poem I remember—it was about this little girl who was a tomboy on the outside, but inside she was something completely different. That was me. It still is. When I was fat and homely, I kept waiting for some little boy to see how funny and smart and generous I was.

''By the time I got prettier, I'd developed this enormous chip on my shoulder. So now I looked like this cute, sexy little airhead, when actually I was an angry, resentful witch. And...I kept waiting for some guy to see how funny and smart and generous I was in spite of all that.''

Remembering the thought that had come to him way back in that truck-stop diner in New Mexico, Jimmy Joe wanted to burst out with, '*I* would have! *Me!*'' It took all the patience and good manners he had in him not to interrupt her.

''Guess what? Nobody ever did. Oh, I had crushes, of course—always on somebody who didn't have a clue. Guys who were attracted to me because of my looks—which was pretty much all of them—got turned off as soon as they found out who I really was. They just weren't expecting somebody who looks like I do to have a brain, I guess. They thought they'd be getting this adorable little someone they could dominate and control, and when they found out I was bossy and independent and headstrong and just as capable as they were—if not more so—boy, did they back off in a hurry.

"So…" She gulped, and suddenly there were tears in her voice. She lowered it to a whisper and went on, hurrying now, determined to get it all said. "I kept waiting for some guy to come along who would see how smart and funny and generous, and headstrong and independent and capable I was, and love me anyway. And no one ever did. I could have settled for just…someone, I suppose, but I've never been much good at compromising." She stopped there for a short huff of dry laughter, then finished in a flat, matter-of-fact tone. "For me it was the right man, or none at all. Eventually, I realized that the right man wasn't going to come along in time, and if I was going to have a child, I'd have to do it without one. So I did."

"Maybe," Jimmy Joe said hoarsely, "you just gave up too soon."

Chapter 16

*"I'm gon' be rollin' into home 'bout twelve,
one, tonight. My wife's gon' be lyin' in bed
a-waitin' for me."*

I-40—Texas

"Oh...Jimmy Joe."

He turned to her then, all primed and ready to take
her in his arms, but when he saw the way she was
looking at him he froze, a terrible fear prickling his
skin. Her eyes were huge and dark with tears; he could
see them glistening, too, on her cheeks.

"Don't you see?" she said, her voice so gentle and
sad it just about broke his heart. "You don't know
who I really am, either, any more than they did. You
don't know me—how could you? You've only seen
me...what—when I was in labor. Weak and helpless
and scared to death and vulnerable. And now with

Amy, when I'm such a soppy, sentimental fool. That's not *me*. I'm not at all like that!''

He would have reached for her right then, pulled her into his arms and murmured reassurances into her mouth, but she put up both hands to ward him off, and continued in a rapid, breathless voice.

''I'm an impossible person to live with. I'm moody, and I really need my privacy, my own space. I'd organize you to death—I'm frighteningly efficient. And a compulsive planner. I always have my Christmas shopping done—and everything wrapped—by mid-October. I'm bossy and argumentative, and I always have to be right. I stick notes on things, and underline in magazines. I…I'm a health nut. I don't eat red meat. And I really do hate country music!''

He studied her as she wound down through the laundry list of her shortcomings, saying nothing to derail her. But as he listened and watched her, he felt the fear slowly leave him, and the quiet joy of certainty come to take its place. He knew he could have kissed her then, and in a very short time thereafter had her in his bed. But it wasn't about that. It never had been. It was more important than that. There was a lot more at stake here than a few passion-filled hours. This was about the rest of his life. Except for the issue of her virginity, he couldn't see how taking her to bed was going to solve anything important.

He didn't think arguing with her was going to solve anything, either. He thought about it—about finally making his pitch like a traveling salesman and telling her all the ways he'd figured out that she could have a life with him here in Georgia and still do the things she liked to do out there in L.A.; how she could start her own business, if she wanted to, and go to Atlanta for shopping and concerts and plays, or to Athens, even to the university.

But he knew this wasn't the right time for that, either. She was right about a couple of things—she did dearly love to argue, and she did hate being wrong. At the moment she was on a roll, and he had an idea if he tried to argue with her she would just dig her heels in and get stubborn about it, more than ever determined to prove she was right.

"Reminds me of one of the great movie lines of all time," he drawled, when he saw she'd finally run down. He paused, shrugged, and delivered it: "'Oh, well...nobody's perfect.'"

She blinked, then let go a misty gust of laughter. He saw a look of confusion flash like a bird shadow across her face.

"Gettin' cold out," he said gently. "Gettin' late. Come on, let's go inside. I'll show you to your room."

He put his hand on her back to guide her through the door he was holding open for her, and felt her tremble. He almost lost it then, all his resolve and patience and self-control. Okay, he thought, so maybe making love to her wouldn't solve anything important between them, but it sure as heck would take care of her trembling, not to mention the hunger that was burning up *his* insides.

He was starting to worry about that, too. If things kept building up in him the way they were, he was afraid that when he finally did make love to her, he might have trouble being as gentle with her as he knew he was going to need to be. This whole thing, in fact, was turning out to be a lot more complicated and difficult than he'd thought it would be. It was going to take just about all the patience and self-discipline he had in him to get it to work out right. But he never doubted that it would. Or that she was worth it.

I really hate this, thought Mirabella. Here she was, all primed to have it out with him once and for all, and he'd left her flat, with nobody to fight with. Now she felt frustrated, and a little foolish.

Also confused. She didn't understand him. She'd seen the way he'd looked at her, the way his eyes had seemed to glow with some deep, inner fire. Everywhere they'd touched her she'd felt hot—as if the sun itself was burning her naked skin. And yet at the same time, she shivered. Chemistry, she thought, then scoffed at herself. *Chemistry, hell. Call it what it is, girl. It's just plain old desire.*

Desire. Oh, yes, she was awash in it, on fire with it. Her body pulsed with it. She wanted him. She could taste him on her tongue. He was in the air she breathed. Her legs felt like melted wax.

And now…he was going to say good-night?

Cold, confused, and wobbly with uncertainty, she picked up Amy's carrier and watched him while he locked up and turned off lights. She offered no objection when he took the carrier from her, but moved ahead of him to the stairs, feeling his hand like a knifepoint at the small of her back. She climbed slowly, breathlessly, wondering if her legs would support her to the top.

"This is my room," he said softly, opening a door

at the top of the stairs. He turned on the light, then stood back out of the way so she could see.

It's nice, she thought. Tidy, like the sleeper in his truck; wholly masculine, but with touches of gentleness and beauty, too, in the shelves full of books and Indian pottery, the Navajo rugs that covered the floor, and in the magnificent, hand-carved four-poster bed.

"What a beautiful bed," she murmured, meaning nothing more than that.

Jimmy Joe glanced at her and nodded. "Bought it from a man up in North Carolina. He told me he carved it from the wood of four-hundred-year-old walnut trees." He waited while she admired it, then said quietly, "It's too big for a man alone. I'd like to share it with you...when you're ready."

But I am ready! She wanted to shout it at him. Why couldn't he see that? Why couldn't she tell him? She suddenly felt as though she were enclosed in glass, walled up inside herself; that there was a door between them that hadn't been opened yet. He held the key— she knew he did. But for some reason, whatever it was, he hadn't used it; not yet. *Please, Jimmy Joe. Please say the words that will make it right.*

He touched her elbow and smiled, just the faintest shadow of his sweet, Jimmy Joe smile. "The guest room's this way," he said.

Jimmy Joe lay awake on the living room sofa listening to his house creak and groan in the stillness of night. It sounded to him like the wind was picking up outside; the rain he'd driven through from Texas to Pensacola would be here by tomorrow. He thought

about that, about the rain and the trip and his truck,
and all the little things he had to do now that he was
home. He thought about them hard, as if they were
big problems he had to solve, trying every way he
could to keep his mind off the woman sleeping upstairs.

It occurred to him that some of those creaks and
groans had taken on the rhythm of footsteps. He
thought it might be J.J. looking for him, or getting up
to use the bathroom or get himself a drink of water.
He waited for the boy to come down the stairs. When
he didn't, he pulled on a pair of sweatpants and went
to investigate.

The door to his bedroom was open. When he looked
inside he saw Mirabella standing beside his bed,
framed in a rectangle of light from the yard lamp outside. She was wearing her nightgown—something
long and slim and white—and he thought she looked
a little like a candle standing there, with her hair the
gleaming flame.

"I was looking for you," she said, her voice soft
and faraway sounding. She threw a bewildered glance
toward the quilt that covered his bed, still smooth and
undisturbed. "You haven't been to bed?"

He moved toward her, feeling his heartbeat grow
stronger with every step he took. He made a gesture,
a small throwaway with his hand. "I don't sleep here
much. Told you, it's too big for one person. Just makes
me feel lonely. Usually I sleep in the guest room. Tonight—" he smiled and shrugged "—I'm on the
couch downstairs."

She shivered when he came up behind her. With a

sigh, he wrapped his arms around her and brought her warm and snug against him. "You said you were lookin' for me," he murmured into her hair. "How come?"

He felt her soften in his arms as she let out the breath she'd been holding. He could barely hear her whisper, "I wanted...to tell you I'm ready. I want...you to make love to me. I want to share this bed with you."

"For tonight?" he asked, holding himself still, "Or from now on?"

She didn't answer. His heart knocked heavily against her back.

He shifted his arms, nestling her more securely against him, and drew a breath. "I have to tell you about this bed," he said. "I told you I bought it up in North Carolina, in the Smoky Mountains, from an old man who'd carved it from the wood of four-hundred-year-old walnut trees. He told me about it, told me it was something special, not just for sleeping in. A marriage bed, he called it. Said it was a bed to last a lifetime, and that I probably wouldn't understand that then, but I would someday.

"Well, I remember thinking, who is this old coot, and who does he think I am—a kid, or something? Shoot, I knew what a marriage bed was for—didn't I already have a child of my own? I thought he was talkin' about sex, of course. But he wasn't. I understand that now.

"See, I always thought I had marriage figured out. When I was a kid, I saw my parents—Daddy always away workin', Mama takin' care of the house, runnin' everything including us kids—and I thought that's what it was—kind of a division of labor, I guess you could call it. Then I got to be in my teens, and the hormones kicked in, and all I could think about was gettin' some girl into bed. And of course there was everybody tellin' me that was wrong, that was supposed to wait for marriage, right? Big revelation—*now* I knew what marriage was really all about. Marriage was so you could have sex without goin' to hell.''

He rocked her gently, as they laughed and trembled together. ''Then…I got Patti into trouble, and we got married, and I found out there was a whole lot more to it than just sex. Hoo boy, was there ever! All of a sudden, marriage was about responsibility, and providing, and taking care of somebody, and when it's your child, that means *forever.*''

''I know,'' Mirabella whispered. ''I know.''

''After Patti…well, I dated some, went to bed with a few. I was looking, I guess. But there was always something missing. I was lonely—sometimes even when I was with somebody. Usually, in fact. And I never knew exactly what it was I was lookin' for. Until you.''

He was shaking harder now, so he held her tighter, too, and laid his cheek against her hair. ''That's when I knew that what I'd been lookin' for was my *mate*— you know, like half of a pair. And that the reason I'd been so lonely was, half of me was missing. And then I found you, and all of a sudden I wasn't lonely anymore, because now I was…whole.''

He turned her suddenly, his hands on her shoulders holding her away from him so he could look into her eyes. Through the blur of her own tears Mirabella saw his face—not just its beauty and sweetness, but also its intelligence and strength, and she thought she was seeing him clearly for the first time.

"And it doesn't *matter* if we're different," he said in a voice gone hoarse with passion. "Night and day, black and white—it doesn't matter, you understand? It's like this rug we're standin' on. Black and white can make one real beautiful whole, when you weave 'em together right."

She could only nod; tears rolled freely down her cheeks, and she made no move to wipe them away. His hands slipped from her shoulders and down her arms, and he took her hands and held them clasped tightly between both of his.

"Marybell...Mirabella, I know I'm not a sophisticated man, or very exciting, and I'm sure never gonna be rich. But I will promise you this—that I will love you and that little girl in there with all my heart and soul until the day I die, and spend every day of my life makin' sure you know it. And I will tell you so again with my last breath. I told you, I'm not good with words—"

"You didn't need many!" It burst from her on the crest of the sob she could no longer contain. "Just those three would have done it!"

"Just—" He looked bewildered for just an instant, and then his smile blossomed. "'I love you,' you mean?"

"*Yes!* I kept waiting for you to say it...dammit." She snatched her hand from him and swiped furiously at her nose, and when that proved futile, sniffed loudly instead. "I love you too," she said soggily.

"Oh, I know that." He took her wet face in his hands and turned it up to his.

"How could you?" She sniffed again. "I didn't know myself. I thought it was just another stupid crush—you know, because there you were, riding to my rescue on your big blue charger, scooping me out of a snowbank and sweeping me up in your arms and saving my life—how could I not fall in love with you? And then I thought it must be chemistry, or hormones, or something. I never dared believe—"

"*Believe*," he growled, and lowered his mouth to hers.

And suddenly she did. Believed in him absolutely, knew with utter certainty that her heart would be safe forever in his keeping, and that she could grow old with him and never have to fear that he would love her less, even when she looked like Granny Calhoun.

"I'm sorry about this virginity thing," she gasped, when his mouth had left hers to travel by slow, melting degrees down the side of her throat. It seemed to her the only relevant issue still unresolved, and it loomed like a mountain in her consciousness. "Of course, technically—"

"Don't worry about it," he murmured. "Not a problem…"

All at once, she believed that, too. *Of course,* she thought, weak-kneed with relief and desire. For some men it would have been, but not Jimmy Joe.

And it wasn't.

She, who had always been envious of the tall and

the slim, and secretly ashamed of her own body's voluptuous curves, now stood dazed and compliant while for the first time in her life the man she adored slowly drew her nightgown over her head. She watched his eyes feast hungrily on the sight of her, and when he told her she was beautiful, for the first time in her life she believed it.

He laughed, and chided her gently for her embarrassment at the predictible response of her nursing breasts to his touch, and lightly, tenderly, lovingly covered them with a towel. "We'll save that for later," he promised huskily. "We have all the time in the world. A lifetime…"

But her legs gave way when his lips brushed her stomach. The melted-wax thing again…

So he drew back the quilt and the blankets and laid her down on the marriage bed that had been carved from the wood of four-hundred-year-old walnut trees, and stretched himself out carefully beside her. He kissed her mouth, deeply and thoroughly, until he felt her body begin to squirm and yearn unconsciously toward him, searching for him in its own natural way. And then he kissed her belly and her thighs and, parting them with gentle stroking, the damp and silky places between.

He heard her gasp, "I…can't," just once, and breathed a smile against her skin. Then he told her with his hands and mouth and tongue that she *could*.

She, who had never believed in anyone but herself, believed now in him. With complete confidence and trust, she gave herself into his hands. How easy it was, then. Like dying, she thought. And shattering…overwhelming…wrenching, too. Like being born.

Contractions, small cataclysms rocked her, then slowly receded. Jimmy Joe held her and murmured to her, telling her how wonderful she was, how sweet and beautiful. And yes, she believed him.

She stroked her hand over his tight, flat belly, pausing when she came to the drawstring of his sweats. He held her hand there for a moment, and asked huskily, "Are you sure you're ready? It's only been three weeks."

"I'm ready," she said firmly. *It's been a lifetime.*

"I'll be careful."

"I know." She found one end of a drawstring tie and pulled it.

He smiled at her, lazy and sure. "You know what you're doin'?"

"I'm a virgin," she replied, "not an idiot." The ties slid through her fingers. Breathless, she lowered her mouth to his belly and slowly drew the sweats over his hips.

"Marybell," he gasped, "what is this?"

"Dessert," she whispered. And then there was silence.

He stood about a minute of it, then grasped her wrists and rolled her over with one swift twist. "If you want me to be gentle," he murmured, pinning her with his legs, "you're gonna have to stop that, right now."

She didn't answer, just gazed at him, her eyes all sleepy and soft. Then she closed them and smiled. Her legs came around him. He whispered her name once more. *"Bella..."* He lowered his head and kissed her and kissed her and kissed her. And while he was kissing her he slipped into her body like a cat burglar and stole her virginity away.

"There, now," he said tenderly. "That wasn't so hard, was it?"

Shaken and relieved, she laughed. And deep inside her he felt it, and with her felt all the newness, wonder and excitement of the very first time. *Her* first time. His, he would always remember as a Christmas night in the sleeper of his snow-bound truck. Shaken himself, he thought of miracles; frightened, he thought of his life if he'd never found her, and with his heart pounding, bowed his head and sought her mouth and kissed her until his world had righted itself again.

He rocked her gently, so gently. Her tender body enfolded and caressed him and he felt every muscle and tremor, every pulse beat, the tiniest flinch and spasm. He knew when she tensed and tightened, and when she relaxed and softened, and when her body began to swell and throb to its own rhythms; when it was time to take them over and make them his...and then theirs. And when he could take them both to the limit—and beyond. And finally...finally, he knew when to let them both go, so that they spun wildly, deliriously out of control, overwhelmed and laughing with the sheer joy of living, and of making and being *in* love.

Quietness and peace came slowly, like twilight settling down after the sun has set in a blaze of glory. In the stillness between sighs, Mirabella heard it—the snuffling, snorting sounds of a baby waking.

"Oh, boy," she murmured, laughing. "Perfect timing."

"I'll get her," Jimmy Joe said. He was already pulling on his sweats, padding across the room in his bare feet.

A few minutes later he was back with Amy tucked expertly in the crook of his arm, a fresh diaper and dry blankets in his other hand. Her heart turned over as she watched him spread out the blankets and change her daughter's diaper while she stretched and gurgled and made faces at him in the soft light of the bedside lamp. When he finished, he scooped Amy up and placed her gently in her waiting arms, then quickly piled up pillows, climbed back into bed and drew Mirabella against him and pulled the blankets around them all.

"I think," said Mirabella drowsily, "I know what the old man meant. About this bed being a marriage bed—a bed for a lifetime. It's this, isn't it? For being together…"

He nodded. "For making love, and just talking…"

"For making plans…"

"Reading out loud to your kids…and grandkids…"

"Cuddling on Sunday mornings…"

"Reading the paper…"

"Making love…"

"Making babies."

"Making babies?" she asked, craning to look at him. "Are you sure?"

"Well," he said, "of course, Amy Jo's mine already, but I wouldn't mind makin' a couple more— long as we do it the old-fashioned way."

She was quiet for a moment. Then she said slowly, "You do realize, don't you, that if I hadn't done what I did, I'd never have met you? If it hadn't been for that idiotic thing I did, I wouldn't have been out there on that interstate, pregnant, in labor, stranded. Then you couldn't have rescued me, and then where would we be?" She shivered suddenly, and his arms tightened around her.

"I don't know," he said, dazed. "I guess you might be right."

Mirabella laughed softly. "Of course I am," she said triumphantly. "I'm always right."

"Okay, eastbound, I'm headin' for the barn."
"Happy trails, westbound. Ten-four..."

* * * * *

LEGACIES . LIES . LOVE .

The Kinards, the Richardses and the Webbers were Seattle's Kennedys, living in elegant Forrester Square—until one fateful night tore these families apart.

Now, twenty years later, memories and secrets are about to be revealed…unless one person has their way!

Coming in October 2003…

THE LAST THING SHE NEEDED

by Top Harlequin Temptation® author

Kate Hoffmann

When Dani O'Malley's childhood friend died, she suddenly found herself guardian to three scared, unruly kids—and terribly overwhelmed! If it weren't for Brad Cullen, she'd be lost. The sexy cowboy had a way with the kids…and with her!

Forrester Square…Legacies. Lies. Love.

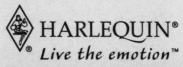

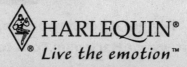

If you enjoyed what you just read,
then we've got an offer you can't resist!

Take 2
bestselling novels FREE!
Plus get a FREE surprise gift!

///////////////////////////////////

Clip this page and mail it to The Best of the Best™

IN U.S.A.	IN CANADA
3010 Walden Ave.	P.O. Box 609
P.O. Box 1867	Fort Erie, Ontario
Buffalo, N.Y. 14240-1867	L2A 5X3

YES! Please send me 2 free Best of the Best™ novels and my free surprise gift. After receiving them, if I don't wish to receive anymore, I can return the shipping statement marked cancel. If I don't cancel, I will receive 4 brand-new novels every month, before they're available in stores! In the U.S.A., bill me at the bargain price of $4.74 plus 25¢ shipping and handling per book and applicable sales tax, if any*. In Canada, bill me at the bargain price of $5.24 plus 25¢ shipping and handling per book and applicable taxes**. That's the complete price and a savings of over 20% off the cover prices—what a great deal! I understand that accepting the 2 free books and gift places me under no obligation ever to buy any books. I can always return a shipment and cancel at any time. Even if I never buy another The Best of the Best™ book, the 2 free books and gift are mine to keep forever.

185 MDN DNWF
385 MDN DNWG

Name	(PLEASE PRINT)	
Address	Apt.#	
City	State/Prov.	Zip/Postal Code

* Terms and prices subject to change without notice. Sales tax applicable in N.Y.
** Canadian residents will be charged applicable provincial taxes and GST.
All orders subject to approval. Offer limited to one per household and not valid to current The Best of the Best™ subscribers.
® are registered trademarks of Harlequin Enterprises Limited.

BOB02-R   ©1998 Harlequin Enterprises Limited